PENGUIN BOOKS

1871

COLLECTED SHORT STORIES

VOLUME I

William Somerset Maugham was born in 1874 and lived in Paris until he was ten. He was educated at King's School, Canterbury, and at Heidelburg University. He afterwards walked the wards of St Thomas's Hospital with a view to practice in medicine, but the success of his first novel, *Liza of Lambeth* (1897), won him over to letters. Something of his hospital experience is reflected, however, in the first of his masterpieces, *Of Human Bondage* (1915), and with *The Moon and Sixpence* (1919) his reputation as a novelist was assured.

His position as one of the most successful playwrights on the London stage was being consolidated simultaneously. His first play, *A Man of Honour* (1903), was followed by a procession of successes just before and after the First World War. (At one point only Bernard Shaw had more plays running at the same time in London.) His theatre career ended with *Sheppey* (1933).

His fame as a short-story writer began with *The Trembling of a Leaf*, sub-titled *Little Stories of the South Sea Islands*, in 1921, after which he published more than ten collections.

Somerset Maugham's general books are fewer in number. They include travel books, such as *On a Chinese Screen* (1922) and *Don Fernando* (1935), essays, criticism, and the self-revealing *The Summing Up* (1938) and *A Writer's Notebook* (1949).

Somerset Maugham became a Companion of Honour in 1954. He died in 1966.

W. Somerset Maugham

COLLECTED SHORT STORIES

VOLUME I

PENGUIN BOOKS

in association with William Heinemann Ltd

Penguin Books Ltd, Harmondsworth, Middlesex, England
Penguin Books Pty Ltd, Ringwood, Victoria, Australia

—

The Complete Short Stories first published in three volumes
by William Heinemann Ltd 1951
Published in four volumes in Penguin Books 1963
This volume reprinted 1964, 1965, 1966

—

Copyright © the Estate of W. Somerset Maugham, 1951

—

Made and printed in Great Britain
by C. Nicholls & Company Ltd
Set in Monotype Times

CONTENTS

PREFACE 7

RAIN 9

THE FALL OF EDWARD BARNARD 46

HONOLULU 75

THE LUNCHEON 97

THE ANT AND THE GRASSHOPPER 101

HOME 105

THE POOL 110

MACKINTOSH 144

APPEARANCE AND REALITY 175

THE THREE FAT WOMEN OF ANTIBES 189

THE FACTS OF LIFE 202

GIGOLO AND GIGOLETTE 219

THE HAPPY COUPLE 235

THE VOICE OF THE TURTLE 248

THE LION'S SKIN 263

THE UNCONQUERED 284

THE ESCAPE 309

THE JUDGEMENT SEAT 313

MR KNOW-ALL 317

THE HAPPY MAN 323

THE ROMANTIC YOUNG LADY 327

THE POINT OF HONOUR 336

THE POET 350

THE MOTHER 354

A MAN FROM GLASGOW 367

BEFORE THE PARTY 377

LOUISE 400

THE PROMISE 406

A STRING OF BEADS 412

THE YELLOW STREAK 418

PREFACE

THIS is the first volume of my collected short stories. In my early youth I wrote a number, but they are so immature that I have preferred not to reprint them. A few are in a book that has long remained out of print, a few others are scattered in various magazines. They are best forgotten. The first of the stories in this collection, *Rain*, was written in 1920 in Hong Kong, but I had hit upon the idea for it during a journey I took in the South Seas during the winter of 1916. The last of my stories was written in New York in 1945 from a brief note that I found by chance among my papers and which I made as far back as 1901. I do not expect ever to write another.

One of the most difficult things that an author has to deal with when he wants to gather together a quantity of stories into a volume is to decide in what order to place them. It is fairly simple when the stories are of about the same length or are placed in the same local (I should have liked to use the word *locale*, but the Oxford Dictionary says that this, though commonly used, is erroneous); then the pattern is easy to form. And it is a satisfaction to an author if he can so arrange his material that the book he finally offers to his readers has a pattern, even though they do not notice it. The pattern of a novel is of course plain; it has a beginning, a middle, and an end; and so, for the matter of that, has a well-constructed story.

But my stories are of very different lengths. Some are as short as sixteen hundred words, some are ten times as long, and one is just over twenty thousand. I have sojourned in most parts of the world, and while I was writing stories I could seldom stay anywhere for any length of time without getting the material for one or more tales. I have written tragic stories and I have written humorous ones. It has been an arduous task to get some kind of symmetry and at least the semblance of a pattern into a collection of a large number of stories of such different lengths, placed in so many different countries, and of such different character; and at the same time to make it as easy as possible for the reader to read them. For though to be read is not the motive which impels the author to write, once he has written his desire is to be read, and in order to achieve that, he must do his best to make what he writes readable.

With this intention, where I could I have followed a group of long stories with a group of short ones, sometimes very short, sometimes of five or six thousand words, and so that the reader should not be required to leap suddenly from China to Peru and back again, I have grouped, as well as I conveniently could, stories of which the local (or locale) was in one particular country. In that way I hoped to give the reader a chance to take his bearings in whatever distant land I chose to lead him to.

RAIN

It was nearly bed-time and when they awoke next morning land would be in sight. Dr Macphail lit his pipe and, leaning over the rail, searched the heavens for the Southern Cross. After two years at the front and a wound that had taken longer to heal than it should, he was glad to settle down quietly at Apia for twelve months at least, and he felt already better for the journey. Since some of the passengers were leaving the ship next day at Pago-Pago they had had a little dance that evening and in his ears hammered still the harsh notes of the mechanical piano. But the deck was quiet at last. A little way off he saw his wife in a long chair talking with the Davidsons, and he strolled over to her. When he sat down under the light and took off his hat you saw that he had very red hair, with a bald patch on the crown, and the red, freckled skin which accompanies red hair; he was a man of forty, thin, with a pinched face, precise and rather pedantic; and he spoke with a Scots accent in a very low, quiet voice.

Between the Macphails and the Davidsons, who were missionaries, there had arisen the intimacy of shipboard, which is due to propinquity rather than to any community of taste. Their chief tie was the disapproval they shared of the men who spent their days and nights in the smoking-room playing poker or bridge and drinking. Mrs Macphail was not a little flattered to think that she and her husband were the only people on board with whom the Davidsons were willing to associate, and even the doctor, shy but no fool, half unconsciously acknowledged the compliment. It was only because he was of an argumentative mind that in their cabin at night he permitted himself to carp.

'Mrs Davidson was saying she didn't know how they'd have got through the journey if it hadn't been for us,' said Mrs Macphail, as she neatly brushed out her transformation. 'She said we were really the only people on the ship they cared to know.'

'I shouldn't have thought a missionary was such a big bug that he could afford to put on frills.'

'It's not frills. I quite understand what she means. It wouldn't have been very nice for the Davidsons to have to mix with all that rough lot in the smoking-room.'

'The founder of their religion wasn't so exclusive,' said Dr Macphail with a chuckle.

'I've asked you over and over again not to joke about religion,' answered his wife. 'I shouldn't like to have a nature like yours, Alec. You never look for the best in people.'

He gave her a sidelong glance with his pale, blue eyes, but did not reply. After many years of married life he had learned that it was more conducive to peace to leave his wife with the last word. He was undressed before she was, and climbing into the upper bunk he settled down to read himself to sleep.

When he came on deck next morning they were close to land. He looked at it with greedy eyes. There was a thin strip of silver beach rising quickly to hills covered to the top with luxuriant vegetation. The coconut trees, thick and green, came nearly to the water's edge, and among them you saw the grass houses of the Samoans; and here and there, gleaming white, a little church. Mrs Davidson came and stood beside him. She was dressed in black and wore round her neck a gold chain, from which dangled a small cross. She was a little woman, with brown, dull hair very elaborately arranged, and she had prominent blue eyes behind invisible pince-nez. Her face was long, like a sheep's, but she gave no impression of foolishness, rather of extreme alertness; she had the quick movements of a bird. The most remarkable thing about her was her voice, high, metallic, and without inflexion; it fell on the ear with a hard monotony, irritating to the nerves like the pitiless clamour of the pneumatic drill.

'This must seem like home to you,' said Dr Macphail, with his thin, difficult smile.

'Ours are low islands, you know, not like these. Coral. These are volcanic. We've got another ten days' journey to reach them.'

'In these parts that's almost like being in the next street at home,' said Dr Macphail facetiously.

'Well, that's rather an exaggerated way of putting it, but one does look at distances differently in the South Seas. So far you're right.'

Dr Macphail sighed faintly.

'I'm glad we're not stationed here,' she went on. 'They say this is a terribly difficult place to work in. The steamers' touching makes the people unsettled; and then there's the naval station; that's bad for the natives. In our district we don't have difficulties like that to contend with. There are one or two traders, of course, but we take care to make them behave, and if they don't we make the place so hot for them they're glad to go.'

Fixing the glasses on her nose she looked at the green island with a ruthless stare.

'It's almost a hopeless task for the missionaries here. I can never be sufficiently thankful to God that we are at least spared that.'

Davidson's district consisted of a group of islands to the North of Samoa; they were widely separated and he had frequently to go long distances by canoe. At these times his wife remained at their headquarters and managed the mission. Dr Macphail felt his heart sink when he considered the efficiency with which she certainly managed it. She spoke of the depravity of the natives in a voice which nothing could hush, but with a vehemently unctuous horror. Her sense of delicacy was singular. Early in their acquaintance she had said to him:

'You know, their marriage customs when we first settled in the islands were so shocking that I couldn't possibly describe them to you. But I'll tell Mrs Macphail and she'll tell you.'

Then he had seen his wife and Mrs Davidson, their deck-chairs close together, in earnest conversation for about two hours. As he walked past them backwards and forwards for the sake of exercise, he had heard Mrs Davidson's agitated whisper, like the distant flow of a mountain torrent, and he saw by his wife's open mouth and pale face that she was enjoying an alarming experience. At night in their cabin she repeated to him with bated breath all she had heard.

'Well, what did I say to you?' cried Mrs Davidson, exultant next morning. 'Did you ever hear anything more dreadful? You don't wonder that I couldn't tell you myself, do you? Even though you are a doctor.'

Mrs Davidson scanned his face. She had a dramatic eagerness to see that she had achieved the desired effect.

'Can you wonder that when we first went there our hearts sank? You'll hardly believe me when I tell you it was impossible to find a single good girl in any of the villages.'

She used the word *good* in a severely technical manner.

'Mr Davidson and I talked it over, and we made up our minds the first thing to do was to put down the dancing. The natives were crazy about dancing.'

'I was not averse to it myself when I was a young man,' said Dr Macphail.

'I guessed as much when I heard you ask Mrs Macphail to have a turn with you last night. I don't think there's any real harm if a man dances with his wife, but I was relieved that she wouldn't. Under the circumstances I thought it better that we should keep ourselves to ourselves.'

'Under what circumstances?'

Mrs Davidson gave him a quick look through her pince-nez, but did not answer his question.

'But among white people it's not quite the same,' she went on, 'though I must say I agree with Mr Davidson, who says he can't understand how a husband can stand by and see his wife in another man's arms, and as far as I'm concerned I've never danced a step since I married. But the native dancing is quite another matter. It's not only immoral in itself, but it distinctly leads to immorality. However, I'm thankful to God that we stamped it out, and I don't think I'm wrong in saying that no one has danced in our district for eight years.'

But now they came to the mouth of the harbour and Mrs Macphail joined them. The ship turned sharply and steamed slowly in. It was a great land-locked harbour big enough to hold a fleet of battleships; and all around it rose, high and steep, the green hills. Near the entrance, getting such breeze as blew from the sea, stood the governor's house in a garden The Stars and Stripes dangled languidly from a flagstaff. They passed two or three trim bungalows, and a tennis court, and then they came to the quay with its warehouses. Mrs Davidson pointed out the schooner, moored two or three hundred yards from the side, which was to take them to Apia. There was a crowd of eager, noisy, and good-humoured natives come from all parts of the island, some from curiosity, others to barter with the travellers on their way to Sydney; and they brought pineapples and huge bunches of bananas, tapa cloths, necklaces of shells or sharks' teeth, *kava*-bowls, and models of war canoes. American sailors, neat and trim, clean-shaven and frank of face, sauntered among them, and there was a little group of officials. While their luggage was being landed the Macphails and Mrs Davidson watched the crowd. Dr Macphail looked at the yaws from which most of the children and the young boys seemed to suffer, disfiguring sores like torpid ulcers, and his professional eyes glistened when he saw for the first time in his experience cases of elephantiasis, men going about with a huge, heavy arm or dragging along a grossly disfigured leg. Men and women wore the lava-lava.

'It's a very indecent costume,' said Mrs Davidson. 'Mr Davidson thinks it should be prohibited by law. How can you expect people to be moral when they wear nothing but a strip of red cotton round their loins?'

'It's suitable enough to the climate,' said the doctor, wiping the sweat off his head.

Now that they were on land the heat, though it was so early in the morning, was already oppressive. Closed in by its hills, not a breath of air came in to Pago-Pago.

'In our islands,' Mrs Davidson went on in her high-pitched tones, 'we've practically eradicated the lava-lava. A few old men still continue to wear it, but that's all. The women have all taken to the Mother Hubbard, and the men wear trousers and singlets. At the beginning of our stay Mr Davidson said in one of his reports: the inhabitants of these islands will never be thoroughly Christianized till every boy of more than ten years is made to wear a pair of trousers.'

But Mrs Davidson had given two or three of her birdlike glances at heavy grey clouds that came floating over the mouth of the harbour. A few drops began to fall.

'We'd better take shelter,' she said.

They made their way with all the crowd to a great shed of corrugated iron, and the rain began to fall in torrents. They stood there for some time and then were joined by Mr Davidson. He had been polite enough to the Macphails during the journey, but he had not his wife's sociability, and had spent much of his time reading. He was a silent, rather sullen man, and you felt that his affability was a duty that he imposed upon himself Christianly; he was by nature reserved and even morose. His appearance was singular. He was very tall and thin, with long limbs loosely jointed; hollow cheeks, and curiously high cheek-bones; he had so cadaverous an air that it surprised you to notice how full and sensual were his lips. He wore his hair very long. His dark eyes, set deep in their sockets, were large and tragic; and his hands with their big, long fingers, were finely shaped; they gave him a look of great strength. But the most striking thing about him was the feeling he gave you of suppressed fire. It was impressive and vaguely troubling. He was not a man with whom any intimacy was possible.

He brought now unwelcome news. There was an epidemic of measles, a serious and often fatal disease among the Kanakas, on the island, and a case had developed among the crew of the schooner which was to take them on their journey. The sick man had been brought ashore and put in hospital on the quarantine station, but telegraphic instructions had been sent from Apia to say that the schooner would not be allowed to enter the harbour till it was certain no other member of the crew was affected.

'It means we shall have to stay here for ten days at least.'

'But I'm urgently needed at Apia,' said Dr Macphail.

'That can't be helped. If no more cases develop on board, the schooner will be allowed to sail with white passengers, but all native traffic is prohibited for three months.'

'Is there a hotel here?' asked Mrs Macphail.

Davidson gave a low chuckle.

'There's not.'

'What shall we do then?'

'I've been talking to the governor. There's a trader along the front who has rooms that he rents, and my proposition is that as soon as the rain lets up we should go along there and see what we can do. Don't expect comfort. You've just got to be thankful if we get a bed to sleep on and a roof over our heads.'

But the rain showed no signs of stopping, and at length with umbrellas and waterproofs they set out. There was no town, but merely a group of official buildings, a store or two, and at the back, among the coconut trees and plantains, a few native dwellings. The house they sought was about five minutes' walk from the wharf. It was a frame house of two storeys, with broad verandas on both floors and a roof of corrugated iron. The owner was a half-caste named Horn, with a native wife surrounded by little brown children, and on the ground-floor he had a store where he sold canned goods and cottons. The rooms he showed them were almost bare of furniture. In the Macphails' there was nothing but a poor, worn bed with a ragged mosquito net, a rickety chair, and a washstand. They looked round with dismay. The rain poured down without ceasing.

'I'm not going to unpack more than we actually need,' said Mrs Macphail.

Mrs Davidson came into the room as she was unlocking a portmanteau. She was very brisk and alert. The cheerless surroundings had no effect on her.

'If you'll take my advice you'll get a needle and cotton and start right in to mend the mosquito net,' she said, 'or you'll not be able to get a wink of sleep tonight.'

'Will they be very bad?' asked Dr Macphail.

'This is the season for them. When you're asked to a party at Government House at Apia you'll notice that all the ladies are given a pillowslip to put their – their lower extremities in.'

'I wish the rain would stop for a moment,' said Mrs Macphail. 'I could try to make the place comfortable with more heart if the sun were shining.'

'Oh, if you wait for that, you'll wait a long time. Pago-Pago is about the rainiest place in the Pacific. You see, the hills, and that bay, they attract the water, and one expects rain at this time of year anyway.'

She looked from Macphail to his wife, standing helplessly in different parts of the room, like lost souls, and she pursed her lips. She saw that she must take them in hand. Feckless people like that made her impatient, but her hands itched to put everything in the order which came so naturally to her.

'Here, you give me a needle and cotton and I'll mend that net of yours, while you go on with your unpacking. Dinner's at one. Dr Macphail, you'd better go down to the wharf and see that your heavy luggage has been put in a dry place. You know what these natives are, they're quite capable of storing it where the rain will beat in on it all the time.'

The doctor put on his waterproof again and went downstairs. At the door Mr Horn was standing in conversation with the quartermaster of the ship they had just arrived in and a second-class passenger whom Dr Macphail had seen several times on board. The quartermaster, a little, shrivelled man, extremely dirty, nodded to him as he passed.

'This is a bad job about the measles, doc,' he said. 'I see you've fixed yourself up already.'

Dr Macphail thought he was rather familiar, but he was a timid man and he did not take offence easily.

'Yes, we've got a room upstairs.'

'Miss Thompson was sailing with you to Apia, so I've brought her along here.'

The quartermaster pointed with his thumb to the woman standing by his side. She was twenty-seven perhaps, plump, and in a coarse fashion pretty. She wore a white dress and a large white hat. Her fat calves in white cotton stockings bulged over the tops of long white boots in glacé kid. She gave Macphail an ingratiating smile.

'The feller's tryin' to soak me a dollar and a half a day for the meanest-sized room,' she said in a hoarse voice.

'I tell you she's a friend of mine, Jo,' said the quartermaster. 'She can't pay more than a dollar, and you've sure got to take her for that.'

The trader was fat and smooth and quietly smiling.

'Well, if you put it like that, Mr Swan, I'll see what I can do about it. I'll talk to Mrs Horn and if we think we can make a reduction we will.'

'Don't try to pull that stuff with me,' said Miss Thompson.

'We'll settle this right now. You get a dollar a day for the room and not one bean more.'

Dr Macphail smiled. He admired the effrontery with which she bargained. He was the sort of man who always paid what he was asked. He preferred to be over-charged than to haggle. The trader sighed.

'Well, to oblige Mr Swan I'll take it.'

'That's the goods,' said Miss Thompson. 'Come right in and have a shot of hooch. I've got some real good rye in that grip if you'll bring it along, Mr Swan. You come along too, doctor.'

'Oh, I don't think I will, thank you,' he answered. 'I'm just going down to see that our luggage is all right.'

He stepped out into the rain. It swept in from the opening of the harbour in sheets and the opposite shore was all blurred. He passed two or three natives clad in nothing but the lava-lava, with huge umbrellas over them. They walked finely, with leisurely movements, very upright; and they smiled and greeted him in a strange tongue as they went by.

It was nearly dinner-time when he got back, and their meal was laid in the trader's parlour. It was a room designed not to live in but for purposes of prestige, and it had a musty, melancholy air. A suite of stamped plush was arranged neatly round the walls, and from the middle of the ceiling, protected from the flies by yellow tissue-paper, hung a gilt chandelier. Davidson did not come.

'I know he went to call on the governor,' said Mrs Davidson, 'and I guess he's kept him to dinner.'

A little native girl brought them a dish of Hamburger steak, and after a while the trader came up to see that they had everything they wanted.

'I see we have a fellow lodger, Mr Horn,' said Dr Macphail.

'She's taken a room, that's all,' answered the trader. 'She's getting her own board.'

He looked at the two ladies with an obsequious air.

'I put her downstairs so she shouldn't be in the way. She won't be any trouble to you.'

'Is it someone who was on the boat?' asked Mrs Macphail.

'Yes, ma'am, she was in the second cabin. She was going to Apia. She has a position as cashier waiting for her.'

'Oh!'

When the trader was gone Macphail said:

'I shouldn't think she'd find it exactly cheerful having her meals in her room.'

'If she was in the second cabin I guess she'd rather,' answered Mrs Davidson. 'I don't exactly know who it can be.'

'I happened to be there when the quartermaster brought her along. Her name's Thompson.'

'It's not the woman who was dancing with the quartermaster last night?' asked Mrs Davidson.

'That's who it must be,' said Mrs Macphail. 'I wondered at the time what she was. She looked rather fast to me.'

'Not good style at all,' said Mrs Davidson.

They began to talk of other things, and after dinner, tired with their early rise, they separated and slept. When they awoke, though the sky was still grey and the clouds hung low, it was not raining and they went for a walk on the high road which the Americans had built along the bay.

On their return they found that Davidson had just come in.

'We may be here for a fortnight,' he said irritably. 'I've argued it out with the governor, but he says there is nothing to be done.'

'Mr Davidson's just longing to get back to his work,' said his wife, with an anxious glance at him.

'We've been away for a year,' he said, walking up and down the veranda. 'The mission has been in charge of native missionaries and I'm terribly nervous that they've let things slide. They're good men, I'm not saying a word against them, God-fearing, devout, and truly Christian men – their Christianity would put many so-called Christians at home to the blush – but they're pitifully lacking in energy. They can make a stand once, they can make a stand twice, but they can't make a stand all the time. If you leave a mission in charge of a native missionary, no matter how trust-worthy he seems, in course of time you'll find he's let abuses creep in.'

Mr Davidson stood still. With his tall, spare form, and his great eyes flashing out of his pale face, he was an impressive figure. His sincerity was obvious in the fire of his gestures and in his deep, ringing voice.

'I expect to have my work cut out for me. I shall act and I shall act promptly. If the tree is rotten it shall be cut down and cast into the flames.'

And in the evening after the high tea which was their last meal, while they sat in the stiff parlour, the ladies working and Dr Macphail smoking his pipe, the missionary told them of his work in the islands.

'When we went there they had no sense of sin at all,' he said. 'They broke the commandments one after the other and never

knew they were doing wrong. And I think that was the most difficult part of my work, to instil into the natives the sense of sin.'

The Macphails knew already that Davidson had worked in the
Solomons for five years before he met his wife. She had been a
missionary in China, and they had become acquainted in Boston,
where they were both spending part of their leave to attend a
missionary congress. On their marriage they had been appointed
to the islands in which they had laboured ever since.

In the course of all the conversations they had had with Mr
Davidson one thing had shone out clearly and that was the man's
unflinching courage. He was a medical missionary, and he was
liable to be called at any time to one or other of the islands in the
group. Even the whaleboat is not so very safe a conveyance in the
stormy Pacific of the wet season, but often he would be sent for
in a canoe, and then the danger was great. In cases of illness or
accident he never hesitated. A dozen times he had spent the whole
night baling for his life, and more than once Mrs Davidson had
given him up for lost.

'I'd beg him not to go sometimes,' she said, 'or at least to wait
till the weather was more settled, but he'd never listen. He's
obstinate, and when he's once made up his mind, nothing can
move him.'

'How can I ask the natives to put their trust in the Lord if I
am afraid to do so myself?' cried Davidson. 'And I'm not, I'm
not. They know that if they send for me in their trouble I'll come
if it's humanly possible. And do you think the Lord is going to
abandon me when I am on his business? The wind blows at his
bidding and the waves toss and rage at his word.'

Dr Macphail was a timid man. He had never been able to get
used to the hurtling of the shells over the trenches, and when he
was operating in an advanced dressing-station the sweat poured
from his brow and dimmed his spectacles in the effort he made to
control his unsteady hand. He shuddered a little as he looked at
the missionary.

'I wish I could say that I've never been afraid,' he said.

'I wish you could say that you believed in God,' retorted the
other.

But for some reason, that evening the missionary's thoughts
travelled back to the early days he and his wife had spent on the
islands.

'Sometimes Mrs Davidson and I would look at one another
and the tears would stream down our cheeks. We worked without
ceasing, day and night, and we seemed to make no progress. I

don't know what I should have done without her then. When I felt my heart sink, when I was very near despair, she gave me courage and hope.'

Mrs Davidson looked down at her work, and a slight colour rose to her thin cheeks. Her hands trembled a little. She did not trust herself to speak.

'We had no one to help us. We were alone, thousands of miles from any of our own people, surrounded by darkness. When I was broken and weary she would put her work aside and take the Bible and read to me till peace came and settled upon me like sleep upon the eyelids of a child, and when at last she closed the book she'd say: "We'll save them in spite of themselves." And I felt strong again in the Lord, and I answered: "Yes, with God's help I'll save them. I must save them."'

He came over to the table and stood in front of it as though it were a lectern.

'You see, they were so naturally depraved that they couldn't be brought to see their wickedness. We had to make sins out of what they thought were natural actions. We had to make it a sin, not only to commit adultery and to lie and thieve, but to expose their bodies, and to dance and not to come to church. I made it a sin for a girl to show her bosom and a sin for a man not to wear trousers.'

'How?' asked Dr Macphail, not without surprise.

'I instituted fines. Obviously the only way to make people realize that an action is sinful is to punish them if they commit it. I fined them if they didn't come to church, and I fined them if they danced. I fined them if they were improperly dressed. I had a tariff, and every sin had to be paid for either in money or work. And at last I made them understand.'

'But did they never refuse to pay?'

'How could they?' asked the missionary.

'It would be a brave man who tried to stand up against Mr Davidson,' said his wife, tightening her lips.

Dr Macphail looked at Davidson with troubled eyes. What he heard shocked him, but he hesitated to express his disapproval.

'You must remember that in the last resort I could expel them from their church membership.'

'Did they mind that?'

Davidson smiled a little and gently rubbed his hands.

'They couldn't sell their copra. When the men fished they got no share of the catch. It meant something very like starvation. Yes, they minded quite a lot.'

'Tell him about Fred Ohlson,' said Mrs Davidson.

The missionary fixed his fiery eyes on Dr Macphail.

'Fred Ohlson was a Danish trader who had been in the islands a good many years. He was a pretty rich man as traders go and he wasn't very pleased when we came. You see, he'd had things very much his own way. He paid the natives what he liked for their copra, and he paid in goods and whisky. He had a native wife, but he was flagrantly unfaithful to her. He was a drunkard. I gave him a chance to mend his ways, but he wouldn't take it. He laughed at me.'

Davidson's voice fell to a deep bass as he said the last words, and he was silent for a minute or two. The silence was heavy with menace.

'In two years he was a ruined man. He'd lost everything he'd saved in a quarter of a century. I broke him, and at last he was forced to come to me like a beggar and beseech me to give him a passage back to Sydney.'

'I wish you could have seen him when he came to see Mr Davidson,' said the missionary's wife. 'He had been a fine, powerful man, with a lot of fat on him, and he had a great big voice, but now he was half the size, and he was shaking all over. He'd suddenly become an old man.'

With abstracted gaze Davidson looked out into the night. The rain was falling again.

Suddenly from below came a sound, and Davidson turned and looked questioningly at his wife. It was the sound of a gramophone, harsh and loud, wheezing out a syncopated tune.

'What's that?' he asked.

Mrs Davidson fixed her pince-nez more firmly on her nose.

'One of the second-class passengers has a room in the house. I guess it comes from there.'

They listened in silence, and presently they heard the sound of dancing. Then the music stopped, and they heard the popping of corks and voices raised in animated conversation.

'I daresay she's giving a farewell party to her friends on board,' said Dr Macphail. 'The ship sails at twelve, doesn't it?'

Davidson made no remark, but he looked at his watch.

'Are you ready?' he asked his wife.

She got up and folded her work.

'Yes, I guess I am,' she answered.

'It's early to go to bed yet, isn't it?' said the doctor.

'We have a good deal of reading to do,' explained Mrs

Davidson. 'Wherever we are, we read a chapter of the Bible before retiring for the night and we study it with the commentaries, you know, and discuss it thoroughly. It's a wonderful training for the mind.'

The two couples bade one another good night. Dr and Mrs Macphail were left alone. For two or three minutes they did not speak.

'I think I'll go and fetch the cards,' the doctor said at last.

Mrs Macphail looked at him doubtfully. Her conversation with the Davidsons had left her a little uneasy, but she did not like to say that she thought they had better not play cards when the Davidsons might come in at any moment. Dr Macphail brought them and she watched him, though with a vague sense of guilt, while he laid out his patience. Below the sound of revelry continued.

It was fine enough next day, and the Macphails, condemned to spend a fortnight of idleness at Pago-Pago, set about making the best of things. They went down to the quay and got out of their boxes a number of books. The doctor called on the chief surgeon of the naval hospital and went round the beds with him. They left cards on the governor. They passed Miss Thompson on the road. The doctor took off his hat, and she gave him a 'Good morning doc,' in a loud, cheerful voice. She was dressed as on the day before, in a white frock, and her shiny white boots with their high heels, her fat legs bulging over the tops of them, were strange things on that exotic scene.

'I don't think she's very suitably dressed, I must say,' said Mrs Macphail. 'She looks extremely common to me.'

When they got back to their house, she was on the veranda playing with one of the trader's dark children.

'Say a word to her,' Dr Macphail whispered to his wife. 'She's all alone here, and it seems rather unkind to ignore her.'

Mrs Macphail was shy, but she was in the habit of doing what her husband bade her.

'I think we're fellow lodgers here,' she said, rather foolishly.

'Terrible, ain't it, bein' cooped up in a one-horse burg like this?' answered Miss Thompson. 'And they tell me I'm lucky to have gotten a room. I don't see myself livin' in a native house, and that's what some have to do. I don't know why they don't have a hotel.'

They exchanged a few more words. Miss Thompson, loud-voiced and garrulous, was evidently quite willing to gossip, but Mrs

Macphail had a poor stock of small talk and presently she said:
'Well, I think we must go upstairs.'

In the evening when they sat down to their high tea, Davidson on coming in said:

'I see that woman downstairs has a couple of sailors sitting there. I wonder how she's gotten acquainted with them.'

'She can't be very particular,' said Mrs Davidson.

They were all rather tired after the idle, aimless day.

'If there's going to be a fortnight of this I don't know what we shall feel like at the end of it,' said Dr Macphail.

'The only thing to do is to portion out the day to different activities,' answered the missionary. 'I shall set aside a certain number of hours to study and a certain number to exercise, rain or fine – in the wet season you can't afford to pay any attention to the rain – and a certain number to recreation.'

Dr Macphail looked at his companion with misgiving. Davidson's programme oppressed him. They were eating Hamburger steak again. It seemed the only dish the cook knew how to make. Then below the gramophone began. Davidson started nervously when he heard it, but said nothing. Men's voices floated up. Miss Thompson's guests were joining in a well-known song and presently they heard her voice too, hoarse and loud. There was a good deal of shouting and laughing. The four people upstairs, trying to make conversation, listened despite themselves to the clink of glasses and the scrape of chairs. More people had evidently come. Miss Thompson was giving a party.

'I wonder how she gets them all in,' said Mrs Macphail suddenly breaking into a medical conversation between the missionary and her husband.

It showed whither her thoughts were wandering. The twitch of Davidson's face proved that, though he spoke of scientific things, his mind was busy in the same direction. Suddenly, while the doctor was giving some experience of practice on the Flanders front, rather prosily, he sprang to his feet with a cry.

'What's the matter, Alfred?' asked Mrs Davidson.

'Of course! It never occurred to me. She's out of Iwelei.'

'She can't be.'

'She came on board at Honolulu. It's obvious. And she's carrying on her trade here. Here.'

He uttered the last word with a passion of indignation.

'What's Iwelei?' asked Mrs Macphail.

He turned his gloomy eyes on her and his voice trembled with horror.

'The plague spot of Honolulu. The Red Light district. It was a blot on our civilization.'

Iwelei was on the edge of the city. You went down side streets by the harbour, in the darkness, across a rickety bridge, till you came to a deserted road, all ruts and holes, and then suddenly you came out into the light. There was parking room for motors on each side of the road, and there were saloons, tawdry and bright, each one noisy with its mechanical piano, and there were barbers' shops and tobacconists. There was a stir in the air and a sense of expectant gaiety. You turned down a narrow alley, either to the right or to the left, for the road divided Iwelei into two parts, and you found yourself in the district. There were rows of little bungalows, trim and neatly painted in green, and the pathway between them was broad and straight. It was laid out like a garden-city. In its respectable regularity, its order and spruceness, it gave an impression of sardonic horror; for never can the search for love have been so systematized and ordered. The pathways were lit by a rare lamp, but they would have been dark except for the lights that came from the open windows of the bungalows. Men wandered about, looking at the women who sat at their windows, reading or sewing, for the most part taking no notice of the passers-by; and like the women they were of all nationalities. There were Americans, sailors from the ships in port, enlisted men off the gunboat, sombrely drunk, and soldiers from the regiments, white and black, quartered on the island; there were Japanese, walking in twos and threes; Hawaiians, Chinese in long robes, and Filipinos in preposterous hats. They were silent and as it were oppressed. Desire is sad.

'It was the most crying scandal of the Pacific,' exclaimed Davidson vehemently. 'The missionaries had been agitating against it for years, and at last the local press took it up. The police refused to stir. You know their argument. They say that vice is inevitable and consequently the best thing is to localize and control it. The truth is, they were paid. Paid. They were paid by the saloon-keepers, paid by the bullies, paid by the women themselves. At last they were forced to move.'

'I read about it in the papers that came on board in Honolulu,' said Dr Macphail.

'Iwelei, with its sin and shame, ceased to exist on the very day we arrived. The whole population was brought before the justices. I don't know why I didn't understand at once what that woman was.'

'Now you come to speak of it,' said Mrs Macphail, 'I

remember seeing her come on board only a few minutes before the boat sailed. I remember thinking at the time she was cutting it rather fine.'

'How dare she come here!' cried Davidson indignantly. 'I'm not going to allow it.'

He strode towards the door.

'What are you going to do?' asked Macphail.

'What do you expect me to? I'm going to stop it. I'm not going to have this house turned into – into . . .'

He sought for a word that should not offend the ladies' ears. His eyes were flashing and his pale face was paler still in his emotion.

'It sounds as though there were three or four men down there,' said the doctor. 'Don't you think it's rather rash to go in just now?'

The missionary gave him a contemptuous look and without a word flung out of the room.

'You know Mr Davidson **very little** if you think the fear of personal danger can stop him in the performance of his duty,' said his wife.

She sat with her hands nervously clasped, a spot of colour on her high cheek-bones, listening to what was about to happen below. They all listened. They heard him clatter down the wooden stairs and throw open the door. The singing stopped suddenly, but the gramophone continued to bray out its vulgar tune. They heard Davidson's voice and then the noise of something heavy falling. The music stopped. He had hurled the gramophone on the floor. Then again they heard Davidson's voice, they could not make out the words, then Miss Thompson's, loud and shrill, then a confused clamour as though several people were shouting together at the top of their lungs. Mrs Davidson gave a little gasp, and she clenched her hands more tightly. Dr Macphail looked uncertainly from her to his wife. He did not want to go down, but he wondered if they expected him to. Then there was something that sounded like a scuffle. The noise now was more distinct. It might be that Davidson was being thrown out of the room. The door was slammed. There was a moment's silence and they heard Davidson come up the stairs again. He went to his room.

'I think I'll go to him,' said Mrs Davidson.

She got up and went out.

'If you want me, just call,' said Mrs Macphail, and then when the other was gone: 'I hope he isn't hurt.'

'Why couldn't he mind his own business?' said Dr Macphail.

They sat in silence for a minute or two and then they both started, for the gramophone began to play once more, defiantly, and mocking voices shouted hoarsely the words of an obscene song.

Next day Mrs Davidson was pale and tired. She complained of headache, and she looked old and wizened. She told Mrs Macphail that the missionary had not slept at all; he had passed the night in a state of frightful agitation and at five had got up and gone out. A glass of beer had been thrown over him and his clothes were stained and stinking. But a sombre fire glowed in Mrs Davidson's eyes when she spoke of Miss Thompson.

'She'll bitterly rue the day when she flouted Mr Davidson,' she said. 'Mr Davidson has a wonderful heart and no one who is in trouble has ever gone to him without being comforted, but he has no mercy for sin, and when his righteous wrath is excited he's terrible.'

'Why, what will he do?' asked Mrs Macphail.

'I don't know, but I wouldn't stand in that creature's shoes for anything in the world.'

Mrs Macphail shuddered. There was something positively alarming in the triumphant assurance of the little woman's manner. They were going out together that morning, and they went down the stairs side by side. Miss Thompson's door was open, and they saw her in a bedraggled dressing-gown, cooking something in a chafing-dish.

'Good morning,' she called. 'Is Mr Davidson better this morning?'

They passed her in silence, with their noses in the air, as if she did not exist. They flushed, however, when she burst into a shout of derisive laughter. Mrs Davidson turned on her suddenly.

'Don't you dare to speak to me,' she screamed. 'If you insult me I shall have you turned out of here.'

'Say, did I ask Mr Davidson to visit with me?'

'Don't answer her,' whispered Mrs Macphail hurriedly.

They walked on till they were out of earshot.

'She's brazen, brazen,' burst from Mrs Davidson.

Her anger almost suffocated her.

And on their way home they met her strolling towards the quay. She had all her finery on. Her great white hat with its vulgar, showy flowers was an affront. She called out cheerily to them as she went by, and a couple of American sailors who were standing there grinned as the ladies set their faces to an icy stare. They got in just before the rain began to fall again.

'I guess she'll get her fine clothes spoilt,' said Mrs Davidson with a bitter sneer.

Davidson did not come in till they were half-way through dinner. He was wet through, but he would not change. He sat, morose and silent, refusing to eat more than a mouthful, and he stared at the slanting rain. When Mrs Davidson told him of their two encounters with Miss Thompson he did not answer. His deepening frown alone showed that he had heard.

'Don't you think we ought to make Mr Horn turn her out of here?' asked Mrs Davidson. 'We can't allow her to insult us.'

'There doesn't seem to be any other place for her to go,' said Macphail.

'She can live with one of the natives.'

'In weather like this a native hut must be a rather uncomfortable place to live in.'

'I lived in one for years,' said the missionary.

When the little native girl brought in the fried bananas which formed the sweet they had every day, Davidson turned to her.

'Ask Miss Thompson when it would be convenient for me to see her,' he said.

The girl nodded shyly and went out.

'What do you want to see her for, Alfred?' asked his wife.

'It's my duty to see her. I won't act till I've given her every chance.'

'You don't know what she is. She'll insult you.'

'Let her insult me. Let her spit on me. She has an immortal soul, and I must do all that is in my power to save it.'

Mrs Davidson's ears rang still with the harlot's mocking laughter.

'She's gone too far.'

'Too far for the mercy of God?' His eyes lit up suddenly and his voice grew mellow and soft. 'Never. The sinner may be deeper in sin than the depth of hell itself, but the love of the Lord Jesus can reach him still.'

The girl came back with the message.

'Miss Thompson's compliments and as long as Rev Davidson don't come in business hours she'll be glad to see him any time.'

The party received it in stony silence, and Dr Macphail quickly effaced from his lips the smile which had come upon them. He knew his wife would be vexed with him if he found Miss Thompson's effrontery amusing.

They finished the meal in silence. When it was over the two ladies got up and took their work. Mrs Macphail was making another of the innumerable comforters which she had turned out since the beginning of the war, and the doctor lit his pipe. But Davidson remained in his chair and with abstracted eyes stared at the table. At last he got up and without a word went out of the room. They heard him go down and they heard Miss Thompson's defiant 'Come in' when he knocked at the door. He remained with her for an hour. And Dr Macphail watched the rain. It was beginning to get on his nerves. It was not like our soft English rain that drops gently on the earth; it was unmerciful and somehow terrible; you felt in it the malignancy of the primitive powers of nature. It did not pour, it flowed. It was like a deluge from heaven, and it rattled on the roof of corrugated iron with a steady persistence that was maddening. It seemed to have a fury of its own. And sometimes you felt that you must scream if it did not stop, and then suddenly you felt powerless, as though your bones had suddenly become soft; and you were miserable and hopeless.

Macphail turned his head when the missionary came back. The two women looked up.

'I've given her every chance. I have exhorted her to repent. She is an evil woman.'

He paused, and Dr Macphail saw his eyes darken and his pale face grow hard and stern.

'Now I shall take the whips with which the Lord Jesus drove the usurers and the money changers out of the Temple of the Most High.'

He walked up and down the room. His mouth was close set, and his black brows were frowning.

'If she fled to the uttermost parts of the earth I should pursue her.'

With a sudden movement he turned round and strode out of the room. They heard him go downstairs again.

'What is he going to do?' asked Mrs Macphail.

'I don't know.' Mrs Davidson took off her pince-nez and wiped them. 'When he is on the Lord's work I never ask him questions.'

She sighed a little.

'What is the matter?'

'He'll wear himself out. He doesn't know what it is to spare himself.'

Dr Macphail learnt the first results of the missionary's activity from the half-caste trader in whose house they lodged. He stopped the doctor when he passed the store and came out to speak to him on the stoop. His fat face was worried.

'The Rev Davidson has been at me for letting Miss Thompson have a room here,' he said, 'but I didn't know what she was when I rented it to her. When people come and ask if I can rent them a room all I want to know is if they've the money to pay for it. And she paid me for hers a week in advance.'

Dr Macphail did not want to commit himself.

'When all's said and done it's your house. We're very much obliged to you for taking us in at all.'

Horn looked at him doubtfully. He was not certain yet how definitely Macphail stood on the missionary's side.

'The missionaries are in with one another,' he said, hesitatingly. 'If they get it in for a trader he may just as well shut up his store and quit.'

'Did he want you to turn her out?'

'No, he said so long as she behaved herself he couldn't ask me to do that. He said he wanted to be just to me. I promised she shouldn't have no more visitors. I've just been and told her.'

'How did she take it?'

'She gave me Hell.'

The trader squirmed in his old ducks. He had found Miss Thompson a rough customer.

'Oh, well, I daresay she'll get out. I don't suppose she wants to stay here if she can't have anyone in.'

'There's nowhere she can go, only a native house, and no native'll take her now, not now that the missionaries have got their knife in her.'

Dr Macphail looked at the falling rain.

'Well, I don't suppose it's any good waiting for it to clear up.'

In the evening when they sat in the parlour Davidson talked to them of his early days at college. He had had no means and had worked his way through by doing odd jobs during the vacations. There was silence downstairs. Miss Thompson was sitting in her little room alone. But suddenly the gramophone began to play. She had set it on in defiance, to cheat her loneliness, but there was no one to sing, and it had a melancholy note. It was like a cry for help. Davidson took no notice. He was in the middle of a long anecdote and without change of expression went on. The gramophone continued. Miss Thompson put on one reel after another. It looked as though the silence of the night were getting on her nerves. It was breathless and sultry. When the Macphails went to bed they could not sleep. They lay side by side with their eyes wide open, listening to the cruel singing of the mosquitoes outside their curtain.

'What's that?' whispered Mrs Macphail at last.

They heard a voice, Davidson's voice, through the wooden partition. It went on with a monotonous, earnest insistence. He was praying aloud. He was praying for the soul of Miss Thompson.

Two or three days went by. Now when they passed Miss Thompson on the road she did not greet them with ironic cordiality or smile; she passed with her nose in the air, a sulky look on her painted face, frowning, as though she did not see them. The trader told Macphail that she had tried to get lodging elsewhere, but had failed. In the evening she played through the various reels of her gramophone, but the pretence of mirth was obvious now. The ragtime had a cracked, heart-broken rhythm as though it were a one-step of despair. When she began to play on Sunday Davidson sent Horn to beg her to stop at once since it was the Lord's day. The reel was taken off and the house was silent except for the steady pattering of the rain on the iron roof.

'I think she's getting a bit worked up,' said the trader next day to Macphail. 'She don't know what Mr Davidson's up to and it makes her scared.'

Macphail had caught a glimpse of her that morning and it struck him that her arrogant expression had changed. There was in her face a hunted look. The half-caste gave him a sidelong glance.

'I suppose you don't know what Mr Davidson is doing about it?' he hazarded.

'No, I don't.'

It was singular that Horn should ask him that question, for he also had the idea that the missionary was mysteriously at work.

He had an impression that he was weaving a net around the woman, carefully, systematically, and suddenly, when everything was ready, would pull the strings tight.

'He told me to tell her', said the trader, 'that if at any time she wanted him she only had to send and he'd come.'

'What did she say when you told her that?'

'She didn't say nothing. I didn't stop. I just said what he said I was to and then I beat it. I thought she might be going to start weepin'.'

'I have no doubt the loneliness is getting on her nerves,' said the doctor. 'And the rain – that's enough to make anyone jumpy,' he continued irritably. 'Doesn't it ever stop in this confounded place?'

'It goes on pretty steady in the rainy season. We have three hundred inches in the year. You see, it's the shape of the bay. It seems to attract the rain from all over the Pacific.'

'Damn the shape of the bay,' said the doctor.

He scratched his mosquito bites. He felt very short-tempered. When the rain stopped and the sun shone, it was like a hot-house, seething, humid, sultry, breathless, and you had a strange feeling that everything was growing with a savage violence. The natives, blithe and childlike by reputation, seemed then, with their tattooing and their dyed hair, to have something sinister in their appearance; and when they pattered along at your heels with their naked feet you looked back instinctively. You felt they might at any moment come behind you swiftly and thrust a long knife between your shoulder-blades. You could not tell what dark thoughts lurked behind their wide-set eyes. They had a little the look of ancient Egyptians painted on a temple wall, and there was about them the terror of what is immeasurably old.

The missionary came and went. He was busy, but the Macphails did not know what he was doing. Horn told the doctor that he saw the governor every day, and once Davidson mentioned him.

'He looks as if he had plenty of determination,' he said, 'but when you come down to brass tacks he has no backbone.'

'I suppose that means he won't do exactly what you want,' suggested the doctor facetiously.

The missionary did not smile.

'I want him to do what's right. It shouldn't be necessary to persuade a man to do that.'

'But there may be differences of opinion about what is right.'

'If a man may a gangrenous foot would you have patience with anyone who hesitated to amputate it?'

'Gangrene is a matter of fact.'

'And Evil?'

What Davidson had done soon appeared. The four of them had just finished their midday meal, and they had not yet separated for the siesta which the heat imposed on the ladies and on the doctor. Davidson had little patience with the slothful habit. The door was suddenly flung open and Miss Thompson came in. She looked round the room and then went up to Davidson.

'You low-down skunk, what have you been saying about me to the governor?'

She was spluttering with rage. There was a moment's pause. Then the missionary drew forward a chair.

'Won't you be seated, Miss Thompson? I've been hoping to have another talk with you.'

'You poor low-life bastard.'

She burst into a torrent of insult, foul and insolent. Davidson kept his grave eyes on her.

'I'm indifferent to the abuse you think fit to heap on me, Miss Thompson,' he said, 'but I must beg you to remember that ladies are present.'

Tears by now were struggling with her anger. Her face was red and swollen as though she were choking.

'What has happened?' asked Dr Macphail.

'A feller's just been in here and he says I gotter beat it on the next boat.'

Was there a gleam in the missionary's eyes? His face remained impassive.

'You could hardly expect the governor to let you stay here under the circumstances.'

'You done it,' she shrieked. 'You can't kid me. You done it.'

'I don't want to deceive you. I urged the governor to take the only possible step consistent with his obligations.'

'Why couldn't you leave me be? I wasn't doin' you no harm.'

'You may be sure that if you had I should be the last man to resent it.'

'Do you think I want to stay on in this poor imitation of a burg? I don't look no busher, do I?'

'In that case I don't see what cause of complaint you have,' he answered.

She gave an inarticulate cry of rage and flung out of the room. There was a short silence.

'It's a relief to know that the governor has acted at last,' said Davidson finally. 'He's a weak man and he shilly-shallied. He said she was only here for a fortnight anyway, and if she went on to Apia, that was under British jurisdiction and had nothing to do with him.'

The missionary sprang to his feet and strode across the room.

'It's terrible the way the men who are in authority seek to evade their responsibility. They speak as though evil that was out of sight ceased to be evil. The very existence of that woman is a scandal and it does not help matters to shift it to another of the

31

islands. In the end I had to speak straight from the shoulder.'

Davidson's brow lowered, and he protruded his firm chin. He looked fierce and determined.

'What do you mean by that?'

'Our mission is not entirely without influence at Washington. I pointed out to the governor that it wouldn't do him any good if there was a complaint about the way he managed things here.'

'When has she got to go?' asked the doctor, after a pause.

'The San Francisco boat is due here from Sydney next Tuesday. She's to sail on that.'

That was in five days' time. It was next day, when he was coming back from the hospital where for want of something better to do Macphail spent most of his mornings, that the half-caste stopped him as he was going upstairs.

'Excuse me, Dr Macphail, Miss Thompson's sick. Will you have a look at her?'

'Certainly.'

Horn led him to her room. She was sitting in a chair idly, neither reading nor sewing, staring in front of her. She wore her white dress and the large hat with the flowers on it. Macphail noticed that her skin was yellow and muddy under her powder, and her eyes were heavy.

'I'm sorry to hear you're not well,' he said.

'Oh, I ain't sick really. I just said that, because I just had to see you. I've got to clear on a boat that's going to 'Frisco.'

She looked at him and he saw that her eyes were suddenly startled. She opened and clenched her hands spasmodically. The trader stood at the door, listening.

'So I understand,' said the doctor.

She gave a little gulp.

'I guess it ain't very convenient for me to go to 'Frisco just now. I went to see the governor yesterday afternoon, but I couldn't get to him. I saw the secretary, and he told me I'd got to take that boat and that was all there was to it. I just had to see the governor, so I waited outside his house this morning, and when he come out I spoke to him. He didn't want to speak to me, I'll say, but I wouldn't let him shake me off, and at last he said he hadn't no objection to my staying here till the next boat to Sydney if the Rev Davidson will stand for it.'

She stopped and looked at Dr Macphail anxiously.

'I don't know exactly what I can do,' he said.

'Well, I thought maybe you wouldn't mind asking him. I swear to God I won't start anything here if he'll just only let me stay.

I won't go out of the house if that'll suit him. It's no more'n a fortnight.'

'I'll ask him.'

'He won't stand for it,' said Horn. 'He'll have you out on Tuesday, so you may as well make up your mind to it.'

'Tell him I can get work in Sydney, straight stuff, I mean. 'Tain't asking very much.'

'I'll do what I can.'

'And come and tell me right away, will you? I can't set down to a thing till I get the dope one way or the other.'

It was not an errand that much pleased the doctor, and, characteristically perhaps, he went about it indirectly. He told his wife what Miss Thompson had said to him and asked her to speak to Mrs Davidson. The missionary's attitude seemed rather arbitrary and it could do no harm if the girl were allowed to stay in Pago-Pago another fortnight. But he was not prepared for the result of his diplomacy. The missionary came to him straightway.

'Mrs Davidson tells me that Thompson has been speaking to you.'

Dr Macphail, thus directly tackled, had the shy man's resentment at being forced out into the open. He felt his temper rising, and he flushed.

'I don't see that it can make any difference if she goes to Sydney rather than to San Francisco, and so long as she promises to behave while she's here it's dashed hard to persecute her.'

The missionary fixed him with his stern eyes.

'Why is she unwilling to go back to San Francisco?'

'I didn't inquire,' answered the doctor with some asperity. 'And I think one does better to mind one's own business.'

Perhaps it was not a very tactful answer.

'The governor has ordered her to be deported by the first boat that leaves the island. He's only done his duty and I will not interfere. Her presence is a peril here.'

'I think you're very harsh and tyrannical.'

The two ladies looked up at the doctor with some alarm, but they need not have feared a quarrel, for the missionary smiled gently.

'I'm terribly sorry you should think that of me, Dr Macphail. Believe me, my heart bleeds for that unfortunate woman, but I'm only trying to do my duty.'

The doctor made no answer. He looked out of the window sullenly. For once it was not raining and across the bay you saw nestling among the trees the huts of a native village.

'I think I'll take advantage of the rain stopping to go out,' he said.

'Please don't bear me malice because I can't accede to your wish,' said Davidson, with a melancholy smile. 'I respect you very much, doctor, and I should be sorry if you thought ill of me.'

'I have no doubt you have a sufficiently good opinion of yourself to bear mine with equanimity,' he retorted.

'That's one on me,' chuckled Davidson.

When Dr Macphail, vexed with himself because he had been uncivil to no purpose, went downstairs, Miss Thompson was waiting for him with her door ajar.

'Well,' she said, 'have you spoken to him?'

'Yes, I'm sorry, he won't do anything,' he answered, not looking at her in his embarrassment.

But then he gave her a quick glance, for a sob broke from her. He saw that her face was white with fear. It gave him a shock of dismay. And suddenly he had an idea.

'But don't give up hope yet. I think it's a shame the way they're treating you and I'm going to see the governor myself.'

'Now?'

He nodded. Her face brightened.

'Say, that's real good of you. I'm sure he'll let me stay if you speak for me. I just won't do a thing I didn't ought all the time I'm here.'

Dr Macphail hardly knew why he had made up his mind to appeal to the governor. He was perfectly indifferent to Miss Thompson's affairs, but the missionary had irritated him, and with him temper was a smouldering thing. He found the governor at home. He was a large, handsome man, a sailor, with a grey toothbrush moustache; and he wore a spotless uniform of white drill.

'I've come to see you about a woman who's lodging in the same house as we are,' he said. 'Her name's Thompson.'

'I guess I've heard nearly enough about her, Dr Macphail,' said the governor, smiling. 'I've given her the order to get out next Tuesday and that's all I can do.'

'I wanted to ask you if you couldn't stretch a point and let her stay here till the boat comes in from San Francisco so that she can go to Sydney. I will guarantee her good behaviour.'

The governor continued to smile, but his eyes grew small and serious.

'I'd be very glad to oblige you, Dr Macphail, but I've given the order and it must stand.'

The doctor put the case as reasonably as he could, but now the governor ceased to smile at all. He listened sullenly, with averted gaze. Macphail saw that he was making no impression.

'I'm sorry to cause any lady inconvenience, but she'll have to sail on Tuesday and that's all there is to it.'

'But what difference can it make?'

'Pardon me, doctor, but I don't feel called upon to explain my official actions except to the proper authorities.'

Macphail looked at him shrewdly. He remembered Davidson's hint that he had used threats, and in the governor's attitude he read a singular embarrassment.

'Davidson's a damned busybody,' he said hotly.

'Between ourselves, Dr Macphail, I don't say that I have formed a very favourable opinion of Mr Davidson, but I am bound to confess that he was within his rights in pointing out to me the danger that the presence of a woman of Miss Thompson's character was to a place like this where a number of enlisted men are stationed among a native population.'

He got up and Dr Macphail was obliged to do so too.

'I must ask you to excuse me. I have an engagement. Please give my respects to Mrs Macphail.'

The doctor left him crestfallen. He knew that Miss Thompson would be waiting for him, and unwilling to tell her himself that he had failed, he went into the house by the back door and sneaked up the stairs as though he had something to hide.

At supper he was silent and ill-at-ease, but the missionary was jovial and animated. Dr Macphail thought his eyes rested on him now and then with triumphant good-humour. It struck him suddenly that Davidson knew of his visit to the governor and of its ill success. But how on earth could he have heard of it? There was something sinister about the power of that man. After supper he saw Horn on the veranda and, as though to have a casual word with him, went out.

'She wants to know if you've seen the governor,' the trader whispered.

'Yes. He wouldn't do anything. I'm awfully sorry, I can't do anything more.'

'I knew he wouldn't. They daren't go against the missionaries.'

'What are you talking about?' said Davidson affably, coming out to join them.

'I was just saying there was no chance of your getting over to Apia for at least another week,' said the trader glibly.

He left them, and the two men returned into the parlour. Mr Davidson devoted one hour after each meal to recreation. Presently a timid knock was heard at the door.

'Come in,' said Mrs Davidson, in her sharp voice.

The door was not opened. She got up and opened it. They saw Miss Thompson standing at the threshold. But the change in her appearance was extraordinary. This was no longer the flaunting hussy who had jeered at them in the road, but a broken, frightened woman. Her hair, as a rule so elaborately arranged, was tumbling untidily over her neck. She wore bedroom slippers and a skirt and blouse. They were unfresh and bedraggled. She stood at the door with the tears streaming down her face and did not dare to enter.

'What do you want?' said Mrs Davidson harshly.

'May I speak to Mr Davidson?' she said in a choking voice.

The missionary rose and went towards her.

'Come right in, Miss Thompson,' he said in cordial tones. 'What can I do for you?'

She entered the room.

'Say, I'm sorry for what I said to you the other day an' for – for everythin' else. I guess I was a bit lit up. I beg pardon.'

'Oh, it was nothing. I guess my back's broad enough to bear a few hard words.'

She stepped towards him with a movement that was horribly cringing.

'You've got me beat. I'm all in. You won't make me go back to 'Frisco?'

His genial manner vanished and his voice grew on a sudden hard and stern.

'Why don't you want to go back there?'

She cowered before him.

'I guess my people live there. I don't want them to see me like this. I'll go anywhere else you say.'

'Why don't you want to go back to San Francisco?'

'I've told you.'

He leaned forward, staring at her, and his great, shining eyes seemed to try to bore into her soul. He gave a sudden gasp.

'The penitentiary.'

She screamed, and then she fell at his feet, clasping his legs.

'Don't send me back there. I swear to you before God I'll be a good woman. I'll give all this up.'

She burst into a torrent of confused supplication and the tears coursed down her painted cheeks. He leaned over her and, lifting her face, forced her to look at him.

'Is that it, the penitentiary?'

'I beat it before they could get me,' she gasped. 'If the bulls grab me it's three years for mine.'

He let go his hold of her and she fell in a heap on the floor, sobbing bitterly. Dr Macphail stood up.

'This alters the whole thing,' he said. 'You can't make her go back when you know this. Give her another chance. She wants to turn over a new leaf.'

'I'm going to give her the finest chance she's ever had. If she repents let her accept her punishment.'

She misunderstood the words and looked up. There was a gleam of hope in her heavy eyes.

'You'll let me go?'

'No. You shall sail for San Francisco on Tuesday.'

She gave a groan of horror and then burst into low, hoarse shrieks which sounded hardly human, and she beat her head passionately on the ground. Dr Macphail sprang to her and lifted her up.

'Come on, you mustn't do that. You'd better go to your room and lie down. I'll get you something.'

He raised her to her feet and partly dragging her, partly carrying her, got her downstairs. He was furious with Mrs Davidson and with his wife because they made no effort to help. The half-caste was standing on the landing and with his assistance he managed to get her on the bed. She was moaning and crying. She was almost insensible. He gave her a hypodermic injection. He was hot and exhausted when he went upstairs again.

'I've got her to lie down.'

The two women and Davidson were in the same positions as when he had left them. They could not have moved or spoken since he went.

'I was waiting for you,' said Davidson, in a strange, distant voice. 'I want you all to pray with me for the soul of our erring sister.'

He took the Bible off a shelf, and sat down at the table at which they had supped. It had not been cleared, and he pushed the tea-pot out of the way. In a powerful voice, resonant and deep, he read to them the chapter in which is narrated the meeting of Jesus Christ with the woman taken in adultery.

'Now kneel with me and let us pray for the soul of our dear sister, Sadie Thompson.'

He burst into a long, passionate prayer in which he implored God to have mercy on the sinful woman. Mrs Macphail and Mrs Davidson knelt with covered eyes. The doctor, taken by surprise, awkward and sheepish, knelt too. The missionary's prayer had a savage eloquence. He was extraordinarily moved, and as he spoke the tears ran down his cheeks. Outside, the pitiless rain fell, fell steadily, with a fierce malignity that was all too human.

At last he stopped. He paused for a moment and said:

'We will now repeat the Lord's prayer.'

They said it and then, following him, they rose from their knees. Mrs Davidson's face was pale and restful. She was comforted and at peace, but the Macphails felt suddenly bashful. They did not know which way to look.

'I'll just go down and see how she is now,' said Dr Macphail.

When he knocked at her door it was opened for him by Horn. Miss Thompson was in a rocking-chair, sobbing quietly.

'What are you doing there?' exclaimed Macphail. 'I told you to lie down.'

'I can't lie down. I want to see Mr Davidson.'

'My poor child, what do you think is the good of it? You'll never move him.'

'He said he'd come if I sent for him.'

Macphail motioned to the trader.

'Go and fetch him.'

He waited with her in silence while the trader went upstairs. Davidson came in.

'Excuse me for asking you to come here,' she said, looking at him sombrely.

'I was expecting you to send for me. I knew the Lord would answer my prayer.'

They stared at one another for a moment and then she looked away. She kept her eyes averted when she spoke.

'I've been a bad woman. I want to repent.'

'Thank God! thank God! He has heard our prayers.'

He turned to the two men.

'Leave me alone with her. Tell Mrs Davidson that our prayers have been answered.

They went out and closed the door behind them.

'Gee whizz,' said the trader.

That night Dr Macphail could not get to sleep till late, and when he heard the missionary come upstairs he looked at his watch. It was two o'clock. But even then he did not go to bed at once, for through the wooden partition that separated their rooms he heard him praying aloud, till he himself, exhausted, fell asleep.

When he saw him next morning he was surprised at his appearance. He was paler than ever, tired, but his eyes shone with inhuman fire. It looked as though he were filled with an overwhelming joy.

'I want you to go down presently and see Sadie,' he said. 'I can't hope that her body is better, but her soul – her soul is transformed.'

The doctor was feeling wan and nervous.

'You were with her very late last night,' he said.

'Yes, she couldn't bear to have me leave her.'

'You look as pleased as Punch,' the doctor said irritably.

Davidson's eyes shone with ecstasy.

'A great mercy has been vouchsafed me. Last night I was privileged to bring a lost soul to the loving arms of Jesus.'

Miss Thompson was again in the rocking-chair. The bed had not been made. The room was in disorder. She had not troubled to dress herself, but wore a dirty dressing-gown, and her hair was tied in a sluttish knot. She had given her face a dab with a wet towel, but it was all swollen and creased with crying. She looked a drab.

She raised her eyes dully when the doctor came in. She was cowed and broken.

'Where's Mr Davidson?' she asked.

'He'll come presently if you want him,' answered Macphail acidly. 'I came here to see how you were.'

'Oh, I guess I'm O.K. You needn't worry about that.'

'Have you had anything to eat?'

'Horn brought me some coffee.'

She looked anxiously at the door.

'D'you think he'll come down soon? I feel as if it wasn't so terrible when he's with me.'

'Are you still going on Tuesday?'

'Yes, he says I've got to go. Please tell him to come right along. You can't do me any good. He's the only one as can help me now.'

'Very well,' said Dr Macphail.

During the next three days the missionary spent almost all his time with Sadie Thompson. He joined the others only to have his meals. Dr Macphail noticed that he hardly ate.

'He's wearing himself out,' said Mrs Davidson pitifully. 'He'll have a breakdown if he doesn't take care, but he won't spare himself.'

She herself was white and pale. She told Mrs Macphail that she had no sleep. When the missionary came upstairs from Miss Thompson he prayed till he was exhausted, but even then he did not sleep for long. After an hour or two he got up and dressed himself, and went for a tramp along the bay. He had strange dreams.

'This morning he told me that he'd been dreaming about the mountains of Nebraska,' said Mrs Davidson.

'That's curious,' said Dr Macphail.

He remembered seeing them from the windows of the train when he crossed America. They were like huge mole-hills, rounded and smooth, and they rose from the plain abruptly. Dr Macphail remembered how it struck him that they were like a woman's breasts.

Davidson's restlessness was intolerable even to himself. But he was buoyed up by a wonderful exhilaration. He was tearing out by the roots the last vestiges of sin that lurked in the hidden corners of that poor woman's heart. He read with her and prayed with her.

'It's wonderful,' he said to them one day at supper. 'It's a true rebirth. Her soul, which was black as night, is now pure and white like the new-fallen snow. I am humble and afraid. Her remorse for all her sins is beautiful. I am not worthy to touch the hem of her garment.'

'Have you the heart to send her back to San Francisco?' said the doctor. 'Three years in an American prison. I should have thought you might have saved her from that.'

'Ah, but don't you see? It's necessary. Do you think my heart doesn't bleed for her? I love her as I love my wife and my sister. All the time that she is in prison I shall suffer all the pain that she suffers.'

'Bunkum,' cried the doctor impatiently.

'You don't understand because you're blind. She's sinned, and she must suffer. I know what she'll endure. She'll be starved and tortured and humiliated. I want her to accept the punishment of man as a sacrifice to God. I want her to accept it joyfully. She has an opportunity which is offered to very few of us. God is very good and very merciful.'

Davidson's voice trembled with excitement. He could hardly articulate the words that tumbled passionately from his lips.

'All day I pray with her and when I leave her I pray again, I pray with all my might and main, so that Jesus may grant her this great mercy. I want to put in her heart the passionate desire to be punished so that at the end, even if I offered to let her go, she would refuse. I want her to feel that the bitter punishment of prison is the thank-offering that she places at the feet of our Blessed Lord, who gave his life for her.'

The days passed slowly. The whole household, intent on the wretched, tortured woman downstairs, lived in a state of unnatural excitement. She was like a victim that was being prepared for the savage rites of a bloody idolatry. Her terror numbed her. She could not bear to let Davidson out of her sight; it was only when he was with her that she had courage, and she hung upon him with a slavish dependence. She cried a great deal, and she read the Bible, and prayed. Sometimes she was exhausted and apathetic. Then she did indeed look forward to her ordeal, for it seemed to offer an escape, direct and concrete, from the anguish she was enduring. She could not bear much longer the vague terrors which now assailed her. With her sins she had put aside all personal vanity, and she slopped about her room, unkempt and dishevelled, in her tawdry dressing-gown. She had not taken off her night-dress for four days, nor put on stockings. Her room was littered and untidy. Meanwhile the rain fell with a cruel persistence. You felt that the heavens must at last be empty of water, but still it poured down, straight and heavy, with a maddening iteration, on the iron roof. Everything was damp and clammy. There was mildew on the walls and on the boots that stood on the floor. Through the sleepless nights the mosquitoes droned their angry chant.

'If it would only stop raining for a single day it wouldn't be so bad,' said Dr Macphail.

They all looked forward to the Tuesday when the boat for San Francisco was to arrive from Sydney. The strain was intolerable. So far as Dr Macphail was concerned, his pity and his resentment were alike extinguished by his desire to be rid of the unfortunate woman. The inevitable must be accepted. He felt he would breathe more freely when the ship had sailed. Sadie Thompson was to be escorted on board by a clerk in the governor's office. This person called on the Monday evening and told Miss Thompson to be prepared at eleven in the morning. Davidson was with her.

'I'll see that everything is ready. I mean to come on board with her myself.'

Miss Thompson did not speak.

When Dr Macphail blew out his candle and crawled cautiously under his mosquito curtains, he gave a sigh of relief.

'Well, thank God that's over. By this time tomorrow she'll be gone.'

'Mrs Davidson will be glad too. She says he's wearing himself to a shadow,' said Mrs Macphail. 'She's a different woman.'

'Who?'

'Sadie. I should never have thought it possible. It makes one humble.'

Dr Macphail did not answer, and presently he fell asleep. He was tired out, and he slept more soundly than usual.

He was awakened in the morning by a hand placed on his arm, and, starting up, saw Horn by the side of his bed. The trader put his finger on his mouth to prevent any exclamation from Dr Macphail and beckoned to him to come. As a rule he wore shabby ducks, but now he was barefoot and wore only the lava-lava of the natives. He looked suddenly savage, and Dr Macphail, getting out of bed, saw that he was heavily tattooed. Horn made him a sign to come on to the veranda. Dr Macphail got out of bed and followed the trader out.

'Don't make a noise,' he whispered. 'You're wanted. Put on a coat and some shoes. Quick.'

Dr Macphail's first thought was that something had happened to Miss Thompson.

'What is it? Shall I bring my instruments?'

'Hurry, please, hurry.'

Dr Macphail crept back into the bedroom, put on a waterproof over his pyjamas, and a pair of rubber-soled shoes. He rejoined the trader, and together they tiptoed down the stairs. The door leading out to the road was open and at it were standing half a dozen natives.

'What is it?' repeated the doctor.

'Come along with me,' said Horn.

He walked out and the doctor followed him. The natives came after them in a little bunch. They crossed the road and came on to the beach. The doctor saw a group of natives standing round some object at the water's edge. They hurried along, a couple of dozen yards perhaps, and the natives opened out as the doctor came up. The trader pushed him forwards. Then he saw, lying half in the water and half out, a dreadful object, the body of Davidson. Dr Macphail bent down – he was not a man to lose his head in an emergency – and turned the body over. The throat was cut from ear to ear, and in the right hand was still the razor with which the deed was done.

'He's quite cold,' said the doctor. 'He must have been dead some time.'

'One of the boys saw him lying there on his way to work just now and came and told me. Do you think he did it himself?'

'Yes. Someone ought to go for the police.'

Horn said something in the native tongue, and two youths started off.

'We must leave him here till they come,' said the doctor.

'They mustn't take him into my house. I won't have him in my house.'

'You'll do what the authorities say,' replied the doctor sharply. 'In point of fact I expect they'll take him to the mortuary.'

They stood waiting where they were. The trader took a cigarette from a fold in his lava-lava and gave one to Dr Macphail. They smoked while they stared at the corpse. Dr Macphail could not understand.

'Why do you think he did it?' asked Horn.

The doctor shrugged his shoulders. In a little while native police came along, under the charge of a marine, with a stretcher, and immediately afterwards a couple of naval officers and a naval doctor. They managed everything in a businesslike manner.

'What about the wife?' said one of the officers.

'Now that you've come I'll go back to the house and get some things on. I'll see that it's broken to her. She'd better not see him till he's been fixed up a little.'

'I guess that's right,' said the naval doctor.

When Dr Macphail went back he found his wife nearly dressed.

'Mrs Davidson's in a dreadful state about her husband,' she said to him as soon as he appeared. 'He hasn't been to bed all night. She heard him leave Miss Thompson's room at two, but he went out. If he's been walking about since then he'll be absolutely dead.'

Dr Macphail told her what had happened and asked her to break the news to Mrs Davidson.

'But why did he do it?' she asked, horror-stricken.

'I don't know.'

'But I can't. I can't.'

'You must.'

She gave him a frightened look and went out. He heard her go into Mrs Davidson's room. He waited a minute to gather himself together and then began to shave and wash. When he was dressed he sat down on the bed and waited for his wife. At last she came.

'She wants to see him,' she said.

'They've taken him to the mortuary. We'd better go down with her. How did she take it?'

'I think she's stunned. She didn't cry. But she's trembling like a leaf.'

'We'd better go at once.'

When they knocked at her door Mrs Davidson came out. She was very pale, but dry-eyed. To the doctor she seemed unnaturally composed. No word was exchanged, and they set out in silence down the road. When they arrived at the mortuary Mrs Davidson spoke.

'Let me go in and see him alone.'

They stood aside. A native opened a door for her and closed it behind her. They sat down and waited. One or two white men came and talked to them in undertones. Dr Macphail told them again what he knew of the tragedy. At last the door was quietly opened and Mrs Davidson came out. Silence fell upon them.

'I'm ready to go back now,' she said.

Her voice was hard and steady. Dr Macphail could not understand the look in her eyes. Her pale face was very stern. They walked back slowly, never saying a word, and at last they came round the bend on the other side of which stood their house. Mrs Davidson gave a gasp, and for a moment they stopped still. An incredible sound assaulted their ears. The gramophone which had been silent for so long was playing, playing ragtime loud and harsh.

'What's that?' cried Mrs Macphail with horror.

'Let's go on,' said Mrs Davidson.

They walked up the steps and entered the hall. Miss Thompson was standing at her door, chatting with a sailor. A sudden change had taken place in her. She was no longer the cowed drudge of the last days. She was dressed in all her finery, in her white dress, with the high shiny boots over which her fat legs bulged in their cotton stockings; her hair was elaborately arranged; and she wore that enormous hat covered with gaudy flowers. Her face was painted, her eyebrows were boldly black, and her lips were scarlet. She held herself erect. She was the flaunting queen that they had known at first. As they came in she broke into a loud, jeering laugh; and then, when Mrs Davidson involuntarily stopped, she collected the spittle in her mouth and spat. Mrs Davidson cowered back, and two red spots rose suddenly to her cheeks. Then, covering her face with her hands, she broke away and ran quickly up the stairs. Dr Macphail was outraged. He pushed past the woman into her room.

'What the devil are you doing?' he cried. 'Stop that damned machine.'

He went up to it and tore the record off. She turned on him.

'Say, doc, you can that stuff with me. What the hell are you doin' in my room?'

'What do you mean?' he cried. 'What d'you mean?'

She gathered herself together. No one could describe the scorn of her expression or the contemptuous hatred she put into her answer.

'You men! You filthy, dirty pigs! You're all the same, all of you. Pigs! Pigs!'

Dr Macphail gasped. He understood.

THE FALL OF EDWARD BARNARD

BATEMAN HUNTER slept badly. For a fortnight on the boat that brought him from Tahiti to San Francisco he had been thinking of the story he had to tell, and for three days on the train he had repeated to himself the words in which he meant to tell it. But in a few hours now he would be in Chicago, and doubts assailed him. His conscience, always very sensitive, was not at ease. He was uncertain that he had done all that was possible, it was on his honour to do much more than the possible, and the thought was disturbing that, in a matter which so nearly touched his own interest, he had allowed his interest to prevail over his quixotry. Self-sacrifice appealed so keenly to his imagination that the inability to exercise it gave him a sense of disillusion. He was like the philanthropist who with altruistic motives builds model dwellings for the poor and finds that he has made a lucrative investment. He cannot prevent the satisfaction he feels in the ten per cent which rewards the bread he had cast upon the waters, but he has an awkward feeling that it detracts somewhat from the savour of his virtue. Bateman Hunter knew that his heart was pure, but he was not quite sure how steadfastly, when he told her his story, he would endure the scrutiny of Isabel Longstaffe's cool grey eyes. They were far-seeing and wise. She measured the standards of others by her own meticulous uprightness and there could be no greater censure than the cold silence with which she expressed her disapproval of a conduct that did not satisfy her exacting code. There was no appeal from her judgement, for, having made up her mind, she never changed it. But Bateman would not have had her different. He loved not only the beauty of her person, slim and straight, with the proud carriage of her head, but still more the beauty of her soul. With her truthfulness, her rigid sense of honour, her fearless outlook, she seemed to him to collect in herself all that was most admirable in his country-women. But he saw in her something more than the perfect type of the American girl, he felt that her exquisiteness was peculiar in a way to her environment, and he was assured that no city in the world could have produced her but Chicago. A pang seized him when he remembered that he must deal so bitter a blow to her pride, and anger flamed up in his heart when he thought of Edward Barnard.

But at last the train steamed in to Chicago and he exulted when he saw the long streets of grey houses. He could hardly bear his impatience at the thought of State and Wabash with their crowded pavements, their hustling traffic, and their noise. He was at home. And he was glad that he had been born in the most important city in the United States. San Francisco was provincial, New York was effete; the future of America lay in the development of its economic possibilities, and Chicago, by its position and by the energy of its citizens, was destined to become the real capital of the country.

'I guess I shall live long enough to see it the biggest city in the world,' Bateman said to himself as he stepped down to the platform.

His father had come to meet him, and after a hearty handshake, the pair of them, tall, slender, and well-made, with the same fine, ascetic features and thin lips, walked out of the station. Mr Hunter's automobile was waiting for them and they got in. Mr Hunter caught his son's proud and happy glance as he looked at the street.

'Glad to be back, son?' he asked.

'I should just think I was,' said Bateman.

His eyes devoured the restless scene.

'I guess there's a bit more traffic here than in your South Sea island,' laughed Mr Hunter. 'Did you like it there?'

'Give me Chicago, dad,' answered Bateman.

'You haven't brought Edward Barnard back with you.'

'No.'

'How was he?'

Bateman was silent for a moment, and his handsome, sensitive face darkened.

'I'd sooner not speak about him, dad,' he said at last.

'That's all right, my son. I guess your mother will be a happy woman today.'

They passed out of the crowded streets in the Loop and drove along the lake till they came to the imposing house, an exact copy of a château on the Loire, which Mr Hunter had built himself some years before. As soon as Bateman was alone in his room he asked for a number on the telephone. His heart leaped when he heard the voice that answered him.

'Good morning, Isabel,' he said gaily.

'Good morning, Bateman.'

'How did you recognize my voice?'

'It is not so long since I heard it last. Besides, I was expecting you.'

'When may I see you?'

'Unless you have anything better to do perhaps you'll dine with us tonight.'

'You know very well that I couldn't possibly have anything better to do.'

'I suppose that you're full of news?'

He thought he detected in her voice a note of apprehension.

'Yes,' he answered.

'Well, you must tell me tonight. Good-bye.'

She rang off. It was characteristic of her that she should be able to wait so many unnecessary hours to know what so immensely concerned her. To Bateman there was an admirable fortitude in her restraint.

At dinner, at which beside himself and Isabel no one was present but her father and mother, he watched her guide the conversation into the channels of an urbane small-talk, and it occurred to him that in just such a manner would a marquise under the shadow of the guillotine toy with the affairs of a day that would know no morrow. Her delicate features, the aristo-cratic shortness of her upper lip, and her wealth of fair hair suggested the marquise again, and it must have been obvious, even if it were not notorious, that in her veins flowed the best blood in Chicago. The dining-room was a fitting frame to her fragile beauty, for Isabel had caused the house, a replica of a palace on the Grand Canal at Venice, to be furnished by an English expert in the style of Louis XV; and the graceful decora-tion linked with the name of that amorous monarch enhanced her loveliness and at the same time acquired from it a more profound significance. For Isabel's mind was richly stored, and her con-versation, however light, was never flippant. She spoke now of the Musicale to which she and her mother had been in the afternoon, of the lectures which an English poet was giving at the Auditorium, of the political situation, and of the Old Master which her father had recently bought for fifty thousand dollars in New York. It comforted Bateman to hear her. He felt that he was once more in the civilized world, at the centre of culture and distinction; and certain voices, troubling and yet against his will refusing to still their clamour, were at last silent in his heart.

'Gee, but it's good to be back in Chicago,' he said.

At last dinner was over, and when they went out of the dining-room Isabel said to her mother:

'I'm going to take Bateman along to my den. We have various things to talk about.'

'Very well, my dear,' said Mrs Longstaffe. 'You'll find your father and me in the Madame du Barry room when you're through.'

Isabel led the young man upstairs and showed him into the room of which he had so many charming memories. Though he knew it so well he could not repress the exclamation of delight which it always wrung from him. She looked round with a smile.

'I think it's a success,' she said. 'The main thing is that it's right. There's not even an ash-tray that isn't of the period.'

'I suppose that's what makes it so wonderful. Like all you do it's so superlatively right.'

They sat down in front of a log fire and Isabel looked at him with calm grave eyes.

'Now what have you to say to me?' she asked.

'I hardly know how to begin.'

'Is Edward Barnard coming back?'

'No.'

There was a long silence before Bateman spoke again, and with each of them it was filled with many thoughts. It was a difficult story he had to tell, for there were things in it which were so offensive to her sensitive ears that he could not bear to tell them, and yet in justice to her, no less than in justice to himself, he must tell her the whole truth.

It had all begun long ago when he and Edward Barnard, still at college, had met Isabel Longstaffe at the tea-party given to introduce her to society. They had both known her when she was a child and they long-legged boys, but for two years she had been in Europe to finish her education and it was with a surprised delight that they renewed acquaintance with the lovely girl who returned. Both of them fell desperately in love with her, but Bateman saw quickly that she had eyes only for Edward, and, devoted to his friend, he resigned himself to the role of confidant. He passed bitter moments, but he could not deny that Edward was worthy of his good fortune, and, anxious that nothing should impair the friendship he so greatly valued, he took care never by a hint to disclose his own feelings. In six months the young couple were engaged. But they were very young and Isabel's father decided that they should not marry at least till Edward graduated. They had to wait a year. Bateman remembered the winter at the end of which Isabel and Edward were to be married, a winter of dances and theatre-parties and of informal gaieties at which he, the constant third, was always present. He loved her no less because she would shortly be his friend's wife; her smile, a gay word she flung him, the confidence of her affection, never ceased to delight him; and he congratulated himself, somewhat complacently, because he did not envy them their happiness. Then an accident happened. A great bank failed, there was a panic on the exchange, and Edward Barnard's father found himself a ruined man. He came home one night, told his wife he was penniless, and after dinner, going into his study, shot himself.

A week later, Edward Barnard, with a tired, white face, went to Isabel and asked her to release him. Her only answer was to throw her arms round his neck and burst into tears.

'Don't make it harder for me, sweet,' he said.

'Do you think I can let you go now? I love you.'

'How can I ask you to marry me? The whole thing's hopeless. Your father would never let you. I haven't a cent.'

'What do I care? I love you.'

He told her his plans. He had to earn money at once, and George Braunschmidt, an old friend of his family, had offered to take him into his own business. He was a South Sea merchant, and he had agencies in many of the islands of the Pacific. He had suggested that Edward should go to Tahiti for a year or two, where under the best of his managers he could learn the details of that varied trade, and at the end of that time he promised the young man a position in Chicago. It was a wonderful opportunity, and when he had finished his explanations Isabel was once more all smiles.

'You foolish boy, why have you been trying to make me miserable?'

His face lit up at her words and his eyes flashed.

'Isabel, you don't mean to say you'll wait for me?'

'Don't you think you're worth it?' she smiled.

'Ah, don't laugh at me now. I beseech you to be serious. It may be for two years.'

'Have no fear. I love you, Edward. When you come back I will marry you.'

Edward's employer was a man who did not like delay and he had told him that if he took the post he offered he must sail that day week from San Francisco. Edward spent his last evening with Isabel. It was after dinner that Mr Longstaffe, saying he wanted a word with Edward, took him into the smoking-room. Mr Longstaffe had accepted good-naturedly the arrangement which his daughter had told him of and Edward could not imagine what mysterious communication he had now to make. He was not a little perplexed to see that his host was embarrassed. He faltered. He talked of trivial things. At last he blurted it out.

'I guess you've heard of Arnold Jackson,' he said, looking at Edward with a frown.

Edward hesitated. His natural truthfulness obliged him to admit a knowledge he would gladly have been able to deny.

'Yes, I have. But it's a long time ago. I guess I didn't pay very much attention.'

'There are not many people in Chicago who haven't heard of Arnold Jackson,' said Mr Longstaffe bitterly, 'and if there are they'll have no difficulty in finding someone who'll be glad to tell them. Did you know he was Mrs Longstaffe's brother?'

'Yes, I knew that.'

'Of course we've had no communication with him for many years. He left the country as soon as he was able to, and I guess the country wasn't sorry to see the last of him. We understand he lives in Tahiti. My advice to you is to give him a wide berth, but if you do hear anything about him Mrs Longstaffe and I would be very glad if you'd let us know.'

'Sure.'

'That was all I wanted to say to you. Now I daresay you'd like to join the ladies.'

There were few families that have not among their members one whom, if their neighbours permitted, they would willingly forget, and they are fortunate when the lapse of a generation or two has invested his vagaries with a romantic glamour. But when he is actually alive, if his peculiarities are not of the kind that can be condoned by the phrase, 'he is nobody's enemy but his own', a safe one when the culprit has no worse to answer for than alcoholism or wandering affections, the only possible course is silence. And it was this which the Longstaffes had adopted towards Arnold Jackson. They never talked of him. They would not even pass through the street in which he had lived. Too kind to make his wife and children suffer for his misdeeds, they had supported them for years, but on the understanding that they should live in Europe. They did everything they could to blot out all recollection of Arnold Jackson and yet were conscious that the story was as fresh in the public mind as when first the scandal burst upon a gaping world. Arnold Jackson was as black a sheep as any family could suffer from. A wealthy banker, prominent in his church, a philanthropist, a man respected by all, not only for his connexions (in his veins ran the blue blood of Chicago), but also for his upright character, he was arrested one day on a charge of fraud; and the dishonesty which the trial brought to light was not the sort which could be explained by a sudden temptation; it was deliberate and systematic. Arnold Jackson was a rogue. When he was sent to the penitentiary for seven years there were few who did not think he had escaped lightly.

When at the end of this last evening the lovers separated it was with many protestations of devotion. Isabel, all tears, was consoled a little by her certainty of Edward's passionate love. It was a strange feeling that she had. It made her wretched to part from him and yet she was happy because he adored her.

This was more than two years ago.

He had written to her by every mail since then, twenty-four letters in all, for the mail went but once a month, and his letters had been all that a lover's letters should be. They were intimate and charming, humorous sometimes, especially of late, and tender. At first they suggested that he was homesick, they were full of his desire to get back to Chicago and Isabel; and, a little anxiously, she wrote begging him to persevere. She was afraid that he might throw up his opportunity and come racing back. She did not want her lover to lack endurance and she quoted to him the lines:

> I could not love thee, dear, so much,
> Loved I not honour more.

But presently he seemed to settle down and it made Isabel very happy to observe his growing enthusiasm to introduce American methods into that forgotten corner of the world. But she knew him, and at the end of the year, which was the shortest time he could possibly stay in Tahiti, she expected to have to use all her influence to dissuade him from coming home. It was much better that he should learn the business thoroughly, and if they had been able to wait a year there seemed no reason why they should not wait another. She talked it over with Bateman Hunter, always the most generous of friends (during those first few days after Edward went she did not know what she would have done without him), and they decided that Edward's future must stand before everything. It was with relief that she found as the time passed that he made no suggestion of returning.

'He's splendid, isn't he?' she exclaimed to Bateman.

'He's white, through and through.'

'Reading between the lines of his letter I know he hates it over there, but he's sticking it out because . . .'

She blushed a little and Bateman, with the grave smile which was so attractive in him, finished the sentence for her.

'Because he loves you.'

'It makes me feel so humble,' she said.

'You're wonderful, Isabel, you're perfectly wonderful.'

But the second year passed and every month Isabel continued to receive a letter from Edward, and presently it began to seem a little strange that he did not speak of coming back. He wrote as though he were settled definitely in Tahiti, and what was more, comfortably settled. She was surprised. Then she read his letters again, all of them, several times; and now, reading between the lines indeed, she was puzzled to notice a change which had escaped her. The later letters were as tender and as delightful as the first, but the tone was different. She was vaguely suspicious of their humour, she had the instinctive mistrust of her sex for that unaccountable quality, and she discerned in them now a flippancy which perplexed her. She was not quite certain that the Edward who wrote to her now was the same Edward that she had known. One afternoon, the day after a mail had arrived from Tahiti, when she was driving with Bateman he said to her:

'Did Edward tell you when he was sailing?'

'No, he didn't mention it. I thought he might have said something to you about it.'

'Not a word.'

'You know what Edward is,' she laughed in reply, 'he has no sense of time. If it occurs to you next time you write you might ask him when he's thinking of coming.'

Her manner was so unconcerned that only Bateman's acute sensitiveness could have discerned in her request a very urgent desire. He laughed lightly.

'Yes. I'll ask him. I can't imagine what he's thinking about.'

A few days later, meeting him again, she noticed that something troubled him. They had been much together since Edward left Chicago; they were both devoted to him and each in his desire to talk of the absent one found a willing listener; the consequence was that Isabel knew every expression of Bateman's face, and his denials now were useless against her keen instinct. Something told her that his harassed look had to do with Edward and she did not rest till she had made him confess.

'The fact is,' he said at last, 'I heard in a roundabout way that Edward was no longer working for Braunschmidt and Co., and yesterday I took the opportunity to ask Mr Braunschmidt himself.'

'Well?'

'Edward left his employment with them nearly a year ago.'

'How strange he should have said nothing about it!'

Bateman hesitated, but he had gone so far now that he was obliged to tell the rest. It made him feel dreadfully embarrassed.

'He was fired.'

'In heaven's name what for?'

'It appears they warned him once or twice, and at last they told him to get out. They say he was lazy and incompetent.'

'Edward?'

They were silent for a while, and then he saw that Isabel was crying. Instinctively he seized her hand.

'Oh, my dear, don't, don't,' he said. 'I can't bear to see it.'

She was so unstrung that she let her hand rest in his. He tried to console her.

'It's incomprehensible, isn't it? It's so unlike Edward. I can't help feeling there must be some mistake.'

She did not say anything for a while, and when she spoke it was hesitatingly.

'Has it struck you that there was anything queer in his letters lately?' she asked, looking away, her eyes all bright with tears.

He did not quite know how to answer.

'I have noticed a change in them,' he admitted. 'He seems to have lost that high seriousness which I admired so much in him. One would almost think that the things that matter – well, don't matter.'

Isabel did not reply. She was vaguely uneasy.

'Perhaps in his answer to your letter he'll say when he's coming home. All we can do is to wait for that.'

Another letter came from Edward for each of them, and still he made no mention of his return; but when he wrote he could not have received Bateman's inquiry. The next mail would bring them an answer to that. The next mail came, and Bateman brought Isabel the letter he had just received; but the first glance of his face was enough to tell her that he was disconcerted. She read it through carefully and then, with slightly tightened lips, read it again.

'It's a very strange letter,' she said. 'I don't quite understand it.'

'One might almost think that he was joshing me,' said Bateman, flushing.

'It reads like that, but it must be unintentional. That's so unlike Edward.'

'He says nothing about coming back.'

'If I weren't so confident of his love I should think . . . I hardly know what I should think.'

It was then that Bateman had broached the scheme which during the afternoon had formed itself in his brain. The firm, founded by his father, in which he was now a partner, a firm which manufactured all manner of motor vehicles, was about to establish agencies in Honolulu, Sydney, and Wellington; and Bateman proposed that himself should go instead of the manager, who had been suggested. He could return by Tahiti; in fact, travelling from Wellington, it was inevitable to do so; and he could see Edward.

'There's some mystery and I'm going to clear it up. That's the only way to do it.'

'Oh, Bateman, how can you be so good and kind?' she exclaimed.

'You know there's nothing in the world I want more than your happiness, Isabel.'

She looked at him and she gave him her hands.

'You're wonderful, Bateman. I didn't know there was anyone in the world like you. How can I ever thank you?'

'I don't want your thanks. I only want to be allowed to help you.'

She dropped her eyes and flushed a little. She was so used to him that she had forgotten how handsome he was. He was as tall as Edward and as well made, but he was dark and pale of face, while Edward was ruddy. Of course she knew he loved her. It touched her. She felt very tenderly towards him.

It was from this journey that Bateman Hunter was now returned.

The business part of it took him somewhat longer than he expected and he had much time to think of his two friends. He had come to the conclusion that it could be nothing serious that prevented Edward from coming home, a pride, perhaps, which made him determined to make good before he claimed the bride he adored; but it was a pride that must be reasoned with. Isabel was unhappy. Edward must come back to Chicago with him and marry her at once. A position could be found for him in the works of the Hunter Motor Traction and Automobile Company. Bateman, with a bleeding heart, exulted at the prospect of giving happiness to the two persons he loved best in the world at the cost of his own. He would never marry. He would be godfather to the children of Edward and Isabel, and many years later when they were both dead he would tell Isabel's daughter how long, long ago he had loved her mother. Bateman's eyes were veiled with tears when he pictured this scene to himself.

Meaning to take Edward by surprise he had not cabled to announce his arrival, and when at last he landed at Tahiti he allowed a youth, who said he was the son of the house, to lead him to the Hôtel de la Fleur. He chuckled when he thought of his friend's amazement on seeing him, the most unexpected of visitors, walk into his office.

'By the way,' he asked, as they went along, 'can you tell me where I shall find Mr Edward Barnard?'

'Barnard?' said the youth. 'I seem to know the name.'

'He's an American. A tall fellow with light brown hair and blue eyes. He's been here over two years.'

'Of course. Now I know who you mean. You mean Mr Jackson's nephew.'

'Whose nephew?'

'Mr Arnold Jackson.'

'I don't think we're speaking of the same person,' answered Bateman, frigidly.

He was startled. It was queer that Arnold Jackson, known apparently to all and sundry, should live here under the disgraceful name in which he had been convicted. But Bateman could not imagine whom it was that he passed off as his nephew. Mrs Longstaffe was his only sister and he had never had a brother. The young man by his side talked volubly in an English that had something in it of the intonation of a foreign tongue, and Bateman, with a sidelong glance, saw, what he had not noticed before, that there was in him a good deal of native blood. A touch of hauteur involuntarily entered into his manner. They reached the hotel. When he had arranged about his room Bateman asked to be directed to the premises of Braunschmidt and Co. They were on the front, facing the lagoon, and, glad to feel the solid earth under his feet after eight days at sea, he sauntered down the sunny road to the water's edge. Having found the place he sought, Bateman sent in his card to the manager and was led through a lofty barn-like room, half store and half warehouse, to an office in which sat a stout, spectacled, bald-headed man.

'Can you tell me where I shall find Mr Edward Barnard? I understand he was in this office for some time.'

'That is so. I don't know just where he is.'

'But I thought he came here with a particular recommendation from Mr Braunschmidt. I know Mr Braunschmidt very well.'

The fat man looked at Bateman with shrewd, suspicious eyes. He called to one of the boys in the warehouse.

'Say, Henry, where's Barnard now, d'you know?'

'He's working at Cameron's, I think,' came the answer from someone who did not trouble to move.

The fat man nodded.

'If you turn to your left when you get out of here you'll come to Cameron's in about three minutes.'

Bateman hesitated.

'I think I should tell you that Edward Barnard is my greatest friend. I was very much surprised when I heard he'd left Braun-schmidt and Co.'

The fat man's eyes contracted till they seemed like pin-points, and their scrutiny made Bateman so uncomfortable that he felt himself blushing.

'I guess Braunschmidt and Co. and Edward Barnard didn't see eye to eye on certain matters,' he replied.

Bateman did not quite like the fellow's manner, so he got up, not without dignity, and with an apology for troubling him bade him good day. He left the place with a singular feeling that the man he had just interviewed had much to tell him, but no intention of telling it. He walked in the direction indicated and soon found himself at Cameron's. It was a trader's store, such as he had passed half a dozen of on his way, and when he entered the first person he saw, in his shirt-sleeves, measuring out a length of trade cotton, was Edward. It gave him a start to see him engaged in so humble an occupation. But he had scarcely appeared when Edward, looking up, caught sight of him, and gave a joyful cry of surprise.

'Bateman! Who ever thought of seeing you here?'

He stretched his arm across the counter and wrung Bateman's hand. There was no self-consciousness in his manner and the embarrassment was all on Bateman's side.

'Just wait till I've wrapped this package.'

With perfect assurance he ran his scissors across the stuff, folded it, made it into a parcel, and handed it to the dark-skinned customer.

'Pay at the desk, please.'

Then, smiling, with bright eyes, he turned to Bateman.

'How did you show up here? Gee, I am delighted to see you. Sit down, old man. Make yourself at home.'

'We can't talk here. Come along to my hotel. I suppose you can get away?'

This he added with some apprehension.

'Of course I can get away. We're not so business-like as all that in Tahiti.' He called out to a Chinese who was standing behind the opposite counter. 'Ah-Ling, when the boss comes tell him a friend of mine's just arrived from America and I've gone out to have a drain with him.'

'All-light,' said the Chinese, with a grin.

Edward slipped on a coat and, putting on his hat, accompanied Bateman out of the store. Bateman attempted to put the matter facetiously.

'I didn't expect to find you selling three and a half yards of rotten cotton to a greasy nigger,' he laughed.

'Braunschmidt fired me, you know, and I thought that would do as well as anything else.'

Edward's candour seemed to Bateman very surprising, but he thought it indiscreet to pursue the subject.

'I guess you won't make a fortune where you are,' he answered, somewhat dryly.

'I guess not. But I earn enough to keep body and soul together, and I'm quite satisfied with that.'

'You wouldn't have been two years ago.'

'We grow wiser as we grow older,' retorted Edward, gaily.

Bateman took a glance at him. Edward was dressed in a suit of shabby white ducks, none too clean, and a large straw hat of native make. He was thinner that he had been, deeply burned by the sun, and he was certainly better-looking than ever. But there was something in his appearance that disconcerted Bateman. He walked with a new jauntiness; there was a carelessness in his demeanour, a gaiety about nothing in particular, which Bateman could not precisely blame, but which exceedingly puzzled him.

'I'm blest if I can see what he's got to be so darned cheerful about,' he said to himself.

They arrived at the hotel and sat on the terrace. A Chinese boy brought them cocktails. Edward was most anxious to hear all the news of Chicago and bombarded his friend with eager questions. His interest was natural and sincere. But the odd thing was that it seemed equally divided among a multitude of subjects. He was as eager to know how Bateman's father was as what Isabel was doing. He talked of her without a shade of embarrassment, but she might just as well have been his sister as his promised wife; and before Bateman had done analysing the exact meaning of Edward's remarks he found that the conversation had drifted to his own work and the buildings his father had lately erected. He was determined to bring the conversation back to Isabel and was looking for the occasion when he saw Edward wave his hand cordially. A man was advancing towards them on the terrace, but Bateman's back was turned to him and he could not see him.

'Come and sit down,' said Edward gaily.

The new-comer approached. He was a very tall, thin man, in white ducks, with a fine head of curly white hair. His face was thin too, long, with a large, hooked nose and a beautiful, expressive mouth.

'This is my old friend Bateman Hunter. I've told you about him,' said Edward, his constant smile breaking on his lips.

'I'm pleased to meet you, Mr Hunter. I used to know your father.'

The stranger held out his hand and took the young man's in a strong, friendly grasp. It was not till then that Edward mentioned the other's name.

'Mr Arnold Jackson.'

Bateman turned white and he felt his hands grow cold. This was the forger, the convict, this was Isabel's uncle. He did not know what to say. He tried to conceal his confusion. Arnold Jackson looked at him with twinkling eyes.

'I daresay my name is familiar to you.'

Bateman did not know whether to say yes or no, and what made it more awkward was that both Jackson and Edward seemed to be amused. It was bad enough to have forced on him the acquaintance of the one man on the island he would rather have avoided, but worse to discern that he was being made a fool of. Perhaps, however, he had reached this conclusion too quickly, for Jackson, without a pause, added:

'I understand you're very friendly with the Longstaffes. Mary Longstaffe is my sister.'

Now Bateman asked himself if Arnold Jackson could think him ignorant of the most terrible scandal that Chicago had ever known. But Jackson put his hand on Edward's shoulder.

'I can't sit down, Teddie,' he said. 'I'm busy. But you two boys had better come up and dine tonight.'

'That'll be fine,' said Edward.

'It's very kind of you, Mr Jackson,' said Bateman, frigidly, 'but I'm here for so short a time; my boat sails tomorrow, you know; I think if you'll forgive me, I won't come.'

'Oh, nonsense. I'll give you a native dinner. My wife's a wonderful cook. Teddie will show you the way. Come early so as to see the sunset. I can give you both a shake-down if you like.'

'Of course we'll come,' said Edward. 'There's always the devil of a row in the hotel on the night a boat arrives and we can have a good yarn up at the bungalow.'

'I can't let you off, Mr Hunter,' Jackson continued with the utmost cordiality. 'I want to hear all about Chicago and Mary.'

He nodded and walked away before Bateman could say another word.

'We don't take refusals in Tahiti,' laughed Edward. 'Besides, you'll get the best dinner on the island.'

'What did he mean by saying his wife was a good cook? I happen to know his wife's in Geneva.'

'That's a long way off for a wife, isn't it?' said Edward. 'And it's a long time since he saw her. I guess it's another wife he's talking about.'

For some time Bateman was silent. His face was set in grave lines. But looking up he caught the amused look in Edward's eyes, and he flushed darkly.

'Arnold Jackson is a despicable rogue,' he said.

'I greatly fear he is,' answered Edward, smiling.

'I don't see how any decent man can have anything to do with him.'

'Perhaps I'm not a decent man.'

'Do you see much of him, Edward?'

'Yes, quite a lot. He's adopted me as his nephew.'

Bateman leaned forward and fixed Edward with his searching eyes.

'Do you like him?'

'Very much.'

'But don't you know, doesn't everyone here know, that he's a forger and that he's been a convict? He ought to be hounded out of civilized society.'

Edward watched a ring of smoke that floated from his cigar into the still, scented air.

'I suppose he is a pretty unmitigated rascal,' he said at last. 'And I can't flatter myself that any repentance for his misdeeds offers one an excuse for condoning them. He was a swindler and a hypocrite. You can't get away from it. I never met a more agreeable companion. He's taught me everything I know.'

'What has he taught you?' cried Bateman in amazement.

'How to live.'

Bateman broke into ironical laughter.

'A fine master. Is it owing to his lessons that you lost the chance of making a fortune and earn your living now by serving behind a counter in a ten-cent store?'

'He has a wonderful personality,' said Edward, smiling good-naturedly. 'Perhaps you'll see what I mean tonight.'

'I'm not going to dine with him if that's what you mean. Nothing would induce me to set foot within that man's house.'

'Come to oblige me, Bateman. We've been friends for so many years, you won't refuse me a favour when I ask it.'

Edward's tone had in it a quality new to Bateman. Its gentleness was singularly persuasive.

'If you put it like that, Edward, I'm bound to come,' he smiled.

Bateman reflected, moreover, that it would be as well to learn what he could about Arnold Jackson. It was plain that he had a great ascendancy over Edward, and if it was to be combated it was necessary to discover in what exactly it consisted. The more he talked with Edward the more conscious he became that a change had taken place in him. He had an instinct that it behoved him to walk warily, and he made up his mind not to broach the real purport of his visit till he saw his way more clearly. He began to talk of one thing and another, of his journey and what he had achieved by it, of politics in Chicago, of this common friend and that, of their days together at college.

At last Edward said he must get back to his work and proposed that he should fetch Bateman at five so that they could drive out together to Arnold Jackson's house.

'By the way, I rather thought you'd be living at this hotel,' said Bateman, as he strolled out of the garden with Edward. 'I understand it's the only decent one here.'

'Not I,' laughed Edward. 'It's a deal too grand for me. I rent a room just outside the town. It's cheap and clean.'

'If I remember right those weren't the points that seemed most important to you when you lived in Chicago.'

'Chicago!'

'I don't know what you mean by that, Edward. It's the greatest city in the world.'

'I know,' said Edward.

Bateman glanced at him quickly, but his face was inscrutable.

'When are you coming back to it?'

'I often wonder,' smiled Edward.

This answer, and the manner of it, staggered Bateman, but before he could ask for an explanation Edward waved to a half-caste who was driving a passing motor.

'Give us a ride down, Charlie,' he said.

He nodded to Bateman, and ran after the machine that had pulled up a few yards in front. Bateman was left to piece together a mass of perplexing impressions.

Edward called for him in a rickety trap drawn by an old mare, and they drove along a road that ran by the sea. On each side of it were plantations, coconut and vanilla; and now and then they saw a great mango, its fruit yellow and red and purple among the massy green of the leaves, now and then they had a glimpse of the lagoon, smooth and blue, with here and there a tiny islet graceful with tall palms. Arnold Jackson's house stood on a little hill and only a path led to it, so they unharnessed the mare and tied her to a tree, leaving the trap by the side of the road. To Bateman it seemed a happy-go-lucky way of doing things. But when they went up to the house they were met by a tall, handsome native woman, no longer young, with whom Edward cordially shook hands. He introduced Bateman to her.

'This is my friend Mr Hunter. We're going to dine with you, Lavina.'

'All right,' she said, with a quick smile. 'Arnold ain't back yet.'

'We'll go down and bathe. Let us have a couple of pareos.'

The woman nodded and went into the house.

'Who is that?' asked Bateman.

'Oh, that's Lavina. She's Arnold's wife.'

Bateman tightened his lips, but said nothing. In a moment the woman returned with a bundle, which she gave to Edward; and the two men, scrambling down a steep path, made their way to a grove of coconut trees on the beach. They undressed and Edward showed his friend how to make the strip of red trade cotton which is called a pareo into a very neat pair of bathing-drawers. Soon they were splashing in the warm, shallow water. Edward was in great spirits. He laughed and shouted and sang. He might have been fifteen. Bateman had never seen him so gay, and afterwards when they lay on the beach, smoking cigarettes, in the limpid air, there was such an irresistible light-heartedness in him that Bateman was taken aback.

'You seem to find life mighty pleasant,' said he.

'I do.'

They heard a soft movement and looking round saw that Arnold Jackson was coming towards them.

'I thought I'd come down and fetch you two boys back,' he said. 'Did you enjoy your bath, Mr Hunter?'

'Very much,' said Bateman.

Arnold Jackson, no longer in spruce ducks, wore nothing but a pareo round his loins and walked barefoot. His body was deeply browned by the sun. With his long, curling white hair and his ascetic face he made a fantastic figure in the native dress, but he bore himself without a trace of self-consciousness.

'If you're ready we'll go right up,' said Jackson.

'I'll just put on my clothes,' said Bateman.

'Why, Teddie, didn't you bring a pareo for your friend?'

'I guess he'd rather wear clothes,' smiled Edward.

'I certainly would,' answered Bateman, grimly, as he saw Edward gird himself in the loincloth and stand ready to start before he himself had got his shirt on.

'Won't you find it rough walking without your shoes?' he asked Edward. 'It struck me the path was a trifle rocky.'

'Oh, I'm used to it.'

'It's a comfort to get into a pareo when one gets back from town,' said Jackson. 'If you were going to stay here I should strongly recommend you to adopt it. It's one of the most sensible costumes I have ever come across. It's cool, convenient, and inexpensive.'

They walked up to the house, and Jackson took them into a large room with white-washed walls and an open ceiling in which a table was laid for dinner. Bateman noticed that it was set for five.

'Eva, come and show yourself to Teddie's friend, and then shake us a cocktail,' called Jackson.

Then he led Bateman to a long low window.

'Look at that,' he said, with a dramatic gesture. 'Look well.'

Below them coconut trees tumbled down steeply to the lagoon, and the lagoon in the evening light had the colour, tender and varied, of a dove's breast. On a creek, at a little distance, were the clustered huts of a native village, and towards the reef was a canoe, sharply silhouetted, in which were a couple of natives fishing. Then, beyond, you saw the vast calmness of the Pacific and twenty miles away, airy and unsubstantial like the fabric of a poet's fancy, the unimaginable beauty of the island which is called Murea. It was all so lovely that Bateman stood abashed.

'I've never seen anything like it,' he said at last.

Arnold Jackson stood staring in front of him, and in his eyes was a dreamy softness. His thin, thoughtful face was very grave. Bateman, glancing at it, was once more conscious of its intense spirituality.

'Beauty,' murmured Arnold Jackson. 'You seldom see beauty

face to face. Look at it well, Mr Hunter, for what you see now you will never see again, since the moment is transitory, but it will be an imperishable memory in your heart. You touch eternity.'

His voice was deep and resonant. He seemed to breathe forth the purest idealism, and Bateman had to urge himself to remember that the man who spoke was a criminal and a cruel cheat. But Edward, as though he heard a sound, turned round quickly.

'Here is my daughter, Mr Hunter.'

Bateman shook hands with her. She had dark, splendid eyes and a red mouth tremulous with laughter; but her skin was brown, and her curling hair, rippling down her shoulders, was coal-black. She wore but one garment, a Mother Hubbard of pink cotton, her feet were bare, and she was crowned with a wreath of white scented flowers. She was a lovely creature. She was like a goddess of the Polynesian spring.

She was a little shy, but not more shy than Bateman, to whom the whole situation was highly embarrassing, and it did not put him at his ease to see this sylph-like thing take a shaker and with a practised hand mix three cocktails.

'Let us have a kick in them, child,' said Jackson.

She poured them out and smiling delightfully handed one to each of the men. Bateman flattered himself on his skill in the subtle art of shaking cocktails and he was not a little astonished on tasting this one, to find that it was excellent. Jackson laughed proudly when he saw his guest's involuntary look of appreciation.

'Not bad, is it? I taught the child myself, and in the old days in Chicago I considered that there wasn't a bar-tender in the city that could hold a candle to me. When I had nothing better to do in the penitentiary I used to amuse myself by thinking out new cocktails, but when you come down to brass tacks there's nothing to beat a dry Martini.'

Bateman felt as though someone had given him a violent blow on the funny-bone and he was conscious that he turned red and then white. But before he could think of anything to say a native boy brought in a great bowl of soup and the whole party sat down to dinner. Arnold Jackson's remark seemed to have aroused in him a train of recollections, for he began to talk of his prison days. He talked quite naturally, without malice, as though he were relating his experiences at a foreign university. He addressed himself to Bateman and Bateman was confused and then confounded. He saw Edward's eyes fixed on him and there was in them a flicker of amusement. He blushed scarlet, for it struck him that Jackson was making a fool of him, and then because he felt absurd – and knew there was no reason why he should – he grew angry. Arnold Jackson was impudent – there was no other word for it – and his callousness, whether assumed or not, was outrageous. The dinner proceeded. Bateman was asked to eat sundry messes, raw fish and he knew not what, which only his civility induced him to swallow, but which he was amazed to find very good eating. Then an incident happened which to Bateman was the most mortifying experience of the evening. There was a little circlet of flowers in front of him, and for the sake of conversation he hazarded a remark about it.

'It's a wreath that Eva made for you,' said Jackson, 'but I guess she was too shy to give it to you.'

Bateman took it up in his hand and made a polite little speech of thanks to the girl.

'You must put it on,' she said, with a smile and a blush.

'I? I don't think I'll do that.'

'It's the charming custom of the country,' said Arnold Jackson. There was one in front of him and he placed it on his hair. Edward did the same.

'I guess I'm not dressed for the part,' said Bateman, uneasily.

'Would you like a pareo?' said Eva quickly. 'I'll get you one in a minute.'

'No, thank you. I'm quite comfortable as I am.'

'Show him how to put it on, Eva,' said Edward.

At that moment Bateman hated his greatest friend. Eva got up from the table and with much laughter placed the wreath on his black hair.

'It suits you very well,' said Mrs Jackson. 'Don't it suit him, Arnold?'

'Of course it does.'

Bateman sweated at every pore.

'Isn't it a pity it's dark?' said Eva. 'We could photograph you all three together.'

Bateman thanked his stars it was. He felt that he must look prodigiously foolish in his blue serge suit and high collar – very neat and gentlemanly – with that ridiculous wreath of flowers on his head. He was seething with indignation, and he had never in his life exercised more self-control than now when he presented an affable exterior. He was furious with that old man, sitting at the head of the table, half-naked, with his saintly face and the flowers on his handsome white locks. The whole position was monstrous.

Then dinner came to an end, and Eva and her mother remained

to clear away while the three men sat on the veranda. It was very warm and the air was scented with the white flowers of the night. The full moon, sailing across an unclouded sky, made a pathway on the broad sea that led to the boundless realms of Forever. Arnold Jackson began to talk. His voice was rich and musical. He talked now of the natives and of the old legends of the country. He told strange stories of the past, stories of hazardous expeditions into the unknown, of love and death, of hatred and revenge. He told of the adventurers who had discovered those distant islands, of the sailors who, settling in them, had married the daughters of great chieftains, and of the beach-combers who had led their varied lives on those silvery shores. Bateman, mortified and exasperated, at first listened sullenly, but presently some magic in the words possessed him and he sat entranced. The mirage of romance obscured the light of common day. Had he forgotten that Arnold Jackson had a tongue of silver, a tongue by which he had charmed vast sums out of the credulous public, a tongue which very nearly enabled him to escape the penalty of his crimes? No one had a sweeter eloquence, and no one had a more acute sense of climax. Suddenly he rose.

'Well, you two boys haven't seen one another for a long time. I shall leave you to have a yarn. Teddie will show you your quarters when you want to go to bed.'

'Oh, but I wasn't thinking of spending the night, Mr Jackson,' said Bateman.

'You'll find it more comfortable. We'll see that you're called in good time.'

Then with a courteous shake of the hand, stately as though he were a bishop in canonicals, Arnold Jackson took leave of his guest.

'Of course I'll drive you back to Papeete if you like,' said Edward, 'but I advise you to stay. It's bully driving in the early morning.'

For a few minutes neither of them spoke. Bateman wondered how he should begin on the conversation which all the events of the day made him think more urgent.

'When are you coming back to Chicago?' he asked, suddenly.

For a moment Edward did not answer. Then he turned rather lazily to look at his friend and smiled.

'I don't know. Perhaps never.'

'What in heaven's name do you mean?' cried Bateman.

'I'm very happy here. Wouldn't it be folly to make a change?'

'Man alive, you can't live here all your life. This is no life for

66

a man. It's a living death. Oh, Edward, come away at once, before it's too late. I've felt that something was wrong. You're infatuated with the place, you've succumbed to evil influences, but it only requires a wrench, and when you're free from these surroundings you'll thank all the gods there be. You'll be like a dope-fiend when he's broken from his drug. You'll see then that for two years you've been breathing poisoned air. You can't imagine what a relief it will be when you fill your lungs once more with the fresh pure air of your native country.'

He spoke quickly, the words tumbling over one another in his excitement, and there was in his voice sincere and affectionate emotion. Edward was touched.

'It is good of you to care so much, old friend.'

'Come with me tomorrow, Edward. It was a mistake that you ever came to this place. This is no life for you.'

'You talk of this sort of life and that. How do you think a man gets the best out of life?'

'Why, I should have thought there could be no two answers to that. By doing his duty, by hard work, by meeting all the obligations of his state and station.'

'And what is his reward?'

'His reward is the consciousness of having achieved what he set out to do.'

'It all sounds a little portentous to me,' said Edward, and in the lightness of the night Bateman could see that he was smiling. 'I'm afraid you'll think I've degenerated sadly. There are several things I think now which I daresay would have seemed outrageous to me three years ago.'

'Have you learnt them from Arnold Jackson?' asked Bateman, scornfully.

'You don't like him? Perhaps you couldn't be expected to. I didn't when I first came. I had just the same prejudice as you. He's a very extraordinary man. You saw for yourself that he makes no secret of the fact that he was in a penitentiary. I do not know that he regrets it or the crimes that led him there. The only complaint he ever made in my hearing was that when he came out his health was impaired. I think he does not know what remorse is. He is completely unmoral. He accepts everything and he accepts himself as well. He's generous and kind.'

'He always was,' interrupted Bateman, 'on other people's money.'

'I've found him a very good friend. Is it unnatural that I should take a man as I find him?'

'The result is that you lose the distinction between right and wrong.'

'No, they remain just as clearly divided in my mind as before, but what has become a little confused in me is the distinction between the bad man and the good one. Is Arnold Jackson a bad man who does good things or a good man who does bad things? It's a difficult question to answer. Perhaps we make too much of the difference between one man and another. Perhaps even the best of us are sinners and the worst of us are saints. Who knows?'

'You will never persuade me that white is black and that black is white,' said Bateman.

'I'm sure I shan't, Bateman.'

Bateman could not understand why the flicker of a smile crossed Edward's lips when he thus agreed with him. Edward was silent for a minute.

'When I saw you this morning, Bateman,' he said then, 'I seemed to see myself as I was two years ago. The same collar, and the same shoes, the same blue suit, the same energy. The same determination. By God, I was energetic. The sleepy methods of this place made my blood tingle. I went about and everywhere I saw possibilities for development and enterprise. There were fortunes to be made here. It seemed to me absurd that the copra should be taken away from here in sacks and the oil extracted in America. It would be far more economical to do all that on the spot, with cheap labour, and save freight, and I saw already the vast factories springing up on the island. Then the way they extracted it from the coconut seemed to me hopelessly inadequate and I invented a machine which divided the nut and scooped out the meat at the rate of two hundred and forty an hour. The harbour was not large enough. I made plans to enlarge it, then to form a syndicate to buy land, put up two or three large hotels, and bungalows for occasional residents; I had a scheme for improving the steamer service in order to attract visitors from California. In twenty years, instead of this half-French, lazy little town of Papeete I saw a great American city with ten-storey buildings and street-cars, a theatre and an opera house, a stock exchange and a mayor.'

'But go ahead, Edward,' cried Bateman, springing up from the chair in excitement. 'You've got the ideas and the capacity. Why, you'll become the richest man between Australia and the States.'

Edward chuckled softly.

'But I don't want to,' he said.

'Do you mean to say you don't want money, big money,

money running into millions? Do you know what you can do with it? Do you know the power it brings? And if you don't care about it for yourself think what you can do, opening new channels for human enterprise, giving occupation to thousands. My brain reels at the visions your words have conjured up.'

'Sit down, then, my dear Bateman,' laughed Edward. 'My machine for cutting the coconuts will always remain unused, and so far as I'm concerned street-cars shall never run in the idle streets of Papeete.'

Bateman sank heavily into his chair.

'I don't understand you,' he said.

'It came upon me little by little. I came to like the life here, with its ease and its leisure, and the people, with their good-nature and their happy smiling faces. I began to think. I'd never had time to do that before. I began to read.'

'You always read.'

'I read for examinations. I read in order to be able to hold my own in conversation. I read for instruction. Here I learned to read for pleasure. I learned to talk. Do you know that conversation is one of the greatest pleasures in life? But it wants leisure. I'd always been too busy before. And gradually all the life that had seemed so important to me began to seem rather trivial and vulgar. What is the use of all this hustle and this constant striving? I think of Chicago now and I see a dark, grey city, all stone – it is like a prison – and a ceaseless turmoil. And what does all that activity amount to? Does one get there the best out of life? Is that what we come into the world for, to hurry to an office, and work hour after hour till night, then hurry home and dine and go to a theatre? Is that how I must spend my youth? Youth lasts so short a time, Bateman. And when I am old, what have I to look forward to? To hurry from my home in the morning to my office and work hour after hour till night, and then hurry home again, and dine and go to a theatre? That may be worth while if you make a fortune; I don't know, it depends on your nature; but if you don't, is it worth while then? I want to make more out of my life than that, Bateman.'

'What do you value in life then?'

'I'm afraid you'll laugh at me. Beauty, truth, and good-ness.'

'Don't you think you can have those in Chicago?'

'Some men can, perhaps, but not I.' Edward sprang up now. 'I tell you when I think of the life I led in the old days I am filled with horror,' he cried violently. 'I tremble with fear when I think of the danger I have escaped. I never knew I had a soul till I found it here. If I had remained a rich man I might have lost it for good and all.'

'I don't know how you can say that,' cried Bateman indignantly. 'We often used to have discussions about it.'

'Yes, I know. They were about as effectual as the discussions of deaf mutes about harmony. I shall never come back to Chicago, Bateman.'

'And what about Isabel?'

Edward walked to the edge of the veranda and leaning over looked intently at the blue magic of the night. There was a slight smile on his face when he turned back to Bateman.

'Isabel is infinitely too good for me. I admire her more than any woman I have ever known. She has a wonderful brain and she's as good as she's beautiful. I respect her energy and her ambition. She was born to make a success of life. I am entirely unworthy of her.'

'She doesn't think so.'

'But you must tell her so, Bateman.'

'I?' cried Bateman. 'I'm the last person who could ever do that.'

Edward had his back to the vivid light of the moon and his face could not be seen. Is it possible that he smiled again?

'It's no good your trying to conceal anything from her, Bateman. With her quick intelligence she'll turn you inside out in five minutes. You'd better make a clean breast of it right away.'

'I don't know what you mean. Of course I shall tell her I've seen you.' Bateman spoke in some agitation. 'Honestly I don't know what to say to her.'

'Tell her that I haven't made good. Tell her that I'm not only poor, but that I'm content to be poor. Tell her I was fired from my job because I was idle and inattentive. Tell her all you've seen tonight and all I've told you.'

The idea which on a sudden flashed through Bateman's brain brought him to his feet and in uncontrollable perturbation he faced Edward.

'Man alive, don't you want to marry her?'

Edward looked at him gravely.

'I can never ask her to release me. If she wishes to hold me to my word I will do my best to make her a good and loving husband.'

'Do you wish me to give her that message, Edward? Oh, I can't. It's terrible. It's never dawned on her for a moment that you don't want to marry her. She loves you. How can I inflict such a mortification on her?'

Edward smiled again.

'Why don't you marry her yourself, Bateman? You've been in love with her for ages. You're perfectly suited to one another. You'll make her very happy.'

'Don't talk to me like that. I can't bear it.'

'I resign in your favour, Bateman. You are the better man.'

There was something in Edward's tone that made Bateman look up quickly, but Edward's eyes were grave and unsmiling. Bateman did not know what to say. He was disconcerted. He wondered whether Edward could possibly suspect that he had come to Tahiti on a special errand. And though he knew it was horrible he could not prevent the exultation in his heart.

'What will you do if Isabel writes and puts an end to her engagement with you?' he said, slowly.

'Survive,' said Edward.

Bateman was so agitated that he did not hear the answer.

'I wish you had ordinary clothes on,' he said, somewhat irritably. 'It's such a tremendously serious decision you're taking. That fantastic costume of yours makes it seem terribly casual.'

'I assure you, I can be just as solemn in a pareo and a wreath of roses, as in a high hat and a cut-away coat.'

Then another thought struck Bateman.

'Edward, it's not for my sake you're doing this? I don't know, but perhaps this is going to make a tremendous difference to my future. You're not sacrificing yourself for me? I couldn't stand for that, you know.'

'No, Bateman, I have learnt not to be silly and sentimental here. I should like you and Isabel to be happy, but I have not the least wish to be unhappy myself.'

The answer somewhat chilled Bateman. It seemed to him a little cynical. He would not have been sorry to act a noble part.

'Do you mean to say you're content to waste your life here? It's nothing less than suicide. When I think of the great hopes you had when we left college it seems terrible that you should be content to be no more than a salesmen in a cheap-John store.'

'Oh, I'm only doing that for the present, and I'm gaining a great deal of valuable experience. I have another plan in my head. Arnold Jackson has a small island in the Paumotas, about a thousand miles from here, a ring of land round a lagoon. He's planted coconut there. He's offered to give it me.'

'Why should he do that?' asked Bateman.

'Because if Isabel releases me I shall marry his daughter.'

'You?' Bateman was thunderstruck. 'You can't marry a half-caste. You wouldn't be so crazy as that.'

'She's a good girl, and she has a sweet and gentle nature. I think she would make me very happy.'

'Are you in love with her?'

'I don't know,' answered Edward reflectively. 'I'm not in love with her as I was in love with Isabel. I worshipped Isabel. I thought she was the most wonderful creature I had ever seen. I was not half good enough for her. I don't feel like that with Eva. She's like a beautiful exotic flower that must be sheltered from bitter winds. I want to protect her. No one ever thought of protecting Isabel. I think she loves me for myself and not for what I may become. Whatever happens to me I shall never disappoint her. She suits me.'

Bateman was silent.

'We must turn out early in the morning,' said Edward at last. 'It's really about time we went to bed.'

Then Bateman spoke and his voice had in it a genuine distress.

'I'm so bewildered, I don't know what to say. I came here because I thought something was wrong. I thought you hadn't succeeded in what you set out to do and were ashamed to come back when you'd failed. I never guessed I should be faced with this. I'm so desperately sorry, Edward. I'm so disappointed. I hoped you would do great things. It's almost more than I can bear to think of you wasting your talents and your youth and your chance in this lamentable way.'

'Don't be grieved, old friend,' said Edward. 'I haven't failed. I've succeeded. You can't think with what zest I look forward to life, how full it seems to me and how significant. Sometimes, when you are married to Isabel, you will think of me. I shall build myself a house on my coral island and I shall live there, looking after my trees – getting the fruit out of the nuts in the same old way that they have done for unnumbered years – I shall grow all sorts of things in my garden, and I shall fish. There will be enough work to keep me busy and not enough to make me dull. I shall have my books and Eva, children, I hope, and above all, the infinite variety of the sea and the sky, the freshness of the dawn and the beauty of the sunset, and the rich magnificence of the night. I shall make a garden out of what so short a while ago was a wilderness. I shall have created something. The years will pass insensibly, and when I am an old man I hope I shall be able to look back on a happy, simple, peaceful life. In my small way

I too shall have lived in beauty. Do you think it is so little to have enjoyed contentment? We know that it will profit a man little if he gain the whole world and lose his soul. I think I have won mine.'

Edward led him to a room in which there were two beds and he threw himself on one of them. In ten minutes Bateman knew by his regular breathing, peaceful as a child's, that Edward was asleep. But for his part he had no rest, he was disturbed in mind, and it was not till the dawn crept into the room, ghostlike and silent, that he fell asleep.

Bateman finished telling Isabel his long story. He had hidden nothing from her except what he thought would wound her or what made himself ridiculous. He did not tell her that he had been forced to sit at dinner with a wreath of flowers round his head and he did not tell her that Edward was prepared to marry her uncle's half-caste daughter the moment she set him free. But perhaps Isabel had keener intuitions than he knew, for as he went on with his tale her eyes grew colder and her lips closed upon one another more tightly. Now and then she looked at him closely, and if he had been less intent on his narrative he might have wondered at her expression.

'What was this girl like?' she asked when he finished. 'Uncle Arnold's daughter. Would you say there was any resemblance between her and me?'

Bateman was surprised at the question.

'It never struck me. You know I've never had eyes for anyone but you and I could never think that anyone was like you. Who could resemble you?'

'Was she pretty?' said Isabel, smiling slightly at his words.

'I suppose so. I daresay some men would say she was very beautiful.'

'Well, it's of no consequence. I don't think we need give her any more of our attention.'

'What are you going to do, Isabel?' he asked then.

Isabel looked down at the hand which still bore the ring Edward had given her on their betrothal.

'I wouldn't let Edward break our engagement because I thought it would be an incentive to him. I wanted to be an inspiration to him. I thought if anything could enable him to achieve success it was the thought that I loved him. I have done all I could. It's hopeless. It would only be weakness on my part not to recognize the facts. Poor Edward, he's nobody's enemy but his own. He was a dear, nice fellow, but there was something

73

lacking in him, I suppose it was backbone. I hope he'll be happy.'

She slipped the ring off her finger and placed it on the table. Bateman watched her with a heart beating so rapidly that he could hardly breathe.

'You're wonderful, Isabel, you're simply wonderful.'

She smiled, and, standing up, held out her hand to him.

'How can I ever thank you for what you've done for me?' she said. 'You have done me a great service. I knew I could trust you.'

He took her hand and held it. She had never looked more beautiful.

'Oh, Isabel, I would do so much more for you than that. You know that I only ask to be allowed to love and serve you.'

'You're so strong, Bateman,' she sighed. 'It gives me such a delicious feeling of confidence.'

'Isabel, I adore you.'

He hardly knew how the inspiration had come to him, but suddenly he clasped her in his arms; she, all unresisting, smiled into his eyes.

'Isabel, you know I wanted to marry you the very first day I saw you,' he cried passionately.

'Then why on earth didn't you ask me?' she replied.

She loved him. He could hardly believe it was true. She gave him her lovely lips to kiss. And as he held her in his arms he had a vision of the works of the Hunter Motor Traction and Automobile Company growing in size and importance till they covered a hundred acres, and of the millions of motors they would turn out, and of the great collection of pictures he would form which should beat anything they had in New York. He would wear horn spectacles. And she, with the delicious pressure of his arms about her, sighed with happiness, for she thought of the exquisite house she would have, full of antique furniture, and of the concerts she would give, and of the *thés dansants*, and the dinners to which only the most cultured people would come.

'Poor Edward,' she sighed.

HONOLULU

THE wise traveller travels only in imagination. An old French-man (he was really a Savoyard) once wrote a book called *Voyage autour de ma chambre*. I have not read it and do not even know what it is about, but the title stimulates my fancy. In such a journey I could circumnavigate the globe. An eikon by the chimneypiece can take me to Russia with its great forests of birch and its white, domed churches. The Volga is wide, and at the end of a straggling village, in the wine-shop, bearded men in rough sheepskin coats sit drinking. I stand on the little hill from which Napoleon first saw Moscow and I look upon the vastness of the city. I will go down and see the people whom I know more intimately than so many of my friends, Alyosha, and Vronsky, and a dozen more. But my eyes fall on a piece of porcelain and I smell the acrid odours of China. I am borne in a chair along a narrow causeway between the padi fields, or else I skirt a tree-clad mountain. My bearers chat gaily as they trudge along in the bright morning and every now and then, distant and mysterious, I heard the deep sound of a monastery bell. In the streets of Peking there is a motley crowd and it scatters to allow passage to a string of camels, stepping delicately, that bring skins and strange drugs from the stony deserts of Mongolia. In England, in London, there are certain afternoons in winter when the clouds hang heavy and low and the light is so bleak that your heart sinks, but then you can look out of your window, and you see the coconut trees crowded upon the beach of a coral island. The strand is silvery and when you walk along in the sunshine it is so dazzling that you can hardly bear to look at it. Overhead the mynah birds are making a great to-do, and the surf beats cease-lessly against the reef. Those are the best journeys, the journeys that you take at your own fireside, for then you lose none of your illusions.

But there are people who take salt in their coffee. They say it gives it a tang, a savour, which is peculiar and fascinating. In the same way there are certain places, surrounded by a halo of romance, to which the inevitable disillusionment which you must experience on seeing them gives a singular spice. You had expected something wholly beautiful and you get an impression which is infinitely more complicated than any that beauty can give you. It is like the weakness in the character of a great man which may make him less admirable but certainly makes him more interesting.

Nothing had prepared me for Honolulu. It is so far away from Europe, it is reached after so long a journey from San Francisco, so strange and so charming associations are attached to the name, that at first I could hardly believe my eyes. I do not know that I had formed in my mind any very exact picture of what I expected, but what I found caused me a great surprise. It is a typical western city. Shacks are cheek by jowl with stone mansions: dilapidated frame houses stand next door to smart stores with plate-glass windows; electric cars rumble noisily along the streets; and motors, Fords, Buicks, Packards, line the pavement. The shops are filled with all the necessities of American civilization. Every third house is a bank and every fifth the agency of a steamship company.

Along the streets crowd an unimaginable assortment of people. The Americans, ignoring the climate, wear black coats and high, starched collars, straw hats, soft hats, and bowlers. The Kanakas, pale brown, with crisp hair, have nothing on but a shirt and a pair of trousers; but the half-breeds are very smart with flaring ties and patent-leather boots. The Japanese, with their obsequious smile, are neat and trim in white duck, while their women walk a step or two behind them, in native dress, with a baby on their backs. The Japanese children, in bright coloured frocks, their little heads shaven, look like quaint dolls. Then there are the Chinese. The men, fat and prosperous, wear their American clothes oddly, but the women are enchanting with their tightly-dressed black hair, so neat that you feel it can never be disarranged, and they are very clean in their tunics and trousers, white, or powder-blue, or black. Lastly there are the Filipinos, the men in huge straw hats, the women in bright yellow muslin with great puffed sleeves.

It is the meeting-place of East and West. The very new rubs shoulders with the immeasurably old. And if you have not found the romance you expected you have come upon something singularly intriguing. All these strange people live close to each other, with different languages and different thoughts; they believe in different gods and they have different values; two passions alone they share, love and hunger. And somehow as you watch them you have an impression of extraordinary vitality. Though the air is so soft and the sky so blue, you have, I know not why, a feeling of something hotly passionate that beats like a throbbing pulse through the crowd. Though the native policeman at the corner, standing on a platform, with a white club to direct the traffic, gives the scene an air of respectability, you cannot but feel that it is a respectability only of the surface; a little below there is darkness and mystery. It gives you just that thrill, with a little catch at the heart, that you have when at night in the forest the silence trembles on a sudden with the low, insistent beating of a drum. You are all expectant of I know not what.

If I have dwelt on the incongruity of Honolulu, it is because just this, to my mind, gives its point to the story I want to tell. It is a story of primitive superstition, and it startles me that anything of the sort should survive in a civilization which, if not very distinguished, is certainly very elaborate. I cannot get over the fact that such incredible things should happen, or at least be thought to happen, right in the middle, so to speak, of telephones, tramcars, and daily papers. And the friend who showed me Honolulu had the same incongruity which I felt from the beginning was its most striking characteristic.

He was an American named Winter and I had brought a letter of introduction to him from an acquaintance in New York. He was a man between forty and fifty, with scanty black hair, grey at the temples, and a sharp-featured, thin face. His eyes had a twinkle in them and his large horn spectacles gave him a demureness which was not a little diverting. He was tall rather than otherwise and very spare. He was born in Honolulu and his father had a large store which sold hosiery and all such goods, from tennis racquets to tarpaulins, as a man of fashion could require. It was a prosperous business and I could well understand the indignation of Winter *père* when his son, refusing to go into it, had announced his determination to be an actor. My friend spent twenty years on the stage, sometimes in New York, but more often on the road, for his gifts were small; but at last, being no fool, he came to the conclusion that it was better to sell sock-suspenders in Honolulu than to play small parts in Cleveland, Ohio. He left the stage and went into the business. I think after the hazardous existence he had lived so long, he thoroughly enjoyed the luxury of driving a large car and living in a beautiful house near the golf-course, and I am quite sure, since he was a man of parts, he managed the business competently. But he could not bring himself entirely to break his connexion with the arts and since he might no longer act he began to paint. He took me to his studio and showed me his work. It was not at all bad, but not what I should have expected from him. He painted nothing but still life, very small pictures, perhaps eight by ten;

and he painted very delicately, with the utmost finish. He had evidently a passion for detail. His fruit pieces reminded you of the fruit in a picture by Ghirlandajo. While you marvelled a little at his patience, you could not help being impressed by his dexterity. I imagine that he failed as an actor because his effects, carefully studied, were neither bold nor broad enough to get across the footlights.

I was entertained by the proprietary, yet ironical air with which he showed me the city. He thought in his heart that there was none in the United States to equal it, but he saw quite clearly that his attitude was comic. He drove me round to the various buildings and swelled with satisfaction when I expressed a proper admiration for their architecture. He showed me the houses of rich men.

'That's the Stubbses' house,' he said. 'It cost a hundred thousand dollars to build. The Stubbses are one of our best families. Old man Stubbs came here as a missionary more than seventy years ago.'

He hesitated a little and looked at me with twinkling eyes through his big round spectacles.

'All our best families are missionary families,' he said. 'You're not very much in Honolulu unless your father or your grandfather converted the heathen.'

'Is that so?'

'Do you know your Bible?'

'Fairly,' I answered.

'There is a text which says: The fathers have eaten sour grapes and the children's teeth are set on edge. I guess it runs differently in Honolulu. The fathers brought Christianity to the Kanaka and the children jumped his land.'

'Heaven helps those who help themselves,' I murmured.

'It surely does. By the time the natives of this island had embraced Christianity they had nothing else they could afford to embrace. The kings gave the missionaries land as a mark of esteem, and the missionaries bought land by way of laying up treasure in heaven. It surely was a good investment. One missionary left the business – I think one may call it a business without offence – and became a land agent, but that is an exception. Mostly it was their sons who looked after the commercial side of the concern. Oh, it's a fine thing to have a father who came here fifty years ago to spread the faith.'

But he looked at his watch.

'Gee, it's stopped. That means it's time to have a cocktail.'

We sped along an excellent road, bordered with red hibiscus, and came back into the town.

'Have you been to the Union Saloon?'

'Not yet.'

'We'll go there.'

I knew it was the most famous spot in Honolulu and I entered it with a lively curiosity. You get to it by a narrow passage from King Street, and in the passage are offices, so that thirsty souls may be supposed bound for one of these just as well as for the saloon. It is a large square room, with three entrances, and opposite the bar, which runs the length of it, two corners have been partitioned off into little cubicles. Legend states that they were built so that King Kalakaua might drink there without being seen by his subjects, and it is pleasant to think that in one or other of these he may have sat over his bottle, a coal-black potentate, with Robert Louis Stevenson. There is a portrait of him, in oils, in a rich gold frame; but there are also two prints of Queen Victoria. On the walls, besides, are old line engravings of the eighteenth century, one of which, and heaven knows how it got there, is after a theatrical picture by De Wilde; and there are oleographs from the Christmas supplements of the *Graphic* and the *Illustrated London News* of twenty years ago. Then there are advertisements of whisky, gin, champagne, and beer; and photographs of baseball teams and of native orchestras.

The place seemed to belong not to the modern, hustling world that I had left in the bright street outside, but to one that was dying. It had the savour of the day before yesterday. Dingy and dimly lit, it had a vaguely mysterious air and you could imagine that it would be a fit scene for shady transactions. It suggested a more lurid time, when ruthless men carried their lives in their hands, and violent deeds diapered the monotony of life.

When I went in, the saloon was fairly full. A group of business men stood together at the bar, discussing affairs, and in a corner two Kanakas were drinking. Two or three men who might have been store-keepers were shaking dice. The rest of the company plainly followed the sea; they were captains of tramps, first mates, and engineers. Behind the bar, busily making the Honolulu cocktail for which the place was famous, served two large half-castes, in white, fat, clean-shaven and dark-skinned, with thick, curly hair and large bright eyes.

Winter seemed to know more than half the company, and when we made our way to the bar a little fat man in spectacles, who was standing by himself, offered him a drink.

'No, you have one with me, Captain,' said Winter.

He turned to me.

'I want you to know Captain Butler.'

The little man shook hands with me. We began to talk, but, my attention distracted by my surroundings, I took small notice of him, and after we had each ordered a cocktail we separated. When we had got into the motor again and were driving away, Winter said to me:

'I'm glad we ran up against Butler. I wanted you to meet him. What did you think of him?'

'I don't know that I thought very much of him at all,' I answered.

'Do you believe in the supernatural?'

'I don't exactly know that I do,' I smiled.

'A very queer thing happened to him a year or two ago. You ought to have him tell you about it.'

'What sort of thing?'

Winter did not answer my question.

'I have no explanation of it myself,' he said. 'But there's no doubt about the facts. Are you interested in things like that?'

'Things like what?'

'Spells and magic and all that.'

'I've never met anyone who wasn't.'

Winter paused for a moment.

'I guess I won't tell you myself. You ought to hear it from his own lips so that you can judge. How are you fixed up for to-night?'

'I've got nothing on at all.'

'Well, I'll get hold of him between now and then and see if we can't go down to his ship.'

Winter told me something about him. Captain Butler had spent all his life on the Pacific. He had been in much better circumstances than he was now, for he had been first officer and then captain of a passenger-boat plying along the coast of California, but he had lost his ship and a number of passengers had been drowned.

'Drink, I guess,' said Winter.

Of course there had been an inquiry, which had cost him his certificate, and then he drifted further afield. For some years he had knocked about the South Seas, but he was now in command of a small schooner which sailed between Honolulu and the various islands of the group. It belonged to a Chinese to whom the fact that his skipper had no certificate meant only that he could be had for lower wages, and to have a white man in charge was always an advantage.

And now that I had heard this about him I took the trouble to remember more exactly what he was like. I recalled his round spectacles and the round blue eyes behind them, and so gradually reconstructed him before my mind. He was a little man, without angles, plump, with a round face like the full moon and a little fat round nose. He had fair short hair, and he was red-faced and clean-shaven. He had plump hands, dimpled on the knuckles, and short fat legs. He was a jolly soul, and the tragic experience he had gone through seemed to have left him unscarred. Though he must have been thirty-four or thirty-five he looked much younger. But after all I had given him but a superficial attention, and now that I knew of this catastrophe, which had obviously ruined his life, I promised myself that when I saw him again I would take more careful note of him. It is very curious to observe the differences of emotional response that you find in different people. Some can go through terrible battles, the fear of imminent death and unimaginable horrors, and preserve their soul unscathed, while with others the trembling of the moon on a solitary sea or the song of a bird in a thicket will cause a convulsion great enough to transform their entire being. Is it due to strength or weakness, want of imagination or instability of character? I do not know. When I called up in my fancy that scene of shipwreck, with the shrieks of the drowning and the terror, and then later, the ordeal of the inquiry, the bitter grief of those who sorrowed for the lost, and the harsh things he must have read of himself in the papers, the shame and the disgrace, it came to me with a shock to remember that Captain Butler had talked with the frank obscenity of a schoolboy of the Hawaiian girls and of Iwelei, the Red Light district, and of his successful adventures. He laughed readily, and one would have thought he could never laugh again. I remembered his shining, white teeth; they were his best feature. He began to interest me, and thinking of him and of his gay insouciance I forgot the particular story, to hear which I was to see him again. I wanted to see him rather to find out if I could a little more what sort of man he was.

Winter made the necessary arrangements and after dinner we went down to the water front. The ships' boat was waiting for us and we rowed out. The schooner was anchored some way across the harbour, not far from the breakwater. We came alongside, and I heard the sound of a ukulele. We clambered up the ladder.

'I guess he's in the cabin,' said Winter, leading the way.

It was a small cabin, bedraggled and dirty, with a table against one side and a broad bench all round upon which slept, I supposed, such passengers as were ill-advised enough to travel in such a ship. A petroleum lamp gave a dim light. The ukulele was being played by a native girl and Butler was lolling on the seat, half lying, with his head on her shoulder and an arm round her waist.

'Don't let us disturb you, Captain,' said Winter, facetiously.

'Come right in,' said Butler, getting up and shaking hands with us. 'What'll you have?'

It was a warm night, and through the open door you saw countless stars in a heaven that was still almost blue. Captain Butler wore a sleeveless undershirt, showing his fat white arms, and a pair of incredibly dirty trousers. His feet were bare, but on his curly head he wore a very old, a very shapeless felt hat.

'Let me introduce you to my girl. Ain't she a peach?'

We shook hands with a very pretty person. She was a good deal taller than the captain, and even the Mother Hubbard, which the missionaries of a past generation had, in the interests of decency, forced on the unwilling natives, could not conceal the beauty of her form. One could not but suspect that age would burden her with a certain corpulence, but now she was graceful and alert. Her brown skin had an exquisite translucency and her eyes were magnificent. Her black hair, very thick and rich, was coiled round her head in a massive plait. When she smiled in a greeting that was charmingly natural, she showed teeth that were small, even, and white. She was certainly a most attractive creature. It was easy to see that the captain was madly in love with her. He could not take his eyes off her; he wanted to touch her all the time. That was very easy to understand; but what seemed to me stranger was that the girl was apparently in love with him. There was a light in her eyes that was unmistakable, and her lips were slightly parted as though in a sigh of desire. It was thrilling. It was even a little moving, and I could not help feeling somewhat in the way. What had a stranger to do with this lovesick pair? I wished that Winter had not brought me. And it seemed to me that the dingy cabin was transfigured and now it seemed a fit and proper scene for such an extremity of passion. I thought I should never forget that schooner in the harbour of Honolulu, crowded with shipping, and yet, under the immensity of the starry sky, remote from all the world. I liked to think of those lovers sailing off together in the night over the empty spaces of the Pacific from one green, hilly island to another. A faint breeze of romance softly fanned my cheek.

And yet Butler was the last man in the world with whom you would have associated romance, and it was hard to see what there was in him to arouse love. In the clothes he wore now he looked podgier than ever, and his round spectacles gave his round face the look of a prim cherub. He suggested rather a curate who had gone to the dogs. His conversation was peppered with the quaintest Americanisms, and it is because I despair of reproducing these that, at whatever loss of vividness, I mean to narrate the story he told me a little later in my own words. Moreover he was unable to frame a sentence without an oath, though a good-natured one, and his speech, albeit offensive only to prudish ears, in print would seem coarse. He was a mirth-loving man, and perhaps that accounted not a little for his successful amours; since women, for the most part frivolous creatures, are excessively bored by the seriousness with which men treat them, and they can seldom resist the buffoon who makes them laugh. Their sense of humour is crude. Diana of Ephesus is always prepared to fling prudence to the winds for the red-nosed comedian who sits on his hat. I realized that Captain Butler had charm. If I had not known the tragic story of the shipwreck I should have thought he had never had a care in his life.

Our host had rung the bell on our entrance and now a Chinese cook came in with more glasses and several bottles of soda. The whisky and the captain's empty glass stood already on the table. But when I saw the Chinese I positively started, for he was certainly the ugliest man I had ever seen. He was very short, but thick-set, and he had a bad limp. He wore a singlet and a pair of trousers that had been white, but were now filthy, and, perched on a shock of bristly, grey hair, an old tweed deer-stalker. It would have been grotesque on any Chinese, but on him it was outrageous. His broad, square face was very flat as though it had been bashed in by a mighty fist, and it was deeply pitted with smallpox; but the most revolting thing in him was a very pronounced harelip which had never been operated on, so that his upper lip, cleft, went up in an angle to his nose, and in the opening was a huge yellow fang. It was horrible. He came in with the end of a cigarette at the corner of his mouth and this, I do not know why, gave him a devilish expression.

He poured out the whisky and opened a bottle of soda.

'Don't drown it, John,' said the captain.

He said nothing, but handed a glass to each of us. Then he went out.

'I saw you lookin' at my Chink,' said Butler, with a grin on his fat, shining face.

'I should hate to meet him on a dark night,' I said.

'He sure is homely,' said the captain, and for some reason he seemed to say it with a peculiar satisfaction. 'But he's fine for one thing, I'll tell the world; you just have to have a drink every time you look at him.'

But my eyes fell on a calabash that hung against the wall over the table, and I got up to look at it. I had been hunting for an old one and this was better than any I had seen outside the museum.

'It was given me by a chief over on one of the islands,' said the captain, watching me. 'I done him a good turn and he wanted to give me something good.'

'He certainly did,' I answered.

I was wondering whether I could discreetly make Captain Butler an offer for it, I could not imagine that he set any store on such an article, when, as though he read my thoughts, he said:

'I wouldn't sell that for ten thousand dollars.'

'I guess not,' said Winter. 'It would be a crime to sell it.'

'Why?' I asked.

'That comes into the story,' returned Winter. 'Doesn't it, Captain?'

'It surely does.'

'Let's hear it then.'

'The night's young yet,' he answered.

The night distinctly lost its youth before he satisfied my curiosity, and meanwhile we drank a great deal too much whisky while Captain Butler narrated his experiences of San Francisco in the old days and of the South Seas. At last the girl fell asleep. She lay curled up on the seat, with her face on her brown arm, and her bosom rose and fell gently with her breathing. In sleep she looked sullen, but darkly beautiful.

He had found her on one of the islands in the group among which, whenever there was cargo to be got, he wandered with his crazy old schooner. The Kanakas have little love for work, and the laborious Chinese, the cunning Japs, have taken the trade out of their hands. Her father had a strip of land on which he grew taro and bananas and he had a boat in which he went fishing. He was vaguely related to the mate of the schooner, and it was he who took Captain Butler up to the shabby little frame house to spend an idle evening. They took a bottle of whisky with them and the ukulele. The captain was not a shy man and when he saw a pretty girl he made love to her. He could speak the native language fluently and it was not long before he had overcome the girl's timidity. They spent the evening singing and dancing, and by the end of it she was sitting by his side and he had his arm round her waist. It happened that they were delayed on the island for several days and the captain, at no time a man to hurry, made no effort to shorten his stay. He was very comfortable in the snug little harbour and life was long. He had a swim round his ship in the morning and another in the evening. There was a chandler's shop on the water front where sailormen could get a drink of whisky, and he spent the best part of the day there, playing cribbage with the half-caste who owned it. At night the mate and he went up to the house where the pretty girl lived and they sang a song or two and told stories. It was the girl's father who suggested that he should take her away with him. They discussed the matter in a friendly fashion, while the girl, nestling against the captain, urged him by the pressure of her hands and her soft smiling glances. He had taken a fancy to her and he was a domestic man. He was a little dull sometimes at sea and it would be very pleasant to have a pretty little creature like that about the old ship. He was of a practical turn too, and he recognized that it would be useful to have someone around to darn his socks and look after his linen. He was tired of having his things washed by a Chink who tore everything to pieces; the natives washed much better, and now and then when the captain went ashore at Honolulu he liked to cut a dash in a smart duck suit. It was only a matter of arranging a price. The father wanted two hundred and fifty dollars, and the captain, never a thrifty man, could not put his hand on such a sum. But he was a generous one, and with the girl's soft face against his, he was not inclined to haggle. He offered to give a hundred and fifty dollars there and then and another hundred in three months. There was a good deal of argument and the parties could not come to any agreement that night, but the idea had fired the captain, and he could not sleep as well as usual. He kept dreaming of the lovely girl and each time he awoke it was with the pressure of her soft, sensual lips on his. He cursed himself in the morning, because a bad night at poker the last time he was at Honolulu had left him so short of ready money. And if the night before he had been in love with the girl, this morning he was crazy about her.

'See here, Bananas,' he said to the mate, 'I've got to have that girl. You go and tell the old man I'll bring the dough up tonight and she can get fixed up. I figure we'll be ready to sail at dawn.'

I have no idea why the mate was known by that eccentric name. He was called Wheeler, but though he had that English surname there was not a drop of white blood in him. He was a tall man, and well-made though inclined to stoutness, but much darker than is usual in Hawaii. He was no longer young, and his crisply curling, thick hair was grey. His upper front teeth were cased in gold. He was very proud of them. He had a marked squint and this gave him a saturnine expression. The captain, who was fond of a joke, found in it a constant source of humour and hesitated the less to rally him on the defect because he realized that the mate was sensitive about it. Bananas, unlike most of the natives, was a taciturn fellow and Captain Butler would have disliked him if it had been possible for a man of his good nature to dislike anyone. He liked to be at sea with someone he could talk to, he was a chatty, sociable creature, and it was enough to drive a missionary to drink to live there day after day with a chap who never opened his mouth. He did his best to wake the mate up, that is to say, he chaffed him without mercy, but it was poor fun to laugh by oneself, and he came to the conclusion that, drunk or sober, Bananas was no fit companion for a white man. But he was a good seaman and the captain was shrewd enough to know the value of a mate he could trust. It was not rare for him to come aboard, when they were sailing, fit for nothing but to fall into his bunk, and it was worth something to know that he could stay there till he had slept his liquor off, since Bananas could be relied on. But he was an unsociable devil, and it would be a treat to have someone he could talk to. That girl would be fine. Besides, he wouldn't be so likely to get drunk when he went ashore if he knew there was a little girl waiting for him when he came on board again.

He went to his friend the chandler and over a peg of gin asked him for a loan. There were one or two useful things a ship's captain could do for a ship's chandler, and after a quarter of an hour's conversation in low tones (there is no object in letting all and sundry know your business), the captain crammed a wad of notes in his hip-pocket, and that night, when he went back to his ship, the girl went with him.

What Captain Butler, seeking for reasons to do what he had already made up his mind to, had anticipated, actually came to pass. He did not give up drinking, but he ceased to drink to excess. An evening with the boys, when he had been away from town two or three weeks, was pleasant enough, but it was pleasant too to get back to his little girl; he thought of her, sleeping so softly, and how, when he got into his cabin and leaned over her, she would open her eyes lazily and stretch out her arms for him: it was as good as a full hand. He found he was saving money, and since he was a generous man he did the right thing by the little girl: he gave her some silver-backed brushes for her long hair, and a gold chain, and a reconstructed ruby for her finger. Gee, but it was good to be alive.

A year went by, a whole year, and he was not tired of her yet. He was not a man who analysed his feelings, but this was so surprising that it forced itself upon his attention. There must be something very wonderful about that girl. He couldn't help seeing that he was more wrapped up in her than ever, and sometimes the thought entered his mind that it might not be a bad thing if he married her.

Then, one day the mate did not come in to dinner or to tea. Butler did not bother himself about his absence at the first meal, but at the second he asked the Chinese cook:

'Where's the mate? He no come tea?'

'No wantchee,' said the Chink.

'He ain't sick?'

'No savvy.'

Next day Bananas turned up again, but he was more sullen than ever, and after dinner the captain asked the girl what was the matter with him. She smiled and shrugged her pretty shoulders. She told the captain that Bananas had taken a fancy to her and he was sore because she had told him off. The captain was a good-humoured man and he was not of a jealous nature; it struck him as exceeding funny that Bananas should be in love. A man who had a squint like that had a precious poor chance. When tea came round he chaffed him gaily. He pretended to speak in the air, so that the mate should not be certain that he knew anything, but he dealt him some pretty shrewd blows. The girl did not think him as funny as he thought himself, and afterwards she begged him to say nothing more. He was surprised at her seriousness. She told him he did not know her people. When their passion was aroused they were capable of anything. She was a little frightened. This was so absurd to him that he laughed heartily.

'If he comes bothering round you, you just threaten to tell me. That'll fix him.'

'Better fire him, I think.'

'Not on your sweet life. I know a good sailor when I see one. But if he don't leave you alone I'll give him the worst licking he's ever had.'

Perhaps the girl had a wisdom unusual in her sex. She knew that it was useless to argue with a man when his mind was made up, for it only increased his stubbornness, and she held her peace. And now on the shabby schooner, threading her way across the silent sea, among those lovely islands, was enacted a dark, tense drama of which the fat little captain remained entirely ignorant. The girl's resistance fired Bananas so that he ceased to be a man, but was simply blind desire. He did not make love to her gently or gaily, but with a black and savage ferocity. Her contempt now was changed to hatred and when he besought her she answered him with bitter, angry taunts. But the struggle went on silently, and when the captain asked her after a little while whether Bananas was bothering her, she lied.

But one night, when they were in Honolulu, he came on board only just in time. They were sailing at dawn. Bananas had been ashore, drinking some native spirit, and he was drunk. The captain, rowing up, heard sounds that surprised him. He scrambled up the ladder. He saw Bananas, beside himself, trying to wrench open the cabin door. He was shouting at the girl. He swore he would kill her if she did not let him in.

'What in hell are you up to?' cried Butler.

The mate let go the handle, gave the captain a look of savage hate, and without a word turned away.

'Stop here. What are you doing with that door?'

The mate still did not answer. He looked at him with sullen, bootless rage.

'I'll teach you not to pull any of your queer stuff with me, you dirty, cross-eyed nigger,' said the captain.

He was a good foot shorter than the mate and no match for him, but he was used to dealing with native crews, and he had his knuckle-duster handy. Perhaps it was not an instrument that a gentleman would use, but then Captain Butler was not a gentleman. Nor was he in the habit of dealing with gentlemen. Before Bananas knew what the captain was at, his right arm had shot out and his fist, with its ring of steel, caught him fair and square on the jaw. He fell like a bull under the pole-axe.

'That'll learn him,' said the captain.

Bananas did not stir. The girl unlocked the cabin door and came out.

'Is he dead?'

'He ain't.'

He called a couple of men and told them to carry the mate to his bunk. He rubbed his hands with satisfaction and his round blue eyes gleamed behind his spectacles. But the girl was strangely silent. She put her arms round him as though to protect him from invisible harm.

It was two or three days before Bananas was on his feet again, and when he came out of his cabin his face was torn and swollen. Through the darkness of his skin you saw the livid bruise. Butler saw him slinking along the deck and called him. The mate went to him without a word.

'See here, Bananas,' he said to him, fixing his spectacles on his slippery nose, for it was very hot. 'I ain't going to fire you for this, but you know now that when I hit, I hit hard. Don't forget it and don't let me have any more funny business.'

Then he held out his hand and gave the mate that good-humoured, flashing smile of his which was his greatest charm. The mate took the outstretched hand and twitched his swollen lips into a devilish grin. The incident in the captain's mind was so completely finished that when the three of them sat at dinner he chaffed Bananas on his appearance. He was eating with difficulty and, his swollen face still more distorted by pain, he looked truly a repulsive object.

That evening, when he was sitting on the upper deck, smoking his pipe, a shiver passed through the captain.

'I don't know what I should be shiverin' for on a night like this,' he grumbled. 'Maybe I've gotten a dose of fever. I've been feelin' a bit queer all day.'

When he went to bed he took some quinine, and next morning he felt better, but a little washed out, as though he were recovering from a debauch.

'I guess my liver's out of order,' he said, and he took a pill.

He had not much appetite that day and towards evening he began to feel very unwell. He tried the next remedy he knew, which was to drink two or three hot whiskies, but that did not seem to help him much, and when in the morning he surveyed himself in the glass he thought he was not looking quite the thing.

'If I ain't right by the time we get back to Honolulu I'll just give Dr Denby a call. He'll sure fix me up.'

He could not eat. He felt a great lassitude in all his limbs. He slept soundly enough, but he awoke with no sense of refreshment; on the contrary he felt a peculiar exhaustion. And the energetic little man, who could not bear the thought of lying in bed, had to make an effort to force himself out of his bunk. After a few days he found it impossible to resist the languor that oppressed him, and he made up his mind not to get up.

'Bananas can look after the ship,' he said. 'He has before now.'

He laughed a little to himself as he thought how often he had lain speechless in his bunk after a night with the boys. That was before he had his girl. He smiled at her and pressed her hand. She was puzzled and anxious. He saw that she was concerned about him and tried to reassure her. He had never had a day's illness in his life and in a week at the outside he would be as right as rain.

'I wish you'd fired Bananas,' she said. 'I've got a feeling that he's at the bottom of this.'

'Damned good thing I didn't, or there'd be no one to sail the ship. I know a good sailor when I see one.' His blue eyes, rather pale now, with the whites all yellow, twinkled. 'You don't think he's trying to poison me, little girl?'

She did not answer, but she had one or two talks with the Chinese cook, and she took great care with the captain's food. But he ate little enough now, and it was only with the greatest difficulty that she persuaded him to drink a cup of soup two or three times a day. It was clear that he was very ill, he was losing weight quickly, and his chubby face was pale and drawn. He suffered no pain, but merely grew every day weaker and more languid. He was wasting away. The round trip on this occasion lasted about four weeks and by the time they came to Honolulu the captain was a little anxious about himself. He had not been out of his bed for more than a fortnight and really he felt too weak to get up and go to the doctor. He sent a message asking him to come on board. The doctor examined him, but could find nothing to account for his condition. His temperature was normal.

'See here, Captain,' he said, 'I'll be perfectly frank with you. I don't know what's the matter with you, and just seeing you like this don't give me a chance. You come into the hospital so that we can keep you under observation. There's nothing organically wrong with you, I know that, and my impression is that a few weeks in hospital ought to put you to rights.'

'I ain't going to leave my ship.'

Chinese owners were queer customers, he said; if he left his ship because he was sick, his owner might fire him, and he couldn't afford to lose his job. So long as he stayed where he was his contract safeguarded him, and he had a first-rate mate.

Besides, he couldn't leave his girl. No man could want a better nurse; if anyone could pull him through she would. Every man had to die once and he only wished to be left in peace. He would not listen to the doctor's expostulations, and finally the doctor gave in.

'I'll write you a prescription', he said doubtfully, 'and see if it does you any good. You'd better stay in bed for a while.'

'There ain't much fear of my getting up, doc,' answered the captain. 'I feel as weak as a cat.'

But he believed in the doctor's prescription as little as did the doctor himself, and when he was alone amused himself by lighting his cigar with it. He had to get amusement out of something, for his cigar tasted like nothing on earth, and he smoked only to persuade himself that he was not too ill to. That evening a couple of friends of his, masters of tramp steamers, hearing he was sick came to see him. They discussed his case over a bottle of whisky and a box of Philippine cigars. One of them remembered how a mate of his had been taken queer just like that and not a doctor in the United States had been able to cure him. He had seen in the paper an advertisement of a patent medicine, and thought there'd be no harm in trying it. That man was as strong as ever he'd been in his life after two bottles. But his illness had given Captain Butler a lucidity which was new and strange, and while they talked he seemed to read their minds. They thought he was dying. And when they left him he was afraid.

The girl saw his weakness. This was her opportunity. She had been urging him to let a native doctor see him, and he had stoutly refused; but now she entreated him. He listened with harassed eyes. He wavered. It was very funny that the American doctor could not tell what was the matter with him. But he did not want her to think that he was scared. If he let a damned nigger come along and look at him, it was to comfort *her*. He told her to do what she liked.

The native doctor came the next night. The captain was lying alone, half awake, and the cabin was dimly lit by an oil lamp. The door was softly opened and the girl came in on tip-toe. She held the door open and someone slipped in silently behind her. The captain smiled at this mystery, but he was so weak now, the smile was no more than a glimmer in his eyes. The doctor was a little, old man, very thin and very wrinkled, with a completely bald head, and the face of a monkey. He was bowed and gnarled like an old tree. He looked hardly human, but his eyes were very bright, and in the half darkness they seemed to glow with a

91

reddish light. He was dressed filthily in a pair of ragged dungarees, and the upper part of his body was naked. He sat down on his haunches and for ten minutes looked at the captain. Then he felt the palms of his hands and the soles of his feet. The girl watched him with frightened eyes. No word was spoken. Then he asked for something that the captain had worn. The girl gave him the old felt hat which the captain used constantly and taking it he sat down again on the floor, clasping it firmly with both hands; and rocking backwards and forwards slowly he muttered some gibberish in a very low tone.

At last he gave a little sigh and dropped the hat. He took an old pipe out of his trouser pocket and lit it. The girl went over to him and sat by his side. He whispered something to her, and she started violently. For a few minutes they talked in hurried undertones, and then they stood up. She gave him money and opened the door for him. He slid out as silently as he had come in. Then she went over to the captain and leaned over him so that she could speak into his ear.

'It's an enemy praying you to death.'

'Don't talk fool stuff, girlie,' he said impatiently.

'It's truth. It's God's truth. That's why the American doctor couldn't do anything. Our people can do that. I've seen it done. I thought you were safe because you were a white man.'

'I haven't an enemy.'

'Bananas.'

'What's he want to pray me to death for?'

'You ought to have fired him before he had a chance.'

'I guess if I ain't got nothing more the matter with me than Bananas' hoodoo I shall be sitting up and taking nourishment in a very few days.'

She was silent for a while and she looked at him intently.

'Don't you know you're dying?' she said to him at last.

That was what the two skippers had thought, but they hadn't said it. A shiver passed across the captain's wan face.

'The doctor says there ain't nothing really the matter with me. I've only to lie quiet for a bit and I shall be all right.'

She put her lips to his ear as if she were afraid that the air itself might hear.

'You're dying, dying, dying. You'll pass out with the old moon.'

'That's something to know.'

'You'll pass out with the old moon unless Bananas dies before.'

He was not a timid man and he had recovered already from

the shock her words, and still more her vehement, silent manner, had given him. Once more a smile flickered in his eyes.

'I guess I'll take my chance, girlie.'

'There's twelve days before the new moon.'

There was something in her tone that gave him an idea.

'See here, my girl, this is all bunk. I don't believe a word of it. But I don't want you to try any of your monkey tricks with Bananas. He ain't a beauty, but he's a first-rate mate.'

He would have said a good deal more, but he was tired out. He suddenly felt very weak and faint. It was always at that hour that he felt worse. He closed his eyes. The girl watched him for a minute and then slipped out of the cabin. The moon, nearly full, made a silver pathway over the dark sea. It shone from an unclouded sky. She looked at it with terror, for she knew that with its death the man she loved would die. His life was in her hands. She could save him, she alone could save him, but the enemy was cunning, and she must be cunning too. She felt that someone was looking at her, and without turning, by the sudden fear that seized her, knew that from the shadow the burning eyes of the mate were fixed upon her. She did not know what he could do; if he could read her thoughts she was defeated already, and with a desperate effort she emptied her mind of all content. His death alone could save her lover, and she could bring his death about. She knew that if he could be brought to look into a calabash in which was water so that a reflection of him was made, and the reflection were broken by hurtling the water, he would die as though he had been struck by lightning; for the reflection was his soul. But none knew better than he the danger, and he could be made to look only by a guile which had lulled his least suspicion. He must never think that he had an enemy who was on the watch to cause his destruction. She knew what she had to do. But the time was short, the time was terribly short. Presently she realized that the mate had gone. She breathed more freely.

Two days later they sailed, and there were ten now before the new moon. Captain Butler was terrible to see. He was nothing but skin and bone, and he could not move without help. He could hardly speak. But she dared do nothing yet. She knew that she must be patient. The mate was cunning, cunning. They went to one of the smaller islands of the group and discharged cargo, and now there were only seven days more. The moment had come to start. She brought some things out of the cabin she shared with the captain and made them into a bundle. She put the bundle in the deck cabin where she and Bananas ate their meals, and at dinner time, when she went in, he turned quickly and she saw that he had been looking at it. Neither of them spoke, but she knew what he suspected. She was making her preparations to leave the ship. He looked at her mockingly. Gradually, as though to prevent the captain from knowing what she was about, she brought everything she owned into the cabin, and some of the captain's clothes, and made them all into bundles. At last Bananas could keep silence no longer. He pointed to a suit of ducks.

'What are you going to do with that?' he asked.

She shrugged her shoulders.

'I'm going back to my island.'

He gave a laugh that distorted his grim face. The captain was dying and she meant to get away with all she could lay hands on.

'What'll you do if I say you can't take those things? They're the captain's.'

'They're no use to you,' she said.

There was a calabash hanging on the wall. It was the very calabash I had seen when I came into the cabin and which we had talked about. She took it down. It was all dusty, so she poured water into it from the water-bottle, and rinsed it with her fingers.

'What are you doing with that?'

'I can sell it for fifty dollars,' she said.

'If you want to take it you'll have to pay me.'

'What d'you want?'

'You know what I want.'

She allowed a fleeting smile to play on her lips. She flashed a quick look at him and quickly turned away. He gave a gasp of desire. She raised her shoulders in a little shrug. With a savage bound he sprang upon her and seized her in his arms. Then she laughed. She put her arms, her soft, round arms, about his neck, and surrendered herself to him voluptuously.

When the morning came she roused him out of a deep sleep. The early rays of the sun slanted into the cabin. He pressed her to his heart. Then he told her that the captain could not last more than a day or two, and the owner wouldn't so easily find another white man to command the ship. If Bananas offered to take less money he would get the job and the girl could stay with him. He looked at her with love-sick eyes. She nestled up against him. She kissed his lips, in the foreign way, in the way the captain had taught her to kiss. And she promised to stay. Bananas was drunk with happiness.

It was now or never.

She got up and went to the table to arrange her hair. There was no mirror and she looked into the calabash, seeking for her reflection. She tidied her beautiful hair. Then she beckoned to Bananas to come to her. She pointed to the calabash.

'There's something in the bottom of it,' she said.

Instinctively, without suspecting anything, Bananas looked full into the water. His face was reflected in it. In a flash she beat upon it violently, with both her hands, so that they pounded on the bottom and the water splashed up. The reflection was broken in pieces. Bananas started back with a sudden hoarse cry and he looked at the girl. She was standing there with a look of triumphant hatred on her face. A horror came into his eyes. His heavy features were twisted in agony, and with a thud, as though he had taken a violent poison, he crumpled up on the ground. A great shudder passed through his body and he was still. She leaned over him callously. She put her hand on his heart and then she pulled down his lower eye-lid. He was quite dead.

She went into the cabin in which lay Captain Butler. There was a faint colour in his cheeks and he looked at her in a startled way.

'What's happened?' he whispered.

They were the first words he had spoken for forty-eight hours.

'Nothing's happened,' she said.

'I feel all funny.'

Then his eyes closed and he fell asleep. He slept for a day and a night, and when he awoke he asked for food. In a fortnight he was well.

It was past midnight when Winter and I rowed back to shore and we had drunk innumerable whiskies and sodas.

'What do you think of it all?' asked Winter.

'What a question! If you mean, have I any explanation to suggest, I haven't.'

'The captain believes every word of it.'

'That's obvious; but, you know, that's not the part that interests me most: whether it's true or not, and what it all means; the part that interests me is that such things should happen to such people. I wonder what there is in that common-place little man to arouse such a passion in that lovely creature. As I watched her, asleep there, while he was telling the story I had some fantastic idea about the power of love being able to work miracles.'

'But that's not the girl,' said Winter.

'What on earth do you mean?'

'Didn't you notice the cook?'

'Of course I did. He's the ugliest man I ever saw.'

'That's why Butler took him. The girl ran away with the Chinese cook last year. This is a new one. He's only had her there about two months.'

'Well, I'm hanged.'

'He thinks this cook is safe. But I wouldn't be too sure in his place. There's something about a Chink, when he lays himself out to please a woman she can't resist him.'

THE LUNCHEON

I CAUGHT sight of her at the play and in answer to her beckoning I went over during the interval and sat down beside her. It was long since I had last seen her and if someone had not mentioned her name I hardly think I would have recognized her. She addressed me brightly.

'Well, it's many years since we first met. How time does fly! We're none of us getting any younger. Do you remember the first time I saw you? You asked me to luncheon.'

Did I remember?

It was twenty years ago and I was living in Paris. I had a tiny apartment in the Latin Quarter overlooking a cemetery and I was earning barely enough money to keep body and soul together. She had read a book of mine and had written to me about it. I answered, thanking her, and presently I received from her another letter saying that she was passing through Paris and would like to have a chat with me; but her time was limited and the only free moment she had was on the following Thursday; she was spending the morning at the Luxembourg and would I give her a little luncheon at Foyot's afterwards? Foyot's is a restaurant at which the French senators eat and it was so far beyond my means that I had never even thought of going there. But I was flattered and I was too young to have learned to say no to a woman. (Few men, I may add, learn this until they are too old to make it of any consequence to a woman what they say.) I had eighty francs (gold francs) to last me the rest of the month and a modest luncheon should not cost more than fifteen. If I cut out coffee for the next two weeks I could manage well enough.

I answered that I would meet my friend – by correspondence – at Foyot's on Thursday at half past twelve. She was not so young as I expected and in appearance imposing rather than attractive. She was in fact a woman of forty (a charming age, but not one that excites a sudden and devastating passion at first sight), and she gave me the impression of having more teeth, white and large and even, than were necessary for any practical purpose. She was talkative, but since she seemed inclined to talk about me I was prepared to be an attentive listener.

I was startled when the bill of fare was brought, for the prices were a great deal higher than I had anticipated. But she reassured me.

'I never eat anything for luncheon,' she said.

'Oh, don't say that!' I answered generously.

'I never eat more than one thing. I think people eat far too much nowadays. A little fish, perhaps. I wonder if they have any salmon.'

Well, it was early in the year for salmon and it was not on the bill of fare, but I asked the waiter if there was any. Yes, a beautiful salmon had just come in, it was the first they had had. I ordered it for my guest. The waiter asked her if she would have something while it was being cooked.

'No,' she answered, 'I never eat more than one thing. Unless you had a little caviare. I never mind caviare.'

My heart sank a little. I knew I could not afford caviare, but I could not very well tell her that. I told the waiter by all means to bring caviare. For myself I chose the cheapest dish on the menu and that was a mutton chop.

'I think you're unwise to eat meat,' she said. 'I don't know how you can expect to work after eating heavy things like chops. I don't believe in overloading my stomach.'

Then came the question of drink.

'I never drink anything for luncheon,' she said.

'Neither do I,' I answered promptly.

'Except white wine,' she proceeded as though I had not spoken. 'These French white wines are so light. They're wonderful for the digestion.'

'What would you like?' I asked, hospitable still, but not exactly effusive.

She gave me a bright and amicable flash of her white teeth.

'My doctor won't let me drink anything but champagne.'

I fancy I turned a trifle pale. I ordered half a bottle. I mentioned casually that my doctor had absolutely forbidden me to drink champagne.

'What are you going to drink, then?'

'Water.'

She ate the caviare and she ate the salmon. She talked gaily of art and literature and music. But I wondered what the bill would come to. When my mutton chop arrived she took me quite seriously to task.

'I see that you're in the habit of eating a heavy luncheon. I'm sure it's a mistake. Why don't you follow my example and just eat one thing? I'm sure you'd feel ever so much better for it.'

'I *am* only going to eat one thing,' I said, as the waiter came again with the bill of fare.

She waved him aside with an airy gesture.

'No, no, I never eat anything for luncheon. Just a bite, I never want more than that, and I eat that more as an excuse for conversation than anything else. I couldn't possibly eat anything more – unless they had some of those giant asparagus. I should be sorry to leave Paris without having some of them.'

My heart sank. I had seen them in the shops and I knew that they were horribly expensive. My mouth had often watered at the sight of them.

'Madame wants to know if you have any of those giant asparagus,' I asked the waiter.

I tried with all my might to will him to say no. A happy smile spread over his broad, priest-like face, and he assured me that they had some so large, so splendid, so tender, that it was a marvel.

'I'm not in the least hungry,' my guest sighed, 'but if you insist I don't mind having some asparagus.'

I ordered them.

'Aren't you going to have any?'

'No, I never eat asparagus.'

'I know there are people who don't like them. The fact is, you ruin your palate by all the meat you eat.'

We waited for the asparagus to be cooked. Panic seized me. It was not a question now how much money I should have left over for the rest of the month, but whether I had enough to pay the bill. It would be mortifying to find myself ten francs short and be obliged to borrow from my guest. I could not bring myself to do that. I knew exactly how much I had and if the bill came to more I made up my mind that I would put my hand in my pocket and with a dramatic cry start up and say it had been picked. Of course it would be awkward if she had not money enough either to pay the bill. Then the only thing would be to leave my watch and say I would come back and pay later.

The asparagus appeared. They were enormous, succulent, and appetizing. The smell of the melted butter tickled my nostrils as the nostrils of Jehovah were tickled by the burned offerings of the virtuous Semites. I watched the abandoned woman thrust them down her throat in large voluptuous mouthfuls and in my polite way I discoursed on the condition of the drama in the Balkans. At last she finished.

'Coffee?' I said.

'Yes, just an ice-cream and coffee,' she answered.

I was past caring now, so I ordered coffee for myself and an ice-cream and coffee for her.

'You know, there's one thing I thoroughly believe in,' she said, as she ate the ice-cream. 'One should always get up from a meal feeling one could eat a little more.'

'Are you still hungry?' I asked faintly.

'Oh, no, I'm not hungry; you see, I don't eat luncheon. I have a cup of coffee in the morning and then dinner, but I never eat more than one thing for luncheon. I was speaking for you.'

'Oh, I see!'

Then a terrible thing happened. While we were waiting for the coffee, the head waiter, with an ingratiating smile on his false face, came up to us bearing a large basket full of huge peaches. They had the blush of an innocent girl; they had the rich tone of an Italian landscape. But surely peaches were not in season then? Lord knew what they cost. I knew too – a little later, for my guest, going on with her conversation, absentmindedly took one.

'You see, you've filled your stomach with a lot of meat' – my one miserable little chop – 'and you can't eat any more. But I've just had a snack and I shall enjoy a peach.'

The bill came and when I paid it I found that I had only enough for a quite inadequate tip. Her eyes rested for an instant on the three francs I left for the waiter and I knew that she thought me mean. But when I walked out of the restaurant I had the whole month before me and not a penny in my pocket.

'Follow my example,' she said as we shook hands, 'and never eat more than one thing for luncheon.'

'I'll do better than that,' I retorted. 'I'll eat nothing for dinner tonight.'

'Humorist!' she cried gaily, jumping into a cab. 'You're quite a humorist!'

But I have had my revenge at last. I do not believe that I am a vindictive man, but when the immortal gods take a hand in the matter it is pardonable to observe the result with complacency. Today she weighs twenty-one stone.

THE ANT AND THE GRASSHOPPER

WHEN I was a very small boy I was made to learn by heart certain of the fables of La Fontaine, and the moral of each was carefully explained to me. Among those I learnt was *The Ant and The Grasshopper*, which is devised to bring home to the young the useful lesson that in an imperfect world industry is rewarded and giddiness punished. In this admirable fable (I apologize for telling something which everyone is politely, but inexactly, supposed to know) the ant spends a laborious summer gathering its winter store, while the grasshopper sits on a blade of grass singing to the sun. Winter comes and the ant is comfortably provided for, but the grasshopper has an empty larder: he goes to the ant and begs for a little food. Then the ant gives him her classic answer:

'What were you doing in the summer time?'

'Saving your presence, I sang, I sang all day, all night.'

'You sang. Why, then go and dance.'

I do not ascribe it to perversity on my part, but rather to the inconsequence of childhood, which is deficient in moral sense, that I could never quite reconcile myself to the lesson. My sympathies were with the grasshopper and for some time I never saw an ant without putting my foot on it. In this summary (and as I have discovered since, entirely human) fashion I sought to express my disapproval of prudence and common sense.

I could not help thinking of this fable when the other day I saw George Ramsay lunching by himself in a restaurant. I never saw anyone wear an expression of such deep gloom. He was staring into space. He looked as though the burden of the whole world sat on his shoulders. I was sorry for him: I suspected at once that his unfortunate brother had been causing trouble again. I went up to him and held out my hand.

'How are you?' I asked.

'I'm not in hilarious spirits,' he answered.

'Is it Tom again?'

He sighed.

'Yes, it's Tom again.'

'Why don't you chuck him? You've done everything in the world for him. You must know by now that he's quite hopeless.'

I suppose every family has a black sheep. Tom had been a sore trial to his for twenty years. He had begun life decently enough:

he went into business, married, and had two children. The Ramsays were perfectly respectable people and there was every reason to suppose that Tom Ramsay would have a useful and honourable career. But one day, without warning, he announced that he didn't like work and that he wasn't suited for marriage. He wanted to enjoy himself. He would listen to no expostulations. He left his wife and his office. He had a little money and he spent two happy years in the various capitals of Europe. Rumours of his doings reached his relations from time to time and they were profoundly shocked. He certainly had a very good time. They shook their heads and asked what would happen when his money was spent. They soon found out: he borrowed. He was charming and unscrupulous. I have never met anyone to whom it was more difficult to refuse a loan. He made a steady income from his friends and he made friends easily. But he always said that the money you spent on necessities was boring; the money that was amusing to spend was the money you spent on luxuries. For this he depended on his brother George. He did not waste his charm on him. George was a serious man and insensible to such enticements. George was respectable. Once or twice he fell to Tom's promises of amendment and gave him considerable sums in order that he might make a fresh start. On these Tom bought a motor-car and some very nice jewellery. But when circumstances forced George to realize that his brother would never settle down and he washed his hands of him, Tom, without a qualm, began to blackmail him. It was not very nice for a respectable lawyer to find his brother shaking cocktails behind the bar of his favourite restaurant or to see him waiting on the box-seat of a taxi outside his club. Tom said that to serve in a bar or to drive a taxi was a perfectly decent occupation, but if George could oblige him with a couple of hundred pounds he didn't mind for the honour of the family giving it up. George paid.

Once Tom nearly went to prison. George was terribly upset. He went into the whole discreditable affair. Really Tom had gone too far. He had been wild, thoughtless, and selfish, but he had never before done anything dishonest, by which George meant illegal; and if he were prosecuted he would assuredly be convicted. But you cannot allow your only brother to go to gaol. The man Tom had cheated, a man called Cronshaw, was vindictive. He was determined to take the matter into court; he said Tom was a scoundrel and should be punished. It cost George an infinite deal of trouble and five hundred pounds to settle the affair. I have never seen him in such a rage as when he heard that Tom and Cronshaw had gone off together to Monte Carlo the moment they cashed the cheque. They spent a happy month there.

For twenty years Tom raced and gambled, philandered with the prettiest girls, danced, ate in the most expensive restaurants, and dressed beautifully. He always looked as if he had just stepped out of a bandbox. Though he was forty-six you would never have taken him for more than thirty-five. He was a most amusing companion and though you knew he was perfectly worthless you could not but enjoy his society. He had high spirits, an unfailing gaiety, and incredible charm. I never grudged the contributions he regularly levied on me for the necessities of his existence. I never lent him fifty pounds without feeling that I was in his debt. Tom Ramsay knew everyone and everyone knew Tom Ramsay. You could not approve of him, but you could not help liking him.

Poor George, only a year older than his scapegrace brother, looked sixty. He had never taken more than a fortnight's holiday in the year for a quarter of a century. He was in his office every morning at nine-thirty and never left it till six. He was honest, industrious, and worthy. He had a good wife, to whom he had never been unfaithful even in thought, and four daughters to whom he was the best of fathers. He made a point of saving a third of his income and his plan was to retire at fifty-five to a little house in the country where he proposed to cultivate his garden and play golf. His life was blameless. He was glad that he was growing old because Tom was growing old too. He rubbed his hands and said:

'It was all very well when Tom was young and good-looking, but he's only a year younger than I am. In four years he'll be fifty. He won't find life so easy then. I shall have thirty thousand pounds by the time I'm fifty. For twenty-five years I've said that Tom would end in the gutter. And we shall see how he likes that. We shall see if it really pays best to work or be idle.'

Poor George! I sympathized with him. I wondered now as I sat down beside him what infamous thing Tom had done. George was evidently very much upset.

'Do you know what's happened now?' he asked me.

I was prepared for the worst. I wondered if Tom had got into the hands of the police at last. George could hardly bring himself to speak.

'You're not going to deny that all my life I've been

hardworking, decent, respectable, and straightforward. After a life of industry and thrift I can look forward to retiring on a small income in gilt-edged securities. I've always done my duty in that state of life in which it has pleased Providence to place me.'

'True.'

'And you can't deny that Tom has been an idle, worthless, dissolute, and dishonourable rogue. If there were any justice he'd be in the workhouse.'

'True.'

George grew red in the face.

'A few weeks ago he became engaged to a woman old enough to be his mother. And now she's died and left him everything she had. Half a million pounds, a yacht, a house in London, and a house in the country.'

George Ramsay beat his clenched fist on the table.

'It's not fair, I tell you, it's not fair. Damn it, it's not fair.'

I could not help it. I burst into a shout of laughter as I looked at George's wrathful face, I rolled in my chair, I very nearly fell on the floor. George never forgave me. But Tom often asks me to excellent dinners in his charming house in Mayfair, and if he occasionally borrows a trifle from me, that is merely from force of habit. It is never more than a sovereign.

HOME

THE farm lay in a hollow among the Somersetshire hills, an old-fashioned stone house surrounded by barns and pens and outhouses. Over the doorway the date when it was built had been carved in the elegant figures of the period, 1673, and the house, grey and weather-beaten, looked as much a part of the landscape as the trees that sheltered it. An avenue of splendid elms that would have been the pride of many a squire's mansion led from the road to the trim garden. The people who lived here were as stolid, sturdy, and unpretentious as the house; their only boast was that ever since it was built from father to son in one unbroken line they had been born and died in it. For three hundred years they had farmed the surrounding land. George Meadows was now a man of fifty, and his wife was a year or two younger. They were both fine, upstanding people in the prime of life; and their children, two sons and three girls, were handsome and strong. They had no new-fangled notions about being gentlemen and ladies; they knew their place and were proud of it. I have never seen a more united household. They were merry, industrious, and kindly. Their life was patriarchal. It had a completeness that gave it a beauty as definite as that of a symphony by Beethoven or a picture by Titian. They were happy and they deserved their happiness. But the master of the house was not George Meadows (not by a long chalk, they said in the village); it was his mother. She was twice the man her son was, they said. She was a woman of seventy, tall, upright, and dignified, with grey hair, and though her face was much wrinkled, her eyes were bright and shrewd. Her word was law in the house and on the farm; but she had humour, and if her rule was despotic it was also kindly. People laughed at her jokes and repeated them. She was a good business woman and you had to get up very early in the morning to best her in a bargain. She was a character. She combined in a rare degree goodwill with an alert sense of the ridiculous.

One day Mrs George stopped me on my way home. She was all in a flutter. (Her mother-in-law was the only Mrs Meadows we knew; George's wife was only known as Mrs George.)

'Whoever do you think is coming here today?' she asked me. 'Uncle George Meadows. You know, him as was in China.'

'Why, I thought he was dead.'

105

'We all thought he was dead.'

I had heard the story of Uncle George Meadows a dozen times, and it had amused me because it had the savour of an old ballad: it was oddly touching to come across it in real life. For Uncle George Meadows and Tom, his younger brother, had both courted Mrs Meadows when she was Emily Green, fifty years and more ago, and when she married Tom, George had gone away to sea.

They heard of him on the China coast. For twenty years now and then he sent them presents; then there was no more news of him; when Tom Meadows died his widow wrote and told him, but received no answer; and at last they came to the conclusion that he must be dead. But two or three days ago to their astonishment they had received a letter from the matron of the sailors' home at Portsmouth. It appeared that for the last ten years George Meadows, crippled with rheumatism, had been an inmate and now, feeling that he had not much longer to live, wanted to see once more the house in which he was born. Albert Meadows, his great-nephew, had gone over to Portsmouth in the Ford to fetch him and he was to arrive that afternoon.

'Just fancy,' said Mrs George, 'he's not been here for more than fifty years. He's never even seen my George, who's fifty-one next birthday.'

'And what does Mrs Meadows think of it?' I asked.

'Well, you know what she is. She sits there and smiles to herself. All she says is, "He was a good-looking young fellow when he left, but not so steady as his brother." That's why she chose my George's father. "But he's probably quietened down by now," she says.'

Mrs George asked me to look in and see him. With the simplicity of a country woman who had never been further from her home than London, she thought that because we had both been in China we must have something in common. Of course I accepted. I found the whole family assembled when I arrived; they were sitting in the great old kitchen, with its stone floor, Mrs Meadows in her usual chair by the fire, very upright, and I was amused to see that she had put on her best silk dress, while her son and his wife sat at the table with their children. On the other side of the fireplace sat an old man, bunched up in a chair. He was very thin and his skin hung on his bones like an old suit much too large for him; his face was wrinkled and yellow and he had lost nearly all his teeth.

I shook hands with him.

'Well, I'm glad to see you've got here safely, Mr Meadows,' I said.

'Captain,' he corrected.

'He walked here,' Albert, his great-nephew, told me. 'When he got to the gate he made me stop the car and said he wanted to walk.'

'And mind you, I've not been out of my bed for two years. They carried me down and put me in the car. I thought I'd never walk again, but when I see them elm trees, I remember my father set a lot of store by them elm trees, I felt I could walk. I walked down that drive fifty-two years ago when I went away and now I've walked back again.'

'Silly, I call it,' said Mrs Meadows.

'It's done me good. I feel better and stronger than I have for ten years. I'll see you out yet, Emily.'

'Don't you be too sure,' she answered.

I suppose no one had called Mrs Meadows by her first name for a generation. It gave me a little shock, as though the old man were taking a liberty with her. She looked at him with a shrewd smile in her eyes and he, talking to her, grinned with his toothless gums. It was strange to look at them, these two old people who had not seen one another for half a century, and to think that all that long time ago he had loved her and she had loved another. I wondered if they remembered what they had felt then and what they had said to one another. I wondered if it seemed to him strange now that for that old woman he had left the home of his fathers, his lawful inheritance, and lived an exile's life.

'Have you ever been married, Captain Meadows?' I asked.

'Not me,' he said, in his quavering voice, with a grin. 'I know too much about women for that.'

'That's what you say,' retorted Mrs Meadows. 'If the truth was known I shouldn't be surprised to hear as how you'd had half a dozen black wives in your day.'

'They're not black in China, Emily, you ought to know better than that, they're yellow.'

'Perhaps that's why you've got so yellow yourself. When I saw you, I said to myself, why, he's got jaundice.'

'I said I'd never marry anyone but you, Emily, and I never have.'

He said this not with pathos or resentment, but as a mere statement of fact, as a man might say, 'I said I'd walk twenty miles and I've done it.' There was a trace of satisfaction in the speech.

'Well, you might have regretted it if you had,' she answered. I talked a little with the old man about China.

'There's not a port in China that I don't know better than you know your coat pocket. Where a ship can go I've been. I could keep you sitting here all day long for six months and not tell you half the things I've seen in my day.'

'Well, one thing you've not done, George, as far as I can see,' said Mrs Meadows, the mocking but not unkindly smile still in her eyes, 'and that's to make a fortune.'

'I'm not one to save money. Make it and spend it; that's my motto. But one thing I can say for myself: if I had the chance of going through my life again I'd take it. And there's not many as'll say that.'

'No, indeed,' I said.

I looked at him with admiration and respect. He was a toothless, crippled, penniless old man, but he had made a success of life, for he had enjoyed it. When I left him he asked me to come and see him again next day. If I was interested in China he would tell me all the stories I wanted to hear.

Next morning I thought I would go and ask if the old man would like to see me. I strolled down the magnificent avenue of elm trees and when I came to the garden saw Mrs Meadows picking flowers. I bade her good morning and she raised herself. She had a huge armful of white flowers. I glanced at the house and I saw that the blinds were drawn: I was surprised, for Mrs Meadows liked the sunshine.

'Time enough to live in the dark when you're buried,' she always said.

'How's Captain Meadows?' I asked her.

'He always was a harum-scarum fellow,' she answered. 'When Lizzie took him a cup of tea this morning she found he was dead.'

'Dead?'

'Yes. Died in his sleep. I was just picking these flowers to put in the room. Well, I'm glad he died in that old house. It always means a lot to them Meadows to do that.'

They had had a good deal of difficulty in persuading him to go to bed. He had talked to them of all the things that had happened to him in his long life. He was happy to be back in his old home. He was proud that he had walked up the drive without assistance, and he boasted that he would live for another twenty years. But fate had been kind: death had written the full-stop in the right place.

Mrs Meadows smelt the white flowers that she held in her arms.

'Well, I'm glad he came back,' she said. 'After I married Tom Meadows and George went away, the fact is I was never quite sure that I'd married the right one.'

THE POOL

When I was introduced to Lawson by Chaplin, the owner of the Hotel Metropole at Apia, I paid no particular attention to him. We were sitting in the lounge over an early cocktail and I was listening with amusement to the gossip of the island.

Chaplin entertained me. He was by profession a mining engineer and perhaps it was characteristic of him that he had settled in a place where his professional attainments were of no possible value. It was, however, generally reported that he was an extremely clever mining engineer. He was a small man, neither fat nor thin, with black hair, scanty on the crown, turning grey, and a small, untidy moustache; his face, partly from the sun and partly from liquor, was very red. He was but a figurehead, for the hotel, though so grandly named but a frame building of two storeys, was managed by his wife, a tall, gaunt Australian of five-and-forty, with an imposing presence and a determined air. The little man, excitable and often tipsy, was terrified of her, and the stranger soon heard of domestic quarrels in which she used her fist and her foot in order to keep him in subjection. She had been known after a night of drunkenness to confine him for twenty-four hours to his own room, and then he could be seen, afraid to leave his prison, talking somewhat pathetically from his veranda to people in the street below.

He was a character, and his reminiscences of a varied life, whether true or not, made him worth listening to, so that when Lawson strolled in I was inclined to resent the interruption. Although not midday, it was clear that he had had enough to drink, and it was without enthusiasm that I yielded to his persistence and accepted his offer of another cocktail. I knew already that Chaplin's head was weak. The next round which in common politeness I should be forced to order would be enough to make him lively, and then Mrs Chaplin would give me black looks.

Nor was there anything attractive in Lawson's appearance. He was a little thin man, with a long, sallow face and a narrow, weak chin, a prominent nose, large and bony, and great shaggy black eyebrows. They gave him a peculiar look. His eyes, very large and very dark, were magnificent. He was jolly, but his jollity did not seem to me sincere; it was on the surface, a mask which he wore to deceive the world, and I suspected that it concealed a mean nature. He was plainly anxious to be thought a 'good sport' and he was hail-fellow-well-met; but, I do not know why, I felt that he was cunning and shifty. He talked a great deal in a raucous voice, and he and Chaplin capped one another's stories of beanos which had become legendary, stories of 'wet' nights at the English Club, of shooting expeditions where an incredible amount of whisky had been consumed, and of jaunts to Sydney of which their pride was that they could remember nothing from the time they landed till the time they sailed. A pair of drunken swine. But even in their intoxication, for by now, after four cocktails each, neither was sober, there was a great difference between Chaplin, rough and vulgar, and Lawson: Lawson might be drunk, but he was certainly a gentleman.

At last he got out of his chair, a little unsteadily.

'Well, I'll be getting along home,' he said. 'See you before dinner.'

'Missus all right?' said Chaplin.

'Yes.'

He went out. There was a peculiar note in the monosyllable of his answer which made me look up.

'Good chap,' said Chaplin flatly, as Lawson went out of the door into the sunshine. 'One of the best. Pity he drinks.'

This from Chaplin was an observation not without humour.

'And when he's drunk he wants to fight people.'

'Is he often drunk?'

'Dead drunk, three or four days a week. It's the island done it, and Ethel.'

'Who's Ethel?'

'Ethel's his wife. Married a half-caste. Old Brevald's daughter. Took her away from here. Only thing to do. But she couldn't stand it, and now they're back again. He'll hang himself one of these days, if he don't drink himself to death. Good chap. Nasty when he's drunk.'

Chaplin belched loudly.

'I'll go and put my head under the shower. I oughtn't to have had that last cocktail. It's always the last one that does you in.'

He looked uncertainly at the staircase as he made up his mind to go to the cubby hole in which was the shower, and then with unnatural seriousness got up.

'Pay you to cultivate Lawson,' he said. 'A well-read chap. You'd be surprised when he's sober. Clever too. Worth talking to.'

Chaplin had told me the whole story in these few speeches.

When I came in towards evening from a ride along the sea-shore Lawson was again in the hotel. He was heavily sunk in one of the cane chairs in the lounge and he looked at me with glassy eyes. It was plain that he had been drinking all the afternoon. He was torpid, and the look on his face was sullen and vindictive. His glance rested on me for a moment, but I could see that he did not recognize me. Two or three other men were sitting there, shaking dice, and they took no notice of him. His condition was evidently too usual to attract attention. I sat down and began to play.

'You're a damned sociable lot,' said Lawson suddenly.

He got out of his chair and waddled with bent knees towards the door. I do not know whether the spectacle was more ridiculous than revolting. When he had gone one of the men sniggered.

'Lawson's fairly soused today,' he said.

'If I couldn't carry my liquor better than that,' said another, 'I'd climb on the waggon and stay there.'

Who would have thought that this wretched object was in his way a romantic figure or that his life had in it those elements of pity and terror which the theorist tells us are necessary to achieve the effect of tragedy?

I did not see him again for two or three days.

I was sitting one evening on the first floor of the hotel on a varanda that overlooked the street when Lawson came up and sank into a chair beside me. He was quite sober. He made a casual remark and then, when I had replied somewhat indifferently, added with a laugh which had in it an apologetic tone:

'I was devilish soused the other day.'

I did not answer. There was really nothing to say. I pulled away at my pipe in the vain hope of keeping the mosquitoes away, and looked at the natives going home from their work. They walked with long steps, slowly, with care and dignity, and the soft patter of their naked feet was strange to hear. Their dark hair, curling or straight, was often white with lime, and then they had a look of extraordinary distinction. They were tall and finely built. Then a gang of Solomon Islanders, indentured labourers, passed by, singing; they were shorter and slighter than the Samoans, coal-black, with great heads of fuzzy hair dyed red. Now and then a white man drove past in his buggy or rode into the hotel yard. In the lagoon two or three schooners reflected their grace in the tranquil water.

'I don't know what there is to do in a place like this except to get soused,' said Lawson at last.

'Don't you like Samoa?' I asked casually, for something to say.

'It's pretty, isn't it?'

The word he chose seemed so inadequate to describe the unimaginable beauty of the island that I smiled, and smiling I turned to look at him. I was startled by the expression in those fine sombre eyes of his, an expression of intolerable anguish; they betrayed a tragic depth of emotion of which I should never have thought him capable. But the expression passed away and he smiled. His smile was simple and a little naïve. It changed his face so that I wavered in my first feeling of aversion from him.

'I was all over the place when I first came out,' he said.

He was silent for a moment.

'I went away for good about three years ago, but I came back.' He hesitated. 'My wife wanted to come back. She was born here, you know.'

'Oh yes.'

He was silent again, and then hazarded a remark about Robert Louis Stevenson. He asked me if I had been up to Vailima. For some reason he was making an effort to be agreeable to me. He began to talk of Stevenson's books, and presently the conversation drifted to London.

'I suppose Covent Garden's still going strong,' he said. 'I think I miss the opera as much as anything here. Have you seen *Tristan and Isolde*?'

He asked me the question as though the answer was really important to him, and when I said, a little casually I daresay, that I had, he seemed pleased. He began to speak of Wagner, not as a musician, but as the plain man who received from him an emotional satisfaction that he could not analyse.

'I suppose Bayreuth was the place to go really,' he said. 'I never had the money, worse luck. But of course one might do worse than Covent Garden, all the lights and the women dressed up to the nines, and the music. The first act of the *Walküre*'s all right, isn't it? And the end of *Tristan*. Golly!'

His eyes were flashing now and his face was lit up so that he hardly seemed the same man. There was a flush on his sallow, thin cheeks, and I forgot that his voice was harsh and unpleasant. There was even a certain charm about him.

'By George, I'd like to be in London tonight. Do you know the Pall Mall restaurant? I used to go there a lot. Piccadilly Circus with the shops all lit up, and the crowd. I think it's stunning to stand there and watch the buses and taxis streaming along as though they'd never stop. And I like the Strand too. What are those lines about God and Charing Cross?'

I was taken aback.

'Thompson's, d'you mean?' I asked.

I quoted them:

> 'And when so sad, thou canst not sadder,
> Cry, and upon thy so sore loss
> Shall shine the traffic of Jacob's ladder
> Pitched between Heaven and Charing Cross.'

He gave a faint sigh.

'I've read *The Hound of Heaven*. It's a bit of all right.'

'It's generally thought so,' I murmured.

'You don't meet anybody here who's read anything. They think it's swank.'

There was a wistful look on his face, and I thought I divined the feeling that made him come to me. I was a link with the world he regretted and a life that he would know no more. Because not so very long before I had been in the London which he loved, he looked upon me with awe and envy. He had not spoken for five minutes perhaps when he broke out with words that startled me by their intensity.

'I'm fed up,' he said. 'I'm fed up.'

'Then why don't you clear out?' I asked.

His face grew sullen.

'My lungs are a bit dicky. I couldn't stand an English winter now.'

At that moment another man joined us on the veranda and Lawson sank into a moody silence.

'It's about time for a drain,' said the newcomer. 'Who'll have a drop of Scotch with me? Lawson?'

Lawson seemed to arise from a distant world. He got up.

'Let's go down to the bar,' he said.

When he left me I remained with a more kindly feeling towards him that I should have expected. He puzzled and interested me. And a few days later I met his wife. I knew they had been married for five or six years, and I was surprised to see that she was still extremely young. When he married her she could not have been more than sixteen. She was adorably pretty. She was no darker than a Spaniard, small and very beautifully made, with tiny hands and feet, and a slight, lithe figure. Her features were lovely; but I think what struck me most was the delicacy of her appearance; the half-castes as a rule have a certain coarseness, they seem a little roughly formed, but she had an exquisite daintiness which took your breath away. There was something extremely civilized about her, so that it surprised you to see her in those surroundings, and you thought of those famous beauties who had set all the world talking at the Court of the Emperor Napoleon III. Though she wore but a muslin frock and a straw hat she wore them with an elegance that suggested the woman of fashion. She must have been ravishing when Lawson first saw her.

He had but lately come out from England to manage the local branch of an English bank, and, reaching Samoa at the beginning of the dry season, he had taken a room at the hotel. He quickly made the acquaintance of all and sundry. The life of the island is pleasant and easy. He enjoyed the long idle talks in the lounge of the hotel and the gay evenings at the English Club when a group of fellows would play pool. He liked Apia straggling along the edge of the lagoon, with its stores and bungalows, and its native village. Then there were week-ends when he would ride over to the house of one planter or another and spend a couple of nights on the hills. He had never before known freedom or leisure. And he was intoxicated by the sunshine. When he rode through the bush his head reeled a little at the beauty that surrounded him. The country was indescribably fertile. In parts the forest was still virgin, a tangle of strange trees, luxuriant undergrowth, and vine; it gave an impression that was mysterious and troubling.

But the spot that entranced him was a pool a mile or two away from Apia to which in the evenings he often went to bathe. There was a little river that bubbled over the rocks in a swift stream, and then, after forming the deep pool, ran on, shallow and crystalline, past a ford made by great stones where the natives came sometimes to bathe or to wash their clothes. The coconut trees, with their frivolous elegance, grew thickly on the banks, all clad with trailing plants, and they were reflected in the green water. It was just such a scene as you might see in Devonshire among the hills and yet with a difference, for it had a tropical richness, a passion, a scented langour which seemed to melt the heart. The water was fresh, but not cold; and it was delicious after the heat of the day. To bathe there refreshed not only the body but the soul.

At the hour when Lawson went, there was not a soul and he lingered for a long time, now floating idly in the water, now drying himself in the evening sun, enjoying the solitude and the friendly silence. He did not regret London then, nor the life that he had abandoned, for life as it was seemed complete and exquisite.

It was here that he first saw Ethel.

Occupied till late by letters which had to be finished for the monthly sailing of the boat next day, he rode down one evening to the pool when the light was almost failing. He tied up his horse and sauntered to the bank. A girl was sitting there. She glanced round as he came and noiselessly slid into the water. She vanished like a naiad startled by the approach of a mortal. He was surprised and amused. He wondered where she had hidden herself. He swam downstream and presently saw her sitting on a rock. She looked at him with uncurious eyes. He called out a greeting in Samoan.

'*Talofa.*'

She answered him, suddenly smiling, and then let herself into the water again. She swam easily and her hair spread out behind her. He watched her cross the pool and climb out on the bank. Like all the natives she bathed in a Mother Hubbard, and the water had made it cling to her slight body. She wrung out her hair, and as she stood there, unconcerned, she looked more than ever like a wild creature of the water or the woods. He saw now that she was half-caste. He swam towards her and, getting out, addressed her in English.

'You're having a late swim.'

She shook back her hair and then let it spread over her shoulders in luxuriant curls.

'I like it when I'm alone,' she said.

'So do I.'

She laughed with a childlike frankness of the native. She slipped a dry Mother Hubbard over her head and, letting down the wet one, stepped out of it. She wrung it out and was ready to go. She paused a moment irresolutely and then sauntered off. The night fell suddenly.

Lawson went back to the hotel and, describing her to the men who were in the lounge shaking dice for drinks, soon discovered who she was. Her father was a Norwegian called Brevald who was often to be seen in the bar of the Hotel Metropole drinking rum and water. He was a little old man, knotted and gnarled like an ancient tree, who had come out to the islands forty years before as mate of a sailing vessel. He had been a blacksmith, a trader, a planter, and at one time fairly well-to-do; but, ruined by the great hurricane of the nineties, he had now nothing to live on but a small plantation of coconut trees. He had had four native wives and, as he told you with a cracked chuckle, more children than he could count. But some had died and some had gone out into the world, so that now the only one left at home was Ethel.

'She's a peach,' said Nelson, the super-cargo of the *Moana*. 'I've given her the glad eye once or twice, but I guess there's nothing doing.'

'Old Brevald's not that sort of a fool, sonny,' put in another, a man called Miller. 'He wants a son-in-law who's prepared to keep him in comfort for the rest of his life.'

It was distasteful to Lawson that they should speak of the girl in that fashion. He made a remark about the departing mail and so distracted their attention. But next evening he went again to the pool. Ethel was there; and the mystery of the sunset, the deep silence of the water, the lithe grace of the coconut trees, added to her beauty, giving it a profundity, a magic, which stirred the heart to unknown emotions. For some reason that time he had the whim not to speak to her. She took no notice of him. She did not even glance in his direction. She swam about the green pool. She dived, she rested on the bank, as though she were quite alone: he had a queer feeling that he was invisible. Scraps of poetry, half forgotten, floated across his memory, and vague recollections of the Greece he had negligently studied in his school days. When she had changed her wet clothes for dry ones and sauntered away he found a scarlet hibiscus where she had been. It was a flower that she had worn in her hair when she came to bathe and, having taken it out on getting into the water, had forgotten or not cared to put in again. He took it in his hands and looked at it with a singular emotion. He had an instinct to keep it, but his sentimentality irritated him, and he flung it away. It gave him quite a little pang to see it float down the stream.

He wondered what strangeness it was in her nature that urged her to go down to this hidden pool when there was no likelihood that anyone should be there. The natives of the islands are devoted to the water. They bathe, somewhere or other, every day, once always, and often twice; but they bathe in bands, laughing and joyous, a whole family together; and you often saw a group of girls, dappled by the sun shining through the trees, with the half-castes among them, splashing about the shallows of the stream. It looked as though there were in this pool some secret which attracted Ethel against her will. Now the night had fallen, mysterious and silent, and he let himself down in the water softly, in order to make no sound, and swam lazily in the warm darkness. The water seemed fragrant still from her slender body. He rode back to the town under the starry sky. He felt at peace with the world.

Now he went every evening to the pool and every evening he saw Ethel. Presently he overcame her timidity. She became playful and friendly. They sat together on the rocks above the pool, where the water ran fast, and they lay side by side on the ledge that overlooked it, watching the gathering dusk envelop it with mystery. It was inevitable that their meetings should become known – in the South Seas everyone seems to know everyone's business – and he was subjected to much rude chaff by the men at the hotel. He smiled and let them talk. It was not even worth while to deny their coarse suggestions. His feelings were absolutely pure. He loved Ethel as a poet might love the moon. He thought of her not as a woman but as something not of this earth. She was the spirit of the pool.

One day at the hotel, passing through the bar, he saw that old Brevald, as ever in his shabby blue overalls, was standing there. Because he was Ethel's father he had a desire to speak to him, so he went in, nodded and, ordering his own drink, casually turned and invited the old man to have one with him. They chatted for a few minutes of local affairs, and Lawson was uneasily conscious that the Norwegian was scrutinizing him with sly blue eyes. His manner was not agreeable. It was sycophantic, and yet behind the cringing air of an old man who had been worsted in his struggle with fate was a shadow of old truculence. Lawson remembered that he had once been captain of a schooner engaged in the slave trade, a blackbirder they call it in the Pacific, and he had a large hernia in the chest which was the result of a wound received in a scrap with Solomon Islanders. The bell rang for luncheon.

'Well, I must be off,' said Lawson.

'Why don't you come along to my place one time?' said Brevald, in his wheezy voice. 'It's not very grand, but you'll be welcome. You know Ethel.'

'I'll come with pleasure.'

'Sunday afternoon's the best time.'

Brevald's bungalow, shabby and bedraggled, stood among the coconut trees of the plantation, a little away from the main road that ran up to Vailima. Immediately around it grew huge plantains. With their tattered leaves they had the tragic beauty of a lovely woman in rags. Everything was slovenly and neglected. Little black pigs, thin and high-backed, rooted about, and chickens clucked noisily as they picked at the refuse scattered here and there. Three or four natives were lounging about the veranda. When Lawson asked for Brevald the old man's cracked voice called out to him, and he found him in the sitting-room smoking an old briar pipe.

'Sit down and make yerself at home,' he said. 'Ethel's just titivating.'

She came in. She wore a blouse and skirt and her hair was done in the European fashion. Although she had not the wild, timid grace of the girl who came down every evening to the pool, she seemed now more usual and consequently more approachable. She shook hands with Lawson. It was the first time he had touched her hand.

'I hope you'll have a cup of tea with us,' she said.

He knew she had been at a mission school, and he was amused, and at the same time touched, by the company manners she was putting on for his benefit. Tea was already set out on the table and in a minute old Brevald's fourth wife brought in the tea-pot. She was a handsome native, no longer very young, and she spoke but a few words of English. She smiled and smiled. Tea was rather a solemn meal, with a great deal of bread and butter and a variety of very sweet cakes, and the conversation was formal. Then a wrinkled old woman came in softly.

'That's Ethel's granny,' said old Brevald, noisily spitting on the floor.

She sat on the edge of a chair, uncomfortably, so that you saw it was unusual for her and she would have been more at ease on the ground, and remained silently staring at Lawson with fixed, shining eyes. In the kitchen behind the bungalow someone began to play the concertina and two or three voices were raised in a hymn. But they sang for the pleasure of the sounds rather than from piety.

When Lawson walked back to the hotel he was strangely happy. He was touched by the higgledy-piggledy way in which those people lived; and in the smiling good-nature of Mrs Brevald, in the little Norwegian's fantastic career, and in the shining mysterious eyes of the old grandmother he found something unusual and fascinating. It was a more natural life than any he had known, it was nearer to the friendly, fertile earth; civilization repelled him at that moment, and by mere contact with these creatures of a more primitive nature he felt a greater freedom.

He saw himself rid of the hotel which already was beginning to irk him, settled in a little bungalow of his own, trim and white, in front of the sea so that he had before his eyes always the multi-coloured variety of the lagoon. He loved the beautiful island. London and England meant nothing to him any more, he was content to spend the rest of his days in that forgotten spot, rich in the best of the world's goods, love and happiness. He made up his mind that whatever the obstacles nothing should prevent him from marrying Ethel.

But there were no obstacles. He was always welcome at the Brevalds' house. The old man was ingratiating and Mrs Brevald smiled without ceasing. He had brief glimpses of natives who seemed somehow to belong to the establishment, and once he found a tall youth in a lava-lava, his body tattooed, his hair white with lime, sitting with Brevald, and was told he was Mrs Brevald's brother's son; but for the most part they kept out of his way. Ethel was delightful with him. The light in her eyes when she saw him filled him with ecstasy. She was charming and naïve. He listened enraptured when she told him of the mission school at which she was educated, and of the sisters. He went with her to the cinema which was given once a fortnight and danced with her at the dance which followed it. They came from all parts of the island for this, since gaieties are few in Upolu; and you saw there all the society of the place, the white ladies keeping a good deal to themselves, the half-castes very elegant in American clothes, the natives, strings of dark girls in white Mother Hub-bards and young men in unaccustomed ducks and white shoes. It was all very smart and gay. Ethel was pleased to show her friends the white admirer who did not leave her side. The rumour was soon spread that he meant to marry her and her friends looked at her with envy. It was a great thing for a half-caste to get a white man to marry her, even the less regular relation was better than nothing, but one could never tell what it would lead to; and Lawson's position as manager of the bank made him one of the catches of the island. If he had not been so absorbed in Ethel he would have noticed that many eyes were fixed on him curiously, and he would have seen the glances of the white ladies and noticed how they put their heads together and gos-siped.

Afterwards, when the men who lived at the hotel were having a whisky before turning in, Nelson burst out with:

'Say, they say Lawson's going to marry that girl.'

'He's a damned fool then,' said Miller.

Miller was a German-American who had changed his name

from Müller, a big man, fat and bald-headed, with a round, clean-shaven face. He wore large gold-rimmed spectacles, which gave him a benign look, and his ducks were always clean and white. He was a heavy drinker, invariably ready to stay up all night with the 'boys', but he never got drunk; he was jolly and affable, but very shrewd. Nothing interfered with his business; he represented a firm in San Francisco, jobbers of the goods sold in the islands, calico, machinery and what not; and his good-fellowship was part of his stock-in-trade.

'He don't know what he's up against,' said Nelson. 'Someone ought to put him wise.'

'If you'll take my advice you won't interfere in what don't concern you,' said Miller. 'When a man's made up his mind to make a fool of himself, there's nothing like letting him.'

'I'm all for having a good time with the girls out here, but when it comes to marrying them – this child ain't taking any, I'll tell the world.'

Chaplin was there, and now he had his say.

'I've seen a lot of fellows do it, and it's no good.'

'You ought to have a talk with him, Chaplin,' said Nelson. 'You know him better than anyone else does.'

'My advice to Chaplin is to leave it alone,' said Miller.

Even in those days Lawson was not popular and really no one took enough interest in him to bother. Mrs Chaplin talked it over with two or three of the white ladies, but they contented themselves with saying that it was a pity; and when he told her definitely that he was going to be married it seemed too late to do anything.

For a year Lawson was happy. He took a bungalow at the point of the bay round which Apia is built, on the borders of a native village. It nestled charmingly among the coconut trees and faced the passionate blue of the Pacific. Ethel was lovely as she went about the little house, lithe and graceful like some young animal of the woods, and she was gay. They laughed a great deal. They talked nonsense. Sometimes one or two of the men at the hotel would come over and spend the evening, and often on a Sunday they would go for a day to some planter who had married a native; now and then one or other of the half-caste traders who had a store in Apia would give a party and they went to it. The half-castes treated Lawson quite differently now. His marriage had made him one of themselves and they called him Bertie. They put their arms through his and smacked him on the back. He liked to see Ethel at these gatherings. Her eyes shone and she laughed. It did him good to see her radiant happiness. Sometimes Ethel's relations would come to the bungalow, old Brevald of course, and her mother, but cousins too, vague native women in Mother Hubbards and men and boys in lava-lavas, with their hair dyed red and their bodies elaborately tattooed. He would find them sitting there when he got back from the bank. He laughed indulgently.

'Don't let them eat us out of hearth and home,' he said.

'They're my own family. I can't help doing something for them when they ask me.'

He knew that when a white man marries a native or a half-caste he must expect her relations to look upon him as a gold mine. He took Ethel's face in his hands and kissed her red lips. Perhaps he could not expect her to understand that the salary which had amply sufficed for a bachelor must be managed with some care when it had to support a wife and a house. Then Ethel was delivered of a son.

It was when Lawson first held the child in his arms that a sudden pang shot through his heart. He had not expected it to be so dark. After all it had but a fourth part of native blood, and there was no reason really why it should not look just like an English baby; but, huddled together in his arms, sallow, its head covered already with black hair, with huge black eyes, it might have been a native child. Since his marriage he had been ignored by the white ladies of the colony. When he came across men in whose houses he had been accustomed to dine as a bachelor, they were a little self-conscious with him; and they sought to cover their embarrassment by an exaggerated cordiality.

'Mrs Lawson well?' they would say. 'You're a lucky fellow. Damned pretty girl.'

But if they were with their wives and met him and Ethel they would feel it awkward when their wives gave Ethel a patronizing nod. Lawson had laughed.

'They're as dull as ditchwater, the whole gang of them,' he said. 'It's not going to disturb my night's rest if they don't ask me to their dirty parties.'

But now it irked him a little.

The little dark baby screwed up its face. That was his son. He thought of the half-caste children in Apia. They had an unhealthy look, sallow and pale, and they were odiously precocious. He had seen them on the boat going to school in New Zealand, and a school had to be chosen which took children with native blood in them; they were huddled together, brazen and yet timid, with traits which set them apart strangely from white people. They spoke the native language among themselves. And when they grew up the men accepted smaller salaries because of their native blood; girls might marry a white man, but boys had no chance; they must marry a half-caste like themselves, or a native. Lawson made up his mind passionately that he would take his son away from the humiliation of such a life. At whatever cost he must get back to Europe. And when he went in to see Ethel, frail and lovely in her bed, surrounded by native women, his determination was strengthened. If he took her away among his own people she would belong more completely to him. He loved her so passionately he wanted her to be one soul and one body with him; and he was conscious that here, with those deep roots attaching her to the native life, she would always keep something from him.

He went to work quietly, urged by an obscure instinct of secrecy, and wrote to a cousin who was a partner in a shipping firm in Aberdeen, saying that his health (on account of which like so many more he had come out to the islands) was so much better, there seemed no reason why he should not return to Europe. He asked him to use what influence he could to get him a job, no matter how poorly paid, on Deeside, where the climate was particularly suitable to such as suffered from diseases of the lungs. It takes five or six weeks for letters to get from Aberdeen to Samoa, and several had to be exchanged. He had plenty of time to prepare Ethel. She was as delighted as a child. He was amused to see how she boasted to her friends that she was going to England; it was a step up for her; she would be quite English there; and she was excited at the interest the approaching departure gave her. When at length a cable came offering him a post in a bank in Kincardineshire she was beside herself with joy.

When, their long journey over, they were settled in the little Scots town with its granite houses Lawson realized how much it meant to him to live once more among his own people. He looked back on the three years he had spent in Apia as exile, and returned to the life that seemed the only normal one with a sigh of relief. It was good to play golf once more, and to fish – to fish properly, that was poor fun in the Pacific when you just threw in your line and pulled out one big sluggish fish after another from the crowded sea – and it was good to see a paper every day with that day's news, and to meet men and women of your own sort, people you could talk to; and it was good to eat meat that was not frozen and to drink milk that was not canned. They were thrown upon their own resources much more than in the Pacific,

and he was glad to have Ethel exclusively to himself. After two
years of marriage he loved her more devotedly than ever, he
could hardly bear her out of his sight, and the need in him grew
urgent for a more intimate communion between them. But it was
strange that after the first excitement of arrival she seemed to
take less interest in the new life than he had expected. She did
not accustom herself to her surroundings. She was a little lethar-
gic. As the fine autumn darkened into winter she complained of
the cold. She lay half the morning in bed and the rest of the day
on a sofa, reading novels sometimes, but more often doing
nothing. She looked pinched.

'Never mind, darling,' he said. 'You'll get used to it very soon.
And wait till the summer comes. It can be almost as hot as in
Apia.'

He felt better and stronger than he had done for years.

The carelessness with which she managed her house had not
mattered in Samoa, but here it was out of place. When anyone
came he did not want the place to look untidy; and, laughing,
chaffing Ethel a little, he set about putting things in order. Ethel
watched him indolently. She spent long hours playing with her
son. She talked to him in the baby language of her own country.
To distract her, Lawson bestirred himself to make friends among
the neighbours, and now and then they went to little parties
where the ladies sang drawing-room ballads and the men beamed
in silent good nature. Ethel was shy. She seemed to sit apart.
Sometimes Lawson, seized with a sudden anxiety, would ask her
if she was happy.

'Yes, I'm quite happy,' she answered.

But her eyes were veiled by some thought he could not guess.
She seemed to withdraw into herself so that he was conscious that
he knew no more of her than when he had first seen her bathing
in the pool. He had an uneasy feeling that she was concealing
something from him, and because he adored her it tortured him.

'You don't regret Apia, do you?' he asked her once.

'Oh, no – I think it's very nice here.'

An obscure misgiving drove him to make disparaging remarks
about the island and the people there. She smiled and did not
answer. Very rarely she received a bundle of letters from Samoa
and then she went about for a day or two with a set, pale face.

'Nothing would induce me ever to go back there,' he said once.
'It's no place for a white man.'

But he grew conscious that sometimes, when he was away,
Ethel cried. In Apia she had been talkative, chatting volubly

about all the little details of their common life, the gossip of the place; but now she gradually became silent, and, though he increased his efforts to amuse her, she remained listless. It seemed to him that her recollections of the old life were drawing her away from him, and he was madly jealous of the island and of the sea, of Brevald, and all the dark-skinned people whom he remembered now with horror. When she spoke of Samoa he was bitter and satirical. One evening late in the spring when the birch trees were bursting into leaf, coming home from a round of golf, he found her not as usual lying on the sofa, but at the window, standing. She had evidently been waiting for his return. She addressed him the moment he came into the room. To his amazement she spoke in Samoan.

'I can't stand it. I can't live here any more. I hate it. I hate it.'

'For God's sake speak in a civilized language,' he said irritably.

She went up to him and clasped her arms around his body awkwardly, with a gesture that had in it something barbaric.

'Let's go away from here. Let's go back to Samoa. If you make me stay here I shall die. I want to go home.'

Her passion broke suddenly and she burst into tears. His anger vanished and he drew her down on his knees. He explained to her that it was impossible for him to throw up his job, which after all meant his bread and butter. His place in Apia was long since filled. He had nothing to go back to there. He tried to put it to her reasonably, the inconveniences of life there, the humiliation to which they must be exposed, and the bitterness it must cause their son.

'Scotland's wonderful for education and that sort of thing. Schools are good and cheap, and he can go to the University at Aberdeen. I'll make a real Scot of him.'

They had called him Andrew. Lawson wanted him to become a doctor. He would marry a white woman.

'I'm not ashamed of being half native,' Ethel said sullenly.

'Of course not, darling. There's nothing to be ashamed of.'

With her soft cheek against his he felt incredibly weak.

'You don't know how much I love you,' he said. 'I'd give anything in the world to be able to tell you what I've got in my heart.'

He sought her lips.

The summer came. The highland valley was green and fragrant and the hills were gay with the heather. One sunny day followed another in that sheltered spot, and the shade of the birch trees was grateful after the glare of the high road. Ethel spoke no more of Samoa and Lawson grew less nervous. He thought that she was resigned to her surroundings, and he felt that his love for her was so passionate that it could leave no room in her heart for any longing. One day the local doctor stopped him in the street.

'I say, Lawson, your missus ought to be careful how she bathes in our highland streams. It's not like the Pacific, you know.'

Lawson was surprised, and had not the presence of mind to conceal the fact.

'I didn't know she was bathing.'

The doctor laughed.

'A good many people have seen her. It makes them talk a bit, you know, because it seems a rum place to choose, the pool up above the bridge, and bathing isn't allowed there, but there's no harm in that. I don't know how she can stand the water.'

Lawson knew the pool the doctor spoke of, and suddenly it occurred to him that in a way it was just like that pool at Upolu where Ethel had been in the habit of bathing every evening. A clear highland stream ran down a sinuous course, rocky, splashing gaily, and then formed a deep, smooth pool, with a little sandy beach. Trees overshadowed it thickly, not coconut trees, but beeches, and the sun played fitfully through the leaves on the sparkling water. It gave him a shock. With his imagination he saw Ethel go there every day and undress on the bank and slip into the water, cold, colder than that of the pool she loved at home, and for a moment regain the feeling of the past. He saw her once more as the strange, wild spirit of the stream, and it seemed to him fantastically that the running water called her. That afternoon he went along to the river. He made his way cautiously among the trees and the grassy path deadened the sound of his steps. Presently he came to a spot from which he could see the pool. Ethel was sitting on the bank, looking down at the water. She sat quite still. It seemed as though the water drew her irresistibly. He wondered what strange thoughts wandered through her head. At last she got up, and for a minute or two she was hidden from his gaze; then he saw her again, wearing a Mother Hubbard, and with her little bare feet she stepped delicately over the mossy bank. She came to the water's edge, and softly, without a splash, let herself down. She swam about quietly, and there was something not quite of a human being in the way she swam. He did not know why it affected him so queerly. He waited till she clambered out. She stood for a moment with the wet folds of her dress clinging to her body, so that its shape was outlined, and then, passing her hands slowly over her breasts, gave a little sigh of delight. Then she disappeared. Lawson turned away and walked back to the village. He had a bitter pain in his heart, for he knew that she was still a stranger to him and his hungry love was destined ever to remain unsatisfied.

He did not make any mention of what he had seen. He ignored the incident completely, but he looked at her curiously, trying to divine what was in her mind. He redoubled the tenderness with which he used her. He sought to make her forget the deep longing of her soul by the passion of his love.

Then one day, when he came home, he was astonished to find her not in the house.

'Where's Mrs Lawson?' he asked the maid.

'She went into Aberdeen, Sir, with the baby,' the maid answered, a little surprised at the question. 'She said she would not be back till the last train.'

'Oh, all right.'

He was vexed that Ethel had said nothing to him about the excursion, but he was not disturbed, since of late she had been in now and again to Aberdeen, and he was glad that she should look at the shops and perhaps visit a cinema. He went to meet the last train, but when she did not come he grew suddenly frightened. He went up to the bedroom and saw at once that her toilet things were no longer in their place. He opened the wardrobe and the drawers. They were half empty. She had bolted.

He was seized with a passion of anger. It was too late that night to telephone to Aberdeen and make inquiries, but he knew already all that his inquiries might have taught him. With fiendish cunning she had chosen a time when they were making up their periodical accounts at the bank and there was no chance that he could follow her. He was imprisoned by his work. He took up a paper and saw that there was a boat sailing for Australia next morning. She must be now well on the way to London. He could not prevent the sobs that were wrung painfully from him.

'I've done everything in the world for her,' he cried, 'and she had the heart to treat me like this. How cruel, how monstrously cruel!'

After two days of misery he received a letter from her. It was written in her school-girl hand. She had always written with difficulty:

Dear Bertie –
I couldn't stand it any more. I'm going home. Good-bye.

Ethel

She did not say a single word of regret. She did not even ask him to come too. Lawson was prostrated. He found out where the ship made its first stop, and, though he knew very well she would not come, sent a cable beseeching her to return. He waited with pitiful anxiety. He wanted her to send him just one word of love; she did not even answer. He passed through one violent phase after another. At one moment he told himself that he was well rid of her, and at the next that he would force her to return by withholding money. He was lonely and wretched. He wanted his boy and he wanted her. He knew that, whatever he pretended to himself, there was only one thing to do and that was to follow her. He could never live without her now. All his plans for the future were like a house of cards and he scattered them with angry impatience. He did not care whether he threw away his chances for the future, for nothing in the world mattered but that he should get Ethel back again. As soon as he could he went into Aberdeen and told the manager of his bank that he meant to leave at once. The manager remonstrated. The short notice was inconvenient. Lawson would not listen to reason. He was determined to be free before the next boat sailed; and it was not until he was on board of her, having sold everything he possessed, that in some measure he regained his calm. Till then to those who had come in contact with him he seemed hardly sane. His last action in England was to cable to Ethel at Apia that he was joining her.

He sent another cable from Sydney, and when at last with the dawn his boat crossed the bar at Apia and he saw once more the white houses straggling along the bay he felt an immense relief. The doctor came on board, and the agent. They were both old acquaintances and he felt kindly towards their familiar faces. He had a drink or two with them for old times' sake, and also because he was desperately nervous. He was not sure if Ethel would be glad to see him. When he got into the launch and approached the wharf he scanned anxiously the little crowd that waited. She was not there and his heart sank, but then he saw Brevald, in his old blue clothes, and his heart warmed towards him.

'Where's Ethel?' he said, as he jumped on shore.

'She's down at the bungalow. She's living with us.'

Lawson was dismayed, but he put on a jovial air.

'Well, have you got room for me? I daresay it'll take a week or two to fix ourselves up.'

'Oh, yes, I guess we can make room for you.'

After passing through the custom-house they went to the hotel and there Lawson was greeted by several of his old friends. There were a good many rounds of drinks before it seemed possible to get away and when they did go at last to Brevald's house they were both rather gay. He clasped Ethel in his arms. He had forgotten all his bitter thoughts in the joy of beholding her once more. His mother-in-law was pleased to see him, and so was the old, wrinkled beldame, her mother; natives and half-castes came in, and they all sat round, beaming on him. Brevald had a bottle of whisky and everyone who came was given a nip. Lawson sat with his little dark-skinned boy on his knees, they had taken his English clothes off him and he was stark, with Ethel by his side in a Mother Hubbard. He felt like a returning prodigal. In the afternoon he went down to the hotel again and when he got back he was more than gay, he was drunk. Ethel and her mother knew that white men got drunk now and then, it was what you expected of them, and they laughed good-naturedly as they helped him to bed.

But in a day or two he set about looking for a job. He knew that he could not hope for such a position as that which he had thrown away to go to England; but with his training he could not fail to be useful to one of the trading firms, and perhaps in the end he would not lose by the change.

'After all, you can't make money in a bank,' he said. 'Trade's the thing.'

He had hopes that he would soon make himself so indispensable that he would get someone to take him into partnership, and there was no reason why in a few years he should not be a rich man.

'As soon as I'm fixed up we'll find ourselves a shack,' he told Ethel. 'We can't go on living here.'

Brevald's bungalow was so small that they were all piled on one another, and there was no chance of ever being alone. There was neither peace nor privacy.

'Well, there's no hurry. We shall be all right here till we find just what we want.'

It took him a week to get settled and then he entered the firm of a man called Bain. But when he talked to Ethel about moving she said she wanted to stay where she was till her baby was born, for she was expecting another child. Lawson tried to argue with her.

'If you don't like it,' she said, 'go and live at the hotel.'

He grew suddenly pale.

'Ethel, how can you suggest that!'

She shrugged her shoulders.

'What's the good of having a house of our own when we can live here.'

He yielded.

When Lawson, after his work, went back to the bungalow he found it crowded with natives. They lay about smoking, sleeping, drinking *kava*; and they talked incessantly. The place was grubby and untidy. His child crawled about, playing with native children, and it heard nothing spoken but Samoan. He fell into the habit of dropping into the hotel on his way home to have a few cocktails, for he could only face the evening and the crowd of friendly natives when he was fortified with liquor. And all the time, though he loved her more passionately than ever, he felt that Ethel was slipping away from him. When the baby was born he suggested that they should get into a house of their own, but Ethel refused. Her stay in Scotland seemed to have thrown her back on her own people, now that she was once more among them, with a passionate zest, and she turned to her native ways with abandon. Lawson began to drink more. Every Saturday night he went to the English Club and got blind drunk.

He had the peculiarity that as he grew drunk he grew quarrelsome and once he had a violent dispute with Bain, his employer. Bain dismissed him, and he had to look out for another job. He was idle for two or three weeks and during these, sooner than sit in the bungalow, he lounged about in the hotel or at the English Club, and drank. It was more out of pity than anything else that Miller, the German-American, took him into his office; but he was a businessman, and though Lawson's financial skill made him valuable, the circumstances were such that he could hardly refuse a smaller salary than he had had before, and Miller did not hesitate to offer it to him. Ethel and Brevald blamed him for taking it, since Pedersen, the half-caste, offered him more. But he resented bitterly the thought of being under the orders of a half-caste. When Ethel nagged him he burst out furiously:

'I'll see myself dead before I work for a nigger.'

'You may have to,' she said.

And in six months he found himself forced to this final humiliation. The passion for liquor had been gaining on him, he was often heavy with drink, and he did his work badly. Miller warned him once or twice and Lawson was not the man to accept remonstrance easily. One day in the midst of an altercation he put on his hat and walked out. But by now his reputation was well known and he could find no one to engage him. For a while he idled, and then he had an attack of delirium tremens. When he recovered, shameful and weak, he could no longer resist the constant pressure and he went to Pedersen and asked him for a job. Pedersen was glad to have a white man in his store and Lawson's skill at figures made him useful.

From that time his degeneration was rapid. The white people gave him the cold shoulder. They were only prevented from cutting him completely by disdainful pity and by a certain dread of his angry violence when he was drunk. He became extremely susceptible and was always on the lookout for affront.

He lived entirely among the natives and half-castes, but he had no longer the prestige of the white man. They felt his loathing for them and they resented his attitude of superiority. He was one of themselves now and they did not see why he should put on airs. Brevald, who had been ingratiating and obsequious, now treated him with contempt. Ethel had made a bad bargain. There were disgraceful scenes and once or twice the two men came to blows. When there was a quarrel Ethel took the part of her family. They found he was better drunk than sober, for when he was drunk he would lie on the bed or on the floor, sleeping heavily.

Then he became aware that something was being hidden from him.

When he got back to the bungalow for the wretched, half-native supper which was his evening meal, often Ethel was not in. If he asked where she was Brevald told him she had gone to spend the evening with one or other of her friends. Once he followed her to the house Brevald had mentioned and found she was not there. On her return he asked her where she had been and she told him her father had made a mistake; she had been to so-and-so's. But he knew that she was lying. She was in her best clothes; her eyes were shining, and she looked lovely.

'Don't try any monkey tricks on me, my girl,' he said, 'or I'll break every bone in your body.'

'You drunken beast,' she said, scornfully.

He fancied that Mrs Brevald and the old grandmother looked at him maliciously and he ascribed Brevald's good humour with him, so unusual those days, to his satisfaction at having something up his sleeve against his son-in-law. And then, his suspicions aroused, he imagined that the white men gave him curious glances. When he came into the lounge of the hotel the sudden silence which fell upon the company convinced him that he had been the subject of the conversation. Something was going on and everyone knew it but himself. He was seized with furious jealousy. He believed that Ethel was carrying on with one of the white men, and he looked at one after the other with scrutinizing eyes; but there was nothing to give him even a hint. He was helpless. Because he could find no one on whom definitely to fix his suspicions, he went about like a raving maniac, looking for someone on whom to vent his wrath. Chance caused him in the end to hit upon the man who of all others least deserved to suffer from his violence. One afternoon, when he was sitting in the hotel by himself, moodily, Chaplin came in and sat down beside him. Perhaps Chaplin was the only man on the island who had any sympathy for him. They ordered drinks and chatted a few minutes about the races that were shortly to be run. Then Chaplin said:

'I guess we shall all have to fork out money for new dresses.'

Lawson sniggered. Since Mrs Chaplin held the purse-strings, if she wanted a new frock for the occasion she would certainly not ask her husband for the money.

'How is your missus?' asked Chaplin, desiring to be friendly.

'What the hell's that got to do with you?' said Lawson, knitting his dark brows.

'I was only asking a civil question.'

'Well, keep your civil questions to yourself.'

Chaplin was not a patient man; his long residence in the tropics, the whisky bottle, and his domestic affairs had given him a temper hardly more under control than Lawson's.

'Look here, my boy, when you're in my hotel you behave like a gentleman or you'll find yourself in the street before you can say knife.'

Lawson's lowering face grew dark and red.

'Let me just tell you once for all and you can pass it on to the others,' he said, panting with rage. 'If any of you fellows come messing round with my wife he'd better look out.'

'Who do you think wants to mess around with your wife?'

'I'm not such a fool as you think. I can see a stone wall in front of me as well as most men, and I warn you straight, that's all. I'm not going to put up with any hanky-panky, not on your life.'

'Look here, you'd better clear out of here, and come back when you're sober.'

'I shall clear out when I choose and not a minute before,' said Lawson.

It was an unfortunate boast, for Chaplin in the course of his experience as a hotel-keeper had acquired a peculiar skill in dealing with gentlemen whose room he preferred to their company, and the words were hardly out of Lawson's mouth before he found himself caught by the collar and arm and hustled not without force into the street. He stumbled down the steps into the blinding glare of the sun.

It was in consequence of this that he had his first violent scene with Ethel. Smarting with humiliation and unwilling to go back to the hotel, he went home that afternoon earlier than usual. He found Ethel dressing to go out. As a rule she lay about in a Mother Hubbard, barefoot, with a flower in her dark hair; but now, in white silk stockings and high-heeled shoes, she was doing up a pink muslin dress which was the newest she had.

'You're making yourself very smart,' he said. 'Where are you going?'

'I'm going to the Crossleys.'

'I'll come with you.'

'Why?' she asked coolly.

'I don't want you to gad about by yourself all the time.'

'You're not asked.'

'I don't care a damn about that. You're not going without me.'

'You'd better lie down till I'm ready.'

She thought he was drunk and if he once settled himself on the bed would quickly drop off to sleep. He sat down on a chair and began to smoke a cigarette. She watched him with increasing irritation. When she was ready he got up. It happened by an unusual chance that there was no one in the bungalow. Brevald was working on the plantation and his wife had gone into Apia. Ethel faced him.

'I'm not going with you. You're drunk.'

'That's a lie. You're not going without me.'

She shrugged her shoulders and tried to pass him, but he caught her by the arm and held her.

'Let me go, you devil,' she said, breaking into Samoan.

'Why do you want to go without me? Haven't I told you I'm not going to put up with any monkey tricks?'

She clenched her fist and hit him in the face. He lost all control of himself. All his love, all his hatred, welled up in him and he was beside himself.

'I'll teach you,' he shouted. 'I'll teach you.'

He seized a riding-whip which happened to be under his hand, and struck her with it. She screamed, and the scream maddened him so that he went on striking her, again and again. Her shrieks rang through the bungalow and he cursed her as he hit. Then he flung her on the bed. She lay there sobbing with pain and terror. He threw the whip away from him and rushed out of the room. Ethel heard him go and she stopped crying. She looked round cautiously, then she raised herself. She was sore, but she had not been badly hurt, and she looked at her dress to see if it was damaged. The native women are not unused to blows. What he had done did not outrage her. When she looked at herself in the glass and arranged her hair, her eyes were shining. There was a strange look in them. Perhaps then she was nearer loving him than she had ever been before.

But Lawson, driven forth blindly, stumbled through the plantation and suddenly exhausted, weak as a child, flung himself on the ground at the foot of a tree. He was miserable and ashamed. He thought of Ethel, and in the yielding tenderness of his love all his bones seemed to grow soft within him. He thought of the past, and of his hopes, and he was aghast at what he had done. He wanted her more than ever. He wanted to take her in his arms. He must go to her at once. He got up. He was so weak that he staggered as he walked. He went into the house and she was sitting in their cramped bedroom in front of her looking-glass.

'Oh, Ethel, forgive me. I'm so awfully ashamed of myself. I didn't know what I was doing.'

He fell on his knees before her and timidly stroked the skirt of her dress.

'I can't bear to think of what I did. It's awful. I think I was mad. There's no one in the world I love as I love you. I'd do anything to save you from pain and I've hurt you. I can never forgive myself, but for God's sake say you forgive me.'

He heard her shrieks still. It was unendurable. She looked at him silently. He tried to take her hands and the tears streamed from his eyes. In his humiliation he hid his face in her lap and his frail body shook with sobs. An expression of utter contempt came over her face. She had the native woman's disdain of a man who abased himself before a woman. A weak creature! And for a moment she had been on the point of thinking there was something in him. He grovelled at her feet like a cur. She gave him a little scornful kick.

'Get out,' she said. 'I hate you.'

He tried to hold her, but she pushed him aside. She stood up. She began to take off her dress. She kicked off her shoes and slid the stockings off her feet, then she slipped on her old Mother Hubbard.

'Where are you going?'

'What's that got to do with you? I'm going down to the pool.'

'Let me come too,' he said.

He asked as though he were a child.

'Can't you even leave me that?'

He hid his face in his hands, crying miserably, while she, her eyes hard and cold, stepped past him and went out.

From that time she entirely despised him; and though, herded together in the small bungalow, Lawson and Ethel with her two children, Brevald, his wife and her mother, and the vague relations and hangers-on who were always in and about, they had to live cheek by jowl, Lawson, ceasing to be of any account, was hardly noticed. He left in the morning after breakfast, and came back only to have supper. He gave up the struggle, and when for want of money he could not go to the English Club he spent the evening playing hearts with old Brevald and the natives. Except when he was drunk he was cowed and listless. Ethel treated him like a dog. She submitted at times to his fits of wild passion, and she was frightened by the gusts of hatred with which they were followed; but when, afterwards, he was cringing and lachrymose she had such a contempt for him that she could have spat in his face. Sometimes he was violent, but now she was prepared for him, and when he hit her she kicked and scratched and bit. They had horrible battles in which he had not always the best of it. Very soon it was known all over Apia that they got on badly. There was little sympathy for Lawson, and at the hotel the general surprise was that old Brevald did not kick him out of the place.

'Brevald's a pretty ugly customer,' said one of the men. 'I shouldn't be surprised if he put a bullet into Lawson's carcass one of these days.'

Ethel still went in the evenings to bathe in the silent pool. It seemed to have an attraction for her that was not quite human, just that attraction you might imagine that a mermaid who had won a soul would have for the cool salt waves of the sea; and sometimes Lawson went also. I do not know what urged him to go, for Ethel was obviously irritated by his presence; perhaps it was because in that spot he hoped to regain the clean rapture which had filled his heart when first he saw her; perhaps only, with the madness of those who love them that love them not, from the feeling that his obstinacy could force love. One day he strolled down there with a feeling that was rare with him now. He felt suddenly at peace with the world. The evening was drawing in and the dusk seemed to cling to the leaves of the coconut trees like a little thin cloud. A faint breeze stirred them noiselessly. A crescent moon jung just over their tops. He made his way to the bank. He saw Ethel in the water floating on her back. Her hair streamed out all round her, and she was holding in her hand a large hibiscus. He stopped a moment to admire her; she was like Ophelia.

'Hullo, Ethel,' he cried joyfully.

She made a sudden movement and dropped the red flower. It floated idly away. She swam a stroke or two till she knew there was ground within her depth and then stood up.

'Go away,' she said. 'Go away.'

He laughed.

'Don't be selfish. There's plenty of room for both of us.'

'Why can't you leave me alone? I want to be by myself.'

'Hang it all, I want to bathe,' he answered, good-humouredly.

'Go down to the bridge. I don't want you here.'

'I'm sorry for that,' he said, smiling still.

He was not in the least angry, and he hardly noticed that she was in a passion. He began to take off his coat.

'Go away,' she shrieked. 'I won't have you here. Can't you even leave me this? Go away.'

'Don't be silly, darling.'

She bent down and picked up a sharp stone and flung it quickly at him. He had no time to duck. It hit him on the temple. With a cry he put his hand to his head and when he took it away it was wet with blood. Ethel stood still, panting with rage. He turned very pale, and without a word, taking up his coat, went away. Ethel let herself fall back into the water and the stream carried her slowly down to the ford.

The stone had made a jagged wound and for some days Lawson went about with a bandaged head. He had invented a likely story to account for the accident when the fellows at the club asked him about it, but he had no occasion to use it. No one referred to the matter. He saw them cast surreptitious glances at his head, but not a word was said. The silence could only mean that they knew how he came by his wound. He was certain now that Ethel had a lover, and they all knew who it was. But there was not the smallest indication to guide him. He never saw Ethel with anyone; no one showed a wish to be with her, or treated him in a manner that seemed strange. Wild rage seized him, and having no one to vent it on he drank more and more heavily. A

little while before I came to the island he had had another attack
of delirium tremens.

I met Ethel at the house of a man called Caster, who lived two
or three miles from Apia with a native wife. I had been playing
tennis with him and when we were tired he suggested a cup of tea.
We went into the house and in the untidy living-room found
Ethel chatting with Mrs Caster.

'Hullo, Ethel,' he said, 'I didn't know you were here.'

I could not help looking at her with curiosity. I tried to see
what there was in her to have excited in Lawson such a devastating passion. But who can explain these things? It was true that
she was lovely; she reminded one of the red hibiscus, the common
flower of the hedgerow in Samoa, with its grace and its languor
and its passion; but what surprised me most, taking into consideration the story I knew even then a good deal of, was her
freshness and simplicity. She was quiet and a little shy. There was
nothing coarse or loud about her; she had not the exuberance
common to the half-caste; and it was almost impossible to
believe that she could be the virago that the horrible scenes
between husband and wife, which were now common knowledge,
indicated. In her pretty pink frock and high-heeled shoes she
looked quite European. You could hardly have guessed at that
dark background of native life in which she felt herself so much
more at home. I did not imagine that she was at all intelligent,
and I should not have been surprised if a man, after living with
her for some time, had found the passion which had drawn him
to her sink into boredom. It suggested itself to me that in her
elusiveness, like a thought that presents itself to consciousness
and vanishes before it can be captured by words, lay her peculiar
charm; but perhaps that was merely fancy, and if I had known
nothing about her I should have seen in her only a pretty little
half-caste like another.

She talked to me of the various things which they talk of to the
stranger in Samoa, of the journey, and whether I had slid down
the water rock at Papaseea, and if I meant to stay in a native
village. She talked to me of Scotland, and perhaps I noticed in her
a tendency to enlarge on the sumptuousness of her establishment
there. She asked me naïvely if I knew Mrs This and Mrs That,
with whom she had been acquainted when she lived in the north.

Then Miller, the fat German-American, came in. He shook
hands all round very cordially and sat down, asking in his loud,
cheerful voice for a whisky and soda. He was very fat and he
sweated profusely. He took off his gold-rimmed spectacles and

wiped them; you saw then that his little eyes, benevolent behind the large round glasses, were shrewd and cunning; the party had been somewhat dull till he came, but he was a good story-teller and a jovial fellow. Soon he had the two women, Ethel and my friend's wife, laughing delightedly at his sallies. He had a reputation on the island of a lady's man, and you could see how this fat, gross fellow, old and ugly, had yet the possibility of fascination. His humour was on a level with the understanding of his company, an affair of vitality and assurance, and his Western accent gave a peculiar point to what he said. At last he turned to me:

'Well, if we want to get back for dinner we'd better be getting. I'll take you along in my machine if you like.'

I thanked him and got up. He shook hands with the others, went out of the room, massive and strong in his walk, and climbed into his car.

'Pretty little thing, Lawson's wife,' I said, as we drove along.

'Too bad the way he treats her. Knocks her about. Gets my dander up when I hear of a man hitting a woman.'

We went on a little. Then he said:

'He was a darned fool to marry her. I said so at the time. If he hadn't, he'd have had the whip hand over her. He's yaller, that's what he is, yaller.'

The year was drawing to its end and the time approached when I was to leave Samoa. My boat was scheduled to sail for Sydney on the fourth of January. Christmas Day had been celebrated at the hotel with suitable ceremonies, but it was looked upon as no more than a rehearsal for New Year, and the men who were accustomed to foregather in the lounge determined on New Year's Eve to make a night of it. There was an uproarious dinner, after which the party sauntered down to the English Club, a simple little frame house, to play pool. There was a great deal of talking, laughing, and betting, but some very poor play, except on the part of Miller, who had drunk as much as any of them, all far younger than he, but had kept unimpaired the keenness of his eye and the sureness of his hand. He pocketed the young men's money with humour and urbanity. After an hour of this I grew tired and went out. I crossed the road and came on to the beach. Three coconut trees grew there, like three moon maidens waiting for their lovers to ride out of the sea, and I sat at the foot of one of them, watching the lagoon and the nightly assemblage of the stars.

I do not know where Lawson had been during the evening, but between ten and eleven he came along to the club. He shambled down the dusty, empty road, feeling dull and bored, and when he reached the club, before going into the billiard-room, went into the bar to have a drink by himself. He had a shyness now about joining the company of white men when there were a lot of them together and needed a stiff dose of whisky to give him confidence. He was standing with the glass in his hand when Miller came in to him. He was in his shirt-sleeves and still held his cue. He gave the bar-tender a glance.

'Get out, Jack,' he said.

The bar-tender, a native in a white jacket and a red lava-lava, without a word slid out of the small room.

'Look here, I've been wanting to have a few words with you, Lawson,' said the big American.

'Well, that's one of the few things you can have free, gratis, and for nothing on this damned island.'

Miller fixed his gold spectacles more firmly on his nose and held Lawson with his cold determined eyes.

'See here, young fellow, I understand you've been knocking Mrs Lawson about again. I'm not going to stand for that. If you don't stop it right now I'll break every bone of your dirty little body.'

Then Lawson knew what he had been trying to find out so long. It was Miller. The appearance of the man, fat, bald-headed, with his round bare face and double chin and the gold spectacles, his age, his benign, shrewd look, like that of a renegade priest, and the thought of Ethel, so slim and virginal, filled him with a sudden horror. Whatever his faults Lawson was no coward, and without a word he hit out violently at Miller. Miller quickly warded the blow with the hand that held the cue, and then with a great swing of his right arm brought his fist down on Lawson's ear. Lawson was four inches shorter than the American and he was slightly built, frail and weakened not only by illness and the enervating tropics, but by drink. He fell like a log and lay half dazed at the foot of the bar. Miller took off his spectacles and wiped them with his handkerchief.

'I guess you know what to expect now. You've had your warning and you'd better take it.'

He took up his cue and went back into the billiard-room. There was so much noise there that no one knew what had happened. Lawson picked himself up. He put his hand to his ear, which was singing still. Then he slunk out of the club.

I saw a man cross the road, a patch of white against the darkness of the night, but did not know who it was. He came down to the beach, passed me sitting at the foot of the tree, and looked down. I saw then that it was Lawson, but since he was doubtless drunk, did not speak. He went on, walked irresolutely two or three steps, and turned back. He came up to me and bending down stared in my face.

'I thought it was you,' he said.

He sat down and took out his pipe.

'It was hot and noisy in the club,' I volunteered.

'Why are you sitting here?'

'I was waiting about for the midnight mass at the Cathedral.'

'If you like I'll come with you.'

Lawson was quite sober. We sat for a while smoking in silence. Now and then in the lagoon was the splash of some big fish, and a little way out towards the opening in the reef was the light of a schooner.

'You're sailing next week, aren't you?' he said.

'Yes.'

'It would be jolly to go home once more. But I could never stand it now. The cold, you know.'

'It's odd to think that in England now they're shivering round the fire,' I said.

There was not even a breath of wind. The balminess of the night was like a spell. I wore nothing but a thin shirt and a suit of ducks. I enjoyed the exquisite languor of the night, and stretched my limbs voluptuously.

'This isn't the sort of New Year's Eve that persuades one to make good resolutions for the future,' I smiled.

He made no answer, but I do not know what train of thought my casual remark had suggested in him, for presently he began to speak. He spoke in a low voice, without any expression, but his accents were educated, and it was a relief to hear him after the twang and the vulgar intonations which for some time had wounded my ears.

'I've made an awful hash of things. That's obvious, isn't it? I'm right down at the bottom of the pit and there's no getting out for me. "*Black as the pit from pole to pole.*"' I felt him smile as he made the quotation. 'And the strange thing is that I don't see how I went wrong.'

I held my breath, for to me there is nothing more awe-inspiring than when a man discovers to you the nakedness of his soul. Then you see that no one is so trivial or debased but that in him is a spark of something to excite compassion.

'It wouldn't be so rotten if I could see that it was all my own fault. It's true I drink, but I shouldn't have taken to that if things had gone differently. I wasn't really fond of liquor. I suppose I ought not to have married Ethel. If I'd kept her it would be all right. But I did love her so.'

His voice faltered.

'She's not a bad lot, you know, not really. It's just rotten luck. We might have been as happy as lords. When she bolted I suppose I ought to have let her go, but I couldn't do that – I was dead stuck on her then; and there was the kid.'

'Are you fond of the kid?' I asked.

'I was. There are two, you know. But they don't mean so much to me now. You'd take them for natives anywhere. I have to talk to them in Samoan.'

'Is it too late for you to start fresh? Couldn't you make a dash for it and leave the place?'

'I haven't the strength. I'm done for.'

'Are you still in love with your wife?'

'Not now. Not now.' He repeated the two words with a kind of horror in his voice. 'I haven't even got that now. I'm down and out.'

The bells of the Cathedral were ringing.

'If you really want to come to the midnight mass we'd better go along,' I said.

'Come on.'

We got up and walked along the road. The Cathedral, all white, stood facing the sea not without impressiveness, and beside it the Protestant chapels had the look of meeting-houses. In the road were two or three cars, and a great number of traps, and traps were put up against the walls at the side. People had come from all parts of the island for the service. and through the great open doors we saw that the place was crowded. The high altar was all ablaze with light. There were a few whites and a good many half-castes, but the great majority were natives. All the men wore trousers, for the Church has decided that the lava-lava is indecent. We found chairs at the back, near the open door, and sat down. Presently, following Lawson's eyes, I saw Ethel come in with a party of half-castes. They were all very much dressed up, the men in high, stiff collars and shiny boots, the women in large, gay hats. Ethel nodded and smiled to her friends as she passed up the aisle. The service began.

When it was over Lawson and I stood on one side for a while to watch the crowd stream out, then he held out his hand.

'Good night,' he said. 'I hope you'll have a pleasant journey home.'

'Oh, but I shall see you before I go.'

He sniggered.

'The question is if you'll see me drunk or sober.'

He turned and left me. I had a recollection of those very large black eyes, shining wildly under the shaggy brows. I paused irresolutely. I did not feel sleepy and I thought I would at all events go along to the club for an hour before turning in. When I got there I found the billiard-room empty, but half-a-dozen men were sitting round a table in the lounge, playing poker. Miller looked up as I came in.

'Sit down and take a hand,' he said.

'All right.'

I bought some chips and began to play. Of course it is the most fascinating game in the world and my hour lengthened out to two, and then to three. The native bar-tender, cheery and wide-awake notwithstanding the time, was at our elbow to supply us with drinks and from somewhere or other he produced a ham and a loaf of bread. We played on. Most of the party had drunk more than was good for them and the play was high and reckless. I played modestly, neither wishing to win nor anxious to lose, but I watched Miller with a fascinated interest. He drank glass for glass with the rest of the company, but remained cool and level-headed. His pile of chips increased in size and he had a neat little paper in front of him on which he had marked various sums lent to players in distress. He beamed amiably at the young men whose money he was taking. He kept up interminably his stream of jest and anecdote, but he never missed a draw, he never let an expression of the face pass him. At last the dawn crept into the windows, gently, with a sort of deprecating shyness, as though it had no business there, and then it was day.

'Well,' said Miller. 'I reckon we've seen the old year out in style. Now let's have a round of jackpots and me for my mosquito net. I'm fifty, remember, I can't keep these late hours.'

The morning was beautiful and fresh when we stood on the veranda, and the lagoon was like a sheet of multicoloured glass. Someone suggested a dip before going to bed, but none cared to bathe in the lagoon, sticky and treacherous to the feet. Miller had his car at the door and he offered to take us down to the pool. We jumped in and drove along the deserted road. When we reached the pool it seemed as though the day had hardly risen there yet. Under the trees the water was all in shadow and the night had the effects of lurking still. We were in great spirits. We had no towels or any costume and in my prudence I wondered how we were going to dry ourselves. None of us had much on and it did not take us long to snatch off our clothes. Nelson, the little super-cargo, was stripped first.

'I'm going down to the bottom,' he said.

He dived and in a moment another man dived too, but shallow, and was out of the water before him. Then Nelson came up and scrambled to the side.

'I say, get me out,' he said.

'What's up?'

Something was evidently the matter. His face was terrified. Two fellows gave him their hands and he slithered up.

'I say, there's a man down there.'

'Don't be a fool. You're drunk.'

'Well, if there isn't I'm in for D.T.s. But I tell you there's a man down there. It just scared me out of my wits.'

Miller looked at him for a moment. The little man was all white. He was actually trembling.

'Come on, Caster,' said Miller to the big Australian, 'we'd better go down and see.'

'He was standing up,' said Nelson, 'all dressed. I saw him. He tried to catch hold of me.'

'Hold your row,' said Miller. 'Are you ready?'

They dived in. We waited on the bank, silent. It really seemed as though they were underwater longer than any men could breathe. Then Caster came up, and immediately after him, red in the face as though he were going to have a fit, Miller. They were pulling something behind them. Another man jumped in to help them, and the three together dragged their burden to the side. They shoved it up. Then we saw that it was Lawson, with a great stone tied up in his coat and bound to his feet.

'He was set on making a good job of it,' said Miller, as he wiped the water from his short-sighted eyes.

MACKINTOSH

HE splashed about for a few minutes in the sea; it was too shallow to swim in and for fear of sharks he could not go out of his depth; then he got out and went into the bath-house for a shower. The coldness of the fresh water was grateful after the heavy stickiness of the salt Pacific, so warm, though it was only just after seven, that to bathe in it did not brace you but rather increased your languor; and when he had dried himself, slipping into a bath-gown, he called out to the Chinese cook that he would be ready for breakfast in five minutes. He walked barefoot across the patch of coarse grass which Walker, the administrator, proudly thought was a lawn, to his own quarters and dressed. This did not take long, for he put on nothing but a shirt and a pair of duck trousers and then went over to his chief's house on the other side of the compound. The two men had their meals together, but the Chinese cook told him that Walker had set out on horseback at five and would not be back for another hour.

Mackintosh had slept badly and he looked with distaste at the paw-paw and the eggs and bacon which were set before him. The mosquitoes had been maddening that night; they flew about the net under which he slept in such numbers that their humming, pitiless and menacing, had the effect of a note, infinitely drawn out, played on a distant organ, and whenever he dozed off he awoke with a start in the belief that one had found its way inside his curtains. It was so hot that he lay naked. He turned from side to side. And gradually the dull roar of the breakers on the reef, so unceasing and so regular that generally you did not hear it, grew distinct on his consciousness, its rhythm hammered on his tired nerves and he held himself with clenched hands in the effort to bear it. The thought that nothing could stop that sound, for it would continue to all eternity, was almost impossible to bear, and, as though his strength were a match for the ruthless forces of nature, he had an insane impulse to do some violent thing. He felt he must cling to his self-control or he would go mad. And now, looking out of the window at the lagoon and the strip of foam which marked the reef, he shuddered with hatred of the brilliant scene. The cloudless sky was like an inverted bowl that hemmed it in. He lit his pipe and turned over the pile of Auckland papers that had come over from Apia a few days before. The newest of them was three weeks old. They gave an impression of incredible dullness.

Then he went into the office. It was a large, bare room with two desks in it and a bench along one side. A number of natives were seated on this, and a couple of women. They gossiped while they waited for the administrator, and when Mackintosh came in they greeted him.

'*Talofa-li.*'

He returned their greeting and sat down at his desk. He began to write, working on a report which the governor of Samoa had been clamouring for and which Walker, with his usual dilatoriness, had neglected to prepare. Mackintosh as he made his notes reflected vindictively that Walker was late with his report because he was so illiterate that he had an invincible distaste for anything to do with pens and paper; and now when it was at last ready, concise and neatly official, he would accept his subordinate's work without a word of appreciation, with a sneer rather or a gibe, and send it on to his own superior as though it were his own composition. He could not have written a word of it. Mackintosh thought with rage that if his chief pencilled in some insertion it would be childish in expression and faulty in language. If he remonstrated or sought to put his meaning into an intelligible phrase, Walker would fly into a passion and cry:

'What the hell do I care about grammar? That's what I want to say and that's how I want to say it.'

At last Walker came in. The natives surrounded him as he entered, trying to get his immediate attention, but he turned on them roughly and told them to sit down and hold their tongues. He threatened that if they were not quiet he would have them all turned out and see none of them that day. He nodded to Mackintosh.

'Hullo, Mac; up at last? I don't know how you can waste the best part of the day in bed. You ought to have been up before dawn like me. Lazy beggar.'

He threw himself heavily into his chair and wiped his face with a large bandana.

'By heaven, I've got a thirst.'

He turned to the policeman who stood at the door, a picturesque figure in his white jacket and lava-lava, the loincloth of the Samoan, and told him to bring *kava.* The *kava* bowl stood on the floor in the corner of the room, and the policeman filled a half coconut shell and brought it to Walker. He poured a few drops on the ground, murmured the customary words to the company, and drank with relish. Then he told the policeman to serve the waiting natives, and the shell was handed to each one in order of birth or importance and emptied with the same ceremonies.

Then he set about the day's work. He was a little man, considerably less than of middle height, and enormously stout; he had a large, fleshy face, clean-shaven, with the cheeks hanging on each side in great dew-laps, and three vast chins; his small features were all dissolved in fat; and, but for a crescent of white hair at the back of his head, he was completely bald. He reminded you of Mr Pickwick. He was grotesque, a figure of fun, and yet, strangely enough, not without dignity. His blue eyes, behind large gold-rimmed spectacles, were shrewd and vivacious, and there was a great deal of determination in his face. He was sixty, but his native vitality triumphed over advancing years. Notwithstanding his corpulence his movements were quick, and he walked with a heavy, resolute tread as though he sought to impress his weight upon the earth. He spoke in a loud, gruff voice.

It was two years now since Mackintosh had been appointed Walker's assistant. Walker, who had been for a quarter of a century administrator of Talua, one of the larger islands in the Samoan group, was a man known in person or by report through the length and breadth of the South Seas; and it was with lively curiosity that Mackintosh looked forward to his first meeting with him. For one reason or another he stayed a couple of weeks at Apia before he took up his post and both at Chaplin's hotel and at the English Club he heard innumerable stories about the administrator. He thought now with irony of his interest in them. Since then he had heard them a hundred times from Walker himself. Walker knew that he was a character and, proud of his reputation, deliberately acted up to it. He was jealous of his 'legend' and anxious that you should know the exact details of any of the celebrated stories that were told of him. He was ludicrously angry with anyone who had told them to the stranger incorrectly.

There was a rough cordiality about Walker which Mackintosh at first found not unattractive, and Walker, glad to have a listener to whom all he said was fresh, gave of his best. He was good-humoured, hearty, and considerate. To Mackintosh, who had lived the sheltered life of a government official in London till at the age of thirty-four an attack of pneumonia, leaving him with the threat of tuberculosis, had forced him to seek a post in the Pacific, Walker's existence seemed extraordinarily romantic. The adventure with which he started on his conquest of circumstance was typical of the man. He ran away to sea when he was fifteen and for over a year was employed in shovelling coal on a collier. He was an undersized boy and both men and mates were kind to him, but the captain for some reason conceived a savage dislike of him. He used the lad cruelly so that, beaten and kicked, he often could not sleep for the pain that racked his limbs. He loathed the captain with all his soul. Then he was given a tip for some race and managed to borrow twenty-five pounds from a friend he had picked up in Belfast. He put it on the horse, an outsider, at long odds. He had no means of repaying the money if he lost, but it never occurred to him that he could lose. He felt himself in luck. The horse won and he found himself with something over a thousand pounds in hard cash. Now his chance had come. He found out who was the best solicitor in the town – the collier lay then somewhere on the Irish coast – went to him, and, telling him that he heard the ship was for sale, asked him to arrange the purchase for him. The solicitor was amused at his small client, he was only sixteen and did not look so old, and, moved perhaps by sympathy, promised not only to arrange the matter for him but to see that he made a good bargain. After a little while Walker found himself the owner of the ship. He went back to her and had what he described as the most glorious moment of his life when he gave the skipper notice and told him that he must get off *his* ship in half an hour. He made the mate captain and sailed on the collier for another nine months, at the end of which he sold her at a profit.

He came out to the islands at the age of twenty-six as a planter. He was one of the few white men settled in Talua at the time of the German occupation and had then already some influence with the natives. The Germans made him administrator, a position which he occupied for twenty years, and when the island was seized by the British he was confirmed in his post. He ruled the island despotically, but with complete success. The prestige of this success was another reason for the interest that Mackintosh took in him.

But the two men were not made to get on. Mackintosh was an ugly man, with ungainly gestures, a tall thin fellow, with a narrow chest and bowed shoulders. He had sallow, sunken cheeks, and his eyes were large and sombre. He was a great reader, and when his books arrived and were unpacked Walker came over to his quarters and looked at them. Then he turned to Mackintosh with a coarse laugh.

'What in Hell have you brought all this muck for?' he asked. Mackintosh flushed darkly.

'I'm sorry you think it muck. I brought my books because I want to read them.'

'When you said you'd got a lot of books coming I thought there'd be something for me to read. Haven't you got any detective stories?'

'Detective stories don't interest me.'

'You're a damned fool then.'

'I'm content that you should think so.'

Every mail brought Walker a mass of periodical literature, papers from New Zealand and magazines from America, and it exasperated him that Mackintosh showed his contempt for these ephemeral publications. He had no patience with the books that absorbed Mackintosh's leisure and thought it only a pose that he read Gibbon's *Decline and Fall* or Burton's *Anatomy of Melancholy*. And since he had never learned to put any restraint on his tongue, he expressed his opinion of his assistant freely. Mackintosh began to see the real man, and under the boisterous good-humour he discerned a vulgar cunning which was hateful; he was vain and domineering, and it was strange that he had notwithstanding a shyness which made him dislike people who were not quite of his kidney. He judged others, naïvely, by their language, and if it was free from the oaths and the obscenity which made up the greater part of his own conversation, he looked upon them with suspicion. In the evening the two men played piquet. He played badly but vaingloriously, crowing over his opponent when he won and losing his temper when he lost. On rare occasions a couple of planters or traders would drive over to play bridge, and then Walker showed himself in what Mackintosh considered a characteristic light. He played regardless of his partner, calling up in his desire to play the hand, and argued interminably, beating down opposition by the loudness of his voice. He constantly revoked, and when he did so said with an ingratiating whine: 'Oh, you wouldn't count it against an old man who can hardly see.' Did he know that his opponents thought it as well to keep on the right side of him and hesitated to insist on the rigour of the game? Mackintosh watched him with an icy contempt. When the game was over, while they smoked their pipes and drank whisky, they would begin telling stories. Walker told with gusto the story of his marriage. He had got so drunk at the wedding feast that the bride had fled and he had never seen her since. He had had numberless adventures, commonplace and sordid, with the women of the island and he described them with a pride in his own prowess which was an offence to Mackintosh's fastidious ears. He was a gross, sensual old man. He thought Mackintosh a poor fellow because he would not share his promiscuous amours and remained sober when the company was drunk.

He despised him also for the orderliness with which he did his official work. Mackintosh liked to do everything just so. His desk was always tidy, his papers were always neatly docketed, he could put his hand on any document that was needed, and he had at his fingers' ends all the regulations that were required for the business of their administration.

'Fudge, fudge,' said Walker. 'I've run this island for twenty years without red tape, and I don't want it now.'

'Does it make it any easier for you that when you want a letter you have to hunt half an hour for it?' answered Mackintosh.

'You're nothing but a damned official. But you're not a bad fellow; when you've been out here a year or two you'll be all right. What's wrong about you is that you won't drink. You would'nt be a bad sort if you got soused once a week.'

The curious thing was that Walker remained perfectly unconscious of the dislike for him which every month increased in the breast of his subordinate. Although he laughed at him, as he grew accustomed to him, he began almost to like him. He had a certain tolerance for the peculiarities of others, and he accepted Mackintosh as a queer fish. Perhaps he like him, unconsciously, because he could chaff him. His humour consisted of coarse banter and he wanted a butt. Mackintosh's exactness, his morality, his sobriety, were all fruitful subjects; his Scots name gave an opportunity for the usual jokes about Scotland; he enjoyed himself thoroughly when two or three men were there and he could make them all laugh at the expense of Mackintosh. He would say ridiculous things about him to the natives, and Mackintosh, his knowledge of Samoan still imperfect, would see their unrestrained mirth when Walker had made an obscene reference to him. He smiled good-humouredly.

'I'll say this for you, Mac,' Walker would say in his gruff loud voice, 'you can take a joke.'

'Was it a joke?' smiled Mackintosh. 'I didn't know.'

'Scots wha hae!' shouted Walker, with a bellow of laughter.
'There's only one way to make a Scotchman see a joke and that's
by a surgical operation.'

Walker little knew that there was nothing Mackintosh could
stand less than chaff. He would wake in the night, the breathless
night of the rainy season, and brood sullenly over the gibe that
Walker had uttered carelessly days before. It rankled. His heart
swelled with rage, and he pictured to himself ways in which he
might get even with the bully. He had tried answering him, but
Walker had a gift of repartee, coarse and obvious, which gave
him an advantage. The dullness of his intellect made him imper-
vious to a delicate shaft. His self-satisfaction made it impossible
to wound him. His loud voice, his bellow of laughter, were
weapons against which Mackintosh had nothing to counter, and
he learned that the wisest thing was never to betray his irritation.
He learned to control himself. But his hatred grew till it was a
monomania. He watched Walker with an insane vigilance. He
fed his own self-esteem by every instance of meanness on Walker's
part, by every exhibition of childish vanity, of cunning, and of
vulgarity. Walker ate greedily, noisily, filthily, and Mackintosh
watched him with satisfaction. He took note of the foolish things
he said and of his mistakes in grammar. He knew that Walker
held him in small esteem, and he found a bitter satisfaction in
his chief's opinion of him; it increased his own contempt for the
narrow, complacent old man. And it gave him a singular pleasure
to know that Walker was entirely unconscious of the hatred he
felt for him. He was a fool who liked popularity, and he blandly
fancied that everyone admired him. Once Mackintosh had over-
heard Walker speaking of him.

'He'll be all right when I've licked him into shape,' he said.
'He's a good dog and he loves his master.'

Mackintosh silently, without a movement of his long, sallow
face, laughed long and heartily.

But his hatred was not blind; on the contrary, it was peculiarly
clear-sighted, and he judged Walker's capabilities with precision.
He ruled his small kingdom with efficiency. He was just and
honest. With opportunities to make money he was a poorer man
than when he was first appointed to his post, and his only support
for his old age was the pension which he expected when at last
he retired from official life. His pride was that with an assistant
and a half-caste clerk he was able to administer the island more
competently than Upolu, the island of which Apia is the chief
town, was administered with its army of functionaries. He had a

few native policemen to sustain his authority, but he made no use of them. He governed by bluff and his Irish humour.

'They insisted on building a jail for me,' he said. 'What the devil do I want a jail for? I'm not going to put the natives in prison. If they do wrong I know how to deal with them.'

One of his quarrels with the higher authorities at Apia was that he claimed entire jurisdiction over the natives of his island. Whatever their crimes he would not give them up to courts competent to deal with them, and several times an angry correspondence had passed between him and the governor at Upolu. For he looked upon the natives as his children. And that was the amazing thing about this coarse, vulgar, selfish man; he loved the island on which he had lived so long with passion, and he had for the natives a strange rough tenderness which was quite wonderful.

He loved to ride about the island on his old grey mare and he was never tired of its beauty. Sauntering along the grassy roads among the coconut trees he would stop every now and then to admire the loveliness of the scene. Now and then he would come upon a native village and stop while the headman brought him a bowl of *kava*. He would look at the little group of bell-shape huts with their high thatched roofs, like beehives, and a smile would spread over his fat face. His eyes rested happily on the spreading green of the bread-fruit trees.

'By George, it's like the garden of Eden.'

Sometimes his rides took him along the coast and through the trees he had a glimpse of the wide sea, empty, with never a sail to disturb the loneliness; sometimes he climbed a hill so that a great stretch of country, with little villages nestling among the tall trees was spread out before him like the kingdom of the world, and he would sit there for an hour in an ecstasy of delight. But he had no words to express his feelings and to relieve them would utter an obscene jest; it was as though his emotion was so violent that he needed vulgarity to break the tension.

Mackintosh observed this sentiment with an icy disdain. Walker had always been a heavy drinker, he was proud of his capacity to see men half his age under the table when he spent a night in Apia, and he had the sentimentality of the toper. He could cry over the stories he read in his magazines and yet would refuse a loan to some trader in difficulties whom he had known for twenty years. He was close with his money. Once Mackintosh said to him:

'No one could accuse you of giving money away.'

151

He took it as a compliment. His enthusiasm for nature was but the drivelling sensibility of the drunkard. Nor had Mackintosh any sympathy for his chief's feelings towards the natives. He loved them because they were in his power, as a selfish man loves his dog, and his mentality was on a level with theirs. Their humour was obscene and he was never at a loss for the lewd remark. He understood them and they understood him. He was proud of his influence over them. He looked upon them as his children and he mixed himself in all their affairs. But he was very jealous of his authority; if he ruled them with a rod of iron, brooking no contradiction, he would not suffer any of the white men on the island to take advantage of them. He watched the missionaries suspiciously and, if they did anything of which he disapproved, was able to make life so unendurable to them that if he could not get them removed they were glad to go of their own accord. His power over the natives was so great that on his word they would refuse labour and food to their pastor. On the other hand he showed the traders no favour. He took care that they should not cheat the natives; he saw that they got a fair reward for their work and their copra and that the traders made no extravagant profit on the wares they sold them. He was merciless to a bargain that he thought unfair. Sometimes the traders would complain at Apia that they did not get fair opportunities. They suffered for it. Walker then hesitated at no calumny, at no outrageous lie, to get even with them, and they found that if they wanted not only to live at peace, but to exist at all, they had to accept the situation on his own terms. More than once the store of a trader obnoxious to him had been burned down, and there was only the appositeness of the event to show that the administrator had instigated it. Once a Swedish half-caste, ruined by the burning, had gone to him and roundly accused him of arson. Walker laughed in his face.

'You dirty dog. Your mother was a native and you try to cheat the natives. If your rotten old store is burned down it's a judgement of Providence; that's what it is, a judgement of Providence. Get out.'

And as the man was hustled out by two native policemen the administrator laughed fatly.

'A judgement of Providence.'

And now Mackintosh watched him enter upon the day's work. He began with the sick, for Walker added doctoring to his other activities, and he had a small room behind the office full of drugs. An elderly man came forward, a man with a crop of curly grey hair, in a blue lava-lava, elaborately tattooed, with the skin of his body wrinkled like a wine-skin.

'What have you come for?' Walker asked him abruptly.

In a whining voice the man said that he could not eat without vomiting and that he had pains here and pains there.

'Go to the missionaries,' said Walker. 'You know that I only cure children.'

'I have been to the missionaries and they do me no good.'

'Then go home and prepare yourself to die. Have you lived so long and still want to go on living? You're a fool.'

The man broke into querulous expostulation, but Walker, pointing to a woman with a sick child in her arms, told her to bring it to his desk. He asked her questions and looked at the child.

'I will give you medicine,' he said. He turned to the half-caste clerk. 'Go into the dispensary and bring me some calomel pills.'

He made the child swallow one there and then and gave another to the mother.

'Take the child away and keep it warm. Tomorrow it will be dead or better.'

He leaned back in his chair and lit his pipe.

'Wonderful stuff, calomel. I've saved more lives with it than all the hospital doctors at Apia put together.'

Walker was very proud of his skill, and with the dogmatism of ignorance had no patience with the members of the medical profession.

'The sort of case I like,' he said, 'is the one that all the doctors have given up as hopeless. When the doctors have said they can't cure you, I say to them, "come to me." Did I ever tell you about the fellow who had a cancer?'

'Frequently,' said Mackintosh.

'I got him right in three months.'

'You've never told me about the people you haven't cured.'

He finished this part of the work and went on to the rest. It was a queer medley. There was a woman who could not get on with her husband and a man who complained that his wife had run away from him.

'Lucky dog,' said Walker. 'Most men wish their wives would too.'

There was a long complicated quarrel about the ownership of a few yards of land. There was a dispute about the sharing out of a catch of fish. There was a complaint against a white trader because he had given short measure. Walker listened attentively to every case, made up his mind quickly, and gave his decision. Then he would listen to nothing more; if the complainant went on he was hustled out of the office by a policeman. Mackintosh listened to it all with sullen irritation. On the whole, perhaps, it might be admitted that rough justice was done, but it exasperated the assistant that his chief trusted his instinct rather than the evidence. He would not listen to reason. He browbeat the witnesses and when they did not see what he wished them to called them thieves and liars.

He left to the last a group of men who were sitting in the corner of the room. He had deliberately ignored them. The party consisted of an old chief, a tall, dignified man with short, white hair, in a new lava-lava, bearing a huge fly wisp as a badge of office, his son, and half a dozen of the important men of the village. Walker had had a feud with them and had beaten them. As was characteristic of him he meant now to rub in his victory, and because he had them down to profit by their helplessness. The facts were peculiar. Walker had a passion for building roads. When he had come to Talua there were but a few tracks here and there, but in course of time he had cut roads through the country, joining the villages together, and it was to this that a great part of the island's prosperity was due. Whereas in the old days it had been impossible to get the produce of the land, copra chiefly, down to the coast where it could be put on schooners or motor launches and so taken to Apia, now transport was easy and simple. His ambition was to make a road right round the island and a great part of it was already built.

'In two years I shall have done it, and then I can die or they can fire me, I don't care.'

His roads were the joy of his heart and he made excursions constantly to see that they were kept in order. They were simple enough, wide tracks, grass-covered, cut through the scrub or through the plantations; but trees had to be rooted out, rocks dug up or blasted, and here and there levelling had been necessary. He was proud that he had surmounted by his own skill such difficulties as they presented. He rejoiced in his disposition of them so that they were not only convenient, but showed off the beauties of the island which his soul loved. When he spoke of his roads he was almost a poet. They meandered through those lovely scenes, and Walker had taken care that here and there they should run in a straight line, giving you a green vista through the tall trees, and here and there should turn and curve so that the heart was rested by the diversity. It was amazing that this coarse and sensual man should exercise so subtle an ingenuity to get the effects which his fancy suggested to him. He had used in making his roads all the fantastic skill of a Japanese gardener. He received a grant from headquarters for the work but took a curious pride in using but a small part of it, and the year before had spent only a hundred pounds of the thousand assigned to him.

'What do they want money for?' he boomed. 'They'll only spend it on all kinds of muck they don't want; what the missionaries leave them, that is to say.'

For no particular reason, except perhaps pride in the economy of his administration and the desire to contrast his efficiency with the wasteful methods of the authorities at Apia, he got the natives to do the work he wanted for wages that were almost nominal. It was owing to this that he had lately had difficulty with the village whose chief men now were come to see him. The chief's son had been in Upolu for a year and on coming back had told his people of the large sums that were paid at Apia for the public works. In long, idle talks he had inflamed their hearts with the desire for gain. He held out to them visions of vast wealth and they thought of the whisky they could buy – it was dear, since there was a law that it must not be sold to natives, and so it cost them double what the white man had to pay for it – they thought of the great sandalwood boxes in which they kept their treasures, and the scented soap and potted salmon, the luxuries for which the Kanaka will sell his soul; so that when the administrator sent for them and told them he wanted a road made from their village to a certain point along the coast and offered them twenty pounds, they asked him a hundred. The chief's son was called Manuma. He was a tall, handsome fellow, copper-coloured, with his fuzzy hair dyed red with lime, a wreath of red berries round his neck, and behind his ear a flower like a scarlet flame against his brown face. The upper part of his body was naked, but to show that he was no longer a savage, since he had lived in Apia, he wore a pair of dungarees instead of a lava-lava. He told them that if they held together the administrator would be obliged to accept their terms. His heart was set on building the road and when he found they would not work for less he would give them what they asked. But they must not move; whatever he said they must not abate their claim; they had asked a hundred and that they must keep to. When they mentioned the figure, Walker burst into a shout of his long, deep-voiced laughter. He told them not to make fools of themselves, but to

set about the work at once. Because he was in a good humour
that day he promised to give them a feast when the road was
finished. But when he found that no attempt was made to start
work, he went to the village and asked the men what silly game
they were playing. Manuma had coached them well. They were
quite calm, they did not attempt to argue – and argument is a
passion with the Kanaka – they merely shrugged their shoulders:
they would do it for a hundred pounds, and if he would not give
them that they would do no work. He could please himself. They
did not care. Then Walker flew into a passion. He was ugly then.
His short fat neck swelled ominously, his red face grew purple,
he foamed at the mouth. He set upon the natives with invective.
He knew well how to wound and how to humiliate. He was
terrifying. The older men grew pale and uneasy. They hesitated.
If it had not been for Manuma, with his knowledge of the great
world, and their dread of his ridicule, they would have yielded.
It was Manuma who answered Walker.

'Pay us a hundred pounds and we will work.'

Walker, shaking his fist at him, called him every name he could
think of. He riddled him with scorn. Manuma sat still and smiled.
There may have been more bravado than confidence in his smile,
but he had to make a good show before the others. He repeated
his words.

'Pay us a hundred pounds and we will work.'

They thought that Walker would spring on him. It would not
have been the first time that he had thrashed a native with his
own hands; they knew his strength, and though Walker was three
times the age of the young man and six inches shorter they did
not doubt that he was more than a match for Manuma. No one
had ever thought of resisting the savage onslaught of the administrator. But Walker said nothing. He chuckled.

'I am not going to waste my time with a pack of fools,' he
said. 'Talk it over again. You know what I have offered. If you
do not start in a week, take care.'

He turned round and walked out of the chief's hut. He untied
his old mare and it was typical of the relations between him and
the natives that one of the elder men hung on to the off stirrup
while Walker from a convenient boulder hoisted himself heavily
into the saddle.

That same night when Walker according to his habit was
strolling along the road that ran past his house, he heard something whizz past him and with a thud strike a tree. Something
had been thrown at him. He ducked instinctively. With a shout,

'Who's that?' he ran towards the place from which the missile had come and he heard the sound of a man escaping through the bush. He knew it was hopeless to pursue in the darkness, and besides he was soon out of breath, so he stopped and made his way back to the road. He looked about for what had been thrown, but could find nothing. It was quite dark. He went quickly back to the house and called Mackintosh and the Chinese boy.

'One of those devils has thrown something at me. Come along and let's find out what it was.'

He told the boy to bring a lantern and the three of them made their way back to the place. They hunted about the ground, but could not find what they sought. Suddenly the boy gave a guttural cry. They turned to look. He held up the lantern, and there, sinister in the light that cut the surrounding darkness, was a long knife sticking into the trunk of a coconut tree. It had been thrown with such force that it required quite an effort to pull it out.

'By George, if he hadn't missed me I'd have been in a nice state.'

Walker handled the knife. It was one of those knives, made in imitation of the sailor knives brought to the islands a hundred years before by the first white men, used to divide the coconuts in two so that the copra might be dried. It was a murderous weapon, and the blade, twelve inches long, was very sharp. Walker chuckled softly.

'The devil, the impudent devil.'

He had no doubt it was Manuma who had flung the knife. He had escaped death by three inches. He was not angry. On the contrary, he was in high spirits; the adventure exhilarated him, and when they got back to the house, calling for drinks, he rubbed his hands gleefully.

'I'll make them pay for this!'

His little eyes twinkled. He blew himself out like a turkey-cock, and for the second time within half an hour insisted on telling Mackintosh every detail of the affair. Then he asked him to play piquet, and while they played he boasted of his intentions. Mackintosh listened with tightened lips.

'But why should you grind them down like this?' he asked. 'Twenty pounds is precious little for the work you want them to do.'

'They ought to be precious thankful I give them anything.'

'Hang it all, it's not your own money. The government allots you a reasonable sum. They won't complain if you spend it.'

'They're a bunch of fools at Apia.'

Mackintosh saw that Walker's motive was merely vanity. He shrugged his shoulders.

'It won't do you much good to score off the fellows at Apia at the cost of your life.'

'Bless you, they wouldn't hurt me, these people. They couldn't do without me. They worship me. Manuma is a fool. He only threw that knife to frighten me.'

The next day Walker rode over again to the village. It was called Matautu. He did not get off his horse. When he reached the chief's house he saw that the men were sitting round the floor in a circle, talking, and he guessed they were discussing again the question of the road. The Samoan huts are formed in this way: trunks of slender trees are placed in a circle at intervals of perhaps five or six feet; a tall tree is set in the middle and from this downwards slopes the thatched roof. Venetian blinds of coconut leaves can be pulled down at night or when it is raining. Ordinarily the hut is open all round so that the breeze can blow through freely. Walker rode to the edge of the hut and called out to the chief.

'Oh, there, Tangatu, your son left his knife in a tree last night. I have brought it back to you.'

He flung it down on the ground in the midst of the circle, and with a low burst of laughter ambled off.

On Monday he went out to see if they had started work. There was no sign of it. He rode through the village. The inhabitants were about their ordinary avocations. Some were weaving mats of the pandanus leaf, one old man was busy with a *kava* bowl, the children were playing, the women went about their household chores. Walker, a smile on his lips, came to the chief's house.

'*Talofa-li*,' said the chief.

'*Talofa*,' answered Walker.

Manuma was making a net. He sat with a cigarette between his lips and looked up at Walker with a smile of triumph.

'You have decided that you will not make the road?'

The chief answered.

'Not unless you pay us one hundred pounds.'

'You will regret it.' He turned to Manuma. 'And you, my lad, I shouldn't wonder if your back was very sore before you're much older.'

He rode away chuckling. He left the natives vaguely uneasy. They feared the fat sinful old man, and neither the missionaries' abuse of him nor the scorn which Manuma had learnt in Apia made them forget that he had a devilish cunning and that no man had ever braved him without in the long run suffering for it. They found out within twenty-four hours what scheme he had devised. It was characteristic. For next morning a great band of men, women, and children came into the village and the chief men said that they had made a bargain with Walker to build the road. He had offered them twenty pounds and they had accepted. Now the cunning lay in this, that the Polynesians have rules of hospitality which have all the force of laws; an etiquette of absolute rigidity made it necessary for the people of the village not only to give lodging to the strangers, but to provide them with food and drink as long as they wished to stay. The inhabitants of Matautu were outwitted. Every morning the workers went out in a joyous band, cut down trees, blasted rocks, levelled here and there and then in the evening tramped back again, and ate and drank, ate heartily, danced, sang hymns, and enjoyed life. For them it was a picnic. But soon their hosts began to wear long faces; the strangers had enormous appetites, and the plantains and the bread-fruit vanished before their rapacity; the alligator-pear trees, whose fruit sent to Apia might sell for good money, were stripped bare. Ruin stared them in the face. And then they found that the strangers were working very slowly. Had they received a hint from Walker that they might take their time? At this rate by the time the road was finished there would not be a scrap of food in the village. And worse than this, they were a laughing-stock; when one or other of them went to some distant hamlet on an errand he found that the story had got there before him, and he was met with derisive laughter. There is nothing the Kanaka can endure less than ridicule. It was not long before much angry talk passed among the sufferers. Manuma was no longer a hero; he had to put up with a good deal of plain speaking, and one day what Walker had suggested came to pass: a heated argument turned into a quarrel and half a dozen of the young men set upon the chief's son and gave him such a beating that for a week he lay bruised and sore on the pandanus mats. He turned from side to side and could find no ease. Every day or two the administrator rode over on his old mare and watched the progress of the road. He was not a man to resist the temptation of taunting the fallen foe, and he missed no opportunity to rub into the shamed inhabitants of Matautu the bitterness of their humiliation. He broke their spirit. And one morning, putting their pride in their pockets – a figure of speech, since pockets they had not – they all set out with the strangers and started working on the road. It was urgent to get it done quickly if they wanted to save any food at all, and the whole village joined in. But they worked silently, with rage and mortification in their hearts, and even the children toiled in silence. The women wept as they carried away bundles of brushwood. When Walker saw them he laughed so much that he almost rolled out of his saddle. The news spread quickly and tickled the people of the island to death. This was the greatest joke of all, the crowning triumph of that cunning old white man whom no Kanaka had ever been able to circumvent; and they came from distant villages, with their wives and children, to look at the foolish folk who had refused twenty pounds to make the road and now were forced to work for nothing. But the harder they worked the more easily went the guests. Why should they hurry, when they were getting good food for nothing and the longer they took about the job the better the joke became? At last the wretched villagers could stand it no longer, and they were come this morning to beg the administrator to send the strangers back to their own homes. If he would do this they promised to finish the road themselves for nothing. For him it was a victory complete and unqualified. They were humbled. A look of arrogant complacence spread over his large, naked face, and he seemed to swell in his chair like a great bullfrog. There was something sinister in his appearance, so that Mackintosh shivered with disgust. Then in his booming tones he began to speak.

'Is it for my good that I make the road? What benefit do you think I get out of it? It is for you, so that you can walk in comfort and carry your copra in comfort. I offered to pay you for your work, though it was for your own sake the work was done. I offered to pay you generously. Now *you* must pay. I will send the people of Manua back to their homes if you will finish the road and pay the twenty pounds that I have to pay them.'

There was an outcry. They sought to reason with him. They told him they had not the money. But to everything they said he replied with brutal gibes. Then the clock struck.

'Dinner time,' he said. 'Turn them all out.'

He raised himself heavily from his chair and walked out of the room. When Mackintosh followed him, he found him already seated at table, a napkin tied round his neck, holding his knife and fork in readiness for the meal the Chinese cook was about to bring. He was in high spirits.

'I did 'em down fine,' he said, as Mackintosh sat down. 'I shan't have much trouble with the roads after this.'

'I suppose you were joking,' said Mackintosh icily.

'What do you mean by that?'

'You're not really going to make them pay twenty pounds?'

'You bet your life I am.'

'I'm not sure you've got any right to.'

'Ain't you? I guess I've got the right to do any damned thing I like on this island.'

'I think you've bullied them quite enough.'

Walker laughed fatly. He did not care what Mackintosh thought.

'When I want your opinion I'll ask for it.'

Mackintosh grew very white. He knew by bitter experience that he could do nothing but keep silence, and the violent effort at self-control made him sick and faint. He could not eat the food that was before him and with disgust he watched Walker shovel meat into his vast mouth. He was a dirty feeder, and to sit at table with him needed a strong stomach. Mackintosh shuddered. A tremendous desire seized him to humiliate that gross and cruel man; he would give anything in the world to see him in the dust, suffering as much as he had made others suffer. He had never loathed the bully with such loathing as now.

The day wore on. Mackintosh tried to sleep after dinner, but the passion in his heart prevented him; he tried to read, but the letters swam before his eyes. The sun beat down pitilessly, and he longed for rain; but he knew that rain would bring no coolness; it would only make it hotter and more steamy. He was a native of Aberdeen and his heart yearned suddenly for the icy winds that whistled through the granite streets of that city. Here he was a prisoner, imprisoned not only by that placid sea, but by his hatred for that horrible old man. He pressed his hands to his aching head. He would like to kill him. But he pulled himself together. He must do something to distract his mind, and since he could not read he thought he would set his private papers in order. It was a job which he had long meant to do and which he had constantly put off. He unlocked the drawer of his desk and took out a handful of letters. He caught sight of his revolver. An impulse, no sooner realized than set aside, to put a bullet through his head and so escape from the intolerable bondage of life flashed through his mind. He noticed that in the damp air the revolver was slightly rusted, and he got an oil-rag and began to clean it. It was while he was thus occupied that he grew aware of someone slinking round the door. He looked up and called:

'Who is there?'

There was a moment's pause, then Manuma showed himself.

'What do you want?'

The chief's son stood for a moment, sullen and silent, and when he spoke it was with a strangled voice.

'We can't pay twenty pounds. We haven't the money.'

'What am I to do?' said Mackintosh. 'You heard what Mr Walker said.'

Manuma began to plead, half in Samoan and half in English. It was a sing-song whine, with the quavering intonations of a beggar, and it filled Mackintosh with disgust. It outraged him that the man should let himself be so crushed. He was a pitiful object.

'I can do nothing,' said Mackintosh irritably. 'You know that Mr Walker is master here.'

Manuma was silent again. He still stood in the doorway.

'I am sick,' he said at last. 'Give me some medicine.'

'What is the matter with you?'

'I do not know. I am sick. I have pains in my body.'

'Don't stand there,' said Mackintosh sharply. 'Come in and let me look at you.'

Manuma entered the little room and stood before the desk.

'I have pains here and here.'

He put his hands to his loins and his face assumed an expression of pain. Suddenly Mackintosh grew conscious that the boy's eyes were resting on the revolver which he had laid on the desk when Manuma appeared in the doorway. There was a silence between the two which to Mackintosh was endless. He seemed to read the thoughts which were in the Kanaka's mind. His heart beat violently. And then he felt as though something possessed him so that he acted under the compulsion of a foreign will. Himself did not make the movements of his body, but a power that was strange to him. His throat was suddenly dry, and he put his hand to it mechanically in order to help his speech. He was impelled to avoid Manuma's eyes.

'Just wait here,' he said, his voice sounded as though someone had seized him by the windpipe, 'and I'll fetch you something from the dispensary.'

He got up. Was it his fancy that he staggered a little? Manuma stood silently, and though he kept his eyes averted, Mackintosh knew that he was looking dully out of the door. It was this other person that possessed him that drove him out of the room, but it was himself that took a handful of muddled papers and threw them on the revolver in order to hide it from view. He went to the dispensary. He got a pill and poured out some blue draught into a small bottle, and then came out into the compound. He did not want to go back into his own bungalow, so he called to Manuma.

'Come here.'

He gave him the drugs and instructions how to take them. He did not know what it was that made it impossible for him to look at the Kanaka. While he was speaking to him he kept his eyes on his shoulder. Manuma took the medicine and slunk out of the gate.

Mackintosh went into the dining-room and turned over once more the old newspapers. But he could not read them. The house was very still. Walker was upstairs in his room asleep, the Chinese cook was busy in the kitchen, the two policemen were out fishing. The silence that seemed to brood over the house was unearthly, and there hammered in Mackintosh's head the question whether the revolver still lay where he had placed it. He could not bring himself to look. The uncertainty was horrible, but the certainty would be more horrible still. He sweated. At last he could stand the silence no longer, and he made up his mind to go down the road to the trader's, a man named Jervis, who had a store about a mile away. He was a half-caste, but even that amount of white blood made him possible to talk to. He wanted to get away from his bungalow, with the desk littered with untidy papers, and underneath them something, or nothing. He walked along the road. As he passed the fine hut of a chief a greeting was called out to him. Then he came to the store. Behind the counter sat the trader's daughter, a swarthy broad-featured girl in a pink blouse and a white drill skirt. Jervis hoped he would marry her. He had money, and he had told Mackintosh that his daughter's husband would be well-to-do. She flushed a little when she saw Mackintosh.

'Father's just unpacking some cases that have come in this morning. I'll tell him you're here.'

He sat down and the girl went out behind the shop. In a moment her mother waddled in, a huge old woman, a chiefess, who owned much land in her own right; and gave him her hand. Her monstrous obesity was an offence, but she managed to convey an impression of dignity. She was cordial without obsequiousness; affable, but conscious of her station.

'You're quite a stranger, Mr Mackintosh. Teresa was saying only this morning: "Why, we never see Mr Mackintosh now."'

He shuddered a little as he thought of himself as that old native's son-in-law. It was notorious that she ruled her husband, notwithstanding his white blood, with a firm hand. Hers was the authority and hers the business head. She might be no more than Mrs Jervis to the white people, but her father had been a chief of the blood royal, and his father and his father's father had ruled as kings. The trader came in, small beside his imposing wife, a dark man with a black beard going grey, in ducks, with handsome eyes and flashing teeth. He was very British, and his conversation was slangy, but you felt he spoke English as a foreign tongue; with his family he used the language of his native mother. He was a servile man, cringing and obsequious.

'Ah, Mr Mackintosh, this is a joyful surprise. Get the whisky, Teresa; Mr Mackintosh will have a gargle with us.'

He gave all the latest news of Apia, watching his guest's eyes the while, so that he might know the welcome thing to say.

'And how is Walker? We've not seen him just lately. Mrs Jervis is going to send him a sucking-pig one day this week.'

'I saw him riding home this morning,' said Teresa.

'Here's how,' said Jervis, holding up his whisky.

Mackintosh drank. The two women sat and looked at him, Mrs Jervis in her black Mother Hubbard, placid and haughty, and Teresa anxious to smile whenever she caught his eye, while the trader gossiped insufferably.

'They were saying in Apia it was about time Walker retired. He ain't so young as he was. Things have changed since he first come to the islands and he ain't changed with them.'

'He'll go too far,' said the old chiefess. 'The natives aren't satisfied.'

'That was a good joke about the road,' laughed the trader. 'When I told them about it in Apia they fair split their sides with laughing. Good old Walker.'

Mackintosh looked at him savagely. What did he mean by talking of him in that fashion? To a half-caste trader he was Mr Walker. It was on his tongue to utter a harsh rebuke for the impertinence. He did not know what held him back.

'When he goes I hope you'll take his place, Mr Mackintosh,' said Jervis. 'We all like you on the island. You understand the natives. They're educated now, they must be treated differently to the old days. It wants an educated man to be administrator now. Walker was only a trader same as I am.'

Teresa's eyes glistened.

'When the time comes if there's anything anyone can do here, you bet your bottom dollar we'll do it. I'd get all the chiefs to go over to Apia and make a petition.'

Mackintosh felt horribly sick. It had not struck him that if anything happened to Walker it might be he who would succeed him. It was true that no one in his official position knew the island so well. He got up suddenly and scarcely taking his leave walked back to the compound. And now he went straight to his room. He took a quick look at his desk. He rummaged among the papers.

The revolver was not there.

His heart thumped violently against his ribs. He looked for the revolver everywhere. He hunted in the chairs and in the drawers. He looked desperately, and all the time he knew he would not find it. Suddenly he heard Walker's gruff, hearty voice.

'What the devil are you up to, Mac?'

He started. Walker was standing in the doorway and instinctively he turned round to hide what lay upon his desk.

'Tidying up?' quizzed Walker. 'I've told 'em to put the grey in the trap. I'm going down to Tafoni to bathe. You'd better come along.'

'All right,' said Mackintosh.

So long as he was with Walker nothing could happen. The place they were bound for was about three miles away, and there was a fresh-water pool, separated by a thin barrier of rock from the sea, which the administrator had blasted out for the natives to bathe in. He had done this at spots round the island, wherever there was a spring; and the fresh water, compared with the sticky warmth of the sea, was cool and invigorating. They drove along the silent grassy road, splashing now and then through fords, where the sea had forced its way in, past a couple of native villages, the bell-shaped huts spaced out roomily and the white chapel in the middle, and at the third village they got out of the trap, tied up the horse, and walked down to the pool. They were accompanied by four or five girls and a dozen children. Soon they were all splashing about, shouting and laughing, while Walker, in a lava-lava, swam to and fro like an unwieldy porpoise. He made lewd jokes with the girls, and they amused themselves by diving under him and wriggling away when he tried to catch them. When he was tired he lay down on a rock, while the girls and children surrounded him; it was a happy family; and the old man, huge, with his crescent of white hair and his shining bald crown, looked like some old sea god. Once Mackintosh caught a queer soft look in his eyes.

'They're dear children,' he said. 'They look upon me as their father.'

And then without a pause he turned to one of the girls and made an obscene remark which sent them all into fits of laughter. Mackintosh started to dress. With his thin legs and thin arms he made a grotesque figure, a sinister Don Quixote, and Walker began to make coarse jokes about him. They were acknowledged with little smothered laughs. Mackintosh struggled with his shirt. He knew he looked absurd, but he hated being laughed at. He stood silent and glowering.

'If you want to get back in time for dinner you ought to come soon.'

'You're not a bad fellow, Mac. Only you're a fool. When you're doing one thing you always want to do another. That's not the way we live.'

But all the same he raised himself slowly to his feet and began to put on his clothes. They sauntered back to the village, drank a bowl of *kava* with the chief, and then, after a joyful farewell from all the lazy villagers, drove home.

After dinner, according to his habit, Walker, lighting his cigar, prepared to go for a stroll. Mackintosh was suddenly seized with fear.

'Don't you think it's rather unwise to go out at night by yourself just now?'

Walker stared at him with his round blue eyes.

'What the devil do you mean?'

'Remember the knife the other night. You've got those fellows' backs up.'

'Pooh! They wouldn't dare.'

'Someone dared before.'

'That was only a bluff. They wouldn't hurt me. They look upon me as a father. They know that whatever I do is for their own good.'

Mackintosh watched him with contempt in his heart. The man's self-complacency outraged him, and yet something, he knew not what, made him insist.

'Remember what happened this morning. It wouldn't hurt you to stay at home just tonight. I'll play piquet with you.'

'I'll play piquet with you when I come back. The Kanaka isn't born yet who can make me alter my plans.'

'You'd better let me come with you.'

'You stay where you are.'

Mackintosh shrugged his shoulders. He had given the man full warning. If he did not heed it that was his own lookout. Walker put on his hat and went out. Mackintosh began to read; but then he thought of something; perhaps it would be as well to have his own whereabouts quite clear. He crossed over to the kitchen and, inventing some pretext, talked for a few minutes with the cook. Then he got out the gramophone and put a record on it, but while it ground out its melancholy tune, some comic song of a London music-hall, his ear was strained for a sound away there in the night. At his elbow the record reeled out its loudness, the words were raucous, but notwithstanding he seemed to be surrounded by an unearthly silence. He heard the dull roar of the breakers against the reef. He heard the breeze sigh, far up, in the leaves of the coconut trees. How long would it be? It was awful.

He heard a hoarse laugh.

'Wonders will never cease. It's not often you play yourself a tune, Mac.'

Walker stood at the window, red-faced, bluff and jovial.

'Well, you see I'm alive and kicking. What were you playing for?'

Walker came in.

'Nerves a bit dicky, eh? Playing a tune to keep your pecker up?'

'I was playing your requiem.'

'What the devil's that?'

''Alf o' bitter an' a pint of stout.'

'A rattling good song too. I don't mind how often I hear it. Now I'm ready to take your money off you at piquet.'

They played and Walker bullied his way to victory, bluffing his opponent, chaffing him, jeering at his mistakes, up to every dodge, browbeating him, exulting. Presently Mackintosh recovered his coolness, and standing outside himself, as it were, he was able to take a detached pleasure in watching the overbearing old man and in his own cold reserve. Somewhere Manuma sat quietly and awaited his opportunity.

Walker won game after game and pocketed his winnings at the end of the evening in high good-humour.

'You'll have to grow a little bit older before you stand much chance against me, Mac. The fact is I have a natural gift for cards.'

'I don't know that there's much gift about it when I happen to deal you fourteen aces.'

'Good cards come to good players,' retorted Walker. 'I'd have won if I'd had your hands.'

He went on to tell long stories of the various occasions on which he had played cards with notorious sharpers and to their consternation had taken all their money from them. He boasted. He praised himself. And Mackintosh listened with absorption. He wanted now to feed his hatred; and everything Walker said, every gesture, made him more detestable. At last Walker got up.

'Well, I'm going to turn in,' he said with a loud yawn. 'I've got a long day tomorrow.'

'What are you going to do?'

'I'm driving over to the other side of the island. I'll start at five, but I don't expect I shall get back to dinner till late.'

They generally dined at seven.

'We'd better make it half past seven then.'

'I guess it would be as well.'

Mackintosh watched him knock the ashes out of his pipe. His vitality was rude and exuberant. It was strange to think that death hung over him. A faint smile flickered in Mackintosh's cold, gloomy eyes.

'Would you like me to come with you?'

'What in God's name should I want that for? I'm using the mare and she'll have enough to do to carry me; she don't want to drag you over thirty miles of road.'

'Perhaps you don't quite realize what the feeling is at Matautu. I think it would be safer if I came with you.'

Walker burst out into contemptuous laughter.

'You'd be a fine lot of use in a scrap. I'm not a great hand at getting the wind up.'

Now the smile passed from Mackintosh's eyes to his lips. It distorted them painfully.

'*Quem deus vult perdere prius dementat.*'

'What the hell is that?' said Walker.

'Latin,' answered Mackintosh as he went out.

And now he chuckled. His mood had changed. He had done all he could and the matter was in the hands of fate. He slept more soundly than he had done for weeks. When he awoke next morning he went out. After a good night he found a pleasant exhilaration in the freshness of the early air. The sea was a more vivid blue, the sky more brilliant, than on most days, the trade wind was fresh, and there was a ripple on the lagoon as the breeze brushed over it like velvet brushed the wrong way. He felt himself stronger and younger. He entered upon the day's work with zest. After luncheon he slept again, and as evening drew on he had the bay saddled and sauntered through the bush. He seemed to see it all with new eyes. He felt more normal. The extraordinary thing was that he was able to put Walker out of his mind altogether. So far as he was concerned he might never have existed.

He returned late, hot after his ride, and bathed again. Then he sat on the veranda, smoking his pipe, and looked at the day declining over the lagoon. In the sunset the lagoon, rosy and purple and green, was very beautiful. He felt at peace with the world and with himself. When the cook came out to say that dinner was ready and to ask whether he should wait, Mackintosh smiled at him with friendly eyes. He looked at his watch.

'It's half past seven. Better not wait. One can't tell when the boss'll be back.'

The boy nodded, and in a moment Mackintosh saw him carry across the yard a bowl of steaming soup. He got up lazily, went into the dining-room, and ate his dinner. Had it happened? The uncertainty was amusing and Mackintosh chuckled in the silence. The food did not seem so monotonous as usual, and even though there was Hamburger steak, the cook's invariable dish when his poor invention failed him, it tasted by some miracle succulent and spiced. After dinner he strolled over lazily to his bungalow to get a book. He liked the intense stillness, and now that the night had fallen the stars were blazing in the sky. He shouted for a lamp and in a moment the Chink pattered over on his bare feet, piercing the darkness with a ray of light. He put the lamp on the desk and noiselessly slipped out of the room. Mackintosh stood rooted to the floor, for there, half hidden by untidy papers, was his revolver. His heart throbbed painfully, and he broke into a sweat. It was done then.

He took up the revolver with a shaking hand. Four of the chambers were empty. He paused a moment and looked suspiciously out into the night, but there was no one there. He quickly slipped four cartridges into the empty chambers and locked the revolver in his drawer.

He sat down to wait.

An hour passed, a second hour passed. There was nothing. He sat at his desk as though he were writing, but he neither wrote nor read. He merely listened. He strained his ears for a sound travelling from a far distance. At last he heard hesitating footsteps and knew it was the Chinese cook.

'Ah-Sung,' he called.

The boy came to the door.

'Boss velly late,' he said. 'Dinner no good.'

Mackintosh stared at him, wondering whether he knew what had happened, and whether, when he knew, he would realize on what terms he and Walker had been. He went about his work, sleek, silent, and smiling, and who could tell his thoughts?

'I expect he's had dinner on the way, but you must keep the soup hot at all events.'

The words were hardly out of his mouth when the silence was suddenly broken into by a confusion, cries, and a rapid patter of naked feet. A number of natives ran into the compound, men and women and children; they crowded round Mackintosh and they all talked at once. They were unintelligible. They were excited and frightened and some of them were crying. Mackintosh pushed his way through them and went to the gateway. Though he had scarcely understood what they said he knew quite well what had happened. And as he reached the gate the dog-cart arrived. The old mare was being led by a tall Kanaka, and in the dog-cart crouched two men, trying to hold Walker up. A little crowd of natives surrounded it.

The mare was led into the yard and the natives surged in after it. Mackintosh shouted to them to stand back and the two policemen, appearing suddenly from God knows where, pushed them violently aside. By now he had managed to understand that some lads, who had been fishing, on their way back to their village had come across the cart on the home side of the ford. The mare was nuzzling about the herbage and in the darkness they could just see the great white bulk of the old man sunk between the seat and the dashboard. At first they thought he was drunk and they peered in, grinning, but then they heard him groan, and guessed that something was amiss. They ran to the village and called for help. It was when they returned, accompanied by half a hundred people, that they discovered Walker had been shot.

With a sudden thrill of horror Mackintosh asked himself whether he was already dead. The first thing at all events was to get him out of the cart, and that, owing to Walker's corpulence, was a difficult job. It took four strong men to lift him. They jolted him and he uttered a dull groan. He was still alive. At last they carried him into the house, up the stairs, and placed him on his bed. Then Mackintosh was able to see him, for in the yard, lit only by half a dozen hurricane lamps, everything had been obscured. Walker's white ducks were stained with blood,

170

and the men who had carried him wiped their hands, red and sticky, on their lava-lavas. Mackintosh held up the lamp. He had not expected the old man to be so pale. His eyes were closed. He was breathing still, his pulse could be just felt but it was obvious that he was dying. Mackintosh had not bargained for the shock of horror that convulsed him. He saw that the native clerk was there, and in a voice hoarse with fear told him to go into the dispensary and get what was necessary for a hypodermic injection. One of the policemen had brought up the whisky, and Mackintosh forced a little into the old man's mouth. The room was crowded with natives. They sat about the floor, speechless now and terrified, and every now and then one wailed aloud. It was very hot, but Mackintosh felt cold, his hands and his feet were like ice, and he had to make a violent effort not to tremble in all his limbs. He did not know what to do. He did not know if Walker was bleeding still, and if he was, how he could stop the bleeding.

The clerk brought the hypodermic needle.

'You give it to him,' said Mackintosh. 'You're more used to that sort of thing than I am.'

His head ached horribly. It felt as though all sorts of little savage things were beating inside it, trying to get out. They watched for the effect of the injection. Presently Walker opened his eyes slowly. He did not seem to know where he was.

'Keep quiet,' said Mackintosh. 'You're at home. You're quite safe.'

Walker's lips outlined a shadowy smile.

'They've got me,' he whispered.

'I'll get Jervis to send his motor-boat to Apia at once. We'll get a doctor out by tomorrow afternoon.'

There was a long pause before the old man answered.

'I shall be dead by then.'

A ghastly expression passed over Mackintosh's pale face. He forced himself to laugh.

'What rot! You keep quiet and you'll be as right as rain.'

'Give me a drink,' said Walker. 'A stiff one.'

With shaking hand Mackintosh poured out whisky and water, half and half, and held the glass while Walker drank greedily. It seemed to restore him. He gave a long sigh and a little colour came into his great fleshy face. Mackintosh felt extraordinarily helpless. He stood and stared at the old man.

'If you'll tell me what to do I'll do it,' he said.

'There's nothing to do. Just leave me alone. I'm done for.'

He looked dreadfully pitiful as he lay on the great bed, a huge, bloated, old man; but so wan, so weak, it was heart-rending. As he rested, his mind seemed to grow clearer.

'You were right, Mac,' he said presently. 'You warned me.'

'I wish to God I'd come with you.'

'You're a good chap, Mac, only you don't drink.'

There was another long silence, and it was clear that Walker was sinking. There was an internal haemorrhage and even Mackintosh in his ignorance could not fail to see that his chief had but an hour or two to live. He stood by the side of the bed stock-still. For half an hour perhaps Walker lay with his eyes closed, then he opened them.

'They'll give you my job,' he said, slowly. 'Last time I was in Apia I told them you were all right. Finish my road. I want to think that'll be done. All round the island.'

'I don't want your job. You'll get all right.'

Walker shook his head wearily.

'I've had my day. Treat them fairly, that's the great thing. They're children. You must always remember that. You must be firm with them, but you must be kind. And you must be just. I've never made a bob out of them. I haven't saved a hundred pounds in twenty years. The road's the great thing. Get the road finished.'

Something very like a sob was wrung from Mackintosh.

'You're a good fellow, Mac. I always liked you.'

He closed his eyes, and Mackintosh thought that he would never open them again. His mouth was so dry that he had to get himself something to drink. The Chinese cook silently put a chair for him. He sat down by the side of the bed and waited. He did not know how long a time passed. The night was endless. Suddenly one of the men sitting there broke into uncontrollable sobbing, loudly, like a child, and Mackintosh grew aware that the room was crowded by this time with natives. They sat all over the floor on their haunches, men and women, staring at the bed.

'What are all these people doing here?' said Mackintosh. 'They've got no right. Turn them out, turn them out, all of them.'

His words seemed to rouse Walker, for he opened his eyes once more, and now they were all misty. He wanted to speak, but he was so weak that Mackintosh had to strain his ears to catch what he said.

'Let them stay. They're my children. They ought to be here.'

Mackintosh turned to the natives.

'Stay where you are. He wants you. But be silent.'

A faint smile came over the old man's white face.

'Come nearer,' he said.

Mackintosh bent over him. His eyes were closed and the words he said were like a wind sighing through the fronds of the coconut trees.

'Give me another drink. I've got something to say.'

This time Mackintosh gave him his whisky neat. Walker collected his strength in a final effort of will.

'Don't make a fuss about this. In ninety-five when there were troubles white men were killed, and the fleet came and shelled the villages. A lot of people were killed who'd had nothing to do with it. They're damned fools at Apia. If they make a fuss they'll only punish the wrong people. I don't want anyone punished.'

He paused for a while to rest.

'You must say it was an accident. No one's to blame. Promise me that.'

'I'll do anything you like,' whispered Mackintosh.

'Good chap. One of the best. They're children. I'm their father. A father don't let his children get into trouble if he can help it.'

A ghost of a chuckle came out of his throat. It was astonishingly weird and ghastly.

'You're a religious chap, Mac. What's that about forgiving them? You know.'

For a while Mackintosh did not answer. His lips trembled.

'Forgive them, for they know not what they do?'

'That's right. Forgive them. I've loved them, you know, always loved them.'

He sighed. His lips faintly moved, and now Mackintosh had to put his ears quite close to them in order to hear.

'Hold my hand,' he said.

Mackintosh gave a gasp. His heart seemed wrenched. He took the old man's hand, so cold and weak, a coarse, rough hand, and held it in his own. And thus he sat until he nearly started out of his seat, for the silence was suddenly broken by a long rattle. It was terrible and unearthly. Walker was dead. Then the natives broke out with loud cries. The tears ran down their faces, and they beat their breasts.

Mackintosh disengaged his hand from the dead man's and staggering like one drunk with sleep he went out of the room. He went to the locked drawer in his writing-desk and took out the revolver. He walked down to the sea and walked into the lagoon; he waded out cautiously, so that he should not trip against a coral rock, till the water came to his arm-pits. Then he put a bullet through his head.

An hour later half a dozen slim brown sharks were splashing and struggling at the spot where he fell.

APPEARANCE AND REALITY

I DO not vouch for the truth of this story, but it was told me by a professor of French literature at an English university, and he was a man of too high a character, I think, to have told it to me unless it were true. His practice was to draw the attention of his students to three French writers who in his opinion combined the qualities that are the mainsprings of the French character. By reading them, he said, you could learn so much about the French people that, if he had the power, he would not trust such of our rulers as have to deal with the French nation to enter upon their offices till they had passed a pretty stiff examination on their works. They are Rabelais, with his *gauloiserie*, which may be described as the ribaldry that likes to call a spade something more than a bloody shovel; La Fontaine, with his *bons sens*, which is just horse sense; and finally Corneille, with his *panache*. This is translated in the dictionaries as the plume, the plume the knight of arms wore on his helmet, but metaphorically it seems to signify dignity and bravado, display and heroism, vainglory and pride. It was *le panache* that made the French gentlemen at Fontenoy say to the officers of King George II, fire first, gentlemen; it was *le panache* that wrung from Cambronne's bawdy lips at Waterloo the phrase: the guard dies but never surrenders; and it is *le panache* that urges an indigent French poet, awarded the Nobel prize, with a splendid gesture to give it all away. My professor was not a frivolous man and to his mind the story I am about to tell brought out so distinctly the three master qualities of the French that it had a high educational value.

I have called it Appearance and Reality. This is the title of what I suppose may be looked upon as the most important philosophical work that my country (right or wrong) produced in the nineteenth century. It is stiff, but stimulating reading. It is written in excellent English, with considerable humour, and even though the lay reader is unlikely to follow with understanding some of its very subtle arguments he has nevertheless the thrilling sensation of walking a spiritual tight-rope over a metaphysical abyss, and he ends the book with a comfortable feeling that nothing matters a hang anyway. There is no excuse for my making use of the title of so celebrated a book except that it so admirably suits my story. Though Lisette was a

175

philosopher only in the sense in which we are all philosophers, that she exercised thought in dealing with the problems of existence, her feeling for reality was so strong and her sympathy for appearance so genuine that she might almost claim to have established that reconcilation of irreconcilables at which the philosophers have for so many centuries been aiming. Lisette was French, and she passed several hours of every working day dressing and undressing herself at one of the most expensive and fashionable establishments in Paris. A pleasant occupation for a young woman who was well aware that she had a lovely figure. She was in short a mannequin. She was tall enough to be able to wear a train with elegance and her hips were so slim that in sports clothes she could bring the scent of heather to your nostrils. Her long legs enabled her to wear pyjamas with distinction, and her slim waist, her little breasts, made the simplest bathing dress a ravishment. She could wear anything. She had a way of huddling herself in a chinchilla coat that made the most sensible persons admit that chinchilla was worth all the money it cost. Fat women, gross women, stumpy women, bony women, shapeless women, old women, plain women, sat in the spacious arm-chairs and because Lisette looked so sweet bought the clothes that so admirably suited her. She had large brown eyes, a large red mouth, and a very clear but slightly freckled skin. It was difficult for her to preserve that haughty, sullen, and coldly indifferent demeanour that appears to be essential to the mannequin as she sails in with deliberate steps, turns round slowly and, with an air of contempt for the universe equalled only by the camel's, sails out. There was the suspicion of a twinkle in Lisette's large brown eyes, and her red lips seemed to tremble as though on the smallest provocation they would break into a smile. It was the twinkle that attracted the attention of Monsieur Raymond Le Sueur.

He was sitting in a spurious Louis XVI chair by the side of his wife (in another) who had induced him to come with her to see the private view of the spring fashions. This was a proof of Monsieur Le Sueur's amiable disposition, for he was an extremely busy man who, one would have thought, had many more important things to do than to sit for an hour and watch a dozen beautiful young women parade themselves in a bewildering variety of costumes. He could not have thought that any of them could possibly make his wife other than she was, and she was a tall, angular woman of fifty, with features considerably larger than life-size. He had not indeed married her for her looks, and she had never, even in the first delirious days of their honeymoon, imagined that he had. He had married her in order to combine the flourishing steel works of which she was the heiress with his equally flourishing manufactory of locomotives. The marriage had been a success. She had provided him with a son who could play tennis nearly as well as a professional, dance quite as well as a gigolo, and hold his own at bridge with any of the experts; and a daughter whom he had been able to dower sufficiently to marry to a very nearly authentic prince. He had reason to be proud of his children. By perseverance and a reasonable integrity he had prospered sufficiently to gain the controlling interest in a sugar refinery, a movie company, a firm that built motor-cars, and a newspaper; and finally he had been able to spend enough money to persuade the free and independent electorate of a certain district to send him to the Senate. He was a man of a dignified presence, a pleasing corpulence, and a sanguine complexion, with a neat grey beard cut square, a bald head, and a roll of fat at the back of his neck. You had no need to look at the red button that adorned his black coat to surmise that he was a person of consequence. He was a man who made up his mind quickly, and when his wife left the dressmaker's to go and play bridge he parted from her, saying that for the sake of exercise he would walk to the Senate, where his duty to his country called him. He did not however go as far as this, but contented himself with taking his exercise up and down a back street into which he rightly surmised the young ladies of the dressmaker's establishment would emerge at the close of business hours. He had barely waited for a quarter of an hour when the appearance of a number of women in groups, some young and pretty, some not so young and far from pretty, apprised him that the moment for which he had been waiting was come, and in two or three minutes Lisette tripped into the street. The Senator was well aware that his appearance and his age made it unlikely that young women would find him attractive at first sight but he had found that his wealth and his position counterbalanced these disadvantages. Lisette had a companion with her, which would possibly have embarrassed a man of less importance, but did not cause the Senator to hesitate for an instant; he went up to her, raising his hat politely, but not so much as to show how bald he was, and bade her good evening.

'*Bonsoir, Mademoiselle*,' he said with an ingratiating smile.

She gave him the shortest possible look and, her full red lips just trembling with a smile, stiffened; she turned her head away and breaking into conversation with her friend, walked on with a very good assumption of supreme indifference. Far from disconcerted, the Senator turned round and followed the two girls at a distance of a few yards. They walked along the little back street, turned into the boulevard and at the Place de la Madeleine took a bus. The Senator was well satisfied. He had drawn a number of correct conclusions. The fact that she was obviously going home with a girl friend proved that she had no accredited admirer. The fact that she had turned away when he had accosted her showed that she was discreet and modest and well-behaved, which he liked young women to be when they were pretty; and her coat and skirt, the plain black hat, and the rayon stockings proclaimed that she was poor and therefore virtuous. In those clothes she looked just as attractive as in the splendid garments he had seen her wearing before. He had a funny little feeling in his heart. He had not had that peculiar sensation, pleasurable and yet oddly painful, for several years, but he recognized it at once.

'It's love, by blue,' he muttered.

He had never expected to feel it again, and squaring his shoulders he walked on with a confident step. He walked to the offices of a private detective and there left instructions that inquiries should be made about a young person called Lisette, who worked as a mannequin at such and such an address; and then, remembering that at the Senate they were discussing the American Debt, took a cab to the impressive building, entered the library, where there was an arm-chair he very much liked, and had a pleasant nap. The information he had asked for reached him three days later. It was cheap at the price. Mademoiselle Lisette Larion lived with a widowed aunt in a two-room apartment in the district of Paris known as the Batignolles. Her father, a wounded hero of the great war, had a *bureau de tabac* in a small country town in the south-west of France. The rent of the flat was two thousand francs. She led a regular life, but was fond of going to the pictures, was not known to have a lover, and was nineteen years old. She was well spoken of by the concierge of the apartments and well liked by her companions at the shop. Obviously she was a very respectable young woman and the Senator could not but think that she was eminently suited to solace the leisure moments of a man who wanted relaxation from the cares of state and the exacting pressure of Big Business.

It is unnecessary to relate in detail the steps that Monsieur Le Sueur took to achieve the end he had in view. He was too

important and too busy to occupy himself with the matter personally, but he had a confidential secretary who was very clever at
dealing with electors who had not made up their minds how to
vote, and who certainly knew how to put before a young woman
who was honest but poor the advantages that might ensue if she
were lucky enough to secure the friendship of such a man as his
employer. The confidential secretary paid the widowed aunt,
Madame Saladin by name, a visit, and told her that Monsieur Le
Sueur, always abreast of the time, had lately begun to take an
interest in films and was indeed about to engage in the production
of a picture. (This shows how much a clever brain can make use
of a fact that an ordinary person would have passed over as
insignificant.) Monsieur Le Sueur had been struck by the appearance of Mademoiselle Lisette at the dressmaker's and the brilliant
way she wore her clothes, and it had occurred to him that she
might very well suit a part he had it in mind for her to play.
(Like all intelligent people the Senator always stuck as close to
the truth as he could.) The confidential secretary then invited
Madame Saladin and her niece to a dinner where they could
make one another's further acquaintance and the Senator could
judge whether Mademoiselle Lisette had the aptitude for the
screen that he suspected. Madame Saladin said she would ask
her niece, but for her part seemed to think the suggestion quite
reasonable.

When Madame Saladin put the proposition before Lisette and explained the rank, dignity, and importance of their generous host,
that young person shrugged her pretty shoulders disdainfully.

'*Cette vieille carpe*,' she said, of which the not quite literal
translation is: that old trout.

'What does it matter if he's an old trout if he gives you a part?'
said Madame Saladin.

'*Et ta sœur*,' said Lisette.

This phrase, which of course means: and your sister, and
sounds harmless enough, and even pointless, is a trifle vulgar
and is used by well-brought-up young women, I think, only if
they want to shock. It expresses the most forcible unbelief, and
the only correct translation into the vernacular is too coarse for
my chaste pen.

'Anyhow, we should get a slap-up dinner,' said Madame
Saladin. 'After all, you're not a child any more.'

'Where did he say we should dine?'

'The Château de Madrid. Everyone knows it's the most
expensive restaurant in the world.'

179

There is no reason why it should not be. The food is very good, the cellar is famous, and its situation makes it on a fine evening of early summer an enchanting place to eat at. A very pretty dimple appeared on Lisette's cheek and a smile on her large red mouth. She had perfect teeth.

'I can borrow a dress from the shop,' she murmured.

A few days later the Senator's confidential secretary fetched them in a taxi and drove Madame Saladin and her engaging niece to the Bois de Boulogne. Lisette looked ravishing in one of the firm's most successful models and Madame Saladin extremely respectable in her own black satin and a hat that Lisette had made for the occasion. The secretary introduced the ladies to Monsieur Le Sueur, who greeted them with the benign dignity of the politician who is behaving graciously to the wife and daughter of a valued constituent; and this is exactly what in his astute way he thought people at adjacent tables who knew him would imagine his guests to be. The dinner passed off very agreeably, and less than a month later Lisette moved into a charming little flat at a convenient distance both from her place of business and from the Senate. It was decorated in the modern style by a fashionable upholsterer. Monsieur Le Sueur wished Lisette to continue to work. It suited him very well that she should have something to do during the hours that he was obliged to devote to affairs, for it would keep her out of mischief, and he very well knew that a woman who has nothing to do all day spends much more money than one who has an occupation. An intelligent man thinks of these things.

But extravagance was a vice to which Lisette was strange. The Senator was fond and generous. It was a source of satisfaction to him that Lisette began very soon to save money. She ran her apartment with thrift and bought her clothes at trade prices, and every month sent a certain sum home to her heroic father, who purchased little plots of land with it. She continued to lead a quiet and modest life and Monsieur Le Sueur was pleased to learn from the concierge, who had a son she wanted to place in a government office, that Lisette's only visitors were her aunt and one or two girls from the shop.

The Senator had never been happier in his life. It was very satisfactory to him to think that even in this world a good action had its reward, for was it not from pure kindness that he had accompanied his wife to the dressmaker's on that afternoon when they were discussing the American Debt at the Senate and thus seen for the first time the charming Lisette? The more he knew her the more he doted on her. She was a delightful companion. She was gay and debonair. Her intelligence was respectable and she could listen cleverly when he discussed business matters or affairs of state with her. She rested him when he was weary and cheered him when he was depressed. She was glad to see him when he came, and he came frequently, generally from five till seven, and sorry when he went away. She gave him the impression that he was not only her lover but her friend. Sometimes they dined together in her apartment, and the well-appointed meal, the genial comfort, gave him a keen appreciation of the charm of domesticity. His friends told the Senator he looked twenty years younger. He felt it. He was conscious of his good fortune. He could not but feel, however, that after a life of honest toil and public service it was only his due.

It was thus a shock to him, after things had been proceeding so happily for nearly two years, on coming back to Paris early one Sunday morning unexpectedly after a visit to his constituency which was to last over the week-end, when he let himself into the apartment with his latchkey, thinking since it was the day of rest to find Lisette in bed, to discover her having breakfast in her bedroom *tête à tête* with a young gentleman he had never seen before who was wearing his (the Senator's) brand new pyjamas. Lisette was surprised to see him. Indeed she gave a distinct start.

'*Tiens*,' she said. 'Where have you sprung from? I didn't expect you till tomorrow.'

'The Ministry has fallen,' he answered mechanically. 'I have been sent for. I am to be offered the Ministry of the Interior.' But that was not what he wanted to say at all. He gave the gentleman who was wearing his pyjamas a furious look. 'Who is that young man?' he cried.

Lisette's large red mouth broke into a most alluring smile.

'My lover,' she answered.

'Do you think I'm a fool?' shouted the Senator. 'I know he's your lover.'

'Why do you ask then?'

Monsieur Le Sueur was a man of action. He went straight up to Lisette and smacked her hard on her right cheek with his left hand and then smacked her hard on the left cheek with his right hand.

'Brute,' screamed Lisette.

He turned to the young man, who had watched this scene of violence with some embarrassment, and, drawing himself to his full height, flung out his arm and with a dramatic finger pointed to the door.

'Get out,' he cried. 'Get out.'

One would have thought, such was the commanding aspect of a man who was accustomed to sway a crowd of angry tax-payers and who could dominate with his frown an annual meeting of disappointed shareholders, that the young man would have made a bolt for the door; but he stood his ground, irresolutely it is true, but he stood his ground; he gave Lisette an appealing look and slightly shrugged his shoulders.

'What are you waiting for?' shouted the Senator. 'Do you want me to use force?'

'He can't go out in his pyjamas,' said Lisette.

'They're not his pyjamas, they're my pyjamas.'

'He's waiting for his clothes.'

Monsieur Le Sueur looked round and on the chair behind him, flung down in a disorderly fashion, was a variety of masculine garments. The Senator gave the young man a look of contempt.

'You may take your clothes, Monsieur,' he said with cold disdain.

The young man picked them up in his arms, gathered up the shoes that were lying about the floor, and quickly left the room. Monsieur Le Sueur had a considerable gift of oratory. Never had he made better use of it than now. He told Lisette what he thought of her. It was not flattering. He painted her ingratitude in the blackest colours. He ransacked an extensive vocabulary in order to find opprobrious names to call her. He called all the powers of heaven to witness that never had a woman repaid with such gross deception an honest man's belief in her. In short he said everything that anger, wounded vanity, and disappointment suggested to him. Lisette did not seek to defend herself. She listened in silence, looking down and mechanically crumbling the roll which the Senator's appearance had prevented her from finishing. He flung an irritated glance at her plate.

'I was so anxious that you should be the first to hear my great news that I came straight here from the station. I was expecting to have my *petit déjeuner* with you, sitting at the end of your bed.'

'My poor dear, haven't you had your breakfast? I'll order some for you at once.'

'I don't want any.'

'Nonsense. With the great responsibility you are about to assume you must keep up your strength.'

She rang and when the maid came told her to bring in hot coffee. It was brought and Lisette poured it out. He would not touch it. She buttered a roll. He shrugged his shoulders and began to eat. Meanwhile he uttered a few remarks on the perfidy of women. She remained silent.

'At all events it is something,' he said, 'that you have not the effrontery to attempt to excuse yourself. You know that I am not a man who can be ill-used with impunity. The soul of generosity when people behave well to me I am pitiless when they behave badly. The very moment I have drunk my coffee I shall leave this apartment for ever.'

Lisette sighed.

'I will tell you now that I had prepared a surprise for you. I had made up my mind to celebrate the second anniversary of our union by settling a sum of money on you sufficient to give you a modest independence if anything happened to me.'

'How much?' asked Lisette sombrely.

'A million francs.'

She sighed again. Suddenly something soft hit the Senator on the back of the head and he gave a start.

'What is that?' he cried.

'He's returning your pyjamas.'

The young man had opened the door, flung the pyjamas at the Senator's head, and quickly closed it again. The Senator disengaged himself from the silk trousers that clung round his neck.

'What a way to return them! It is obvious that your friend has no education.'

'Of course he has not your distinction,' murmured Lisette.

'And has he my intelligence?'

'Oh, no.'

'Is he rich?'

'Penniless.'

'Then, name of a name, what is it you see in him?'

'He's young,' smiled Lisette.

The Senator looked down at his plate and a tear rose in his eyes and rolled down his cheek into the coffee. Lisette gave him a kindly look.

'My poor friend, one can't have everything in this life,' she said.

'I knew I was not young. But my situation, my fortune, my vitality. I thought it made up. There are women who only like men of a certain age. There are celebrated actresses who look upon it as an honour to be the little friend of a Minister. I am too well brought up to throw your origins in your face, but the fact remains that you are a mannequin and I took you out of an apartment of which the rent is only two thousand francs a year. It was a step up for you.'

'The daughter of poor but honest parents, I have no reason to be ashamed of my origins, and it is not because I have earned my living in a humble sphere that you have the right to reproach me.'

'Do you love this boy?'

'Yes.'

'And not me?'

'You too. I love you both, but I love you differently. I love you because you are so distinguished and your conversation is instructive and interesting. I love you because you are kind and generous. I love him because his eyes are so big and his hair waves and he dances divinely. It's very natural.'

'You know that in my position I cannot take you to places where they dance and I daresay when he's as old as I am he'll have no more hair than I have.'

'That may well be true,' Lisette agreed, but she did not think it much mattered.

'What will your aunt, the respectable Madame Saladin, say to you when she hears what you have done?'

'It will not be exactly a surprise to her.'

'Do you mean to say that worthy woman countenances your conduct? *O tempora, o mores!* How long then has this been going on?'

'Since I first went to the shop. He travels for a big silk firm in Lyons. He came in one day with his samples. We liked the look of one another.'

'But your aunt was there to defend you from the temptations to which a young girl is exposed in Paris. She should never have allowed you to have anything to do with this young man.'

'I did not ask her permission.'

'It is enough to bring the grey hairs of your poor father to the grave. Had you no thought of that wounded hero whose services to his country have been rewarded with a licence to sell tobacco? Do you forget that as Minister of the Interior the department is under my control? I should be within my rights if I revoked the licence on account of your flagrant immorality.'

'I know you are too great a gentleman to do a dastardly thing like that.'

He waved his hand in an impressive, though perhaps too dramatic a manner.

'Don't be afraid, I will never stoop so low as to revenge myself on one who has deserved well of his country for the misdeeds of a creature my sense of dignity forces me to despise.'

He went on with his interrupted breakfast. Lisette did not speak and there was silence between them. But his appetite satisfied, his mood changed; he began to feel sorry for himself rather than angry with her, and with a strange ignorance of woman's heart he thought to arouse Lisette's remorse by exhibiting himself as an object of pity.

'It is hard to break a habit to which one has grown accustomed. It was a relief and a solace to me to come here when I could snatch a moment from my many occupations. Will you regret me a little, Lisette?'

'Of course.'

He gave a deep sigh.

'I should never have thought you capable of so much deception.'

'It is the deception that rankles,' she murmured thoughtfully. 'Men are funny in that way. They cannot forgive being made fools of. It is because they are so vain. They attach importance to things that are of no consequence.'

'Do you call it a matter of no consequence that I should find you having breakfast with a young man wearing my pyjamas?'

'If he were my husband and you were my lover you would think it perfectly natural.'

'Obviously. For then I should be deceiving him and my honour would be secure.'

'In short, I have only to marry him to make the situation perfectly regular.'

For a moment he did not understand. Then her meaning flashed across his clever brain and he gave her a quick look. Her lovely eyes had the twinkle he always found so alluring and on her large red mouth was the suspicion of a roguish smile.

'Do not forget that as a member of the Senate I am by all the traditions of the Republic the authorized mainstay of morality and good behaviour.'

'Does that weigh very heavily with you?'

He stroked his handsome square beard with a composed and dignified gesture.

'Not a row of beans,' he replied, but the expression he used had a Gallic breadth that would perhaps have given his more conservative supporters something of a shock.

'Would he marry you?' he asked.

'He adores me. Of course he would marry me. If I told him I had a *dot* of a million francs he would ask nothing better.'

Monsieur Le Sueur gave her another look. When in a moment of anger he told her it had been his intention to settle a million francs on her he had exaggerated a good deal in the desire to make her see how much her treachery was costing her. But he was not the man to draw back when his dignity was concerned.

'It is much more than a young man in his position of life could aspire to. But if he adores you he would be always at your side.'

'Didn't I tell you that he was a commercial traveller? He can only come to Paris for the week-end.'

'That of course is a horse of another colour,' said the Senator. 'It would naturally be a satisfaction to him to know that during his absence I should be there to keep an eye on you.'

'A considerable satisfaction,' said Lisette.

To facilitate the conversation she rose from her seat and made herself comfortable on the Senator's knees. He pressed her hand tenderly.

'I am very fond of you, Lisette,' he said. 'I should not like you to make a mistake. Are you sure he will make you happy?'

'I think so.'

'I will have proper inquiries made. I would never consent to your marrying anyone not of exemplary character and unimpeachable morality. For all our sakes we must make quite sure about this young man whom we are preparing to bring into our lives.'

Lisette raised no objection. She was aware that the Senator liked to do things with order and method. He now prepared to leave her. He wanted to break his important news to Madame Le Sueur, and he had to get in touch with various persons in the parliamentary group to which he belonged.

'There is only one more thing,' he said, as he bade Lisette an affectionate farewell, 'if you marry I must insist on your giving up your work. The place of a wife is the home, and it is against all my principles that a married woman should take the bread out of a man's mouth.'

Lisette reflected that a strapping young man would look rather funny walking round the room, with his hips swaying, to show off the latest models, but she respected the Senator's principles.

'It shall be as you wish, darling,' she said.

The inquiries he made were satisfactory and the marriage took place on a Saturday morning as soon as the legal formalities were completed. Monsieur Le Sueur, Minister of the Interior, and Madame Saladin were witnesses. The bridegroom was a slim young man with a straight nose, fine eyes, and black waving hair brushed straight back from his forehead. He looked more like a tennis-player than a traveller in silk. The Mayor, impressed by the august presence of the Minister of the Interior, made according to French practice a speech which he sought to render eloquent. He began by telling the married couple what presumably they knew already. He informed the bridegroom that he was the son of worthy parents and was engaged in an honourable profession. He congratulated him on entering the bonds of matrimony at an age when many young men thought only of their pleasures. He reminded the bride that her father was a hero of the great war, whose glorious wounds had been rewarded by a concession to sell tobacco, and he told her that she had earned a decent living since her arrival in Paris in an establishment that was one of the glories of French taste and luxury. The Mayor was of a literary turn and he briefly mentioned various celebrated lovers of fiction, Romeo and Juliet whose short but legitimate union had been interrupted by a regrettable misunderstanding, Paul and Virginia who had met her death at sea rather than sacrifice her modesty by taking off her clothes, and finally Daphnis and Chloe who had not consummated their marriage till it was sanctioned by the legitimate authority. He was so moving that Lisette shed a few tears. He paid a compliment to Madame Saladin whose example and precept had preserved her young and beautiful niece from the dangers that are likely to befall a young girl alone in a great city, and finally he congratulated the happy pair on the honour that the Minister of the Interior had done them in consenting to be a witness at the ceremony. It was a testimony to their own probity that this captain of industry and eminent statesman should find time to perform a humble office to persons in their modest sphere, and it proved not only the excellence of his heart but his lively sense of duty. His action showed that he appreciated the importance of early marriage, affirmed the security of the family, and emphasized the desirability of producing offspring to increase the power, influence and consequence of the fair land of France. A very good speech indeed.

The wedding breakfast was held at the Château de Madrid, which had sentimental associations for Monsieur Le Sueur. It has been mentioned already that among his many interests the Minister (as we must now call him) was interested in a firm of motor-cars. His wedding present to the bridegroom was a very nice two-seater of his own manufacture, and in this, when lunch was over, the young couple started off for their honeymoon. This could only last over the week-end since the young man had to get back to his work, which would take him to Marseilles, Toulon, and Nice. Lisette kissed her aunt and she kissed Monsieur Le Sueur.

'I shall expect you at five on Monday,' she whispered to him.

'I shall be there,' he answered.

They drove away and for a moment Monsieur Le Sueur and Madame Saladin looked at the smart yellow roadster.

'As long as he makes her happy,' sighed Madame Saladin, who was not used to champagne at lunch and felt unreasonably melancholy.

'If he does not make her happy he will have me to count with,' said Monsieur Le Sueur impressively.

His car drove up.

'*Au revoir, chère Madame.* You will get a bus at the Avenue de Neuilly.'

He stepped into his car and as he thought of the affairs of state that awaited his attention he sighed with content. It was evidently much more fitting to his situation that his mistress should be, not just a little mannequin in a dressmaker's shop, but a respectable married woman.

THE THREE FAT WOMEN OF ANTIBES

ONE was called Mrs Richman and she was a widow. The second was called Mrs Sutcliffe; she was American and she had divorced two husbands. The third was called Miss Hickson and she was a spinster. They were all in the comfortable forties and they were all well off. Mrs Sutcliffe had the odd first name of Arrow. When she was young and slender she had liked it well enough. It suited her and the jests it occasioned though too often repeated were very flattering; she was not disinclined to believe that it suited her character too: it suggested directness, speed, and purpose. She liked it less now that her delicate features had grown muzzy with fat, that her arms and shoulders were so substantial and her hips so massive. It was increasingly difficult to find dresses to make her look as she liked to look. The jests her name gave rise to now were made behind her back and she very well knew that they were far from obliging. But she was by no means resigned to middle age. She still wore blue to bring out the colour of her eyes and, with the help of art, her fair hair had kept its lustre. What she liked about Beatrice Richman and Frances Hickson was that they were both so much fatter than she, it made her look quite slim; they were both of them older and much inclined to treat her as a little young thing. It was not disagreeable. They were good-natured women and they chaffed her pleasantly about her beaux; they had both given up the thought of that kind of nonsense, indeed Miss Hickson had never given it a moment's consideration, but they were sympathetic to her flirtations. It was understood that one of these days Arrow would make a third man happy.

'Only you mustn't get any heavier, darling,' said Mrs Richman.

'And for goodness' sake make certain of his bridge,' said Miss Hickson.

They saw for her a man of about fifty, but well-preserved and of distinguished carriage, an admiral on the retired list and a good golfer, or a widower without encumbrances, but in any case with a substantial income. Arrow listened to them amiably, and kept to herself the fact that this was not at all her idea. It was true that she would have liked to marry again, but her fancy turned to a dark slim Italian with flashing eyes and a sonorous title or to a Spanish don of noble lineage; and not a day more than thirty. There were times when, looking at herself in her mirror, she was certain she did not look any more than that herself.

They were great friends, Miss Hickson, Mrs Richman, and Arrow Sutcliffe. It was their fat that had brought them together and bridge that had cemented their alliance. They had met first at Carlsbad, where they were staying at the same hotel and were treated by the same doctor who used them with the same ruthlessness. Beatrice Richman was enormous. She was a handsome woman, with fine eyes, rouged cheeks, and painted lips. She was very well content to be a widow with a handsome fortune. She adored her food. She liked bread and butter, cream, potatoes, and suet puddings, and for eleven months of the year ate pretty well everything she had a mind to, and for one month went to Carlsbad to reduce. But every year she grew fatter. She upbraided the doctor, but got no sympathy from him. He pointed out to her various plain and simple facts.

'But if I'm never to eat a thing I like, life isn't worth living,' she expostulated.

He shrugged his disapproving shoulders. Afterwards she told Miss Hickson that she was beginning to suspect he wasn't so clever as she had thought. Miss Hickson gave a great guffaw. She was that sort of woman. She had a deep bass voice, a large flat sallow face from which twinkled little bright eyes; she walked with a slouch, her hands in her pockets, and when she could do so without exciting attention smoked a long cigar. She dressed as like a man as she could.

'What the deuce should I look like in frills and furbelows?' she said. 'When you're as fat as I am you may just as well be comfortable.'

She wore tweeds and heavy boots and whenever she could went about bareheaded. But she was as strong as an ox and boasted that few men could drive a longer ball than she. She was plain of speech, and she could swear more variously than a stevedore. Though her name was Frances she preferred to be called Frank. Masterful, but with tact, it was her jovial strength of character that held the three together. They drank their waters together, had their baths at the same hour, they took their strenuous walks together, pounded about the tennis court with a professional to make them run, and ate at the same table their sparse and regulated meals. Nothing impaired their good humour but the scales, and when one or other of them weighed as much on one day as she had the day before neither Frank's coarse jokes, the *bonhomie* of Beatrice, nor Arrow's pretty kittenish ways sufficed to dispel the gloom. Then drastic measures were resorted to, the culprit went to bed for twenty-four hours and nothing passed her lips but the doctor's famous vegetable soup which tasted like hot water in which a cabbage had been well rinsed.

Never were three women greater friends. They would have been independent of anyone else if they had not needed a fourth at bridge. They were fierce, enthusiastic players and the moment the day's cure was over they sat down at the bridge table. Arrow, feminine as she was, played the best game of the three, a hard, brilliant game, in which she showed no mercy and never conceded a point or failed to take advantage of a mistake. Beatrice was solid and reliable. Frank was dashing; she was a great theorist, and had all the authorities at the tip of her tongue. They had long arguments over the rival systems. They bombarded one another with Culbertson and Sims. It was obvious that not one of them ever played a card without fifteen good reasons, but it was also obvious from the subsequent conversation that there were fifteen equally good reasons why she should not have played it. Life would have been perfect, even with the prospect of twenty-four hours of that filthy soup when the doctor's rotten (Beatrice) bloody (Frank) lousy (Arrow) scales pretended one hadn't lost an ounce in two days, if only there had not been this constant difficulty of finding someone to play with them who was in their class.

It was for this reason that on the occasion with which this narrative deals Frank invited Lena Finch to come and stay with them at Antibes. They were spending some weeks there on Frank's suggestion. It seemed absurd to her, with her common sense, that immediately the cure was over Beatrice who always lost twenty pounds should by giving way to her ungovernable appetite put it all on again. Beatrice was weak. She needed a person of strong will to watch her diet. She proposed then that on leaving Carlsbad they should take a house at Antibes, where they could get plenty of exercise – everyone knew that nothing slimmed you like swimming – and as far as possible could go on with the cure. With a cook of their own they could at least avoid things that were obviously fattening. There was no reason why they should not all lose several pounds more. It seemed a very good idea. Beatrice knew what was good for her, and she could resist temptation well enough if temptation was not put right under her nose. Besides, she liked gambling, and a flutter at the Casino two or three times a week would pass the time very pleasantly. Arrow adored Antibes, and she would be looking her best after a month at Carlsbad. She could just pick and choose among the young Italians, the passionate Spaniards, the gallant Frenchmen, and the long-limbed English who sauntered about all day in bathing trunks and gay-coloured dressing-gowns. The plan worked very well. They had a grand time. Two days a week they ate nothing but hard-boiled eggs and raw tomatoes and they mounted the scales every morning with light hearts. Arrow got down to eleven stone and felt just like a girl; Beatrice and Frank by standing in a certain way just avoided the thirteen. The machine they had bought registered kilogrammes, and they got extraordinarily clever at translating these in the twinkling of an eye to pounds and ounces.

But the fourth at bridge continued to be the difficulty. This person played like a fool, the other was so slow that it drove you frantic, one was quarrelsome, another was a bad loser, a third was next door to a crook. It was strange how hard it was to find exactly the player you wanted.

One morning when they were sitting in pyjamas on the terrace overlooking the sea, drinking their tea (without milk or sugar) and eating a rusk prepared by Dr Hudebert and guaranteed not to be fattening, Frank looked up from her letters.

'Lena Finch is coming down to the Riviera,' she said.

'Who's she?' asked Arrow.

'She married a cousin of mine. He died a couple of months ago and she's just recovering from a nervous breakdown. What about asking her to come here for a fortnight?'

'Does she play bridge?' asked Beatrice.

'You bet your life she does,' boomed Frank in her deep voice. 'And a damned good game too. We should be absolutely independent of outsiders.'

'How old is she?' asked Arrow.

'Same age as I am.'

'That sounds all right.'

It was settled. Frank, with her usual decisiveness, stalked out as soon as she had finished her breakfast to send a wire, and three days later Lena Finch arrived. Frank met her at the station. She was in deep but not obtrusive mourning for the recent death of her husband. Frank had not seen her for two years. She kissed her warmly and took a good look at her.

'You're very thin, darling,' she said.

Lena smiled bravely.

'I've been through a good deal lately. I've lost a lot of weight.'

Frank sighed, but whether from sympathy with her cousin's sad loss, or from envy, was not obvious.

Lena was not, however, unduly depressed, and after a quick bath was quite ready to accompany Frank to Eden Roc. Frank introduced the stranger to her two friends and they sat down in what was known as the Monkey House. It was an enclosure covered with glass overlooking the sea, with a bar at the back, and it was crowded with chattering people in bathing costumes, pyjamas, or dressing-gowns, who were seated at the tables having drinks. Beatrice's soft heart went out to the lorn widow, and Arrow, seeing that she was pale, quite ordinary to look at, and probably forty-eight, was prepared to like her very much. A waiter approached them.

'What will you have, Lena dear?' Frank asked.

'Oh, I don't know, what you all have, a dry Martini or a White Lady.'

Arrow and Beatrice gave her a quick look. Everyone knows how fattening cocktails are.

'I daresay you're tired after your journey,' said Frank kindly.

She ordered a dry Martini for Lena and a mixed lemon and orange juice for herself and her two friends.

'We find alcohol isn't very good in all this heat,' she explained.

'Oh, it never affects me at all,' Lena answered airily. 'I like cocktails.'

Arrow went very slightly pale under her rouge (neither she nor Beatrice ever wet their faces when they bathed and they thought it absurd of Frank, a woman of her size, to pretend she liked diving) but she said nothing. The conversation was gay and easy, they all said the obvious things with gusto, and presently they strolled back to the villa for luncheon.

In each napkin were two little antifat rusks. Lena gave a bright smile as she put them by the side of her plate.

'May I have some bread?' she asked.

The grossest indecency would not have fallen on the ears of those three women with such a shock. Not one of them had eaten bread for ten years. Even Beatrice, greedy as she was, drew the line there. Frank, the good hostess, recovered herself first.

'Of course, darling,' she said and turning to the butler asked him to bring some.

'And some butter,' said Lena in that pleasant easy way of hers.

There was a moment's embarrassed silence.

'I don't know if there's any in the house,' said Frank, 'but I'll inquire. There may be some in the kitchen.'

'I adore bread and butter, don't you?' said Lena, turning to Beatrice.

Beatrice gave a sickly smile and an evasive reply. The butler brought a long crisp roll of French bread. Lena slit it in two and plastered it with the butter which was miraculously produced. A grilled sole was served.

'We eat very simply here,' said Frank. 'I hope you won't mind.'

'Oh, no, I like my food very plain,' said Lena as she took some butter and spread it over her fish. 'As long as I can have bread and butter and potatoes and cream I'm quite happy.'

The three friends exchanged a glance. Frank's great sallow face sagged a little and she looked with distaste at the dry, insipid sole on her plate. Beatrice came to the rescue.

'It's such a bore, we can't get cream here,' she said. 'It's one of the things one has to do without on the Riviera.'

'What a pity,' said Lena.

The rest of the luncheon consisted of lamb cutlets, with the fat carefully removed so that Beatrice should not be led astray, and spinach boiled in water, with stewed pears to end up with. Lena tasted her pears and gave the butler a look of inquiry. That resourceful man understood her at once and though powdered sugar had never been served at that table before handed her without a moment's hesitation a bowl of it. She helped herself liberally. The other three pretended not to notice. Coffee was served and Lena took three lumps of sugar in hers.

'You have a very sweet tooth,' said Arrow in a tone which she struggled to keep friendly.

'We think saccharine so much more sweetening,' said Frank, as she put a tiny tablet of it into her coffee.

'Disgusting stuff,' said Lena.

Beatrice's mouth drooped at the corners, and she gave the lump sugar a yearning look.

'Beatrice,' boomed Frank sternly.

Beatrice stifled a sigh, and reached for the saccharine.

Frank was relieved when they could sit down to the bridge table. It was plain to her that Arrow and Beatrice were upset. She wanted them to like Lena and she was anxious that Lena should enjoy her fortnight with them. For the first rubber Arrow cut with the newcomer.

'Do you play Vanderbilt or Culbertson?' she asked her.

'I have no conventions,' Lena answered in a happy-go-lucky way, 'I play by the light of nature.'

'I play strict Culbertson,' said Arrow acidly.

The three fat women braced themselves to the fray. No

conventions indeed! They'd learn her. When it came to bridge even Frank's family feeling was forgotten and she settled down with the same determination as the others to trim the stranger in their midst. But the light of nature served Lena very well. She had a natural gift for the game and great experience. She played with imagination, quickly, boldly, and with assurance. The other players were in too high a class not to realize very soon that Lena knew what she was about, and since they were all thoroughly good-natured, generous women, they were gradually mollified. This was real bridge. They all enjoyed themselves. Arrow and Beatrice began to feel more kindly towards Lena, and Frank, noticing this, heaved a fat sigh of relief. It was going to be a success.

After a couple of hours they parted, Frank and Beatrice to have a round of golf, and Arrow to take a brisk walk with a young Prince Roccamare whose acquaintance she had lately made. He was very sweet and young and good-looking. Lena said she would rest.

They met again just before dinner.

'I hope you've been all right, Lena dear,' said Frank. 'I was rather conscience-stricken at leaving you with nothing to do all this time.'

'Oh, don't apologize. I had a lovely sleep and then I went down to Juan and had a cocktail. And d'you know what I discovered? You'll be so pleased. I found a dear little tea-shop where they've got the most beautiful thick fresh cream. I've ordered half a pint to be sent every day. I thought it would be my little contribution to the household.'

Her eyes were shining. She was evidently expecting them to be delighted.

'How very kind of you,' said Frank, with a look that sought to quell the indignation that she saw on the faces of her two friends. 'But we never eat cream. In this climate it makes one so bilious.'

'I shall have to eat it all myself then,' said Lena cheerfully.

'Don't you ever think of your figure?' Arrow asked with icy deliberation.

'The doctor said I must eat.'

'Did he say you must eat bread and butter and potatoes and cream?'

'Yes. That's what I thought you meant when you said you had simple food.'

'You'll get simply enormous,' said Beatrice.

Lena laughed gaily.

'No, I shan't. You see, nothing ever makes me fat. I've always eaten everything I wanted to and it's never had the slightest effect on me.'

The stony silence that followed this speech was only broken by the entrance of the butler.

'*Mademoiselle est servie*,' he announced.

They talked the matter over late that night, after Lena had gone to bed, in Frank's room. During the evening they had been furiously cheerful, and they had chaffed one another with a friendliness that would have taken in the keenest observer. But now they dropped the mask. Beatrice was sullen, Arrow was spiteful and Frank was unmanned.

'It's not very nice for me to sit there and see her eat all the things I particularly like,' said Beatrice plaintively.

'It's not very nice for any of us,' Frank snapped back.

'You should never have asked her here,' said Arrow.

'How was I to know?' cried Frank.

'I can't help thinking that if she really cared for her husband she would hardly eat so much,' said Beatrice. 'He's only been buried two months. I mean, I think you ought to show some respect for the dead.'

'Why can't she eat the same as we do?' asked Arrow viciously. 'She's a guest.'

'Well, you heard what she said. The doctor told her she must eat.'

'Then she ought to go to a sanatorium.'

'It's more than flesh and blood can stand, Frank,' moaned Beatrice.

'If I can stand it you can stand it.'

'She's your cousin, she's not our cousin,' said Arrow. 'I'm not going to sit there for fourteen days and watch that woman make a hog of herself.'

'It's so vulgar to attach all this importance to food,' Frank boomed, and her voice was deeper than ever. 'After all the only thing that counts really is spirit.'

'Are you calling *me* vulgar, Frank?' asked Arrow with flashing eyes.

'No, of course she isn't,' interrupted Beatrice.

'I wouldn't put it past you to go down in the kitchen when we're all in bed and have a good square meal on the sly.'

Frank sprang to her feet.

'How dare you say that, Arrow! I'd never ask anybody to do what I'm not prepared to do myself. Have you known me all these years and do you think me capable of such a mean thing?'

'How is it you never take off any weight then?'

Frank gave a gasp and burst into a flood of tears.

'What a cruel thing to say! I've lost pounds and pounds.'

She wept like a child. Her vast body shook and great tears splashed on her mountainous bosom.

'Darling, I didn't mean it,' cried Arrow.

She threw herself on her knees and enveloped what she could of Frank in her own plump arms. She wept and the mascara ran down her cheeks.

'D'you mean to say I don't look thinner?' Frank sobbed. 'After all I've gone through.'

'Yes, dear, of course you do,' cried Arrow through her tears. 'Everybody's noticed it.'

Beatrice, though naturally of a placid disposition, began to cry gently. It was very pathetic. Indeed, it would have been a hard heart that failed to be moved by the sight of Frank, that lion-hearted woman, crying her eyes out. Presently, however, they dried their tears and had a little brandy and water, which every doctor had told them was the least fattening thing they could drink, and then they felt much better. They decided that Lena should have the nourishing food that had been ordered her and they made a solemn resolution not to let it disturb their equanimity. She was certainly a first-rate bridge player and after all it was only for a fortnight. They would do whatever they could to make her stay enjoyable. They kissed one another warmly and separated for the night feeling strangely uplifted. Nothing should interfere with the wonderful friendship that had brought so much happiness into their three lives.

But human nature is weak. You must not ask too much of it. They ate grilled fish while Lena ate macaroni sizzling with cheese and butter; they ate grilled cutlets and boiled spinach while Lena ate *pâté de foie gras*; twice a week they ate hard-boiled eggs and raw tomatoes, while Lena ate peas swimming in cream and potatoes cooked in all sorts of delicious ways. The chef was a good chef and he leapt at the opportunity afforded him to send up one dish more rich, tasty and succulent than the other.

'Poor Jim,' sighed Lena, thinking of her husband, 'he loved French cooking.'

The butler disclosed the fact that he could make half a dozen kinds of cocktail and Lena informed them that the doctor had recommended her to drink burgundy at luncheon and champagne at dinner. The three fat women persevered. They were gay, chatty and even hilarious (such is the natural gift that women have for deception) but Beatrice grew limp and forlorn, and Arrow's tender blue eyes acquired a steely glint. Frank's deep voice grew more raucous. It was when they played bridge that the strain showed itself. They had always been fond of talking over their hands, but their discussion had been friendly. Now a distinct bitterness crept in and sometimes one pointed out a mistake to another with quite unnecessary frankness. Discussion turned to argument and argument to altercation. Sometimes the session ended in angry silence. Once Frank accused Arrow of deliberately letting her down. Two or three times Beatrice, the softest of the three, was reduced to tears. On another occasion Arrow flung down her cards and swept out of the room in a pet. Their tempers were getting frayed. Lena was the peacemaker.

'I think it's such a pity to quarrel over bridge,' she said. 'After all, it's only a game.'

It was all very well for her. She had had a square meal and half a bottle of champagne. Besides, she had phenomenal luck. She was winning all their money. The score was put down in a book after each session, and hers mounted up day after day with unfailing regularity. Was there no justice in the world? They began to hate one another. And though they hated her too they could not resist confiding in her. Each of them went to her separately and told her how detestable the others were. Arrow said she was sure it was bad for her to see so much of women so much older than herself. She had a good mind to sacrifice her share of the lease and go to Venice for the rest of the summer. Frank told Lena that with her masculine mind it was too much to expect that she could be satisfied with anyone so frivolous as Arrow and so frankly stupid as Beatrice.

'I must have intellectual conversation,' she boomed. 'When you have a brain like mine you've got to consort with your intellectual equals.'

Beatrice only wanted peace and quiet.

'Really I hate women,' she said. 'They're so unreliable; they're so malicious.'

By the time Lena's fortnight drew to its close the three fat women were barely on speaking terms. They kept up appearances before Lena, but when she was not there made no pretences. They had got past quarrelling. They ignored one another, and when this was not possible treated each other with icy politeness.

Lena was going to stay with friends on the Italian Riviera and Frank saw her off by the same train as that by which she had arrived. She was taking away with her a lot of their money.

'I don't know how to thank you,' she said, as she got into the carriage. 'I've had a wonderful visit.'

If there was one thing that Frank Hickson prided herself on more than on being a match for any man it was that she was a gentlewoman, and her reply was perfect in its combination of majesty and graciousness.

'We've all enjoyed having you here, Lena,' she said. 'It's been a real treat.'

But when she turned away from the departing train she heaved such a vast sigh of relief that the platform shook beneath her. She flung back her massive shoulders and strode home to the villa.

'Ouf!' she roared at intervals. 'Ouf!'

She changed into her one-piece bathing-suit, put on her espadrilles and a man's dressing-gown (no nonsense about it), and went to Eden Roc. There was still time for a bathe before luncheon. She passed through the Monkey House, looking about her to say good morning to anyone she knew, for she felt on a sudden at peace with mankind, and then stopped dead still. She could not believe her eyes. Beatrice was sitting at one of the tables, by herself; she wore the pyjamas she had bought at Molyneux's a day or two before, she had a string of pearls round her neck, and Frank's quick eyes saw that she had just had her hair waved; her cheeks, her eyes, her lips were made up. Fat, nay vast, as she was, none could deny that she was an extremely handsome woman. But what was she doing? With the slouching gait of the Neanderthal man which was Frank's characteristic walk she went up to Beatrice. In her black bathing-dress Frank looked like the huge cetacean which the Japanese catch in the Torres Straits and which the vulgar call a sea-cow.

'Beatrice, what are you doing?' she cried in her deep voice.

It was like the roll of thunder in the distant mountains. Beatrice looked at her coolly.

'Eating,' she answered.

'Damn it, I can see you're eating.'

In front of Beatrice was a plate of *croissants* and a plate of butter, a pot of strawberry jam, coffee, and a jug of cream. Beatrice was spreading butter thick on the delicious hot bread, covering this with jam, and then pouring the thick cream over all.

'You'll kill yourself,' said Frank.

'I don't care,' mumbled Beatrice with her mouth full.

'You'll put on pounds and pounds.'

'Go to hell!'

She actually laughed in Frank's face. My God, how good those *croissants* smelt!

'I'm disappointed in you, Beatrice. I thought you had more character.'

'It's your fault. That blasted woman. You would have her down. For a fortnight I've watched her gorge like a hog. It's more than flesh and blood can stand. I'm going to have one square meal if I bust.'

The tears welled up to Frank's eyes. Suddenly she felt very weak and womanly. She would have liked a strong man to take her on his knee and pet her and cuddle her and call her little baby names. Speechless she sank down on a chair by Beatrice's side. A waiter came up. With a pathetic gesture she waved towards the coffee and *croissants*.

'I'll have the same,' she sighed.

She listlessly reached out her hand to take a roll, but Beatrice snatched away the plate.

'No, you don't,' she said. 'You wait till you get your own.'

Frank called her a name which ladies seldom apply to one another in affection. In a moment the waiter brought her *croissants*, butter, jam, and coffee.

'Where's the cream, you fool?' she roared like a lioness at bay.

She began to eat. She ate gluttonously. The place was beginning to fill up with bathers coming to enjoy a cocktail or two after having done their duty by the sun and the sea. Presently Arrow strolled along with Prince Roccamare. She had on a beautiful silk wrap which she held tightly round her with one hand in order to look as slim as possible and she bore her head high so that he should not see her double chin. She was laughing gaily. She felt like a girl. He had just told her (in Italian) that her eyes made the blue of the Mediterranean look like pea-soup. He left her to go into the men's room to brush his sleek black hair and they arranged to meet in five minutes for a drink. Arrow walked on to the women's room to put a little more rouge on her cheeks and a little more red on her lips. On her way she caught sight of Frank and Beatrice. She stopped. She could hardly believe her eyes.

'My God!' she cried. 'You beasts. You hogs.' She seized a chair. 'Waiter.'

Her appointment went clean out of her head. In the twinkling of an eye the waiter was at her side.

'Bring me what these ladies are having,' she ordered.

Frank lifted her great heavy head from her plate.

'Bring me some *pâté de foie gras*,' she boomed.

'Frank!' cried Beatrice.

'Shut up.'

'All right. I'll have some too.'

The coffee was brought and the hot rolls and cream and the *pâté de foie gras* and they set to. They spread the cream on the *pâté* and they ate it. They devoured great spoonfuls of jam. They crunched the delicious crisp bread voluptuously. What was love to Arrow then? Let the Prince keep his palace in Rome and his castle in the Apennines. They did not speak. What they were about was much too serious. They ate with solemn, ecstatic fervour.

'I haven't eaten potatoes for twenty-five years,' said Frank in a far-off brooding tone.

'Waiter,' cried Beatrice, 'bring fried potatoes for three.'

'*Très bien, Madame.*'

The potatoes were brought. Not all the perfumes of Arabia smelt so sweet. They ate them with their fingers.

'Bring me a dry Martini,' said Arrow.

'You can't have a dry Martini in the middle of a meal, Arrow,' said Frank.

'Can't I? You wait and see.'

'All right then. Bring me a double dry Martini,' said Frank.

'Bring three double dry Martinis,' said Beatrice.

They were brought and drunk at a gulp. The women looked at one another and sighed. The misunderstandings of the last fortnight dissolved and the sincere affection each had for the others welled up again in their hearts. They could hardly believe that they had ever contemplated the possibility of severing a friendship that had brought them so much solid satisfaction. They finished the potatoes.

'I wonder if they've got any chocolate éclairs,' said Beatrice.

'Of course they have.'

And of course they had. Frank thrust one whole into her huge mouth, swallowed it and seized another, but before she ate it she looked at the other two and plunged a vindictive dagger into the heart of the monstrous Lena.

'You can say what you like, but the truth is she played a damned rotten game of bridge, really.'

'Lousy,' agreed Arrow.

But Beatrice suddenly thought she would like a meringue.

THE FACTS OF LIFE

It was Henry Garnet's habit on leaving the city of an afternoon to drop in at his club and play bridge before going home to dinner. He was a pleasant man to play with. He knew the game well and you could be sure that he would make the best of his cards. He was a good loser; and when he won was more inclined to ascribe his success to his luck than to his skill. He was indulgent, and if his partner made a mistake could be trusted to find an excuse for him. It was surprising then on this occasion to hear him telling his partner with unnecessary sharpness that he had never seen a hand worse played; and it was more surprising still to see him not only make a grave error himself, an error of which you would never have thought him capable, but when his partner, not unwilling to get a little of his own back, pointed it out, insist against all reason and with considerable heat that he was perfectly right. But they were all old friends, the men he was playing with, and none of them took his ill-humour very seriously. Henry Garnet was a broker, a partner in a firm of repute, and it occurred to one of them that something had gone wrong with some stock he was interested in.

'How's the market today?' he asked.

'Booming. Even the suckers are making money.'

It was evident that stocks and shares had nothing to do with Henry Garnet's vexation; but something was the matter; that was evident too. He was a hearty fellow, who enjoyed excellent health; he had plenty of money; he was fond of his wife, and devoted to his children. As a rule he had high spirits, and he laughed easily at the nonsense they were apt to talk while they played; but today he sat glum and silent. His brows were crossly puckered and there was a sulky look about his mouth. Presently, to ease the tension, one of the others mentioned a subject upon which they all knew Henry Garnet was glad to speak.

'How's your boy, Henry? I see he's done pretty well in the tournament.'

Henry Garnet's frown grew darker.

'He's done no better than I expected him to.'

'When does he come back from Monte?'

'He got back last night.'

'Did he enjoy himself?'

202

'I suppose so; all I know is that he made a damned fool of himself.'

'Oh. How?'

'I'd rather not talk about it if you don't mind.'

The three men looked at him with curiosity. Henry Garnet scowled at the green baize.

'Sorry, old boy. Your call.'

The game proceeded in a strained silence. Garnet got his bid, and when he played his cards so badly that he went three down not a word was said. Another rubber was begun and in the second game Garnet denied a suit.

'Having none?' his partner asked him.

Garnet's irritability was such that he did not even reply, and when at the end of the hand it appeared that he had revoked, and that his revoke cost the rubber, it was not to be expected that his partner should let his carelessness go without remark.

'What the devil's the matter with you, Henry?' he said. 'You're playing like a fool.'

Garnet was disconcerted. He did not so much mind losing a big rubber himself, but he was sore that his inattention should have made his partner lose too. He pulled himself together.

'I'd better not play any more. I thought a few rubbers would calm me, but the fact is I can't give my mind to the game. To tell you the truth I'm in a hell of a temper.'

They all burst out laughing.

'You don't have to tell us that, old boy. It's obvious.'

Garnet gave them a rueful smile.

'Well, I bet you'd be in a temper if what's happened to me had happened to you. As a matter of fact I'm in a damned awkward situation, and if any of you fellows can give me any advice how to deal with it I'd be grateful.'

'Let's have a drink and you tell us all about it. With a K.C., a Home Office official and an eminent surgeon – if we can't tell you how to deal with a situation, nobody can.'

The K.C. got up and rang the bell for a waiter.

'It's about that damned boy of mine,' said Henry Garnet.

Drinks were ordered and brought. And this is the story that Henry Garnet told them.

The boy of whom he spoke was his only son. His name was Nicholas and of course he was called Nicky. He was eighteen. The Garnets had two daughters besides, one of sixteen and the other of twelve, but however unreasonable it seemed, for a father is generally supposed to like his daughters best, and though he did all he could not to show his preference, there was no doubt that the greater share of Henry Garnet's affection was given to his son. He was kind, in a chaffing, casual way, to his daughters, and gave them handsome presents on their birthdays and at Christmas; but he doted on Nicky. Nothing was too good for him. He thought the world of him. He could hardly take his eyes off him. You could not blame him, for Nicky was a son that any parent might have been proud of. He was six foot two, lithe but muscular, with broad shoulders and a slim waist, and he held himself gallantly erect; he had a charming head, well placed on the shoulders, with pale brown hair that waved slightly, blue eyes with long dark lashes under well-marked eyebrows, a full red mouth, and a tanned, clean skin. When he smiled he showed very regular and very white teeth. He was not shy, but there was a modesty in his demeanour that was attractive. In social intercourse he was easy, polite, and quietly gay. He was the offspring of nice, healthy, decent parents, he had been well brought up in a good home, he had been sent to a good school, and the general result was as engaging a specimen of young manhood as you were likely to find in a long time. You felt that he was as honest, open, and virtuous as he looked. He had never given his parents a moment's uneasiness. As a child he was seldom ill and never naughty. As a boy he did everything that was expected of him. His school reports were excellent. He was wonderfully popular, and he ended his career, with a creditable number of prizes, as head of the school and captain of the football team. But this was not all. At the age of fourteen Nicky had developed an unexpected gift for lawn tennis. This was a game that his father not only was fond of, but played very well, and when he discerned in the boy the promise of a tennis-player he fostered it. During the holidays he had him taught by the best professionals and by the time he was sixteen he had won a number of tournaments for boys of his age. He could beat his father so badly that only parental affection reconciled the older player to the poor show he put up. At eighteen Nicky went to Cambridge and Henry Garnet conceived the ambition that before he was through with the university he should play for it. Nicky had all the qualifications for becoming a great tennis-player. He was tall, he had a long reach, he was quick on his feet, and his timing was perfect. He realized instinctively where the ball was coming and, seemingly without hurry, was there to take it. He had a powerful serve, with a nasty break that made it difficult to return, and his forehand drive, low, long, and accurate, was deadly. He was not so good on the backhand and his volleying was wild, but all through the summer before he went to Cambridge Henry Garnet made him work on these points under the best teacher in England. At the back of his mind, though he did not even mention it to Nicky, he cherished a further ambition, to see his son play at Wimbledon, and who could tell, perhaps be chosen to represent his country in the Davis Cup. A great lump came into Henry Garnet's throat as he saw in fancy his son leap over the net to shake hands with the American champion whom he had just defeated, and walk off the court to the deafening plaudits of the multitude.

As an assiduous frequenter of Wimbledon Henry Garnet had a good many friends in the tennis world, and one evening he found himself at a City dinner sitting next to one of them, a Colonel Brabazon, and in due course began talking to him of Nicky and what chance there might be of his being chosen to play for his university during the following season.

'Why don't you let him go down to Monte Carlo and play in the spring tournament there?' said the Colonel suddenly.

'Oh, I don't think he's good enough for that. He's not nineteen yet, he only went up to Cambridge last October; he wouldn't stand a chance against all those cracks.'

'Of course, Austin and von Cramm and so on would knock spots off him, but he might snatch a game or two; and if he got up against some of the smaller fry there's no reason why he shouldn't win two or three matches. He's never been up against any of the first-rate players and it would be wonderful practice for him. He'd learn a lot more than he'll ever learn in the seaside tournaments you enter him for.'

'I wouldn't dream of it. I'm not going to let him leave Cambridge in the middle of a term. I've always impressed upon him that tennis is only a game and it mustn't interfere with work.'

Colonel Brabazon asked Garnet when the term ended.

'That's all right. He'd only have to cut about three days. Surely that could be arranged. You see, two of the men we were depending on have let us down, and we're in a hole. We want to send as good a team as we can. The Germans are sending their best players and so are the Americans.'

'Nothing doing, old boy. In the first place Nicky's not good enough, and secondly, I don't fancy the idea of sending a kid like that to Monte Carlo without anyone to look after him. If I could get away myself I might think of it, but that's out of the question.'

'I shall be there. I'm going as the non-playing captain of the English team. I'll keep an eye on him.'

'You'll be busy, and besides, it's not a responsibility I'd like to ask you to take. He's never been abroad in his life, and to tell you the truth, I shouldn't have a moment's peace all the time he was there.'

They left it at that and presently Henry Garnet went home. He was so flattered by Colonel Brabazon's suggestion that he could not help telling his wife.

'Fancy his thinking Nicky's as good as that. He told me he'd seen him play and his style was fine. He only wants more practice to get into the first flight. We shall see the kid playing in the semi-finals at Wimbledon yet, old girl.'

To his surprise Mrs Garnet was not so much opposed to the notion as he would have expected.

'After all the boy's eighteen. Nicky's never got into mischief yet and there's no reason to suppose he will now.'

'There's his work to be considered; don't forget that. I think it would be a very bad precedent to let him cut the end of term.'

'But what can three days matter? It seems a shame to rob him of a chance like that. I'm sure he'd jump at it if you asked him.'

'Well, I'm not going to. I haven't sent him to Cambridge just to play tennis. I know he's steady, but it's silly to put temptation in his way. He's much too young to go to Monte Carlo by himself.'

'You say he won't have a chance against these crack players, but you can't tell.'

Henry Garnet sighed a little. On the way home in the car it had struck him that Austin's health was uncertain and that von Cramm had his off-days. Supposing, just for the sake of argument, that Nicky had a bit of luck like that – then there would be no doubt that he would be chosen to play for Cambridge. But of course that was all nonsense.

'Nothing doing, my dear. I've made up my mind and I'm not going to change it.'

Mrs Garnet held her peace. But next day she wrote to Nicky, telling him what had happened, and suggested to him what she would do in his place if, wanting to go, he wished to get his father's consent. A day or two later Henry Garnet received a letter from his son. He was bubbling over with excitement. He had seen his tutor, who was a tennis-player himself, and the Provost of his college, who happened to know Colonel Brabazon, and no objection would be made to his leaving before the end of term; they both thought it an opportunity that shouldn't be missed. He didn't see what harm he could come to, and if only, just this once, his father would stretch a point, well, next term, he promised faithfully, he'd work like blazes. It was a very pretty letter. Mrs Garnet watched her husband read it at the breakfast table; she was undisturbed by the frown on his face. He threw it over to her.

'I don't know why you thought it necessary to tell Nicky something I told you in confidence. It's too bad of you. Now you've thoroughly unsettled him.'

'I'm sorry. I thought it would please him to know that Colonel Brabazon had such a high opinion of him. I don't see why one should only tell people the disagreeable things that are said about them. Of course I made it quite clear that there could be no question of his going.'

'You've put me in an odious position. If there's anything I hate it's for the boy to look upon me as a spoil-sport and a tyrant.'

'Oh, he'll never do that. He may think you rather silly and unreasonable, but I'm sure he'll understand that it's only for his own good that you're being so unkind.'

'Christ,' said Henry Garnet.

His wife had a great inclination to laugh. She knew the battle was won. Dear, oh dear, how easy it was to get men to do what you wanted. For appearance sake Henry Garnet held out for forty-eight hours, but then he yielded, and a fortnight later Nicky came to London. He was to start for Monte Carlo next morning, and after dinner, when Mrs Garnet and her elder daughter had left them, Henry took the opportunity to give his son some good advice.

'I don't feel quite comfortable about letting you go off to a place like Monte Carlo at your age practically by yourself,' he finished, 'but there it is and I can only hope you'll be sensible. I don't want to play the heavy father, but there are three things especially that I want to warn you against: one is gambling, don't gamble; the second is money, don't lend anyone money; and the third is women, don't have anything to do with women. If you don't do any of those three things you can't come to much harm, so remember them well.'

'All right, father,' Nicky smiled.

'That's my last word to you. I know the world pretty well and believe me, my advice is sound.'

'I won't forget it. I promise you.'

'That's a good chap. Now let's go up and join the ladies.'

Nicky beat neither Austin nor von Cramm in the Monte Carlo tournament, but he did not disgrace himself. He snatched an unexpected victory over a Spanish player and gave one of the Austrians a closer match than anyone had thought possible. In the mixed doubles he got into the semi-finals. His charm conquered everyone and he vastly enjoyed himself. It was generally allowed that he showed promise, and Colonel Brabazon told him that when he was a little older and had had more practice with first-class players he would be a credit to his father. The tournament came to an end and the day following he was to fly back to London. Anxious to play his best he had lived very carefully, smoking little and drinking nothing, and going to bed early; but on his last evening he thought he would like to see something of the life in Monte Carlo of which he had heard so much. An official dinner was given to the tennis-players and after dinner with the rest of them he went into the Sporting Club. It was the first time he had been there. Monte Carlo was very full and the rooms were crowded. Nicky had never before seen roulette played except in the pictures; in a maze he stopped at the first table he came to; chips of different sizes were scattered over the green cloth in what looked like a hopeless muddle; the croupier gave the wheel a sharp turn and with a flick threw in the little white ball. After what seemed an endless time the ball stopped and another croupier with a broad, indifferent gesture raked in the chips of those who had lost.

Presently Nicky wandered over to where they were playing *trente et quarante*, but he couldn't understand what it was all about and he thought it dull. He saw a crowd in another room and sauntered in. A big game of baccara was in progress and he was immediately conscious of the tension. The players were protected from the thronging bystanders by a brass rail; they sat round the table, nine on each side, with the dealer in the middle and the croupier facing him. Big money was changing hands. The dealer was a member of the Greek Syndicate. Nicky looked at his impassive face. His eyes were watchful, but his expression never changed whether he won or lost. It was a terrifying, strangely impressive sight. It gave Nicky, who had been thriftily brought up, a peculiar thrill to see someone risk a thousand pounds on the turn of a card and when he lost make a little joke and laugh. It was all terribly exciting. An acquaintance came up to him.

'Been doing any good?' he asked.

'I haven't been playing.'

'Wise of you. Rotten game. Come and have a drink.'

'All right.'

While they were having it Nicky told his friends that this was the first time he had ever been in the rooms.

'Oh, but you must have one little flutter before you go. It's idiotic to leave Monte without having tried your luck. After all it won't hurt you to lose a hundred francs or so.'

'I don't suppose it will, but my father wasn't any too keen on my coming at all and one of the three things he particularly advised me not to do was to gamble.'

But when Nicky left his companion he strolled back to one of the tables where they were playing roulette. He stood for a while looking at the losers' money being raked-in by the croupier and the money that was won paid out to the winners. It was impossible to deny that it was thrilling. His friend was right, it did seem silly to leave Monte without putting something on the table just once. It would be an experience, and at his age you had to have all the experience you could get. He reflected that he hadn't promised his father not to gamble, he'd promised him not to forget his advice. It wasn't quite the same, was it? He took a hundred-franc note out of his pocket and rather shyly put it on number eighteen. He chose it because that was his age. With a wildly beating heart he watched the wheel turn; the little white ball whizzed about like a small demon of mischief; the wheel went round more slowly, the little white ball hesitated, it seemed about to stop, it went on again; Nicky could hardly believe his eyes when it fell into number eighteen. A lot of chips were passed over to him and his hands trembled as he took them. It seemed to amount to a lot of money. He was so confused that he never thought of putting anything on the following round; in fact he had no intention of playing any more, once was enough; and he was surprised when eighteen again came up. There was only one chip on it.

'By George, you've won again,' said a man who was standing near to him.

'Me? I hadn't got anything on.'

'Yes, you had. Your original stake. They always leave it on unless you ask for it back. Didn't you know?'

Another packet of chips was handed over to him. Nicky's head reeled. He counted his gains: seven thousand francs. A queer sense of power seized him; he felt wonderfully clever. This was the easiest way of making money that he had ever heard of. His frank, charming face was wreathed in smiles. His bright eyes met those of a woman standing by his side. She smiled.

'You're in luck,' she said.

She spoke English, but with a foreign accent.

'I can hardly believe it. It's the first time I've ever played.'

'That explains it. Lend me a thousand francs, will you? I've lost everything I've got. I'll give it you back in half an hour.'

'All right.'

She took a large red chip from his pile and with a word of thanks disappeared. The man who had spoken to him before grunted.

'You'll never see that again.'

Nicky was dashed. His father had particularly advised him not to lend anyone money. What a silly thing to do! And to somebody he'd never seen in his life. But the fact was, he felt at that moment such a love for the human race that it had never occurred to him to refuse. And that big red chip, it was almost impossible to realize that it had any value. Oh well, it didn't matter, he still had six thousand francs, he'd just try his luck once or twice more and if he didn't win he'd go home. He put a chip on sixteen, which was his elder sister's age, but it didn't come up; then on twelve, which was his younger sister's, and that didn't come up either; he tried various numbers at random, but without success. It was funny, he seemed to have lost his knack. He thought he would try just once more and then stop; he won. He had made up all his losses and had something over. At the end of an hour, after various ups and downs, having experienced such thrills as he had never known in his life, he found himself with so many chips that they would hardly go in his pockets. He decided to go. He went to the changers' office and he gasped when twenty thousand-franc notes were spread out before him. He had never had so much money in his life. He put it in his pocket and was turning away when the woman to whom he had lent the thousand francs came up to him.

'I've been looking for you everywhere,' she said. 'I was afraid you'd gone. I was in a fever, I didn't know what you'd think of me. Here's your thousand francs and thank you so much for the loan.'

Nicky, blushing scarlet, stared at her with amazement. How he had misjudged her! His father had said, don't gamble; well, he had, and he'd made twenty thousand francs; and his father had said, don't lend anyone money; well, he had, he'd lent quite a lot to a total stranger, and she'd returned it. The fact was that he wasn't nearly such a fool as his father thought: he'd had an instinct that he could lend her the money with safety, and you see, his instinct was right. But he was so obviously taken aback that the little lady was forced to laugh.

'What is the matter with you?' she asked.

'To tell you the truth I never expected to see the money back.'

'What did you take me for? Did you think I was a – cocotte?'

Nicky reddened to the roots of his wavy hair.

'No, of course not.'

'Do I look like one?'

'Not a bit.'

She was dressed very quietly, in black, with a string of gold beads round her neck; her simple frock showed off a neat, slight figure; she had a pretty little face and a trim head. She was made up, but not excessively, and Nicky supposed that she was not more than three or four years older than himself. She gave him a friendly smile.

'My husband is in the administration in Morocco, and I've come to Monte Carlo for a few weeks because he thought I wanted a change.'

'I was just going,' said Nicky because he couldn't think of anything else to say.

'Already!'

'Well, I've got to get up early tomorrow. I'm going back to London by air.'

'Of course. The tournament ended today, didn't it? I saw you play, you know, two or three times.'

'Did you? I don't know why you should have noticed me.'

'You've got a beautiful style. And you looked very sweet in your shorts.'

Nicky was not an immodest youth, but it did cross his mind that perhaps she had borrowed that thousand francs in order to scrape acquaintance with him.

'Do you ever go to the Knickerbocker?' she asked.

'No. I never have.'

'Oh, but you mustn't leave Monte Carlo without having been there. Why don't you come and dance a little? To tell you the truth, I'm starving with hunger and I should adore some bacon and eggs.'

Nicky remembered his father's advice not to have anything to do with women, but this was different; you had only to look at the pretty little thing to know at once that she was perfectly respectable. Her husband was in what corresponded, he supposed, to the Civil Service. His father and mother had friends who were Civil Servants and they and their wives sometimes came to dinner. It was true that the wives were neither so young nor so pretty as this one, but she was just as ladylike as they were. And after winning twenty thousand francs he thought it wouldn't be a bad idea to have a little fun.

'I'd love to go with you,' he said. 'But you won't mind if I don't stay very long. I've left instructions at my hotel that I'm to be called at seven.'

'We'll leave as soon as ever you like.'

Nicky found it very pleasant at the Knickerbocker. He ate his bacon and eggs with appetite. They shared a bottle of champagne. They danced, and the little lady told him he danced beautifully. He knew he danced pretty well, and of course she was easy to dance with. As light as a feather. She laid her cheek against his and when their eyes met there was in hers a smile that made his heart go pit-a-pat. A coloured woman sang in a throaty, sensual voice. The floor was crowded.

'Have you ever been told that you're very good-looking?' she asked.

'I don't think so,' he laughed. 'Gosh,' he thought, 'I believe she's fallen for me.'

Nicky was not such a fool as to be unaware that women often liked him, and when she made that remark he pressed her to him a little more closely. She closed her eyes and a faint sigh escaped her lips.

'I suppose it wouldn't be quite nice if I kissed you before all these people,' he said.

'What do you think they would take me for?'

It began to grow late and Nicky said that really he thought he ought to be going.

'I shall go too,' she said. 'Will you drop me at my hotel on your way?'

Nicky paid the bill. He was rather surprised at its amount, but with all that money he had in his pocket he could afford not to care, and they got into a taxi. She snuggled up to him and he kissed her. She seemed to like it.

'By Jove,' he thought, 'I wonder if there's anything doing.'

It was true that she was a married woman, but her husband was in Morocco, and it certainly did look as if she'd fallen for him. Good and proper. It was true also that his father had warned him to have nothing to do with women, but, he reflected again, he hadn't actually promised he wouldn't, he'd only promised not to forget his advice. Well, he hadn't; he was bearing it in mind that very minute. But circumstances alter cases. She was a sweet little thing; it seemed silly to miss the chance of an adventure when it was handed to you like that on a tray. When they reached the hotel he paid off the taxi.

'I'll walk home,' he said. 'The air will do me good after the stuffy atmosphere of that place.'

'Come up a moment,' she said. 'I'd like to show you the photo of my little boy.'

'Oh, have you got a little boy?' he exclaimed, a trifle dashed.

'Yes, a sweet little boy.'

He walked upstairs after her. He didn't in the least want to see the photograph of her little boy, but he thought it only civil to pretend he did. He was afraid he'd made a fool of himself; it occurred to him that she was taking him up to look at the photograph in order to show him in a nice way that he'd made a mistake. He'd told her he was eighteen.

'I suppose she thinks I'm just a kid.'

He began to wish he hadn't spent all that money on champagne at the night-club.

But she didn't show him the photograph of her little boy after all. They had no sooner got into her room than she turned to him, flung her arms round his neck, and kissed him full on the lips. He had never in all his life been kissed so passionately.

'Darling,' she said.

For a brief moment his father's advice once more crossed Nicky's mind and then he forgot it.

Nicky was a light sleeper and the least sound was apt to wake him. Two or three hours later he awoke and for a moment could not imagine where he was. The room was not quite dark, for the door of the bathroom was ajar, and the light in it had been left on. Suddenly he was conscious that someone was moving about the room. Then he remembered. He saw that it was his little friend, and he was on the point of speaking when something in the way she was behaving stopped him. She was walking very cautiously, as though she were afraid of waking him; she stopped once or twice and looked over at the bed. He wondered what she was after. He soon saw. She went over to the chair on which he had placed his clothes and once more looked in his direction. She waited for what seemed to him an interminable time. The silence was so intense that Nicky thought he could hear his own heart beating. Then, very slowly, very quietly, she took up his coat, slipped her hand into the inside pocket and drew out all those beautiful thousand-franc notes that Nicky had been so proud to win. She put the coat back and placed some other clothes on it so that it should look as though it had not been disturbed, then, with the bundle of notes in her hand, for an appreciable time stood once more stock-still. Nicky had repressed an instinctive impulse to jump up and grab her, it was partly surprise that had kept him quiet, partly the notion that he was in a strange hotel, in a foreign country, and if he made a row he didn't know what might happen. She looked at him. His eyes were partly closed and he was sure that she thought he was asleep. In the silence she could hardly fail to hear his regular breathing. When she had reassured herself that her movements had not disturbed him she stepped, with infinite caution, across the room. On a small table in the window a cineraria was growing in a pot. Nicky watched her now with his eyes wide open. The plant was evidently placed quite loosely in the pot, for taking it by the stalks she lifted it out; she put the banknotes in the bottom of the pot and replaced the plant. It was an excellent hiding-place. No one could have guessed that anything was concealed under that richly-flowering plant. She pressed the earth down with her fingers and then, very slowly, taking care not to make the smallest noise, crept across the room and slipped back into bed.

'*Chéri*,' she said, in a caressing voice.

Nicky breathed steadily, like a man immersed in deep sleep. The little lady turned over on her side and disposed herself to slumber. But though Nicky lay so still his thoughts worked busily. He was extremely indignant at the scene he had just witnessed, and to himself he spoke his thoughts with vigour.

'She's nothing but a damned tart. She and her dear little boy and her husband in Morocco. My eye! She's a rotten thief, that's what she is. Took me for a mug. If she thinks she's going to get away with anything like that, she's mistaken.'

He had already made up his mind what he was going to do with the money he had so cleverly won. He had long wanted a car of his own, and had thought it rather mean of his father not to have given him one. After all, a feller doesn't always want to drive about in the family bus. Well, he'd just teach the old man a lesson and buy one himself. For twenty thousand francs, two hundred pounds roughly, he could get a very decent second-hand car. He meant to get the money back, but just then he didn't quite know how. He didn't like the idea of kicking up a row, he was a stranger, in a hotel he knew nothing of; it might very well be that the beastly woman had friends there, he didn't mind facing anyone in a fair fight, but he'd look pretty foolish if someone pulled a gun on him. He reflected besides, very sensibly, that he had no proof the money was his. If it came to a show-down and she swore it was hers, he might very easily find himself hauled off to a police-station. He really didn't know what to do. Presently by her regular breathing he knew that the little lady was asleep. She must have fallen asleep with an easy mind, for she had done her job without a hitch. It infuriated Nicky that she should rest so peacefully while he lay awake worried to death. Suddenly an idea occurred to him. It was such a good one that it was only by the exercise of all his self-control that he prevented himself from jumping out of bed and carrying it out at once. Two could play at her game. She'd stolen his money; well, he'd steal it back again, and they'd be all square. He made up his mind to wait quite quietly until he was sure that deceitful woman was sound asleep. He waited for what seemed to him a very long time. She did not stir. Her breathing was as regular as a child's.

'Darling,' he said at last.

No answer. No movement. She was dead to the world. Very slowly, pausing after every movement, very silently, he slipped out of bed. He stood still for a while, looking at her to see whether he had disturbed her. Her breathing was as regular as before. During the time he was waiting he had taken note care-fully of the furniture in the room so that in crossing it he should not knock against a chair or a table and make a noise. He took a couple of steps and waited, he took a couple of steps more; he was very light on his feet and made no sound as he walked; he took fully five minutes to get to the window, and here he waited again. He started, for the bed slightly creaked, but it was only because the sleeper turned in her sleep. He forced himself to wait till he had counted one hundred. She was sleeping like a log. With infinite care he seized the cineraria by the stalks and gently pulled it out of the pot; he put his other hand in, his heart beat nineteen to the dozen as his fingers touched the notes, his hand closed on them and he slowly drew them out. He replaced the plant and in his turn carefully pressed down the earth. While he was doing all this he had kept one eye on the form lying in the bed. It remained still. After another pause he crept softly to the chair on which his clothes were lying. He first put the bundle of notes in his coat pocket and then proceeded to dress. It took him a good quarter of an hour, because he could afford to make no sound. He had been wearing a soft shirt with his dinner jacket, and he congratulated himself on this, because it was easier to put on silently than a stiff one. He had some difficulty in tying his tie without a looking-glass, but he very wisely reflected that it didn't really matter if it wasn't tied very well. His spirits were rising. The whole thing now began to seem rather a lark. At length he was completely dressed except for his shoes, which he took in his hand; he thought he would put them on when he got into the passage. Now he had to cross the room to get to the door. He reached it so quietly that he could not have disturbed the lightest sleeper. But the door had to be unlocked. He turned the key very slowly; it creaked.

'Who's that?'

The little woman suddenly sat up in bed. Nicky's heart jumped to his mouth. He made a great effort to keep his head.

'It's only me. It's six o'clock and I've got to go. I was trying not to wake you.'

'Oh, I forgot.'

She sank back on to the pillow.

'Now that you're awake I'll put on my shoes.'

He sat down on the edge of the bed and did this.

'Don't make a noise when you go out. The hotel people don't like it. Oh, I'm so sleepy.'

'You go right off to sleep again.'

'Kiss me before you go.' He bent down and kissed her. 'You're a sweet boy and a wonderful lover. *Bon voyage*.'

Nicky did not feel quite safe till he got out of the hotel. The dawn had broken. The sky was unclouded, and in the harbour the yachts and the fishing-boats lay motionless on the still water. On the quay fishermen were getting ready to start on their day's work. The streets were deserted. Nicky took a long breath of the sweet morning air. He felt alert and well. He also felt as pleased as Punch. With a swinging stride, his shoulders well thrown back, he walked up the hill and along the gardens in front of the Casino – the flowers in that clear light had a dewy brilliance that was delicious – till he came to his hotel. Here the day had already begun. In the hall porters with mufflers round their necks and berets on their heads were busy sweeping. Nicky went up to his room and had a hot bath. He lay in it and thought with satisfaction that he was not such a mug as some people might think. After his bath he did his exercises, dressed, packed, and went down to breakfast. He had a grand appetite. No continental breakfast for him! He had grapefruit, porridge, bacon and eggs, rolls fresh from the oven, so crisp and delicious they melted in your mouth, marmalade, and three cups of coffee. Though feeling perfectly well before, he felt better after that. He lit the pipe he had recently learnt to smoke, paid his bill and stepped into the car that was waiting to take him to the aerodrome on the other side of Cannes. The road as far as Nice ran over the hills and below him was the blue sea and the coast-line. He couldn't help thinking it damned pretty. They passed through Nice, so gay and friendly in the early morning, and presently they came to a long stretch of straight road that ran by the sea. Nicky had paid his bill, not with the money he had won the night before, but with the money his father had given him; he had changed a thousand francs to pay for supper at the Knickerbocker, but that deceitful little woman had returned him the thousand francs he had lent her, so that he still had twenty thousand-franc notes in his pocket. He thought he would like to have a look at them. He had so nearly lost them that they had a double value for him. He took them out of his hip-pocket into which for safety's sake he had stuffed them when he put on the suit he was travelling in, and counted them one by one. Something very strange had happened to them. Instead of there being twenty notes as there should have been there were twenty-six. He couldn't understand it at all. He counted them twice more. There was no doubt about it; somehow or other he had twenty-six thousand francs instead of the twenty he should have had. He couldn't make it out. He asked himself if it was possible that he had won more at the Sporting Club than he had realized. But no, that was out of the question; he distinctly remembered the man at the desk laying the notes out in four rows of five, and he had counted them himself. Suddenly the explanation occurred to him; when he had put his hand into the flower-pot, after taking out the cineraria, he had grabbed everything he felt there. The flower-pot was the little hussy's money-box and he had taken out not only his own money, but her savings as well. Nicky leant back in the car and burst into a roar of laughter. It was the funniest thing he had ever heard in his life. And when he thought of her going to the flower-pot some time later in the morning when she awoke, expecting to find the money she had so cleverly got away with, and finding, not only that it wasn't there, but that her own had gone too, he laughed more than ever. And so far as he was concerned there was nothing to do about it; he neither knew her name, nor the name of the hotel to which she had taken him. He couldn't return her money even if he wanted to.

'It serves her damned well right,' he said.

This then was the story that Henry Garnet told his friends over the bridge-table, for the night before, after dinner when his wife and daughter had left them to their port, Nicky had narrated it in full.

'And you know what infuriated me is that he's so damned pleased with himself. Talk of a cat swallowing a canary. And d'you know what he said to me when he'd finished? He looked at me with those innocent eyes of his and said: "You know, father, I can't help thinking there was something wrong about the advice you gave me. You said, don't gamble; well, I did, and I made a packet; you said, don't lend money; well, I did, and I got it back; and you said, don't have anything to do with women; well, I did, and I made six thousand francs on the deal."'

It didn't make it any better for Henry Garnet that his three companions burst out laughing.

'It's all very well for you fellows to laugh, but you know, I'm in a damned awkward position. The boy looked up to me, he respected me, he took whatever I said as gospel truth, and now, I saw it in his eyes, he just looks upon me as a drivelling old fool. It's no good my saying one swallow doesn't make a summer; he doesn't see that it was just a fluke, he thinks the whole thing was due to his own cleverness. It may ruin him.'

'You do look a bit of a damned fool, old man,' said one of the others. 'There's no denying that, is there?'

'I know I do, and I don't like it. It's so dashed unfair. Fate has no right to play one tricks like that. After all, you must admit that my advice was good.'

'Very good.'

'And the wretched boy ought to have burnt his fingers. Well, he hasn't. You're all men of the world, you tell me how I'm to deal with the situation now.'

But they none of them could.

'Well, Henry, if I were you I wouldn't worry,' said the lawyer. 'My belief is that your boy's born lucky, and in the long run that's better than to be born clever or rich.'

GIGOLO AND GIGOLETTE

THE bar was crowded. Sandy Westcott had had a couple of cocktails and he was beginning to feel hungry. He looked at his watch. He had been asked to dinner at half past nine and it was nearly ten. Eva Barrett was always late and he would be lucky if he got anything to eat by ten-thirty. He turned to the barman to order another cocktail and caught sight of a man who at that moment came up to the bar.

'Hullo, Cotman,' he said. 'Have a drink?'

'I don't mind if I do, sir.'

Cotman was a nice-looking fellow, of thirty perhaps, short, but with so good a figure that he did not look it, very smartly dressed in a double-breasted dinner jacket, a little too much waisted, and a butterfly tie a good deal too large. He had a thick mat of black, wavy hair, very sleek and shiny, brushed straight back from his forehead, and large flashing eyes. He spoke with great refinement, but with a Cockney accent.

'How's Stella?' asked Sandy.

'Oh, she's all right. Likes to have a lay-down before the show, you know. Steadies the old nerves, she says.'

'I wouldn't do that stunt of hers for a thousand pounds.'

'I don't suppose you would. No one can do it but her, not from that height, I mean, and only five foot of water.'

'It's the most sick-making thing I've ever seen.'

Cotman gave a little laugh. He took this as a compliment. Stella was his wife. Of course she did the trick and took the risk, but it was he who had thought of the flames, and it was the flames that had taken the public fancy and made the turn the huge success it was. Stella dived into a tank from the top of a ladder sixty feet high, and as he said, there were only five feet of water in the tank. Just before she dived they poured enough petrol on to cover the surface and he set it alight; the flames soared up and she dived straight into them.

'Paco Espinel tells me it's the biggest draw the Casino has ever had,' said Sandy.

'I know. He told me they'd served as many dinners in July as they generally do in August. And that's you, he says to me.'

'Well, I hope you're making a packet.'

'Well, I can't exactly say that. You see, we've got our contract and naturally we didn't know it was going to be a riot, but Mr

219

Espinel's talking of booking us for next month, and I don't mind telling you he's not going to get us on the same terms or anything like it. Why, I had a letter from an agent only this morning saying they wanted us to go to Deauville.'

'Here are my people,' said Sandy.

He nodded to Cotman and left him. Eva Barrett sailed in with the rest of her guests. She had gathered them together downstairs. It was a party of eight.

'I knew we should find you here, Sandy,' she said. 'I'm not late, am I?'

'Only half an hour.'

'Ask them what cocktails they want and then we'll dine.'

While they were standing at the bar, emptying now, for nearly everyone had gone down to the terrace for dinner, Paco Espinel passed through and stopped to shake hands with Eva Barrett. Paco Espinel was a young man who had run through his money and now made his living by arranging the turns with which the Casino sought to attract visitors. It was his duty to be civil to the rich and great. Mrs Chaloner Barrett was an American widow of vast wealth; she not only entertained expensively, but also gambled. And after all, the dinners and suppers and the two cabaret shows that accompanied them were only provided to induce people to lose their money at the tables.

'Got a good table for me, Paco?' said Eva Barrett.

'The best.' His eyes, fine, dark Argentine eyes, expressed his admiration of Mrs Barrett's opulent, ageing charms. This also was business. 'You've seen Stella?'

'Of course. Three times. It's the most terrifying thing I've ever seen.'

'Sandy comes every night.'

'I want to be in at the death. She's bound to kill herself one of these nights and I don't want to miss that if I can help it.'

Paco laughed.

'She's been such a success, we're going to keep her on another month. All I ask is that she shouldn't kill herself till the end of August. After that she can do as she likes.'

'Oh, God, have I got to go on eating trout and roast chicken every night till the end of August?' cried Sandy.

'You brute, Sandy,' said Eva Barrett. 'Come on, let's go in to dinner. I'm starving.'

Paco Espinel asked the barman if he'd seen Cotman. The barman said he'd had a drink with Mr Westcott.

'Oh, well, if he comes in here again, tell him I want a word with him.'

Mrs Barrett paused at the top of the steps that led down to the terrace long enough for the press representative, a little haggard woman with an untidy head, to come up with her note-book. Sandy whispered the names of the guests. It was a representative Riviera party. There was an English Lord and his Lady, long and lean both of them, who were prepared to dine with anyone who would give them a free meal. They were certain to be as tight as drums before midnight. There was a gaunt Scotch woman, with a face like a Peruvian mask that has been battered by the storms of ten centuries, and her English husband. Though a broker by profession, he was bluff, military, and hearty. He gave you an impression of such integrity that you were almost more sorry for him than for yourself when the good thing he had put you on to as a special favour turned out to be a dud. There was an Italian countess who was neither Italian nor a countess, but played a beautiful game of bridge, and there was a Russian prince who was ready to make Mrs Barrett a princess and in the meantime sold champagne, motor-cars, and Old Masters on commission. A dance was in progress, and Mrs Barrett, waiting for it to end, surveyed with a look which her short upper lip made scornful the serried throng on the dance floor. It was a gala night and the dining tables were crowded together. Beyond the terrace the sea was calm and silent. The music stopped and the head waiter, affably smiling, came up to guide her to her table. She swept down the steps with majestic gait.

'We shall have quite a good view of the dive,' she said as she sat down.

'I like to be next door to the tank,' said Sandy, 'so that I can see her face.'

'Is she pretty?' asked the Countess.

'It's not that. It's the expression of her eyes. She's scared to death every time she does it.'

'Oh, I don't believe that,' said the City gentleman, Colonel Goodhart by name, though no one had ever discovered how he came by the title. 'I mean, the whole bally stunt's only a trick. There's no danger really, I mean.'

'You don't know what you're talking about. Diving from that height in as little water as that, she's got to turn like a flash the moment she touches the water. And if she doesn't do it right she's bound to bash her head against the bottom and break her back.'

'That's just what I'm telling you, old boy,' said the Colonel, 'it's a trick. I mean, there's no argument.'

'If there's no danger there's nothing to it, anyway,' said Eva Barrett. 'It's over in a minute. Unless she's risking her life it's the biggest fraud of modern times. Don't say we've come to see this over and over again and it's only a fake.'

'Pretty well everything is. You can take my word for that.'

'Well, you ought to know,' said Sandy.

If it occurred to the Colonel that this might be a nasty dig he admirably concealed it. He laughed.

'I don't mind saying I know a thing or two,' he admitted. 'I mean, I've got my eyes peeled all right. You can't put much over on me.'

The tank was on the far left of the terrace, and behind it, supported by stays, was an immensely tall ladder at the top of which was a tiny platform. After two or three dances more, when Eva Barrett's party were eating asparagus, the music stopped and the lights were lowered. A spot was turned on the tank. Cotman was visible in the brilliance. He ascended half a dozen steps so that he was on a level with the top of the tank.

'Ladies and gentlemen,' he cried out, in a loud clear voice, 'you are now going to see the most marvellous feat of the century. Madam Stella, the greatest diver in the world, is about to dive from a height of sixty feet into a lake of flames five foot deep. This is a feat that has never been performed before, and Madam Stella is prepared to give one hundred pounds to anyone who will attempt it. Ladies and gentlemen, I have the honour to present Madam Stella.'

A little figure appeared at the top of the steps that led on to the terrace, ran quickly up to the tank, and bowed to the applauding audience. She wore a man's silk dressing-gown and on her head a bathing-cap. Her thin face was made up as if for the stage. The Italian countess looked at her through her *face-à-main*.

'Not pretty,' she said.

'Good figure,' said Eva Barrett. 'You'll see.'

Stella slipped out of her dressing-gown and gave it to Cotman. He went down the steps. She stood for a moment and looked at the crowd. They were in darkness and she could only see vague white faces and white shirt-fronts. She was small, beautifully made, with legs long for her body and slim hips. Her bathing costume was very scanty.

'You're quite right about the figure, Eva,' said the Colonel.

'Bit undeveloped, of course, but I know you girls think that's quite the thing.'

Stella began to climb the ladder and the spot-light followed her. It seemed an incredible height. An attendant poured petrol on the surface of the water. Cotman was handed a flaming torch. He watched Stella reach the top of the ladder and settle herself on the platform.

'Ready?' he cried.

'Yes.'

'Go,' he shouted.

And as he shouted he seemed to plunge the burning torch into the water. The flames sprang up, leaping high, and really terrifying to look at. At the same moment Stella dived. She came down like a streak of lightning and plunged through the flames, which subsided a moment after she had reached the water. A second later she was at the surface and jumped out to a roar, a storm of applause. Cotman wrapped the dressing-gown round her. She bowed and bowed. The applause went on. Music struck up. With a final wave of the hand she ran down the steps and between the tables to the door. The lights went up and the waiters hurried along with their neglected service.

Sandy Westcott gave a sigh. He did not know whether he was disappointed or relieved.

'Top hole,' said the English peer.

'It's a bally fake,' said the Colonel, with his British pertinacity. 'I bet you anything you like.'

'It's over so quickly,' said her English ladyship. 'I mean, you don't get your money's worth really.'

Anyhow it wasn't her money. That it never was. The Italian countess leaned forward. She spoke fluent English, but with a strong accent.

'Eva, my darling, who are those extraordinary people at the table near the door under the balcony?'

'Packet of fun, aren't they?' said Sandy. 'I simply haven't been able to take my eyes off them.'

Eva Barrett glanced at the table the Countess indicated, and the Prince, who sat with his back to it, turned round to look.

'They can't be true,' cried Eva. 'I must ask Angelo who they are.'

Mrs Barrett was the sort of woman who knew the head waiters of all the principal restaurants in Europe by their first names. She told the waiter who was at that moment filling her glass to send Angelo to her.

It was certainly an odd pair. They were sitting by themselves at a small table. They were very old. The man was big and stout, with a mass of white hair, great bushy white eyebrows, and an enormous white moustache. He looked like the late King Humbert of Italy, but much more like a king. He sat bolt upright. He wore full evening dress, with a white tie and a collar that has been out of fashion for hard on thirty years. His companion was a little old lady in a black satin ball dress, cut very low, and tight at the waist. Round her neck were several chains of coloured beads. She wore what was obviously a wig, and a very ill-fitting one at that; it was very elaborate, all curls and sausages, and raven black. She was outrageously made-up, bright blue under the eyes and on the eyelids, the eyebrows heavily black, a great patch of very pink rouge on each cheek, and the lips a livid scarlet. The skin hung loosely on her face in deep wrinkles. She had large bold eyes and they darted eagerly from table to table. She was taking everything in, and every other minute called the old man's attention to someone or other. The appearance of the couple was so fantastic in that fashionable crowd, the men in dinner jackets, the women in thin, pale-coloured frocks, that many eyes were turned on them. The staring did not seem to incommode the old lady. When she felt certain persons were looking at her she raised her eyebrows archly, smiled and rolled her eyes. She seemed on the point of acknowledging applause.

Angelo hurried up to the good customer that Eva Barrett was.

'You wished to see me, my lady?'

'Oh, Angelo, we're simply dying to know who those absolutely marvellous people are at the next table to the door.'

Angelo gave a look and then assumed a deprecating air. The expression of his face, the movement of his shoulders, the turn of his spine, the gesture of his hands, probably even the twiddle of his toes, all indicated a half-humorous apology.

'You must overlook them, my lady.' He knew of course that Mrs Barrett had no right to be thus addressed, just as he knew that the Italian countess was neither Italian nor a countess and that the English lord never paid for a drink if anyone else would pay for it, but he also knew that to be thus addressed did not displease her. 'They begged me to give them a table because they wanted to see Madam Stella do her dive. They were in the profession themselves once. I know they're not the sort of people one expects to see dining here, but they made such a point of it I simply hadn't the heart to refuse.'

'But I think they're a perfect scream. I adore them.'

'I've known them for many years. The man indeed is a compatriot of mine.' The head waiter gave a condescending little laugh. 'I told them I'd give them a table on the condition that they didn't dance. I wasn't taking any risks, my lady.'

'Oh, but I should have loved to see them dance.'

'One has to draw the line somewhere, my lady,' said Angelo gravely.

He smiled, bowed again and withdrew.

'Look,' cried Sandy, 'they're going.'

The funny old couple were paying their bill. The old man got up and put round his wife's neck a large white, but not too clean, feather boa. She rose. He gave her his arm, holding himself very erect, and she, small in comparison, tripped out beside him. Her black satin dress had a long train, and Eva Barrett (who was well over fifty) screamed with joy.

'Look, I remember my mother wearing a dress like that when I was in the schoolroom.'

The comic pair walked, still arm in arm, through the spacious rooms of the Casino till they came to the door. The old man addressed a commissionaire.

'Be so good as to direct me to the artistes' dressing-rooms. We wish to pay our respects to Madam Stella.'

The commissionaire gave them a look and summed them up. They were not people with whom it was necessary to be very polite.

'You won't find her there.'

'She has not gone? I thought she gave a second performance at two?'

'That's true. They might be in the bar.'

'It won't 'urt us just to go an' 'ave a look, Carlo,' said the old lady.

'Right-o, my love,' he answered with a great roll of the R.

They walked slowly up the great stairs and entered the bar. It was empty but for the deputy-barman and a couple sitting in two arm-chairs in the corner. The old lady released her husband's arm and tripped up with outstretched hands.

''Ow are you, dear? I felt I just 'ad to come and congratulate you, bein' English same as you are. And in the profession meself. It's a grand turn, my dear, it deserves to be a success.' She turned to Cotman. 'And this is your 'usband?'

Stella got out of her arm-chair and a shy smile broke on her lips as she listened with some confusion to the voluble old lady.

'Yes, that's Syd.'

'Pleased to meet you,' he said.

'And this is mine,' said the old lady, with a little dig of the elbow in the direction of the tall white-haired man. 'Mr Penezzi. 'E's a count really, and I'm the Countess Penezzi by rights, but when we retired from the profession we dropped the title.'

'Will you have a drink?' said Cotman.

'No, you 'ave one with us,' said Mrs Penezzi, sinking into an arm-chair. 'Carlo, you order.'

The barman came, and after some discussion three bottles of beer were ordered. Stella would not have anything.

'She never has anything till after the second show,' explained Cotman.

Stella was slight and small, about twenty-six, with light brown hair, cut short and waved, and grey eyes. She had reddened her lips, but wore little rouge on her face. Her skin was pale. She was not very pretty, but she had a neat little face. She wore a very simple evening frock of white silk. The beer was brought and Mr Penezzi, evidently not very talkative, took a long swig.

'What was your line?' asked Syd Cotman, politely.

Mrs Penezzi gave him a rolling glance of her flashing, made-up eyes and turned to her husband.

'Tell 'em who I am, Carlo,' she said.

'The 'uman cannon-ball,' he announced.

Mrs Penezzi smiled brightly and with a quick, birdlike glance looked from one to the other. They stared at her in dismay.

'Flora,' she said. 'The 'uman cannon-ball.'

She so obviously expected them to be impressed that they did not quite know what to do. Stella gave her Syd a puzzled look. He came to the rescue.

'It must have been before our time.'

'Naturally it was before your time. Why, we retired from the profession definitely the year poor Queen Victoria died. It made quite a sensation when we did too. But you've 'eard of me, of course.' She saw the blank look on their faces; her tone changed a little. 'But I was the biggest draw in London. At the Old Aquarium, that was. All the swells came to see me. The Prince of Wales and I don't know who all. I was the talk of the town. Isn't that true, Carlo?'

'She crowded the Aquarium for a year.'

'It was the most spectacular turn they'd ever 'ad there. Why, only a few years ago I went up and introduced meself to Lady de Bathe. Lily Langtry, you know. She used to live down 'ere. She remembered me perfectly. She told me she'd seen me ten times.'

'What did you do?' asked Stella.

'I was fired out of a cannon. Believe me, it was a sensation. And after London I went all over the world with it. Yes, my dear, I'm an old woman now and I won't deny it. Seventy-eight Mr Penezzi is and I shall never see seventy again, but I've 'ad me portrait on every 'oardin' in London. Lady de Bathe said to me: My dear, you was as celebrated as I was. But you know what the public is, give 'em a good thing and they go mad over it, only they want change; 'owever good it is, they get sick of it and then they won't go and see it any more. It'll 'appen to you, my dear, same as it 'appened to me. It comes to all of us. But Mr Penezzi always 'ad 'is 'ead screwed on 'is shoulders the right way. Been in the business since 'e was so 'igh. Circus, you know. Ring-master. That's 'ow I first knew 'im. I was in a troupe of acro-backs. Trapeze act, you know. 'E's a fine-lookin' man now, but you should 'ave seen 'im then, in 'is Russian boots, and ridin' breeches, and a tight-fittin' coat with frogs all down the front of it, crackin' 'is long whip as 'is 'orses galloped round the ring, the 'andsomest man I ever see in my life.'

Mr Penezzi did not make any remark, but thoughtfully twisted his immense white moustache.

'Well, as I was tellin' you, 'e was never one to throw money about and when the agents couldn't get us bookin's any more 'e said, let's retire. An 'e was quite right, after 'avin' been the biggest star in London, we couldn't go back to circus work any more, I mean, Mr Penezzi bein' a count really, 'e 'ad 'is dignity to think of, so we come down 'ere and we bought a 'ouse and started a pension. It always 'ad been Mr Penezzi's ambition to do something like that. Thirty-five years we been 'ere now. We 'aven't done so badly not until the last two or three years, and the slump came, though visitors are very different from what they was when we first started, the things they want, electric-light and runnin' water in their bedrooms and I don't know what all. Give them a card, Carlo. Mr Penezzi does the cookin' 'imself, and if ever you want a real 'ome from 'ome, you'll know where to find it. I like professional people and we'd 'ave a rare lot to talk about, you and me, dearie. Once a professional always a pro-fessional, I say.'

At that moment the head barman came back from his supper. He caught sight of Syd.

'Oh, Mr Cotman, Mr Espinel was looking for you, wants to see you particularly.'

'Oh, where is he?'

'You'll find him around somewhere.'

'We'll be going,' said Mrs Penezzi, getting up. 'Come and 'ave lunch with us one day, will you? I'd like to show you my old photographs and me press cuttin's. Fancy you not 'avin' 'eard of the 'uman cannon-ball. Why, I was as well known as the Tower of London.'

Mrs Penezzi was not vexed at finding that these young people had never even heard of her. She was simply amused.

They bade one another good-bye, and Stella sank back again into her chair.

'I'll just finish my beer,' said Syd, 'and then I'll go and see what Paco wants. Will you stay here, ducky, or would you like to go to your dressing-room?'

Stella's hands were tightly clenched. She did not answer. Syd gave her a look and then quickly glanced away.

'Perfect riot, that old girl,' he went on, in his hearty way. 'Real figure of fun. I suppose it's true what she said. It's difficult to believe, I must say. Fancy 'er drawing all London, what, forty year ago? And the funny thing is, her thinking anybody remembered. Seemed as though she simply couldn't understand us not having heard of her even.'

He gave Stella another glance, from the corner of his eye so that she should not see he was looking at her, and he saw she was crying. He faltered. The tears were rolling down her pale face. She made no sound.

'What's the matter, darling?'

'Syd, I can't do it again tonight,' she sobbed.

'Why on earth not?'

'I'm afraid.'

He took her hand.

'I know you better than that,' he said. 'You're the bravest little woman in the world. Have a brandy, that'll pull you together.'

'No, that'd only make it worse.'

'You can't disappoint your public like that.'

'That filthy public. Swine who eat too much and drink too much. A pack of chattering fools with more money than they know what to do with. I can't stick them. What do they care if I risk my life?'

'Of course, it's the thrill they come for, there's no denying that,' he replied uneasily. 'But you know and I know, there's no risk, not if you keep your nerve.'

'But I've lost my nerve, Syd. I shall kill myself.'

She had raised her voice a little, and he looked round quickly at the barman. But the barman was reading the *Éclaireur de Nice* and paying no attention.

'You don't know what it looks like from up there, the top of the ladder, when I look down at the tank. I give you my word, tonight I thought I was going to faint. I tell you I can't do it again tonight, you've got to get me out of it, Syd.'

'If you funk it tonight it'll be worse tomorrow.'

'No, it won't. It's having to do it twice kills me. The long wait and all that. You go and see Mr Espinel and tell him I can't give two shows a night. It's more than my nerves'll stand.'

'He'll never stand for that. The whole supper trade depends on you. It's only to see you they come in then at all.'

'I can't help it, I tell you I can't go on.'

He was silent for a moment. The tears still streamed down her pale little face, and he saw that she was quickly losing control of herself. He had felt for some days that something was up and he had been anxious. He had tried not to give her an opportunity to talk. He knew obscurely that it was better for her not to put into words what she felt. But he had been worried. For he loved her.

'Anyhow Espinel wants to see me,' he said.

'What about?'

'I don't know. I'll tell him you can't give the show more than once a night and see what he says. Will you wait here?'

'No, I'll go along to the dressing-room.'

Ten minutes later he found her there. He was in great spirits and his step was jaunty. He burst open the door.

'I've got grand news for you, honey. They're keeping us on next month at twice the money.'

He sprang forward to take her in his arms and kiss her, but she pushed him away.

'Have I got to go on again tonight?'

'I'm afraid you must. I tried to make it only one show a night, but he wouldn't hear of it. He says it's quite essential you should do the supper turn. And after all, for double the money, it's worth it.'

She flung herself down on the floor and this time burst into a storm of tears.

'I can't, Syd, I can't. I shall kill myself.'

He sat down on the floor and raised her head and took her in his arms and petted her.

'Buck up, darling. You can't refuse a sum like that. Why, it'll keep us all the winter and we shan't have to do a thing. After all there are only four more days to the end of July and then it's only August.'

'No, no, no. I'm frightened. I don't want to die, Syd. I love you.'

'I know you do, darling, and I love you. Why, since we married I've never looked at another woman. We've never had money like this before and we shall never get it again. You know what these things are, we're a riot now, but we can't expect it to go on for ever. We've got to strike while the iron's hot.'

'D'you want me to die, Syd?'

'Don't talk so silly. Why, where should I be without you? You mustn't give way like this. You've got your self-respect to think of. You're famous all over the world.'

'Like the human cannon-ball was,' she cried with a laugh of fury.

'That damned old woman,' he thought.

He knew that was the last straw. Bad luck, Stella taking it like that.

'That was an eye-opener to me,' she went on. 'What do they come and see me over and over again for? On the chance they'll see me kill myself. And a week after I'm dead they'll have forgotten even my name. That's what the public is. When I looked at that painted old hag I saw it all. Oh, Syd, I'm so miserable.' She threw her arms round his neck and pressed her face to his. 'Syd, it's no good, I can't do it again.'

'Tonight, d'you mean? If you really feel like that about it, I'll tell Espinel you've had a fainting fit. I daresay it'll be all right just for once.'

'I don't mean tonight, I mean never.'

She felt him stiffen a little.

'Syd dear, don't think I'm being silly. It's not just today, it's been growing on me. I can't sleep at night thinking of it, and when I do drop off I see myself standing at the top of the ladder and looking down. Tonight I could hardly get up it, I was trembling so, and when you lit the flames and said go, something seemed to be holding me back. I didn't even know I'd jumped. My mind was a blank till I found myself on the platform and heard them clapping. Syd, if you loved me you wouldn't want me to go through such torture.'

He sighed. His own eyes were wet with tears. For he loved her devotedly.

'You know what it means,' he said. 'The old life. Marathons and all.'

'Anything's better than this.'

The old life. They both remembered it. Syd had been a dancing gigolo since he was eighteen, he was very good-looking in his dark Spanish way and full of life, old women and middle-aged women were glad to pay to dance with him, and he was never out of work. He had drifted from England to the Continent and there he had stayed, going from hotel to hotel, to the Riviera in the winter, to watering-places in France in the summer. It wasn't a bad life they led, there were generally two or three of them together, the men, and they shared a room in cheap lodgings. They didn't have to get up till late and they only dressed in time to go to the hotel at twelve to dance with stout women who wanted to get their weight down. Then they were free till five, when they went to the hotel again and sat at a table, the three of them together, keeping a sharp eye open for anyone who looked a likely client. They had their regular customers. At night they went to the restaurant and the house provided them with quite a decent meal. Between the courses they danced. It was good money. They generally got fifty or a hundred francs from anyone they danced with. Sometimes a rich woman, after dancing a good deal with one of them for two or three nights, would give him as much as a thousand francs. Sometimes a middle-aged woman would ask one to spend a night with her, and he would get two hundred and fifty francs for that. There was always the chance of a silly old fool losing her head, and then there were platinum and sapphire rings, cigarette-cases, clothes, and a wristwatch to be got. One of Syd's friends had married one of them, who was old enough to be his mother, but she gave him a car and money to gamble with, and they lived in a beautiful villa at Biarritz. Those were the good days when everybody had money to burn. The slump came and hit the gigolos hard. The hotels were empty, and the clients didn't seem to want to pay for the pleasure of dancing with a nice-looking young fellow. Often and often Syd passed a whole day without earning the price of a drink, and more than once a fat old girl who weighed a ton had had the nerve to give him ten francs. His expenses didn't go down, for he had to be smartly dressed or the manager of the hotel made remarks, washing cost a packet, and you'd be surprised the amount of linen he needed; then shoes, those floors were terribly hard on shoes, and they had to look new. He had his room to pay for and his lunch.

It was then he met Stella. It was at Évian, and the season was disastrous. She was a swimming instructress. She was Australian, and a beautiful diver. She gave exhibitions every morning and afternoon. At night she was engaged to dance at the hotel. They dined together at a little table in the restaurant apart from the guests, and when the band began to play they danced together to induce the customers to come on to the floor. But often no one followed them and they danced by themselves. Neither of them got anything much in the way of paying partners. They fell in love with one another, and at the end of the season got married

They had never regretted it. They had gone through hard times. Even though for business reasons (elderly ladies didn't so much like the idea of dancing with a married man when his wife was there) they concealed their marriage, it was not so easy to get a hotel job for the pair of them, and Syd was far from being able to earn enough to keep Stella, even in the most modest pension, without working. The gigolo business had gone to pot. They went to Paris and learnt a dancing act, but the competition was fearful and cabaret engagements were very hard to get. Stella was a good ballroom dancer, but the rage was for acrobatics, and however much they practised she never managed to do anything startling. The public was sick of the apache turn. They were out of a job for weeks at a time. Syd's wrist-watch, his gold cigarette-case, his platinum ring, all went up the spout. At last they found themselves in Nice reduced to such straits that Syd had to pawn his evening clothes. It was a catastrophe. They were forced to enter for the Marathon that an enterprising manager was starting. Twenty-four hours a day they danced, resting every hour for fifteen minutes. It was frightful. Their legs ached, their feet were numb. For long periods they were unconscious of what they were doing. They just kept time to the music, exerting themselves as little as possible. They made a little money, people gave them sums of a hundred francs, or two hundred, to encourage them, and sometimes to attract attention they roused themselves to give an exhibition dance. If the public was in a good humour this might bring in a decent sum. They grew terribly tired. On the eleventh day Stella fainted and had to give up. Syd went on by himself, moving, moving without pause, grotesquely, without a partner. That was the worst time they had ever had. It was the final degradation. It had left with them a recollection of horror and misery.

But it was then that Syd had his inspiration. It had come to him while he was slowly going round the hall by himself. Stella always said she could dive in a saucer. It was just a trick.

'Funny how ideas come,' he said afterwards. 'Like a flash of lightning.'

He suddenly remembered having seen a boy set fire to some petrol that had been spilt on the pavement, and the sudden blaze-up. For of course it was the flames on the water and the spectacular dive into them that had caught the public fancy. He stopped dancing there and then; he was too excited to go on. He talked it over with Stella, and she was enthusiastic. He wrote to an agent who was a friend of his; everyone liked Syd, he was a nice little man, and the agent put up the money for the apparatus. He got them an engagement at a circus in Paris, and the turn was a success. They were made. Engagements followed here and there, Syd bought himself an entire outfit of new clothes, and the climax came when they got a booking for the summer casino on the coast. It was no exaggeration of Syd's when he said that Stella was a riot.

'All our troubles are over, old girl,' he said fondly. 'We can put a bit by now for a rainy day, and when the public's sick of this I'll just think of something else.'

And now, without warning, at the top of their boom, Stella wanted to chuck it. He didn't know what to say to her. It broke his heart to see her so unhappy. He loved her more now even than when he had married her. He loved her because of all they'd gone through together; after all, for five days once they'd had nothing to eat but a hunk of bread each and a glass of milk, and he loved her because she'd taken him out of all that; he had good clothes to wear again and his three meals a day. He couldn't look at her; the anguish in her dear grey eyes was more than he could bear. Timidly she stretched out her hand and touched his. He gave a deep sigh.

'You know what it means, honey. Our connexion in the hotels has gone west, and the business is finished, anyway. What there is'll go to people younger than us. You know what these old women are as well as I do; it's a boy they want, and besides, I'm not tall enough really. It didn't matter so much when I was a kid. It's no good saying I don't look my age because I do.'

'Perhaps we can get into pictures.'

He shrugged his shoulders. They'd tried that before when they were down and out.

'I wouldn't mind what I did. I'd serve in a shop.'

'D'you think jobs can be had for the asking?'

She began to cry again.

'Don't, honey. It breaks my heart.'

'We've got a bit put by.'

'I know we have. Enough to last us six months. And then it'll mean starvation. First popping the bits and pieces, and then the clothes'll have to go, same as they did before. And then dancing in lowdown joints for our supper and fifty francs a night. Out of a job for weeks together. And Marathons whenever we hear of one. And how long will the public stand for them?'

'I know you think I'm unreasonable, Syd.'

He turned and looked at her now. There were tears in her eyes. He smiled, and the smile he gave her was charming and tender.

'No, I don't, ducky. I want to make you happy. After all, you're all I've got. I love you.'

He took her in his arms and held her. He could feel the beating of her heart. If Stella felt like that about it, well, he must just make the best of it. After all, supposing she were killed? No, no, let her chuck it and be damned to the money. She made a little movement.

'What is it, honey?'

She released herself and stood up. She went over to the dressing-table.

'I expect it's about time for me to be getting ready,' she said.

He started to his feet.

'You're not going to do a show tonight?'

'Tonight, and every night till I kill myself. What else is there? I know you're right, Syd. I can't go back to all that other, stinking rooms in fifth-rate hotels and not enough to eat. Oh, that Marathon. Why did you bring that up? Being tired and dirty for days at a time and then having to give up because flesh and blood just couldn't stand it. Perhaps I can go on another month and then there'll be enough to give you a chance of looking round.'

'No, darling. I can't stand for that. Chuck it. We'll manage somehow. We starved before; we can starve again.'

She slipped out of her clothes, and for a moment stood naked but for her stockings, looking at herself in the glass. She gave her reflection a hard smile.

'I mustn't disappoint my public,' she sniggered.

THE HAPPY COUPLE

I DON'T know that I very much liked Landon. He was a member of a club I belonged to, and I had often sat next to him at lunch. He was a judge at the Old Bailey, and it was through him I was able to get a privileged seat in court when there was an interesting trial that I wanted to attend. He was an imposing figure on the bench in his great full-bottomed wig, his red robes, and his ermine tippet; and with his long, white face, thin lips, and pale blue eyes, a somewhat terrifying one. He was just, but harsh; and sometimes it made me uncomfortable to hear the bitter scolding he gave a convicted prisoner whom he was about to sentence to a long term of imprisonment. But his acid humour at the lunch-table and his willingness to discuss the cases he had tried made him sufficiently good company for me to disregard the slight malaise 1 felt in his presence. I asked him once whether he did not feel a certain uneasiness of mind after he had sent a man to the gallows. He smiled as he sipped his glass of port.

'Not at all. The man's had a fair trial; I've summed up as fairly as I could, and the jury has found him guilty. When I condemn him to death, I sentence him to a punishment he richly deserves; and when the court rises, I put the case out of my head. Nobody but a sentimental fool would do anything else.'

I knew he liked to talk to me, but I never thought he looked upon me as anything but a club acquaintance, so I was not a little surprised when one day I received a telegram from him saying that he was spending his vacation on the Riviera, and would like to stay with me for two or three days on his way to Italy. 1 wired that I should be glad to see him. But it was with a certain trepidation that I met him at the station.

On the day of his arrival, to help me out, I asked Miss Gray, a neighbour and an old friend of mine, to dinner. She was of mature age, but charming, and she had a flow of lively conversation which I knew nothing could discourage. I gave them a very good dinner, and though I had no port to offer the judge, I was able to provide him with a good bottle of Montrachet and an even better bottle of Mouton Rothschild. He enjoyed them both; and I was glad of that, because when I had offered him a cocktail, he had refused with indignation.

'I have never understood,' he said, 'how people presumably

civilized can indulge in a habit that is not only barbarous but disgusting.'

I may state that this did not deter Miss Gray and me from having a couple of dry Martinis, though it was with impatience and distaste that he watched us drink them.

But the dinner was a success. The good wine and Miss Gray's sprightly chatter combined to give Landon a geniality I had never before seen in him. It was plain to me that notwithstanding his austere appearance he liked feminine society; and Miss Gray in a becoming dress, with her neat head only just touched with grey and her delicate features, her sparkling eyes, was still alluring. After dinner the judge, with some old brandy still further to mellow him, let himself go, and for a couple of hours held us entranced while he told us of celebrated trials in which he had been concerned. I was not surprised therefore that when Miss Gray asked us to lunch with her next day, Landon, even before I could answer, accepted with alacrity.

'A very nice woman,' he said when she had left us. 'And a head on her shoulders. She must have been very pretty as a girl. She's not bad now. Why isn't she married?'

'She always says nobody asked her.'

'Stuff and nonsense! Women ought to marry. Too many of these women about who want their independence. I have no patience with them.'

Miss Gray lived in a little house facing the sea at St Jean, which is a couple of miles from my own house at Cap Ferrat. We drove down next day at one and were shown into her sitting-room.

'I have a surprise for you,' she said to me, as we shook hands. 'The Craigs are coming.'

'You've got to know them at last.'

'Well, I thought it was too absurd that we should live next door to one another, and bathe from the same beach every day and not speak. So I forced myself on them, and they've promised to come to lunch today. I wanted you to meet them, to see what you make of them.' She turned to Landon. 'I hope you don't mind.'

But he was on his best behaviour.

'I'm sure I shall be delighted to meet any friends of yours, Miss Gray,' he said.

'But they're not friends of mine. I've seen a lot of them, but I never spoke to them till yesterday. It'll be a treat for them to meet an author and a celebrated judge.'

I had heard a good deal of the Craigs from Miss Gray during

the previous three weeks. They had taken the cottage next to hers, and at first she feared they would be a nuisance. She liked her own company and did not want to be bothered with the trivialities of social intercourse. But she very quickly discovered that the Craigs were as plainly disinclined to strike up an acquaintance with her as she with them. Though in that little place they could not but meet two or three times a day, the Craigs never by so much as a glance gave an indication that they had ever seen her before. Miss Gray told me she thought it very tactful of them to make no attempt to intrude upon her privacy, but I had an idea that she was not affronted, a little puzzled rather, that they apparently wanted to know her as little as she wanted to know them. I had guessed some time before that she would not be able to resist making the first advance. On one occasion, while we were walking we passed them, and I was able to have a good look at them. Craig was a handsome man, with a red, honest face, a grey moustache, and thick strong grey hair. He held himself well, and there was a bluff heartiness of manner about him that suggested a broker who had retired on a handsome fortune. His wife was a woman hard of visage, tall, and of masculine appearance, with dull, fair hair too elaborately dressed, a large nose, a large mouth, and a weather-beaten skin. She was not only plain but grim. Her clothes, pretty, flimsy and graceful, sat oddly upon her, for they would better have suited a girl of eighteen, and Mrs Craig was certainly forty. Miss Gray told me they were well cut and expensive. I thought he looked commonplace and she looked disagreeable, and I told Miss Gray she was lucky that they were obviously disposed to keep themselves to themselves.

'There's something rather sweet about them,' she answered.
'What?'
'They love one another. And they adore the baby.'

For they had a child that was not more than a year old; and from this Miss Gray had concluded that they had not long been married. She liked to watch them with their baby. A nurse took it out every morning in a pram, but before this, father and mother spent an ecstatic quarter of an hour teaching it to walk. They stood a few yards apart and urged the child to flounder from one to the other; and each time it tumbled into the parental arms it was lifted up and rapturously embraced. And when finally it was tucked up in the smart pram, they hung over it with charming baby talk, and watched it out of sight as though they couldn't bear to let it go.

Miss Gray used often to see them walking up and down the

lawn of their garden arm in arm; they did not talk, as though they were so happy to be together that conversation was unnecessary; and it warmed her heart to observe the affection which that dour, unsympathetic woman so obviously felt for her tall, handsome husband. It was a pretty sight to see Mrs Craig brush an invisible speck of dust off his coat, and Miss Gray was convinced that she purposely made holes in his socks in order to have the pleasure of darning them. And it looked as though he loved her as much as she loved him. Every now and then he would give her a glance, and she would look up at him and smile, and he gave her cheek a little pat. Because they were no longer young, their mutual devotion was peculiarly touching.

I never knew why Miss Gray had never married; I felt as certain as the judge that she had had plenty of chances; and I asked myself, when she talked to me about the Craigs, whether the sight of this matrimonial felicity didn't give her a slight pang. I suppose complete happiness is very rare in this world, but these two people seemed to enjoy it, and it may be that Miss Gray was so strangely interested in them only because she could not quite suppress the feeling in her heart that by remaining single she had missed something.

Because she didn't know what their first names were, she called them Edwin and Angelina. She made up a story about them. She told it to me one day; and when I ridiculed it, she was quite short with me. This, as far as I can remember, is how it went: They had fallen in love with one another years before – perhaps twenty years – when Angelina, a young girl then, had the fresh grace of her teens and Edwin was a brave youth setting out joyously on the journey of life. And since the gods, who are said to look upon young love with kindliness, nevertheless do not bother their heads with practical matters, neither Edwin nor Angelina had a penny. It was impossible for them to marry, but they had courage, hope, and confidence. Edwin made up his mind to go out to South America or Malaya or where you like, make his fortune and return to marry the girl who had patiently waited for him. It couldn't take more than two or three years, five at the utmost; and what is that, when you're twenty and the whole of life is before you? Meanwhile of course Angelina would live with her widowed mother.

But things didn't pan out according to schedule. Edwin found it more difficult than he had expected to make a fortune; in fact, he found it hard to earn enough money to keep body and soul together, and only Angelina's love and her tender letters gave him the heart to continue the struggle. At the end of five years he was not much better off than when he started. Angelina would willingly have joined him and shared his poverty, but it was impossible for her to leave her mother, bed-ridden as she was, poor thing, and there was nothing for them to do but have patience. And so the years passed slowly, and Edwin's hair grew grey, and Angelina became grim and haggard. Hers was the harder lot, for she could do nothing but wait. The cruel glass showed such charms as she had possessed slipping away from her one by one; and at last she discovered that youth, with a mocking laugh and a pirouette, had left her for good. Her sweetness turned sour from long tending of a querulous invalid; her mind was narrowed by the society of the small town in which she lived. Her friends married and had children, but she remained a prisoner to duty.

She wondered if Edwin still loved her. She wondered if he would ever come back. She often despaired. Ten years went by, and fifteen, and twenty. Then Edwin wrote to say that his affairs were settled, and he had made enough money for them to live upon in comfort, and if she were still willing to marry him, he would return at once. By a merciful interposition of providence, Angelina's mother chose that very moment to abandon a world in which she had made herself a thorough nuisance. But when after so long a separation they met, Angelina saw with dismay that Edwin was as young as ever. It's true his hair was grey, but it infinitely became him. He had always been good-looking, but now he was a very handsome man in the flower of his age. She felt as old as the hills. She was conscious of her narrowness, her terrible provincialism, compared with the breadth he had acquired by his long sojourn in foreign countries. He was gay and breezy as of old, but her spirit was crushed. The bitterness of life had warped her soul. It seemed monstrous to bind that alert and active man to her by a promise twenty years old, and she offered him his release. He went deathly pale.

'Don't you care for me any more?' he cried brokenly.

And she realized on a sudden – oh, the rapture, oh, the relief! – that to him she was just the same as she had ever been. He had thought of her always as she was; her portrait had been, as it were, stamped on his heart, so that now, when the real woman stood before him, she was to him, still eighteen.

So they were married.

'I don't believe a word of it,' I said when Miss Gray had brought her story to its happy ending.

'I insist on your believing it,' she said. 'I'm convinced it's true, and I haven't the smallest doubt that they'll live happily together to a ripe old age.' Then she made a remark that I thought rather shrewd. 'Their love is founded on an illusion, perhaps; but since it has to them all the appearance of reality, what does it matter?'

While I have told you this idyllic story of Miss Gray's invention, the three of us, our hostess, Landon, and myself, waited for the Craigs to come.

'Have you ever noticed that if people live next door to you, they're invariably late?' Miss Gray asked the judge.

'No, I haven't,' he answered acidly. 'I'm always punctual myself, and I expect other people to be punctual.'

'I suppose it's no good offering you a cocktail?'

'None whatever, madam.'

'But I have some sherry that they tell me isn't bad.'

The judge took the bottle out of her hands and looked at the label. A faint smile broke on his thin lips.

'This is a civilized drink, Miss Gray. With your permission I will help myself. I never knew a woman yet who knew how to pour out a glass of wine. One should hold a woman by the waist, but a bottle by the neck.'

While he was sipping the old sherry with every sign of satisfaction, Miss Gray glanced out of the window.

'Oh, that's why the Craigs are late. They were waiting for the baby to come back.'

I followed her eyes and saw that the nurse had just pushed the pram past Miss Gray's house on her way home. Craig took the baby out of the pram and lifted it high in the air. The baby, trying to tug at his moustache, crowed gleefully. Mrs Craig stood by, watching, and the smile on her face made her harsh features almost pleasant. The window was open, and we heard her speak.

'Come along, darling,' she said, 'we're late.'

He put the baby back in the pram, and they came up to the door of Miss Gray's house and rang the bell. The maid showed them in. They shook hands with Miss Gray, and because I was standing near, she introduced me to them. Then she turned to the judge.

'And this is Sir Edward Landon – Mr and Mrs Craig.'

One would have expected the judge to move forward with an outstretched hand, but he remained stock-still. He put his eyeglass up to his eye, that eyeglass that I had on more than one occasion seen him use with devastating effect in court, and stared at the newcomers.

'Gosh, what a dirty customer,' I said to myself.

He let the glass drop from his eye.

'How do you do,' he said. 'Am I mistaken in thinking that we've met before?'

The question turned my eyes to the Craigs. They stood side by side close to one another, as though they had drawn together for mutual protection. They did not speak. Mrs Craig looked terrified. Craig's red face was darkened by a purple flush, and his eyes appeared almost to start out of his head. But that only lasted a second.

'I don't think so,' he said in a rich, deep voice. 'Of course I've heard of you, Sir Edward.'

'More people know Tom Fool than Tom Fool knows,' said he.

Miss Gray meanwhile had been giving the cocktail-shaker a shake, and now she handed cocktails to her two guests. She had noticed nothing. I didn't know what it all meant; in fact, I wasn't sure it meant anything. The incident, if incident there was, passed so quickly that I was half inclined to think that I had read into the strangers' momentary embarrassment on being introduced to a celebrated man something for which there was no foundation. I set about making myself pleasant. I asked them how they liked the Riviera and if they were comfortable in their house. Miss Gray joined in, and we chatted, as one does with strangers, of commonplace things. They talked easily and pleasantly. Mrs Craig said how much they enjoyed the bathing and complained of the difficulty of getting fish at the seaside. I was aware that the judge did not join in the conversation, but looked down at his feet as though he were unconscious of the company.

Lunch was announced. We went into the dining-room. We were only five, and it was a small round table, so the conversation could not be anything but general. I must confess that it was carried on chiefly by Miss Gray and myself. The judge was silent, but he often was, for he was a moody creature, and I paid no attention. I noticed that he ate the omelette with good appetite, and when it was passed round again took a second helping. The Craigs struck me as a little shy, but that didn't surprise me, and as the second course was produced they began to talk more freely. It didn't strike me that they were very amusing people; they didn't seem interested in very much besides their baby, the vagaries of the two Italian maids they had, and an occasional flutter at Monte Carlo; and I couldn't help thinking that Miss Gray had erred in making their acquaintance. Then suddenly something happened: Craig rose abruptly from his chair and fell headlong to the floor. We jumped up. Mrs Craig threw herself down, over her husband, and took his head in her hands.

'It's all right, George,' she cried in an agonized tone. 'It's all right!'

'Put his head down,' I said. 'He's only fainted.'

I felt his pulse and could feel nothing. I said he had fainted, but I wasn't sure it wasn't a stroke. He was the sort of heavy, plethoric man who might easily have one. Miss Gray dipped her napkin into water and dabbed his forehead. Mrs Craig seemed distraught. Then I noticed that Landon had remained quietly sitting in his chair.

'If he's fainted, you're not helping him to recover by crowding round him,' he said acidly.

Mrs Craig turned her head and gave him a look of bitter hatred.

'I'll ring up the doctor,' said Miss Gray.

'No, I don't think that's necessary,' I said. 'He's coming to.'

I could feel his pulse growing stronger, and in a minute or two he opened his eyes. He gasped when he realized what had happened, and tried to struggle to his feet.

'Don't move,' I said. 'Lie still a little longer.'

I got him to drink a glass of brandy, and the colour came back to his face.

'I feel all right now,' he said.

'We'll get you into the next room, and you can lie on the sofa for a bit.'

'No, I'd sooner go home. It's only a step.'

He got up from the floor.

'Yes, let's go back,' said Mrs Craig. She turned to Miss Gray. 'I'm so sorry; he's never done anything like this before.'

They were determined to go, and I thought myself it was the best thing for them to do.

'Put him to bed and keep him there, and he'll be as right as rain tomorrow.'

Mrs Craig took one of his arms and I took the other; Miss Gray opened the door, and though still a bit shaky, he was able to walk. When we arrived at the Craigs' home, I offered to go in and help undress him; but they would neither of them hear of it. I went back to Miss Gray's and found them at dessert.

'I wonder why he fainted,' Miss Gray was saying. 'All the windows are open, and it's not particularly hot today.'

'I wonder,' said the judge.

I noticed that his thin pale face bore an expression of some complacency. We had our coffee; and then, since the judge and I were going to play golf, we got into the car and drove up the hill to my house.

'How did Miss Gray get to know those people?' Landon asked me. 'They struck me as rather second-rate. I shouldn't have thought they were very much her mark.'

'You know women. She likes her privacy, and when they settled in next door, she was quite decided that she wouldn't have anything to do with them; but when she discovered that they didn't want to have anything to do with her, she couldn't rest till she'd made their acquaintance.'

I told him the story she had invented about her neighbours. He listened with an expressionless face.

'I'm afraid your friend Miss Gray is a sentimental donkey, my dear fellow,' he said when I had come to an end. 'I tell you, women ought to marry. She'd soon have had all that nonsense knocked out of her if she'd had half a dozen brats.'

'What do you know about the Craigs?' I asked.

He gave me a frigid glance.

'I? Why should I know anything about them? I thought they were very ordinary people.'

I wish I knew how to describe the strong impression he gave me, both by the glacial austerity of his look and by the rasping finality of his tone, that he was not prepared to say anything more. We finished the drive in silence.

Landon was well on in his sixties, and he was the kind of golfer who never hits a long ball but is never off the straight, and he was a deadly putter, so, though he gave me strokes, he beat me handsomely. After dinner I took him in to Monte Carlo, where he finished the evening by winning a couple of thousand francs at the roulette table. These successive events put him into a remarkably good humour.

'A very pleasant day,' he said when we parted for the night. 'I've thoroughly enjoyed it.'

I spent the next morning at work, and we did not meet till lunch. We were just finishing when I was called to the telephone.

When I came back, my guest was drinking a second cup of coffee.

'That was Miss Gray,' I said.

'Oh? What had she to say?'

'The Craigs have done a bolt. They disappeared last night.

The maids live in the village; and when they came this morning, they found the house empty. They'd skipped – the Craigs, the nurse, and the baby – and taken their luggage with them. They left money on the table for the maids' wages, the rent to the end of their tenancy, and the tradesmen's bills.'

The judge said nothing. He took a cigar from the box, examined it carefully and then lit it with deliberation.

'What have you got to say about that?' I asked.

'My dear fellow, are you obliged to use these American phrases? Isn't English good enough for you?'

'Is that an American phrase? It expresses exactly what I mean. You can't imagine I'm such a fool as not to have noticed that you and the Craigs had met before; and if they've vanished into thin air like figments of the imagination, it's a fairly reasonable conclusion that the circumstances under which you met were not altogether pleasant.'

The judge gave a little chuckle, and there was a twinkle in his cold blue eyes.

'That was a very good brandy you gave me last night,' he said. 'It's against my principles to drink liqueurs after lunch, but it's a very dull man who allows his principles to enslave him, and for once I think I should enjoy one.'

I sent for the brandy and watched the judge while he poured himself out a generous measure. He took a sip with obvious satisfaction.

'Do you remember the Wingford murder?' he asked me.

'No.'

'Perhaps you weren't in England at the time. Pity – you might have come to the trial. You'd have enjoyed it. It caused a lot of excitement; the papers were full of it.

'Miss Wingford was a rich spinster of mature age who lived in the country with a companion. She was a healthy woman for her age; and when she died rather suddenly, her friends were surprised. Her physician, a fellow called Brandon, signed the certificate and she was duly buried. The will was read, and it appeared that she had left everything she had, something between sixty and seventy thousand pounds, to her companion. The relations were very sore, but there was nothing they could do about it. The will had been drawn up by her lawyer and witnessed by his clerk and Dr Brandon.

'But Miss Wingford had a maid who had been with her for thirty years and had always understood that she would be remembered in the will; she claimed that Miss Wingford had promised to leave her well provided for, and when she found that she wasn't even mentioned she flew into a passion. She told the nephew and the two neices who had come down for the funeral that she was sure Miss Wingford had been poisoned, and she said that if they didn't go to the police, she'd go herself. Well, they didn't do that, but they went to see Dr Brandon. He laughed. He said that Miss Wingford had had a weak heart and he'd been treating her for years. She died just as he had always expected her to die, peacefully in her sleep; and he advised them not to pay any attention to what the maid said. She had always hated the companion, a Miss Starling, and had been jealous of her. Dr Brandon was highly respected; he had been Miss Wingford's doctor for a long time, and the two nieces, who'd stayed with her often, knew him well. He was not profiting by the will, and there seemed no reason to doubt his word, so the family thought there was nothing to do but make the best of a bad job and went back to London.

'But the maid went on talking; she talked so much that at last the police, much against their will, I must admit, were obliged to take notice, and an order to exhume the body was made. There was an inquest, and it was found that Miss Wingford had died from an overdose of veronal. The coroner's jury found that it had been administered by Miss Starling, and she was arrested. A detective was sent down from Scotland Yard, and he got together some unexpected evidence. It appeared that there'd been a good deal of gossip about Miss Starling and Dr Brandon. They'd been seen a lot together in places in which there was no reason for them to be except that they wanted to be together, and the general impression in the village was that they were only waiting for Miss Wingford to die to get married. That put a very different complexion on the case. To make a long story short, the police got enough evidence in their opinion to justify them in arresting the doctor and charging him and Miss Starling with the murder of the old lady.'

The judge took another sip of brandy.

'The case came up for trial before me. The case for the prosecution was that the accused were madly in love with one another and had done the poor old lady to death so that they could marry on the fortune Miss Starling had wheedled her employer into leaving her. Miss Wingford always had a cup of cocoa when she went to bed, which Miss Starling prepared for her; and the counsel for the prosecution claimed that it was in this that Miss Starling had dissolved the tablets that caused Miss Wingford's death. The accused elected to give evidence on their own behalf, and they made a miserable showing in the witness-box. They lied their heads off. Though witnesses testified they had seen them walking together at night with their arms round one another's waists, though Brandon's maid testified she had seen them kissing one another in the doctor's house, they swore they were no more than friends. And oddly enough, medical evidence proved that Miss Starling was *virgo intacta*.

'Brandon admitted that he had given Miss Wingford a bottle of veronal tablets because she complained of sleeplessness, but declared he had warned her never to take more than one, and then only when absolutely necessary. The defence sought to prove that she had taken the tablets either by accident or because she wanted to commit suicide. That didn't hold water for a moment. Miss Wingford was a jolly, normal old lady who thoroughly enjoyed life; and her death occurred two days before the expected arrival of an old friend for a week's visit. She hadn't complained to the maid of sleeping badly – in fact, her maid had always thought her a very good sleeper. It was impossible to believe that she had accidentally taken a sufficient number of tablets to kill herself. Personally, I had no doubt that it was a put-up job between the doctor and the companion. The motive was obvious and sufficient. I summed up and I hope summed up fairly; but it was my duty to put the facts before the jury, and to my mind the facts were damning. The jury filed out. I don't suppose you know that when you are sitting on the bench, you somehow get the feeling of the court. You have to be on your guard against it, to be sure it doesn't influence you. I never had it more strongly than on that day that there wasn't a soul in court who wasn't convinced that those two people had committed the crime with which they were charged. I hadn't the shadow of a doubt that the jury would bring in a verdict of guilty. Juries are incalculable. They were out for three hours, and when they came back I knew at once that I was mistaken. In a murder case, when a jury is going to bring in a verdict of guilty they won't look at the prisoner; they look away. I noticed that three or four of the jurymen glanced at the two prisoners in the dock. They brought in a verdict of not guilty. The real names of Mr and Mrs Craig are Dr and Mrs Brandon. I'm just as certain as I am that I'm sitting here that they committed between them a cruel and heartless murder and richly deserved to be hanged.'

'What do you think made the jury find them not guilty?'

'I've asked myself that; and do you know the only explanation

I can give? The fact that it was conclusively proved that they had never been lovers. And if you come to think of it, that's one of the most curious features of the whole case. That woman was prepared to commit murder to get the man she loved, but she wasn't prepared to have an illicit love-affair with him.'

'Human nature is very odd, isn't it?'

'Very,' said Landon, helping himself to another glass of brandy.

THE VOICE OF THE TURTLE

FOR some time I could not make up my mind if I liked Peter
Melrose or not. He had had a novel published that had caused
some stir among the rather dreary but worthy people who are
always on the lookout for new talent. Elderly gentlemen with
nothing much to do but go to luncheon parties praised it with
girlish enthusiasm, and wiry little women who didn't get on with
their husbands thought it showed promise. I read a few reviews.
They contradicted one another freely. Some of the critics claimed
that with this first novel the author had sprung into the front rank
of English novelists: others reviled it. I did not read it. I have
learnt by experience that when a book makes a sensation it is just
as well to wait a year before you read it. It is astonishing how
many books then you need not read at all. But it chanced that one
day I met Peter Melrose. With some misgiving I had accepted an
invitation to a sherry party. It was in the top flat of a converted
house in Bloomsbury, and I was a trifle out of breath when I had
climbed four flights of stairs. My hostesses were two women,
much over life-size, in early middle life, the sort of women who
know all about the insides of motor-cars and like a good tramp in
the rain, but very feminine for all that, fond of eating out of paper
bags. The drawing-room, which they called 'our workshop',
though being of independent means neither had ever done a
stroke of work in her life, was large and bare, furnished with
rustless-steel chairs, which looked as though they could with
difficulty support the very substantial weight of their owners,
glass-topped tables, and a vast divan covered with zebra-skin. On
the walls were book-shelves, and pictures by the better-known
English imitators of Cézanne, Braque, and Picasso. In the shelves,
besides a number of 'curious' books of the eighteenth century
(for pornography is ageless) there were only the works of living
authors, mostly first editions, and it was indeed to sign some of
my own that I had been asked to the party.

It was quite small. There was but one other woman, who might
have been a younger sister of my hostesses, for, though stout, she
was not quite so stout, though tall, not quite so tall, and though
hearty, not quite so hearty. I did not catch her name, but she
answered to that of Boofuls. The only man besides myself was
Peter Melrose. He was quite young, twenty-two or twenty-three,
of the middle height, but with an ungainly figure that made him

look squat. He had a reddish skin that seemed to fit over the bones of his face too tightly, a rather large semitic nose, though he was not a Jew, and alert green eyes under bushy eyebrows. His brown hair, cut very short, was scurfy. He was dressed in the brown Norfolk jacket and grey flannel trousers that are worn by the art students who wander hatless along King's Road, Chelsea. An uncouth young man. Nor was there much to attract in his manner. He was self-assertive, disputatious and intolerant. He had a hearty contempt for his fellow-writers which he expressed with zest. The satisfaction he gave me by his breezy attacks on reputations which for my part I considered exaggerated, but prudently held my tongue about, was only lessened by the conviction that no sooner was my back turned than he would tear my own to shreds. He talked well. He was amusing and sometimes witty. I should have laughed at his sallies more easily if those three ladies had not been so unreasonably convulsed by them. They roared with laughter at what he said, whether it was funny or whether it was inept. He said many silly things, for he talked without stopping, but he also said some very clever ones. He had a point of view, crude and not so original as he thought, but sincere. But the most striking thing about him was his eager, impetuous vitality; it was like a hot flame that burnt him with an unendurable fury. It even shed a glow on those about him. He had something, if only that, and when I left it was with a slight sense of curiosity at what would come of him. I did not know if he had talent; so many young things can write a clever novel – that means nothing; but it seemed to me that as a man he was not quite like everybody else. He was the sort of person who at thirty, when time had softened his asperity and experience had taught him that he was not quite so intelligent as he thought, would turn into an interesting and agreeable fellow. But I never expected to see him again.

It was with surprise that I received two or three days later a copy of his novel with a very flattering dedication. I read it. It was obviously autobiographical. The scene was a small town in Sussex, and the characters of the upper middle class that strives to keep up appearances on an inadequate income. The humour was rather brutal and rather vulgar. It grated on me, for it consisted chiefly of mockery at people because they were old and poor. Peter Melrose did not know how hard those misfortunes are to bear, and that the efforts made to cope with them are more deserving of sympathy than of derision. But there were descriptions of places, little pictures of a room or impressions of the countryside, which were excellently done. They showed tenderness and a sense of the spiritual beauty of material things. The book was written easily, without affectation, and with a pleasant feeling for the sound of words. But what made it indeed somewhat remarkable, so that I understood why it had attracted attention, was the passion that quivered in the love story of which the plot, such as it was, consisted. It was, as is the modern fashion, more than a trifle coarse and, again in the modern fashion, it tailed off vaguely, without any particular result, so that everything was left in the end pretty much as it had been in the beginning; but you did get the impression of young love, idealistic and yet vehemently sexual; it was so vivid and so deeply felt that it took your breath away. It seemed to throb on the printed page like the pulse of life. It had no reticence. It was absurd, scandalous, and beautiful. It was like a force of nature. That was passion all right. There is nothing, anywhere, so moving and so awe-inspiring.

I wrote to Peter Melrose and told him what I thought of his book, then suggested that we might lunch together. He rang me up next day and we made a date.

I found him unaccountably shy when we sat down opposite one another at a table in a restaurant. I gave him a cocktail. He talked glibly enough, but I could not help seeing that he was ill at ease. I gained the impression that his self-assurance was a pose assumed to conceal, from himself, maybe, a diffidence that tortured him. His manners were brusque and awkward. He would say a rude thing and then laugh nervously to cover his own embarrassment. Though he pretended to be so sure of himself he wanted all the time to be reassured by you. By irritating you, by saying the things he thought would annoy, he tried to force from you some admission, tacit it might be, that he was as wonderful as he longed to think himself. He wanted to despise the opinion of his fellows, and nothing was more important to him. I thought him rather an odious young man, but I did not mind that. It is very natural that clever young men should be rather odious. They are conscious of gifts that they do not know how to use. They are exasperated with the world that will not recognize their merit. They have something to give, and no hand is stretched out to receive it. They are impatient for the fame they regard as their due. No, I do not mind odious young men; it is when they are charming that I button up the pockets of my sympathy.

Peter Melrose was extremely modest about his book. He

blushed through his reddish skin when I praised what I liked in it, and accepted my strictures with a humility that was almost embarrassing. He had made very little money out of it, and his publishers were giving him a small monthly allowance in advance of royalties on the next one. This he had just started, but he wanted to get away to write it in peace, and knowing I lived on the Riviera he asked me if I could tell him of a quiet place where he could bathe and live cheaply. I suggested that he should come and spend a few days with me so that he could look about till he found something to suit him. His green eyes sparkled when I proposed this and he flushed.

'Shouldn't I be an awful nuisance?'

'No. I shall be working. All I can offer you is three meals a day and a room to sleep in. It'll be very dull, but you can do exactly what you like.'

'It sounds grand. May I let you know if I decide to come?'

'Of course.'

We separated, and a week or two later I went home. This was in May. Early in June I received a letter from Peter Melrose asking, if I had really meant what I said when I invited him to spend a few days with me, whether he might arrive on such and such a date. Well, at the time I had meant it, but now, a month later, I remembered that he was an arrogant and ill-bred youth, whom I had seen but twice and wasn't in the least interested in, and I didn't mean it any longer. It seemed to me very likely that he would be bored stiff. I lived a very quiet life and saw few people. And I thought it would be a great strain on my nerves if he were as rude as I knew he could be, and I as his host felt it behoved me to keep my temper. I saw myself driven beyond endurance, and ringing the bell to have his clothes packed and the car brought round to take him away within half an hour. But there was nothing to do about it. It would save him the cost of board and lodging to spend a short period with me, and if he was tired and unhappy as he said in his letter it might be that it would do him good. I sent him a wire and shortly afterwards he arrived.

He looked very hot and grubby in his grey flannel trousers and brown tweed coat when I met him at the station, but after a swim in the pool he changed into white shorts and a Cochet shirt. He looked then quite absurdly young. He had never been out of England before. He was excited. It was touching to see his delight. He seemed, amid those unaccustomed surroundings, to lose his sense of himself, and he was simple, boyish and modest.

I was agreeably surprised. In the evening, after dinner, sitting in the garden, with only the croaking of the little green frogs to break the silence, he began talking to me of his novel. It was a romantic story about a young writer and a celebrated *prima donna*. The theme was reminiscent of Ouida, the last thing I should have expected this hard-boiled youth to write, and I was tickled; it was odd how the fashion completed the circle and returned generation after generation to the same themes. I had no doubt that Peter Melrose would treat it in a very modern way, but there it was, the same old story as had entranced sentimental readers in the three-volume novels of the eighties. He proposed to set it in the beginning of the Edwardian era, which to the young has already acquired the fantastic, far-away feeling of a past age. He talked and talked. He was not unpleasant to listen to. He had no notion that he was putting into fiction his own day-dreams, the comic and touching day-dreams of a rather unattractive, obscure young man who sees himself beloved, to the admiration of the whole world, by an incredibly beautiful, celebrated, and magnificent woman. I always enjoyed the novels of Ouida, and Peter's idea did not at all displease me. With his charming gift of description, his vivid, ingenuous way of looking at material things, fabrics, pieces of furniture, walls, trees, flowers, and his power of representing the passion of life, the passion of love, that thrilled every fibre of his own uncouth body, I had a notion that he might well produce something exuberant, absurd, and poetical. But I asked him a question.

'Have you ever known a *prima donna*?'

'No, but I've read all the autobiographies and memoirs that I could find. I've gone into it pretty thoroughly. Not only the obvious things, you know, but I've hunted around in all sorts of byways to get the revealing touch or the suggestive anecdote.'

'And have you got what you wanted?'

'I think so.'

He began to describe his heroine to me. She was young and beautiful, wilful it is true and with a quick temper, but magnanimous. A woman on the grand scale. Music was her passion; there was music not only in her voice, but in her gestures and in her inmost thoughts. She was devoid of envy, and her appreciation of art was such that when another singer had done her an injury she forgave her when she heard her sing a role beautifully. She was of a wonderful generosity, and would give away everything she possessed when a story of misfortune touched her soft heart. She was a great lover, prepared to sacrifice the world for the man she loved. She was intelligent and well-read. She was tender, unselfish, and disinterested. In fact she was much too good to be true.

'I think you'd better meet a *prima donna*,' I said at last.

'How can I?'

'Have you ever heard of La Falterona?'

'Of course I have. I've read her memoirs.'

'She lives just along the coast. I'll ring her up and ask her to dinner.'

'Will you really? It would be wonderful.'

'Don't blame me if you don't find her quite what you expect.'

'It's the truth I want.'

Everyone has heard of La Falterona. Not even Melba had a greater reputation. She had ceased now to sing in opera, but her voice was still lovely, and she could fill a concert hall in any part of the world. She went for long tours every winter, and in summer rested in a villa by the sea. On the Riviera people are neighbours if they live thirty miles from one another, and for some years I had seen a good deal of La Falterona. She was a woman of ardent temperament, and she was celebrated not only for her singing, but for her love affairs: she never minded talking about them, and I had often sat entranced for hours while with the humour which to me was her most astonishing characteristic she regaled me with lurid tales of royal or very opulent adorers. I was satisfied that there was at least a measure of truth in them. She had been married, for short periods, three or four times, and in one of these unions had annexed a Neapolitan prince. Thinking that to be known as La Falterona was grander than any title, she did not use his name (to which indeed she had no right, since after divorcing him she had married somebody else); but her silver, her cutlery, and her dinner-service were heavily decorated with a coat of arms and a crown, and her servants invariably addressed her as *madame la princesse*. She claimed to be a Hungarian, but her English was perfect; she spoke it with a slight accent (when she remembered), but with an intonation suggestive, I had been told, of Kansas City. This she explained by saying that her father was a political exile who had fled to America when she was no more than a child; but she did not seem quite sure whether he was a distinguished scientist who had got into trouble for his liberal views, or a Magyar of high rank who had brought down on his head the imperial wrath because he had had a love affair with an Archduchess. It depended on whether she was just an artist among artists, or a great lady among persons of noble birth.

With me she was not natural, for that she could never have been if she had tried, but franker than with anyone else. She had a natural and healthy contempt for the arts. She genuinely looked upon the whole thing as a gigantic bluff, and deep down in her heart was an amused sympathy for all the people who were able to put it over on the public. I will admit that I looked forward to the encounter between Peter Melrose and La Falterona with a good deal of sardonic amusement.

She liked coming to dine with me because she knew the food was good. It was the only meal she ate in the day, for she took great care of her figure, but she liked that one to be succulent and ample. I asked her to come at nine, knowing that was the earliest hour she dreamt of eating, and ordered dinner for half past. She turned up at a quarter to ten. She was dressed in apple-green satin, cut very low in front, with no back at all, and she wore a string of huge pearls, a number of expensive-looking rings, and on her left arm diamond and emerald bracelets from the wrist to the elbow. Two or three of them were certainly real. On her raven-black hair was a thin circlet of diamonds. She could not have looked more splendid if she had been going to a ball at Stafford House in the old days. We were in white ducks.

'How grand you are,' I said. 'I told you it wasn't a party.'

She flashed a look of her magnificent black eyes at Peter.

'Of course it's a party. You told me your friend was a writer of talent. I am only an interpreter.' She ran one finger down her flashing bracelets. 'This is the homage I pay to the creative artist.'

I did not utter the vulgar monosyllable that rose to my lips, but offered her what I knew was her favourite cocktail. I was privileged to call her Maria, and she always called me Master. This she did, first because she knew it made me feel a perfect fool, and secondly because, though she was in point of fact not more than two or three years younger than I, it made it quite clear that we belonged to different generations. Sometimes, however, she also called me you dirty swine. This evening she certainly might very well have passed for thirty-five. She had those rather large features which somehow do not seem to betray age. On the stage she was a beautiful woman, and even in private life, notwithstanding her big nose, large mouth, and fleshy face, a good-looking one. She wore a brown make-up, with dark rouge, and her lips were vividly scarlet. She looked very Spanish and, I suspected, felt it, for her accent at the beginning of dinner was quite Sevillian. I wanted her to talk so that Peter should get his money's worth, and I knew there was but one subject in the world that she could talk about. She was in point of fact a stupid woman who had acquired a line of glib chatter which made people on first meeting her think she was as brilliant as she looked; but it was merely a performance she gave, and you soon discovered that she not only did not know what she was talking about, but was not in the least interested in it. I do not think she had ever read a book in her life. Her knowledge of what was going on in the world was confined to what she was able to gather by looking at the pictures in the illustrated press. Her passion for music was complete bunkum. Once at a concert to which I went with her she slept all through the Fifth Symphony, and I was charmed to hear her during the interval telling people that Beethoven stirred her so much that she hesitated to come and hear him, for with those glorious themes singing through her head, it meant that she wouldn't sleep a wink all night. I could well believe she would lie awake, for she had had so sound a nap during the Symphony that it could not but interfere with her night's rest.

But there was one subject in which her interest never failed. She pursued it with indefatigable energy. No obstacle prevented her from returning to it; no chance word was so remote that she could not use it as a stepping-stone to come back to it, and in effecting this she displayed a cleverness of which one would never have thought her capable. On this subject she could be witty, vivacious, philosophic, tragic and inventive. It enabled her to exhibit all the resources of her ingenuity. There was no end to its ramifications, and no limit to its variety. This subject was herself. I gave her an opening at once and then all I had to do was to make suitable interjections. She was in great form. We were dining on the terrace and a full moon was obligingly shining on the sea in front of us. Nature, as though she knew what was proper to the occasion, had set just the right scene. The view was framed by two tall black cypresses, and all round us on the terrace the orange trees in full flower exhaled their heady perfume. There was no wind, and the candles on the table flamed with a steady softness. It was a light that exactly suited La Falterona. She sat between us, eating heartily and thoroughly appreciating the champagne, and she was enjoying herself. She gave the moon a glance. On the sea was a broad pathway of silver.

'How beautiful nature is,' she said. 'My God, the scenery one has to play in. How can they expect one to sing? You know, really, the sets at Covent Garden are a disgrace. The last time I sang Juliet I just told them I wouldn't go on unless they did something about the moon.'

Peter listened to her in silence. He ate her words. She was better value than I had dared to hope. She got a little tight not only on the champagne but on her own loquaciousness. To listen to her you would have thought she was a meek and docile creature against whom the whole world was in conspiracy. Her life had been one long bitter struggle against desperate odds. Managers treated her vilely, impresarios played foul tricks on her, singers combined to ruin her, critics bought by the money of her enemies wrote scandalous things about her, lovers for whom she had sacrificed everything used her with base ingratitude; and yet, by the miracle of her genius and her quick wits, she had discomfited them all. With joyous glee, her eyes flashing, she told us how she had defeated their machinations and what disaster had befallen the wretches who stood in her way. I wondered how she had the nerve to tell the disgraceful stories she told. Without the smallest consciousness of what she was doing she showed herself vindictive and envious, hard as nails, incredibly vain, cruel, selfish, scheming, and mercenary. I stole a glance now and then at Peter. I was tickled at the confusion he must be experiencing when he compared his ideal picture of the *prima donna* with the ruthless reality. She was a woman without a heart. When at last she left us I turned to Peter with a smile.

'Well,' I said, 'at all events you've got some good material.'

'I know, and it all fits in so beautifully,' he said with enthusiasm.

'Does it?' I exclaimed, taken aback.

'She's exactly like my woman. She'll never believe that I'd sketched out the main lines of the character before I'd ever seen her.'

I stared at him in amazement.

'The passion for art. The disinterestedness. She had that same nobility of soul that I saw in my mind's eye. The small-minded, the curious, the vulgar put every obstacle in her way and she sweeps them all aside by the greatness of her purpose and the purity of her ends.' He gave a little happy laugh. 'Isn't it wonderful how nature copies art? I swear to you, I've got her to the life.'

I was about to speak; I held my tongue; though I shrugged a spiritual shoulder I was touched. Peter had seen in her what he was determined to see. There was something very like beauty in his illusion. In his own way he was a poet. We went to bed, and two or three days later, having found a pension to his liking, he left me.

In course of time his book appeared, and like most second novels by young people it had but a very moderate success. The critics had overpraised his first effort and now were unduly censorious. It is of course a very different thing to write a novel about yourself and the people you have known from childhood and to write one about persons of your own invention. Peter's was too long. He had allowed his gift for word-painting to run away with him, the humour was still rather vulgar; but he had reconstructed the period with skill, and the romantic story had that same thrill of real passion which in his first book had so much impressed me.

After the dinner at my house I did not see La Falterona for more than a year. She went for a long tour in South America and did not come down to the Riviera till late in the summer. One night she asked me to dine with her. We were alone but for her companion-secretary, an Englishwoman, Miss Glaser by name, whom La Falterona bullied and ill-treated, hit and swore at, but whom she could not do without. Miss Glaser was a haggard person of fifty, with grey hair and a sallow, wrinkled face. She was a queer creature. She knew everything there was to be known about La Falterona. She both adored and hated her. Behind her back she could be extremely funny at her expense, and the imitation she gave in secret of the great singer with her admirers was the most richly comic thing I have ever heard. But she watched over her like a mother. It was she who, sometimes by wheedling, sometimes by sheer plainness of speech, caused La Falterona to behave herself something like a human being. It was she who had written the singer's exceedingly inaccurate memoirs.

La Falterona wore pale-blue satin pyjamas (she liked satin) and, presumably to rest her hair, a green silk wig; except for a few rings, a pearl necklace, a couple of bracelets, and a diamond brooch at her waist, she wore no jewellery. She had much to tell me of her triumphs in South America. She talked on and on. She had never been in more superb voice and the ovations she had received were unparalleled. The concert halls were sold out for every performance, and she had made a packet.

'Is it true or is it not true, Glaser?' cried Maria with a strong South American accent.

'Most of it,' said Miss Glaser.

La Falterona had the objectionable habit of addressing her

companion by her surname. But it must long since have ceased to annoy the poor woman, so there was not much point in it.

'Who was that man we met in Buenos Aires?'

'Which man?'

'You fool, Glaser. You remember perfectly. The man I was married to once.'

'Pepe Zapata,' Miss Glaser replied without a smile.

'He was broke. He had the impudence to ask me to give him back a diamond necklace he'd given me. He said it had belonged to his mother.'

'It wouldn't have hurt you to give it him,' said Miss Glaser. 'You never wear it.'

'Give it him back?' cried La Falterona, and her astonishment was such that she spoke the purest English. 'Give it him back? You're crazy.'

She looked at Miss Glaser as though she expected her there and then to have an attack of acute mania. She got up from the table, for we had finished our dinner.

'Let us go outside,' she said. 'If I hadn't the patience of an angel I'd have sacked that woman long ago.'

La Falterona and I went out, but Miss Glaser did not come with us. We sat on the veranda. There was a magnificent cedar in the garden, and its dark branches were silhouetted against the starry sky. The sea, almost at our feet, was marvellously still. Suddenly La Falterona gave a start.

'I almost forgot. Glaser, you fool,' she shouted, 'why didn't you remind me?' And then again to me: 'I'm furious with you.'

'I'm glad you didn't remember till after dinner,' I answered.

'That friend of yours and his book.'

I didn't immediately grasp what she was talking about.

'What friend and what book?'

'Don't be so stupid. An ugly little man with a shiny face and a bad figure. He wrote a book about me.'

'Oh! Peter Melrose. But it's not about you.'

'Of course it is. Do you take me for a fool? He had the impudence to send it me.'

'I hope you had the decency to acknowledge it.'

'Do you think I have the time to acknowledge all the books twopenny-halfpenny authors send me? I expect Glaser wrote to him. You had no right to ask me to dinner to meet him. I came to oblige you, because I thought you liked me for myself, I didn't know I was just being made use of. It's awful that one can't trust one's oldest friends to behave like gentlemen. I'll never dine with you again so long as I live. Never, never, never.'

She was working herself into one of her tantrums, so I interrupted her before it was too late.

'Come off it, my dear,' I said. 'In the first place the character of the singer in that book, which I suppose is the one you're referring to . . .'

'You don't suppose I'm referring to the charwoman, do you?'

'Well, the character of the singer was roughed out before he'd even seen you, and besides, it isn't in the least like you.'

'How d'you mean, it's not like me? All my friends have recognized me. I mean, it's the most obvious portrait.'

'Mary,' I expostulated.

'My name is Maria and no one knows it better than you, and if you can't call me Maria you can call me Madame Falterona or Princess.'

I paid no attention to this.

'Did you read the book?'

'Of course I read it. When everyone told me it was about me.'

'But the boy's heroine, the *prima donna*, is twenty-five.'

'A woman like me is ageless.'

'She's musical to her finger-tips, gentle as a dove, and a miracle of unselfishness; she's frank, loyal, and disinterested. Is that the opinion you have of yourself?'

'And what is *your* opinion of me?'

'Hard as nails, absolutely ruthless, a born intriguer, and as self-centred as they make 'em.'

She then called me a name which a lady does not habitually apply to a gentleman who, whatever his faults, has never had his legitimacy called in question. But though her eyes flashed I could see that she was not in the least angry. She accepted my description of her as complimentary.

'And what about the emerald ring? Are you going to deny that I told him that?'

The story of the emerald ring was this: La Falterona was having a passionate love-affair with the Crown Prince of a powerful state and he had made her a present of an emerald of immense value. One night they had a quarrel, high words passed, and some reference being made to the ring she tore it off her finger and flung it in the fire. The Crown Prince, being a man of thrifty habit, with a cry of consternation, threw himself on his knees and began raking out the coals till he recovered the ring. La Falterona watched him scornfully as he grovelled on the floor. She didn't give much away herself, but she could not bear economy in others. She finished the story with these splendid words:

'After that I *couldn't* love him.'

The incident was picturesque and had taken Peter's fancy. He had used it very neatly.

'I told you both about that in the greatest confidence and I've never told it to a soul before. It's a scandalous breach of confidence to have put it into a book. There are no excuses either for him or for you.'

'But I've heard you tell the story dozens of times. And it was told me by Florence Montgomerie about herself and the Crown Prince Rudolf. It was one of her favourite stories too. Lola Montez used to tell it about herself and the King of Bavaria. I have little doubt that Nell Gwyn told it about herself and Charles II. It's one of the oldest stories in the world.'

She was taken aback, but only for an instant.

'I don't see anything strange in its having happened more than once. Everyone knows that women are passionate and that men are as mean as cat's-meat. I could show you the emerald if you liked. I had to have it reset, of course.'

'With Lola Montez it was pearls,' I said ironically. 'I believe they were considerably damaged.'

'Pearls?' She gave that brilliant smile of hers. 'Have I ever told you about Benjy Riesenbaum and the pearls? You might make a story out of it.'

Benjy Riesenbaum was a person of great wealth, and it was common knowledge that for a long time he had been the Falterona's lover. In fact it was he who had bought her the luxurious little villa in which we were now sitting.

'He'd given me a very handsome string in New York. I was singing at the Metropolitan, and at the end of the season we travelled back to Europe together. You never knew him, did you?'

'No.'

'Well, he wasn't bad in some ways, but he was insanely jealous. We had a row on the boat because a young Italian officer was paying me a good deal of attention. Heaven knows, I'm the easiest woman in the world to get on with, but I will not be bullied by any man. After all, I have my self-respect to think of. I told him where he got off, if you understand what I mean, and he slapped my face. On deck if you please. I don't mind telling you I was mad. I tore the string of pearls off my neck and flung it in the sea. "They cost fifty thousand dollars," he gasped. He went white. I drew myself up to my full height. "I only valued them because I loved you," I said. And I turned on my heel.'

'You were a fool,' I said.

'I wouldn't speak to him for twenty-four hours. At the end of that time I had him eating out of my hand. When we got to Paris the first thing he did was to go to Cartier's and buy me another just as good.'

She began to giggle.

'Did you say I was a fool? I'd left the real string in the bank in New York, because I knew I was going back next season. It was an imitation one that I threw in the sea.'

She started to laugh, and her laugh was rich and joyous and like a child's. That was the sort of trick that thoroughly appealed to her. She chortled with glee.

'What fools men are,' she gasped. 'And you, you thought I'd throw a real string into the sea.'

She laughed and laughed. At last she stopped. She was excited.

'I want to sing. Glaser, play an accompaniment.'

A voice came from the drawing-room.

'You can't sing after all that food you walloped down.'

'Shut up, you old cow. Play something, I tell you.'

There was no reply, but in a moment Miss Glaser began to play the opening bars of one of Schumann's songs. It was no strain on the voice, and I guessed that Miss Glaser knew what she was doing when she chose it. La Falterona began to sing, in an undertone, but as she heard the sounds come from her lips and found that they were clear and pure she let herself go. The song finished. There was silence. Miss Glaser had heard that La Falterona was in magnificent voice, and she sensed that she wished to sing again. The *prima donna* was standing in the window, with her back to the lighted room, and she looked out at the darkly shining sea. The cedar made a lovely pattern against the sky. The night was soft and balmy. Miss Glaser played a couple of bars. A cold shiver ran down my spine. La Falterona gave a little start as she recognized the music, and I felt her gather herself together:

> *Mild und leise wie er lächelt*
> *Wie das Auge er öffnet.*

It was Isolde's death song. She had never sung in Wagner, fearing the strain on her voice, but this, I suppose, she had often sung in concerts. It did not matter now that instead of an orchestral accompaniment she had only the thin tinkle of a piano. The notes of the heavenly melody fell upon the still air and travelled over the water. In that too romantic scene, in that starry night, the effect was shattering. La Falterona's voice, even now, was exquisite in its quality, mellow and crystalline; and she sang with wonderful emotion, so tenderly, with such tragic, beautiful anguish that my heart melted within me. I had a most awkward lump in my throat when she finished, and looking at her I saw that tears were streaming down her face. I did not want to speak. She stood quite still looking out at that ageless sea.

What a strange woman! I thought then that I would sooner have her as she was, with her monstrous faults, than as Peter Melrose saw her, a pattern of all the virtues. But then people blame me because I rather like people who are a little worse than is reasonable. She was hateful, of course, but she was irresistible.

THE LION'S SKIN

A GOOD many people were shocked when they read that Captain Forestier had met his death in a forest fire when trying to save his wife's dog, which had been accidentally shut up in the house. Some said they never knew he had it in him; others said it was exactly what they would have expected of him, but of these some meant it in one way and some in another. After the tragic occurrence Mrs Forestier found shelter in the villa of some people called Hardy, whose acquaintance she and her husband had but lately made. Captain Forestier had not liked them, at any rate he had not liked Fred Hardy, but she felt that if he had lived through that terrible night he would have changed his mind. He would have realized how much good there was in Hardy notwithstanding his reputation, and like the great gentleman he was he would not have hesitated to admit that he had been mistaken. Mrs Forestier did not know how she could ever have kept her reason after the loss of the man who was everything in the world to her but for the Hardy's wonderful kindness. In her immense distress their unfailing sympathy had been her only consolation. They, who had been almost eye-witnesses of her husband's great sacrifice, knew as did no one else how wonderful he had been. She could never forget the words dear Fred Hardy had used when he was breaking the dreadful news to her. It was these words that had enabled her not only to bear the frightful disaster, but to face the desolate future with the courage with which she well knew that brave man, that gallant gentleman, whom she had loved so well, would have wished her to face it.

Mrs Forestier was a very nice woman. Kindly people often say that of a woman when they can say nothing about her, and it has come to be looked upon as cold praise. I do not mean it as such. Mrs Forestier was neither charming, beautiful, nor intelligent; on the contrary she was absurd, homely and foolish; yet the more you knew her, the more you liked her, and when asked why, you found yourself forced to repeat that she was a very nice woman. She was as tall as the average man; she had a large mouth and a great hooked nose, pale-blue, short-sighted eyes, and big ugly hands. Her skin was lined and weather-beaten, but she made up heavily, and her hair, which she wore long, was dyed golden, tightly marcelled and elaborately dressed. She did everything she could to counteract the aggressive masculinity of her appearance, and succeeded only in looking like a vaudeville artist doing a female impersonation. Her voice was a woman's voice, but you were always expecting her, at the end of the number as it were, to break into a deep bass, and tearing off that golden wig, discover a man's bald pate. She spent a great deal of money on her clothes, which she got from the most fashionable dressmakers in Paris, but though a woman of fifty she had an unfortunate taste for choosing dresses that looked exquisite on pretty little mannequins in the flower of their youth. She always wore a great quantity of rich jewels. Her movements were awkward and her gestures clumsy. If she went into a drawing-room where there was a valuable piece of jade she managed to sweep it on the floor; if she lunched with you and you had a set of glasses you treasured she was almost certain to smash one of them to atoms.

Yet this ungainly exterior sheltered a tender, romantic, and idealistic soul. It took you some time to discover this, for when first you knew her you took her for a figure of fun, and then when you knew her better (and had suffered from her clumsiness) she exasperated you; but when you did discover it, you thought yourself very stupid not to have known it all the time, for then it looked out at you through those pale-blue, near-sighted eyes, rather shyly, but with a sincerity that only a fool could miss. Those dainty muslins and spring-like organdies, those virginal silks, clothed not the uncouth body but the fresh, girlish spirit. You forgot that she broke your china and looked like a man dressed up as a woman, you saw her as she saw herself, as indeed she really was if reality were visible, as a dear little thing with a heart of gold. When you came to know her you found her as simple as a child; she was touchingly grateful for any attention you paid her; her own kindness was infinite, you could ask her to do anything for you, however tiresome, and she would do it as though by giving her the opportunity to put herself out you rendered her a service. She had a rare capacity for disinterested love. You knew that never an unkind nor a malicious thought had once passed through her head. And having granted all that you said over again that Mrs Forestier was a very nice woman.

Unfortunately she was also a damned fool. This you discovered when you met her husband. Mrs Forestier was American and Captain Forestier was English. Mrs Forestier was born in Portland, Oregon, and had never been to Europe till the war of 1914, when, her first husband having recently died, she joined a hospital unit and came to France. She was not rich by American standards, but by our English ones in affluent circumstances. From the way the Foresters lived I should guess that she had something like thirty thousand dollars a year. Except that she undoubtedly gave the wrong medicines to the wrong men, put on their bandages so that they were worse than useless, and broke every utensil that was breakable, I am sure that she was an admirable nurse. I do not think she ever found work too revolting for her to do it without hesitation; she certainly never spared herself and was surely never out of temper; I have a notion that many a poor wretch had cause to bless the tenderness of her heart, and it may be that not a few took the last bitter step into the unknown with more courage because of the loving-kindness of her golden soul. It was during the last year of the war that Captain Forestier came under her care, and soon after peace was declared they married. They settled down in a handsome villa on the hills behind Cannes, and in a short time became conspicuous in the social life of the Riviera. Captain Forestier played bridge well and was a keen golfer. He was not a bad tennis player either. He had a sailing boat, and in the summer the Foresters gave very nice parties between the islands. After seventeen years of marriage Mrs Forestier still adored her good-looking husband, and you were unlikely to know her long without being told in that slow Western drawl of hers the full story of their courtship.

'It was a case of love at first sight,' she said. 'He was brought in when I happened to be off duty, and when I came on and found him lying in one of my beds, oh, my dear, I felt such a pang in my heart, for a moment I thought I'd been overworking and had strained it. He was the handsomest man I'd ever seen in my life.'

'Was he badly wounded?'

'Well, he wasn't exactly wounded. You know, it's a most extraordinary thing, he went all through the war, he was under fire for months at a time, and of course he risked his life twenty times a day, he's one of those men who simply doesn't know what fear is; but he never even got a scratch. He had carbuncles.'

It seemed an unromantic ailment on which to start a passionate attachment. Mrs Forestier was a trifle prudish, and though Captain Forestier's carbuncles greatly interested her she always found it a little difficult to tell you exactly where they were.

'They were right down at the bottom of his back, even farther really, and he hated to have me dress them. Englishmen are curiously modest, I've noticed that over and over again, and it mortified him terribly. You'd have thought being on those terms, if you know what I mean, from our first acquaintance it would have made us more intimate. But somehow it didn't. He was very stand-offish with me. When I used to get to his bed on my round I was so breathless and my heart beat so I couldn't make out what was the matter with me. I'm not naturally a clumsy woman, I never drop things or break anything; but you wouldn't believe it, when I had to give Robert his medicine I used to drop the spoon and break the glass, I couldn't imagine what he must be thinking of me.'

It was almost impossible not to laugh when Mrs Forestier told you this. She smiled rather sweetly.

'I suppose it sounds very absurd to you, but you see I'd never felt that way before. When I married my first husband – well, he was a widower with grown-up children, he was a fine man and one of the most prominent citizens in the state, but somehow it was different.'

'And how did you eventually discover that you were in love with Captain Forestier?'

'Well, I don't ask you to believe me, I know it sounds funny, but the fact is that one of the other nurses told me, and as soon as she did of course I knew it was true. I was terribly upset at first. You see, I knew nothing about him. Like all Englishmen he was very reserved and for all I knew he had a wife and half a dozen children.'

'How did you find out he hadn't?'

'I asked him. The moment he told me he was a bachelor I made up my mind that by hook or by crook I was going to marry him. He suffered agonies, poor darling; you see, he had to lie on his face almost all the time, lying on his back was torture, and as to sitting down – well, of course he couldn't even think of that. But I don't believe his agonies were worse than mine. Men like clinging silks and soft, fluffy things, you know what I mean, and I was at such a disadvantage in my nurse's uniform. The matron, one of those New England spinsters, couldn't bear make-up, and in those days I didn't make up anyway; my first husband never liked it; and then my hair wasn't as pretty as it is now. He used to look at me with those wonderful blue eyes of his, and I felt he must be thinking I looked a perfect sight. He was very low and I thought I ought to do all I could to cheer him up, so whenever I had a few minutes to spare I'd go and talk to him. He said he couldn't bear the thought of a strong, husky chap like he was lying in bed week after week while all his pals were in the trenches. You couldn't talk to him without realizing that he was one of those men who never feel the joy of life so intensely as when the bullets are whistling all round them, and the next moment may be their last. Danger was a stimulant to him. I don't mind telling you that when I used to write down his temperature on the chart I added a point or two so that the doctors should think him a little worse than he was. I knew he was doing his damnedest to get them to discharge him, and I thought it only fair to him to make sure that they wouldn't. He used to look at me thoughtfully while I talked away and I know he looked forward to our little chats. I told him that I was a widow and had no one dependent on me, and I told him that I was thinking of settling down in Europe after the war. Gradually he thawed a little. He didn't say much about himself, but he began to chaff me, he has a great sense of humour, you know, and sometimes I really began to think he rather liked me. At last they reported him fit for duty. To my surprise he asked me to dine with him on his last evening. I managed to get leave from the matron and we drove in to Paris. You can't imagine how handsome he looked in his uniform. I've never seen anyone look so distinguished. Aristocratic to his finger-tips. Somehow or other he wasn't in such good spirits as I'd expected. He'd been crazy to get back to the front.

'"Why are you so down tonight?" I asked him. "After all, you've got your wish at last."

'"I know I have," he said. "If for all that I'm a bit blue, can't you guess why?"

'I simply dared not think what he meant. I thought I'd better make a little joke.

'"I'm not very good at guessing," I said, with a laugh. "If you want me to know you'd better tell me."

'He looked down and I could see he was nervous.

'"You've been most awfully good to me," he said. "I can never begin to thank you for all your kindness. You're the grandest woman I've ever known."

'It upset me terribly to hear him say that. You know how funny Englishmen are; he'd never paid me a compliment before.

'"I've only done what any competent nurse would have," I said.

'"Shall I ever see you again?" he said.

'"That's up to you," I said.

'I hoped he didn't hear the tremble in my voice.

'"I hate leaving you," he said.

267

'I really could hardly speak.

'"Need you?" I said.

'"So long as my King and Country want me I am at their service."'

When Mrs Forestier reached this point her pale blue eyes filled with tears.

'"But the war can't last for ever," I said.

'"When the war ends," he answered, "supposing a bullet hasn't put an end to me, I shan't have a penny. I don't even know how I shall set about earning my living. You're a very rich woman; I'm a pauper."

'"You're an English gentleman," I said.

'"Will that matter very much when the world has been made safe for democracy?" he said bitterly.

'I was just crying my eyes out by then. Everything he said was so beautiful. Of course I saw what he meant. He didn't think it honourable to ask me to marry him. I felt he'd sooner die than let me think he was after my money. He was a fine man. I knew that I wasn't worthy of him, but I saw that if I wanted him I must go out and get him myself.

'"It's no good pretending I'm not crazy about you, because I am," I said.

'"Don't make it harder for me," he said hoarsely.

'I thought I should die, I loved him so much when he said that. It told me all I wanted to know. I stretched out my hand.

'"Will you marry me, Robert?" I said, very simply.

'"Eleanor," he said.

'It was then he told me that he'd loved me from the first day he ever saw me. At first he hadn't taken it seriously, he thought I was just a nurse and perhaps he'd have an affair with me, and then when he found out that I wasn't that sort of woman and had a certain amount of money, he made up his mind that he must conquer his love. You see, he thought that marriage was quite out of the question.'

Probably nothing flattered Mrs Forestier more than the idea that Captain Forestier had wanted to have a slap and tickle with her. It was certain that no one else had ever made dishonourable proposals to her, and though Forestier hadn't either, the conviction that he had entertained the notion was a never-failing source of satisfaction to her. When they were married Eleanor's relations, hard-bitten Western people, had suggested that her husband should go to work rather than live on her money, and

Captain Forestier was all for it. The only stipulation he made was this:

'There are some things a gentleman can't do, Eleanor. Anything else I'll do gladly. God knows, I don't attach any importance to that sort of thing, but if one's a sahib one can't help it, and damn it all, especially in these days, one does owe something to one's class.'

Eleanor thought he had done enough in risking his life for his country in one bloody battle after another during four long years, but she was too proud of him to let it be said that he was a fortune-hunter who had married her for her money, and she made up her mind not to object if he found something to do that was worth his while. Unfortunately, the only jobs that offered were not very important. But he did not turn them down on his own responsibility.

'It's up to you, Eleanor,' he told her. 'You've only got to say the word and I'll take it. It would make my poor old governor turn in his grave to see me do it, but that can't be helped. My first duty is to you.'

Eleanor wouldn't hear of it, and gradually the idea of his working was dropped. The Forestiers lived most of the year in their villa on the Riviera. They seldom went to England; Robert said it was no place for a gentleman since the war, and all the good fellows, white men every one of them, that he used to go about with when he was 'one of the boys', had been killed. He would have liked to spend his winters in England, three days a week with the Quorn, that was the life for a man, but poor Eleanor, she would be so out of it in that hunting set, he couldn't ask her to make the sacrifice. Eleanor was prepared to make any sacrifice, but Captain Forestier shook his head. He wasn't as young as he had been, and his hunting days were over. He was quite satisfied to breed Sealyhams and raise Buff Orpingtons. They had a good deal of land; the house stood on the top of a hill, on a plateau, surrounded on three sides by forest, and in front they had a garden. Eleanor said he was never so happy as when he was walking round the estate in an old tweed suit with the kennel-man, who also looked after the chickens. It was then you saw in him all those generations of country squires that he had behind him. It touched and amused Eleanor to see the long talks he had with the kennel-man about the Buff Orpingtons; it was for all the world as if he were discussing the pheasants with his head keeper: and he fussed over the Sealyhams as much as if they had been the pack of hounds you couldn't help feeling he would have been so much more at home with. Captain Forestier's great-grandfather had been one of the bucks of the Regency. It was he who had ruined the family so that the estates had to be sold. They had a wonderful old place in Shropshire, they'd had it for centuries, and Eleanor, even though it no longer belonged to them, would have liked to go and see it; but Captain Forestier said it would be too painful to him and would never take her.

The Forestiers entertained a good deal. Captain Forestier was a connoisseur of wines and was proud of his cellar.

'His father was well known to have the best palate in England,' said Eleanor, 'and he's inherited it.'

Most of their friends were Americans, French, and Russians. Robert found them on the whole more interesting than the English, and Eleanor liked everybody he liked. Robert did not think the English quite up to their mark. Most of the people he had known in the old days belonged to the shooting, hunting, and fishing set; they, poor devils, were all broke now, and though, thank God, he wasn't a snob, he didn't half like the idea of his wife getting herself mixed up with a lot of *nouveaux riches* no one had ever heard of. Mrs Forestier was not nearly so particular, but she respected his prejudices and admired his exclusiveness.

'Of course he has his whims and fancies,' she said, 'but I think it's only loyal on my part to defer to them. When you know the sort of people he comes from you can't help seeing how natural it is he should have them. The only time I've ever seen him vexed in all the years we've been married was when once a gigolo came up to me in the Casino and asked me to dance. Robert nearly knocked him down. I told him the poor little thing was only doing his job, but he said he wasn't going to have a damned swine like that even asking his wife to dance.'

Captain Forestier had high moral standards. He thanked God that he wasn't narrow-minded, but one had to draw the line somewhere; and just because he lived on the Riviera he didn't see why he should hob-nob with drunks, wastrels, and perverts. He had no indulgence for sexual irregularities and would not allow Eleanor to frequent women of doubtful reputation.

'You see,' said Eleanor, 'he's a man of complete integrity; he's the cleanest man I've ever known; and if sometimes he seems a little intolerant you must always remember that he never asks of others what he isn't prepared to do himself. After all, one

270

can't help admiring a man whose principles are so high and who's prepared to stick to them at any cost.'

When Captain Forestier told Eleanor that such and such a man, whom you met everywhere, and who you thought was rather pleasant, wasn't a pukkah sahib, she knew it was no good insisting. She knew that in her husband's judgement that finished him, and she was prepared to abide by it. After nearly twenty years of marriage she was sure of one thing, if of no other, and this was that Robert Forestier was the perfect type of an English gentleman.

'And I don't know that God has ever created anything finer than that,' she said.

The trouble was that Captain Forestier was almost too perfect a type of the English gentleman. He was at forty-five (he was two or three years younger than Eleanor) still a very handsome man, with his wavy, abundant grey hair and his handsome moustache; he had the weather-beaten, healthy, tanned skin of a man who is much in the open air. He was tall, lean, and broad-shouldered. He looked every inch a soldier. He had a bluff, hearty way with him and a loud, frank laugh. In his conversation, in his manner, in his dress he was so typical that you could hardly believe it. He was so much of a country gentleman that he made you think rather of an actor giving a marvellous performance of the part. When you saw him walking along the Croisette, a pipe in his mouth, in plus-fours and just the sort of tweed coat he would have worn on the moors, he looked so like an English sportsman that it gave you quite a shock. And his conversation, the way he dogmatized, the platitudinous inanity of his statements, his amiable, well-bred stupidity, were all so characteristic of the retired officer that you could hardly help thinking he was putting it on.

When Eleanor heard that the house at the bottom of their hill had been taken by a Sir Frederick and Lady Hardy she was much pleased. It would be nice for Robert to have as a near neighbour someone of his own class. She made inquiries about them from her friends in Cannes. It appeared that Sir Frederick had lately come into the baronetcy on the death of an uncle and was come to the Riviera for two or three years while he was paying off the death duties. He was said to have been very wild in his youth, he was well on in the fifties when he came to Cannes, but now he was respectably married, to a very nice little woman, and had two small boys. It was a pity that Lady Hardy had been an actress. for Robert was apt to be a little stuffy about actresses but everyone said that she was very well-mannered and ladylike, and you would never have guessed she had been on the stage. The Forestiers met her first at a tea-party to which Sir Frederick did not go, and Robert acknowledged that she seemed a very decent sort of person; so Eleanor, wishing to be neighbourly, invited them both to luncheon. A day was arranged. The Forestiers had asked a good many people to meet them, and the Hardys were rather late. Eleanor took an immediate fancy to Sir Frederick. He looked much younger than she expected, he hadn't a white hair on his close-cropped head; indeed there was about him something boyish that was rather attractive. He was slightly built, not as tall as she was; and he had bright friendly eyes and a ready smile. She noticed that he wore the same Guards tie that Robert sometimes wore; he was not nearly so well-dressed as Robert, who always looked as though he had stepped out of a show-window, but he wore his old clothes as though it didn't much matter what one wore. Eleanor could quite believe he had been a trifle wild as a young man. She was not inclined to blame him.

'I must introduce my husband to you,' she said.

She called him. Robert was talking to some of the other guests on the terrace, and hadn't noticed the Hardys come in. He came forward and in his affable, hearty way, with a grace that always charmed Eleanor, shook hands with Lady Hardy. Then he turned to Sir Frederick. Sir Frederick gave him a puzzled look.

'Haven't we met before?' he said.

Robert looked at him coolly.

'I don't think so.'

'I could have sworn I knew your face.'

Eleanor felt her husband stiffen and at once realized that something was going wrong. Robert laughed.

'It sounds terribly rude, but to the best of my belief I've never set eyes on you in my life. We may have run across one another in the war. One met such hosts of fellers, then, didn't one? Will you have a cocktail, Lady Hardy?'

During luncheon Eleanor noticed that Hardy kept looking at Robert. He was evidently trying to place him. Robert was busy with the women on either side of him and did not catch the glances. He was making efforts to entertain his neighbours; and his loud, ringing laugh rang through the room. He was a wonderful host. Eleanor had always admired his sense of social duty; however dull the women were he was sitting next to he gave them of his best. But when their guests had gone Robert's gaiety dropped from him like a cloak from his shoulders. She had a feeling that he was upset.

'Was the princess very boring?' she asked kindly.

'She's a malignant old cat, but otherwise she was all right.'

'Funny that Sir Frederick thought he knew you.'

'I've never set eyes on him in my life. But I know all about him. I wouldn't have more to do with him than you can help if I were you, Eleanor. I don't think he's quite our mark.'

'But it's one of the oldest baronetcies in England. We looked it out in *Who's Who*.'

'He's a disreputable scamp. I didn't dream that the Captain Hardy,' Robert corrected himself, 'the Fred Hardy I used to know about in the old days was now Sir Frederick. I would never have allowed you to ask him to my house.'

'Why, Robert? I'm bound to tell you that I thought him very attractive.'

For once Eleanor thought her husband rather unreasonable.

'A great many women have found him so, and a pretty penny it's cost them.'

'You know how people talk. One really can't believe everything one hears.'

He took one of her hands in his and looked earnestly into her eyes.

'Eleanor, you know I'm not the sort of chap to say anything against another chap behind his back, and I'd rather not tell you what I know about Hardy; I can only ask you to take my word for it that he isn't a proper person for you to know.'

This was an appeal to which Eleanor was incapable of turning a deaf ear. It thrilled her to know that Robert placed such confidence in her: he knew that in a crisis he had only to call on her loyalty and she would not fail him.

'No one can be better aware than I, Robert,' she answered gravely, 'of your perfect integrity; I know that if you could tell me you would, but even if you wanted to now I wouldn't let you; it would look as if I had less confidence in you than you have in me. I am willing to abide by your judgement. I promise you that the Hardys shall never darken these doors again.'

But Eleanor often lunched out without Robert, when he was playing golf, and so frequently met the Hardys. She was very stiff with Sir Frederick, because if Robert disapproved of him, she must too; but he either did not notice or did not care. He went out of his way to be nice to her and she found him easy to get on with. It was difficult to dislike a man who plainly thought that no woman was better than she should be, but very sweet for all that, and who had such delightful manners. It might be that he was an improper man for her to know, but she couldn't help liking the look in his brown eyes. It was a mocking look, which put you on your guard, and yet so caressing that you could not think he meant you harm. But the more Eleanor heard about him, the more she realized how right Robert was. He was an unprincipled rascal. They mentioned the names of women who had sacrificed everything for his sake and whom he had thrown aside without ceremony the moment he was tired of them. He seemed to have settled down now, and to be devoted to his wife and children; but can the leopard change his spots? It was only too probable that Lady Hardy had more to put up with than anyone suspected.

Fred Hardy was a bad lot. Pretty women, *chemin de fer*, and an unlucky knack for backing the wrong horse had landed him in the bankruptcy court by the time he was twenty-five, and he had been forced to resign his commission. He had seen no shame then in allowing women no longer in their first youth, who found his charm irresistible, to supply his wants. But the war came, he rejoined his regiment, and got a D.S.O. Then he went out to Kenya, where he found occasion to become co-respondent in a notorious divorce case; he left Kenya over some trouble with a cheque. His ideas of honesty were lax. It was unsafe to buy a car or a horse off him, and you did much better to keep away from the champagnes he warmly recommended to you. When with his persuasive charm he put before you a speculation by which you and he would make a fortune, you could only be sure that whatever he made out of it you would make nothing. He was in turn a motor-salesman, an outside broker, a commission agent, and an actor. Were there any justice in the world he should have ended if not in gaol at least in the gutter. But by one of fate's monstrous tricks, having at last inherited his baronetcy and an adequate income, having married when well over forty a pretty, clever wife to whom were in due course born two healthy and handsome children, the future offered him affluence, position, and respectability. He had never taken life any more seriously than he took women, and life had been as kind to him as women. If he thought of his past it was with complacency; he had had a good time, he had enjoyed his ups and downs; and now, with good health and a clear conscience, he was prepared to settle down as a country gentleman, damn it, bring up the kids as kids should be brought up; and when the old buffer who sat for his constituency pegged out, by George, go into Parliament himself.

'I could tell them a thing or two they don't know,' he said.

He was probably right, but he did not stop to reflect that perhaps they were not things they much wanted to know.

One afternoon, about sunset, Fred Hardy went into one of the bars on the Croisette. He was a sociable creature and did not care to drink alone, so he looked around to see if there were anyone he knew. He caught sight of Robert, who had been playing golf and was waiting there for Eleanor.

'Hulloa, Bob, what about having a tiddly?'

Robert gave a start. No one on the Riviera called him Bob. When he saw who it was he answered stiffly:

'I've got a drink, thanks.'

'Have another. My old lady don't approve of my drinking between meals, but when I can manage to get away from her I generally slip in and have one about this time. I don't know what you think about it, but my feeling is that God made six o'clock for man to have a drink at.'

He flung himself into a great leather arm-chair next to the one Robert was sitting in and called a waiter. He gave Robert his good-natured, engaging smile.

'A lot of water has passed under the bridges since first we met, old boy, hasn't it?'

Robert, frowning a little, shot a look at him which an observer might have described as wary.

'I don't know exactly what you mean. To the best of my belief we met for the first time three or four weeks ago when you and your wife were good enough to come and have lunch with us.'

'Come off it, Bob. I knew I'd seen you before. I was puzzled at first and then it flashed across me. You were the car-washer at that garage off Bruton Street where I used to keep my car.'

Captain Forestier gave a hearty laugh.

'I'm sorry, but you've made a mistake. I never heard anything so ridiculous.'

'I've got a damned good memory and I never forget a face. I bet you haven't forgotten me either. Many's the half-crown I've given you for fetching the car away from my flat when I didn't want to be bothered to bring it round to the garage myself.'

'You're talking absolute rot. I'd never seen you in my life till you came to my house.'

Hardy grinned cheerfully.

'You know I've always been a Kodak-fiend. I've got albums of snaps that I've taken at one time and another. Would it surprise you to learn that I've found a snap of you standing by a two-seater I'd just bought? A damned good-looking fellow you were in those days even though you had overalls on and your face was none too clean. Of course you've broadened out, your hair's grey and you've got a moustache, but it's the same chap. Unmistakably.'

Captain Forestier looked at him coolly.

'You must have been misled by an accidental resemblance. It was somebody else you gave your half-crowns to.'

'Well, where were you then, if you weren't a car-washer at the Bruton Garage between 1913 and 1914?'

'I was in India.'

'With your regiment?' asked Fred Hardy with another grin.

'I was shooting.'

'You liar.'

Robert flushed deeply.

'This isn't quite the place to choose for a scrap, but if you think I'm going to stay here to be insulted by a drunken swine like you, you're mistaken.'

'Wouldn't you like to hear what else I know about you? You know how things come back to one, and I've remembered quite a lot.'

'I'm not in the least interested. I tell you that you're making an absolute mistake. You're confusing me with somebody else.'

But he made no attempt to go.

'You were a bit of a slacker even in those days. I remember once, when I was going into the country early, I'd told you to have my car washed by nine and it wasn't ready, so I kicked up a row and old Thompson told me then your father had been a pal of his and he'd taken you on out of charity because you were down and out. Your father had been a wine waiter at one of the clubs, White's or Brooks's, I forget which, and you'd been a page-boy there yourself. You enlisted in the Coldstream Guards, if I remember right, and some chap bought you out and made you his valet.'

'It's too fantastic,' said Robert scornfully.

'And I remember, when I was home on leave once and went to the garage, old Thompson told me you'd enlisted in the A.S.C. You weren't going to take any more risks than you could help, were you? You've been drawing the long bow a bit, haven't you, with all those stories I hear of your gallantry in the trenches? I suppose you did get a commission, or is that a fake too?'

'Of course I got a commission.'

'Well, a lot of funny people did in those days, but you know, old boy, if it was in the A.S.C. I wouldn't wear a Guards tie if I were you.'

Captain Forestier instinctively put his hand up to his tie, and Fred Hardy, watching him with his mocking eyes, was pretty sure that notwithstanding his tan he went white.

'It's no business of yours what tie I wear.'

'Don't get snotty, old boy. There's no reason to get up on your hind legs. I've got the goods on you, but I'm not going to give you away, so why don't you come clean?'

'I've got nothing to come clean about. I tell you it's all an absurd mistake. And I should tell you that if I find that you've been spreading these lying stories about me, I shall immediately start proceedings for slander.'

'Stow it, Bob. I'm not going to spread any stories. You don't think I care? I think the whole thing's rather a lark. I've got no ill-feeling towards you. I've been a bit of an adventurer myself; I admire you for carrying off such a stupendous bluff. Starting as a page-boy and then being a trooper, a valet, and a car-washer, and there you are, a fine gentleman, with a grand house, entertaining all the big bugs of the Riviera, winning golf tournaments; vice-president of the Sailing Club, and I don't know what all. You're It in Cannes and no mistake. It's stupendous. I've done some pretty rum things in my day, but the nerve you must have; old boy, I take off my hat to you.'

'I wish I deserved your compliments. I don't. My father was in the Indian cavalry and I was at least born a gentleman. I may not have had a very distinguished career, but I certainly have nothing to be ashamed of.'

'Oh, come off it, Bob. I shan't split, you know, not even to my old lady. I never tell women anything that they don't know already. Believe me, I'd have got into even worse scrapes than I have if I hadn't made a rule of that. I should have thought you'd be glad to have someone around that you could be yourself with. Isn't it a strain never to let up? Silly of you to keep me at arm's length. I haven't got anything on you, old boy. It's true I'm a bart and a landed proprietor now, but I've been in some pretty tight places in my time, and it's a wonder to me that I've kept out of gaol.'

'It's a wonder to a good many other people.'

Fred Hardy broke into a guffaw.

'That's one on me, old boy. All the same, if you don't mind

my saying so, I think it was a bit thick your telling your wife I wasn't a proper person for her to associate with.'

'I never said anything of the sort.'

'Oh yes, you did. She's a grand old girl, but a bit garrulous, or am I mistaken?'

'I'm not prepared to discuss my wife with a man like you,' said Captain Forestier, coldly.

'Oh, don't be so damned gentlemanly with me, Bob. We're a couple of bums and that's all there is to it. We could have some grand times together if you'd only have a little sense. You're a liar, a humbug, and a cheat, but you seem to be very decent to your wife, and that's something in your favour. She just dotes upon you, doesn't she? Funny, women are. She's a very nice woman, Bob.'

Robert's face grew red, he clenched his fist and half rose from his chair.

'Damn you, stop talking about my wife. If you mention her name again I swear I'll knock you down.'

'Oh no, you won't. You're too great a gentleman to hit a feller smaller than yourself.'

Hardy had said these words mockingly, watching Robert, and quite ready to dodge if that great fist struck out; he was astounded at their effect. Robert sank back into his chair and unclenched his fist.

'You're right. But only a mean hound would trade on it.'

The reply was so theatrical that Fred Hardy began to chuckle, but then he saw that the man meant it. He was deadly serious. Fred Hardy was no fool; he could hardly have lived for twenty-five years on his wits in tolerable comfort unless he had had them all about him. And now, in amazement, staring at that heavy, powerful man, who looked so like the typical English sportsman, sunk back in the chair, he had a sudden flash of comprehension. He was no common swindler who had got hold of a silly woman to keep him in luxury and idleness. She was only a means to a greater end. He had been captivated by an ideal and in pursuit of it had stuck at nothing. Perhaps the notion had come to him when he was a page-boy in a smart club; the members, with their lounging ease, their casual manner, may have seemed very wonderful to him; and afterwards as a trooper, as a valet, as a car-washer, the many men he ran across, belonging to a different world and seen through a haze of hero-worship, had filled him perhaps with admiration and envy. He wanted to be like them. He wanted to be one of them. That was the ideal that haunted his dreams. He wanted – it was grotesque, it was pathetic – he wanted to be a gentleman. The war, with the commission it brought him, gave him his chance. Eleanor's money provided the means. That wretched fellow had spent twenty years pretending to be something the only value of which was that it wasn't a pretence. That was grotesque too; that was pathetic. Without meaning to, Fred Hardy uttered the thought that passed through his head.

'Poor old chap,' he said.

Forestier looked at him quickly. He could not understand what those words meant nor the tone in which they were said. He flushed.

'What d'you mean by that?'

'Nothing. Nothing.'

'I don't think we need continue this conversation. Apparently there's nothing I can say to persuade you that you're mistaken. I can only repeat that there's not a word of truth in it. I am not the fellow you think I am.'

'All right, old boy, have it your own way.'

Forestier called the waiter.

'D'you want me to pay for your drink?' he asked icily.

'Yes, old boy.'

Forestier somewhat grandly gave the waiter a note and told him to keep the change, then without a word, without giving Fred Hardy another look, stalked out of the bar.

They did not meet again till the night on which Robert Forestier lost his life.

The winter passed into spring, and the gardens on the Riviera were ablaze with colour. The hillsides were primly gay with wild flowers. The spring passed into summer. In the towns along the Riviera the streets were hot with a bright, eager heat that made the blood run faster; and women walked about in great straw hats and pyjamas. The beaches were crowded. Men in trunks and women almost naked lay in the sun. In the evening the bars on the Croisette were thronged by a restless, chattering crowd as many-coloured as the flowers of spring. It had not rained for weeks. There had been several forest fires along the coast, and Robert Forestier in his hearty, joking way had several times said that they would stand a pretty thin chance if they had a fire in their woods. One or two people had advised him to cut down some of the trees at the back of his house; but he couldn't bear to: they had been in poor condition when the Forestiers bought the place, but now that the dead wood had been cut away year by year, that they had been given air and kept clean of pests, they were magnificent.

'Why, it would be like having my leg chopped off to cut one of 'em down. They must be the best part of a hundred years old.'

On the fourteenth of July the Forestiers went over to a gala dinner at Monte Carlo, and they gave their staff leave to go to Cannes. It was the national holiday, and in Cannes they danced in the open air under the plane trees, there were fireworks, and from far and near the people came in to have a good time. The Hardys had sent their servants out too, but they were sitting at home, and their two little boys were in bed. Fred was playing patience and Lady Hardy was working at a piece of tapestry to cover a chair. Suddenly there was a ring of the bell and a loud knocking on the door.

'Who the devil's that?'

Hardy went to the door and found a boy who told him that fire had broken out in the Forestiers' woods. Some men had gone up from the village and were fighting it, but they needed all the help they could get, and would he come.

'Of course I'll come.' He hurried back to his wife and told her. 'Wake the kids and let them come up and see the fun. By George, after all this drought it'll be a blaze.'

He bolted out. The boy told him they had telephoned to the police station and they were going to send along the soldiers. Someone was trying to get through to Monte Carlo and let Captain Forestier know.

'It'll take him an hour to get here,' said Hardy.

As they ran they saw the glow in the sky, and when they came to the top of the hill, the leaping flames. There was no water and the only thing was to try to beat them out. Already a number of men were at work. Hardy joined them. But you had no sooner beat out the flames in one bush than another began to crackle and before you could look had turned into a fiery torch. The heat was terrific, and the workers, unable to support it, were slowly driven back. A breeze was blowing, and the sparks were carried from tree to bush. After weeks of drought everything was as dry as tinder, and the moment a spark fell the tree, the bush, went up in flames. If it had not been terrifying, it would have been awe-inspiring to see a great fir-tree, sixty feet high, blazing like matchwood. The fire roared like the fire in a factory furnace. The best way to put a stop to it was by cutting down trees and brushwood, but the men were few, and but two or three had axes. The only hope was in the troops, who were used to dealing with the forest fires, and the troops did not come.

'Unless they get here soon we shall never save the house,' said Hardy.

He caught sight of his wife, who had come up with the two boys, and waved to them. Already he was black with grime, and the sweat was pouring down his face. Lady Hardy ran up.

'Oh, Fred, the dogs and the chickens.'

'By George, yes.'

The kennels and the chicken-run were at the back of the house, in a clearing that had been cut in the woods, and the wretched animals were already frantic with terror. Hardy let them out and they rushed to safety. They could only be left to shift for themselves. They must be rounded up later. The blaze could be seen now from far away. But the troops did not come, and the small body of helpers were powerless against the advancing flames.

'If those damned soldiers don't get here soon the house is for it,' said Hardy. 'I think we'd better get what we can out of it.'

It was a stone house, but there were wooden verandas all round it, and they would burn like kindling. The Forestiers' servants had come by now. He got them together, his wife gave a hand, and the two boys; they carried out on to the lawn in front such things as were portable, linen and silver, clothes, ornaments, pictures, pieces of furniture. At last the troops came, two lorry-loads of them, and set about systematically digging trenches and felling trees. There was an officer in charge and Hardy, pointing out the danger to the house, begged him first of all to cut down the trees that surrounded it.

'The house must look after itself,' he said. 'I've got to prevent the fire spreading beyond the hill.'

The lights of a car were seen speeding along the winding road, and a few minutes later Forestier and his wife sprang out of it.

'Where are the dogs?' he cried.

'I've let them out,' said Hardy.

'Oh, it's you.'

At first in that filthy fellow, his face begrimed with soot and sweat, he had not recognized Fred Hardy. He frowned angrily.

'I thought the house might catch. I've got everything out I could.'

Forestier looked at the blazing forest.

'Well, that's the end of my trees,' he said.

'The soldiers are working on the side of the hill. They're

trying to save the next property. We'd better go along and see if we can save anything.'

'I'll go. You needn't,' Forestier cried irritably.

On a sudden Eleanor gave an anguished cry.

'Oh, look. The house.'

From where they stood they could see a veranda at the back suddenly burst into flames.

'That's all right, Eleanor. The house can't burn. It'll only get the woodwork. Take my coat; I'm going along to help the soldiers.'

He took off his dinner jacket and handed it to his wife.

'I'll come with you,' said Hardy. 'Mrs Forestier, you'd better go along to where your things are. I think we've got everything out that's valuable.'

'Thank heaven, I was wearing most of my jewellery.'

Lady Hardy was a woman of sense.

'Mrs Forestier, let's get the servants together and carry what we can down to our house.'

The two men walked towards where the soldiers were at work.

'It's very decent of you to have got that stuff out of my house,' said Robert, stiffly.

'Not at all,' answered Fred Hardy.

They had not gone far when they heard somebody calling. They looked round and vaguely saw a woman running after them.

'*Monsieur, Monsieur.*'

They stopped and the woman, her arms outstretched, rushed up. It was Eleanor's maid. She was distraught.

'*La petite Judy.* Judy. I shut her up when we went out. She's on heat. I put her in the servants' bathroom.'

'My God!' cried Forestier.

'What is it?'

'Eleanor's dog. I must save her at any cost.'

He turned round and started to run back to the house. Hardy caught hold of his arm to hold him.

'Don't be a damned fool, Bob. The house is burning. You can't go into it.'

Forestier struggled to release himself.

'Let me go, damn you. D'you think I'm going to let a dog be burned alive?'

'Oh, shut up. This is no time for play-acting!'

Forestier shook Hardy off, but Hardy sprang on him and seized him round the middle. Forestier with his clenched fist hit

Hardy in the face as hard as he could. Hardy staggered, releasing his hold, and Forestier hit him again; Hardy fell to the ground.

'You rotten bounder. I'll show you how a gentleman behaves.'

Fred Hardy picked himself up slowly and felt his face. It hurt him.

'God, the black eye I'm going to have tomorrow.' He was shaken and a trifle dazed. The maid suddenly broke into a storm of hysterical tears. 'Shut up, you slut,' he cried crossly. 'And don't say a word to your mistress.'

Forestier was nowhere to be seen. It was more than an hour before they were able to get at him. They found him lying on the landing outside the bathroom, dead, with the dead Sealyham in his arms. Hardy looked at him for a long time before speaking.

'You fool,' he muttered between his teeth, angrily. 'You damned fool!'

That imposture of his had paid him out at last. Like a man who cherishes a vice till it gets a stranglehold on him so that he is its helpless slave, he had lied so long that he had come to believe his own lies. Bob Forestier had pretended for so many years to be a gentleman that in the end, forgetting that it was all a fake, he had found himself driven to act as in that stupid, conventional brain of his he thought a gentleman must act. No longer knowing the difference between sham and real, he had sacrificed his life to a spurious heroism. But Fred Hardy had to break the news to Mrs Forestier. She was with his wife, in their villa at the bottom of the hill, and she still thought that Robert was with the soldiers cutting down trees and clearing the brushwood. He told her as gently as he could, but he had to tell her, and he had to tell her everything. At first it seemed as though she could not grasp the sense of what he said.

'Dead?' she cried. 'Dead? My Robert?'

Then Fred Hardy, the rip, the cynic, the unscrupulous ruffian, took her hands in his and said the words that alone enabled her to bear her anguish.

'Mrs Forestier, he was a very gallant gentleman.'

THE UNCONQUERED

HE came back into the kitchen. The man was still on the floor, lying where he had hit him, and his face was bloody. He was moaning. The woman had backed against the wall and was staring with terrified eyes at Willi, his friend, and when he came in she gave a gasp and broke into loud sobbing. Willi was sitting at the table, his revolver in his hand, with a half empty glass of wine beside him. Hans went up to the table, filled his glass and emptied it at a gulp.

'You look as though you'd had trouble, young fellow,' said Willi with a grin.

Hans's face was blood-stained and you could see the gashes of five sharp finger-nails. He put his hand gingerly to his cheek.

'She'd have scratched my eyes out if she could, the bitch. I shall have to put some iodine on. But she's all right now. You go along.'

'I don't know. Shall I? It's getting late.'

'Don't be a fool. You're a man, aren't you? What if it is getting late? We lost our way.'

It was still light and the westering sun streamed into the kitchen windows of the farm-house. Willi hesitated a moment. He was a little fellow, dark and thin-faced, a dress designer in civil life, and he didn't want Hans to think him a cissy. He got up and went towards the door through which Hans had come. When the woman saw what he was going to do she gave a shriek and sprang forwards.

'*Non, non,*' she cried.

With one step Hans was in front of her. He seized her by the shoulders and flung her violently back. She tottered and fell. He took Willi's revolver.

'Stop still, both of you,' he rasped in French, but with his guttural German accent. He nodded his head towards the door. 'Go on. I'll look after them.'

Willi went out, but in a moment was back again.

'She's unconscious.'

'Well, what of it?'

'I can't. It's no good.'

'Stupid, that's what you are. *Ein Weibchen.* A woman.'

Willi flushed.

'We'd better be getting on our way.'

284

Hans shrugged a scornful shoulder.

'I'll just finish the bottle of wine and then we'll go.'

He was feeling at ease and it would have been pleasant to linger. He had been on the job since morning and after so many hours on his motor-cycle his limbs ached. Luckily they hadn't far to go, only to Soissons – ten or fifteen kilometres. He wondered if he'd have the luck to get a bed to sleep in. Of course all this wouldn't have happened if the girl hadn't been a fool. They had lost their way, he and Willi, they had stopped a peasant working in a field and he had deliberately misled them, and they found themselves on a side road. When they came to the farm they stopped to ask for a direction. They'd asked very politely, for orders were to treat the French population well as long as they behaved themselves. The door was opened for them by the girl and she said she didn't know the way to Soissons, so they pushed in; then the woman, her mother, Hans guessed, told them. The three of them, the farmer, his wife and daughter, had just finished supper and there was a bottle of wine on the table. It reminded Hans that he was as thirsty as the devil. The day had been sweltering and he hadn't had a drink since noon. He asked them for a bottle of wine and Willi had added that they would pay them well for it. Willi was a good little chap, but soft. After all, they were the victors. Where was the French army? In headlong flight. And the English, leaving everything behind, had scuttled like rabbits back to their island. The conquerors took what they wanted, didn't they? But Willi had worked at a Paris dressmaker's for two years. It's true he spoke French well, that's why he had his present job, but it had done something to him. A decadent people. It did a German no good to live among them.

The farmer's wife put a couple of bottles of wine on the table and Willi took twenty francs out of his pocket and gave it to her. She didn't even say thank you. Hans's French wasn't as good as Willi's, but he could make himself understood, and he and Willi spoke it together all the time. Willi corrected his mistakes. It was because Willi was so useful to him in this way that he had made him his friend, and he knew that Willi admired him. He admired him because he was so tall, slim, and broad-shouldered, because his curly hair was so fair and his eyes so blue. He never lost an opportunity to practise his French, and he tried to talk now, but those three French people wouldn't meet him half-way. He told them that he was a farmer's son himself and when the war was over was going back to the farm. He had been sent to school in Munich because his mother wanted him to go into business, but his heart wasn't in it, and so after matriculating he had gone to an agricultural college.

'You came here to ask your way and now you know it,' said the girl. 'Drink up your wine and go.'

He had hardly looked at her before. She wasn't pretty, but she had fine dark eyes and a straight nose. Her face was very pale. She was plainly dressed, but somehow she didn't look quite like what she evidently was. There was a sort of distinction about her. Ever since the war started he'd heard fellows talk about the French girls. They had something the German girls hadn't. Chic, Willi said it was, but when he asked him just what he meant by that Willi could only say that you had to see it to understand. Of course he'd heard others say that they were mercenary and hard as nails. Well, they'd be in Paris in a week and he'd find out for himself. They said the High Command had already arranged for houses for the men to go to.

'Finish your wine and let's go,' said Willi.

But Hans was feeling comfortable and didn't want to be hurried.

'You don't look like a farmer's daughter,' he said to the girl.

'And so what?' she answered.

'She's a teacher,' said her mother.

'Then you've had a good education.' She shrugged her shoulders, but he went on good-humouredly in his bad French. 'You ought to understand that this is the best thing that has ever happened to the French people. We didn't declare war. You declared war. And now we're going to make France a decent country. We're going to put order into it. We're going to teach you to work. You'll learn obedience and discipline.'

She clenched her fists and looked at him, her eyes black with hatred. But she did not speak.

'You're drunk, Hans,' said Willi.

'I'm as sober as a judge. I'm only telling them the truth and they may just as well know it at once.'

'He's right,' she cried out, unable any longer to contain herself. 'You're drunk. Now go. Go.'

'Oh, you understand German, do you? All right, I'll go. But you must give me a kiss first.'

She took a step back to avoid him, but he seized her wrist.

'Father,' she cried. 'Father.'

The farmer flung himself on the German. Hans let go of her and with all his might hit him in the face. He crumpled up on the floor. Then, before she could escape him, he caught the girl in his arms. She gave him a swinging blow on the cheek. . . . He chuckled grimly.

'Is that how you take it when a German soldier wants to kiss you? You'll pay for this.'

With his great strength he pinioned her arms and was dragging her out of the door, but her mother rushed at him and catching him by the clothes tried to pull him away. With one arm holding the girl close to him, with the flat of his other hand he gave the woman a great push and she staggered back to the wall.

'Hans, Hans,' cried Willi.

'Shut up, damn you.'

He put his hands over the girl's mouth to stop her shrieking and carried her out of the room. That was how it had happened and you had to admit that she'd brought it on herself. She shouldn't have slapped him. If she'd given him the kiss he'd asked for he'd have gone away. He gave a glance at the farmer still lying where he had fallen and he could hardly help laughing at his funny face. There was a smile in his eyes when he looked at the woman cowering against the wall. Was she afraid it was her turn next? Not likely. He remembered a French proverb.

'*C'est le premier pas qui coûte*. There's nothing to cry about, old woman. It had to come sooner or later.' He put his hand to his hip pocket and pulled out a wallet. 'Look, here's a hundred francs so that mademoiselle can buy herself a new dress. There's not much left of that one.' He placed the note on the table and put his helmet back on his head. 'Let's go.'

They slammed the door behind them and got on their motor-cycles. The woman went into the parlour. Her daughter was lying on the divan. She was lying as he had left her and she was weeping bitterly.

Three months later Hans found himself in Soissons again. He had been in Paris with the conquering army and had ridden through the Arc de Triomphe on his motor-cycle. He had advanced with the army first to Tours and then to Bordeaux. He'd seen very little fighting. The only French soldiers he'd seen were prisoners. The campaign had been the greatest spree he could ever have imagined. After the armistice he had spent a month in Paris. He'd sent picture postcards to his family in Bavaria and bought them all presents. Willi, because he knew the city like the palm of his hand, had stayed on, but he and the rest of his unit were sent to Soissons to join the force that was holding it. It was a nice little town and he was comfortably billeted. Plenty to eat and champagne for less than a mark a bottle in German money. When he was ordered to proceed there it had occurred to him that it would be fun to go and have a look at the girl he'd had. He'd take her a pair of silk stockings to show there was no ill-feeling. He had a good bump of locality and he thought he would be able to find the farm without difficulty. So one afternoon, when he had nothing to do, he put the silk stockings in his pocket and got on his machine. It was a lovely autumn day, with hardly a cloud in the sky, and it was pretty, undulating country that he rode through. It had been fine and dry for so long that, though it was September, not even the restless poplars gave sign that the summer was drawing to an end. He took one wrong turning, which delayed him, but for all that he got to the place he sought in less than half an hour. A mongrel dog barked at him as he walked up to the door. He did not knock, but turned the handle and stepped in. The girl was sitting at the table peeling potatoes. She sprang to her feet when she saw the uniformed man.

'What d'you want?' Then she recognized him. She backed to the wall, clutching the knife in her hands. 'It's you. *Cochon*.'

'Don't get excited. I'm not going to hurt you. Look. I've brought you some silk stockings.'

'Take them away and take yourself off with them.'

'Don't be silly. Drop that knife. You'll only get hurt if you try to be nasty. You needn't be afraid of me.'

'I'm not afraid of you,' she said.

She let the knife fall to the floor. He took off his helmet and sat down. He reached out with his foot and drew the knife towards him.

'Shall I peel some of your potatoes for you?' She did not answer. He bent down for the knife and then took a potato out of the bowl and went to work on it. Her face hard, her eyes hostile, she stood against the wall and watched him. He smiled at her disarmingly. 'Why do you look so cross? I didn't do you much harm, you know. I was excited, we all were, they'd talked of the invincible French army and the Maginot line . . .' he finished the sentence with a chuckle. 'And the wine went to my head. You might have fared worse. Women have told me that I'm not a bad-looking fellow.'

She looked him up and down scornfully.

'Get out of here.'

'Not until I choose.'

'If you don't go my father will go to Soissons and complain to the general.'

'Much he'll care. Our orders are to make friends with the population. What's your name?'

'That's not your business.'

There was a flush in her cheeks now and her angry eyes were blazing. She was prettier than he remembered her. He hadn't done so badly. She had a refinement that suggested the city-dweller rather than the peasant. He remembered her mother saying she was a teacher. Because she was almost a lady it amused him to torment her. He felt strong and healthy. He passed his hand through his curly blond hair, and giggled when he thought that many girls would have jumped at the chance she had had. His face was so deeply tanned by the summer that his eyes were startlingly blue.

'Where are your father and mother?'

'Working in the fields.'

'I'm hungry. Give me a bit of bread and cheese and a glass of wine. I'll pay.'

She gave a harsh laugh.

'We haven't seen cheese for three months. We haven't enough bread to stay our hunger. The French took our horses a year ago and now the Boches have taken our cows, our pigs, our chickens, everything.'

'Well, they paid you for them.'

'Can we eat the worthless paper they gave us?'

She began to cry.

'Are you hungry?'

'Oh, no,' she answered bitterly, 'we can eat like kings on potatoes and bread and turnips and lettuce. Tomorrow my father's going to Soissons to see if he can buy some horse meat.'

'Listen, Miss. I'm not a bad fellow. I'll bring you a cheese, and I think I can get hold of a bit of ham.'

'I don't want your presents. I'll starve before I touch the food you swine have stolen from us.'

'We'll see,' he said good-humouredly.

He put on his hat, got up, and with an *Au revoir, mademoiselle*, walked out.

He wasn't supposed to go joy-riding round the country and he had to wait to be sent on an errand before he was able to get to the farm again. It was ten days later. He walked in as unceremoniously as before and this time he found the farmer and his wife in the kitchen. It was round about noon and the woman was stirring a pot on the stove. The man was seated at table. They gave him a glance when he came in, but there was no surprise in it. Their daughter had evidently told them of his visit. They did not speak. The woman went on with her cooking, and the man, a surly look on his face, stared at the oil-cloth on the table. But it required more than this to disconcert the good-humoured Hans.

'*Bonjour, la compagnie*,' he said cheerfully. 'I've brought you a present.'

He undid the package he had with him and set out a sizable piece of Gruyère cheese, a piece of pork, and a couple of tins of sardines. The woman turned round and he smiled when he saw the light of greed in her eyes. The man looked at the foodstuff sullenly. Hans gave him his sunny grin.

'I'm sorry we had a misunderstanding the first time I came here. But you shouldn't have interfered.'

At that moment the girl came in.

'What are you doing here?' she cried harshly. Then her eyes fell on the things he had brought. She swept them together and flung them at him. 'Take them away. Take them.'

But her mother sprang forward.

'Annette, you're crazy.'

'I won't take his presents.'

'It's our own food that they've stolen from us. Look at the sardines. They're Bordeaux sardines.'

She picked the things up. Hans looked at the girl with a mocking smile in his light blue eyes.

'Annette's your name, is it? A pretty name. Do you grudge your parents a little food? You said you hadn't had cheese for three months. I couldn't get any ham; I did the best I could.'

The farmer's wife took the lump of meat in her hands and pressed it to her bosom. You felt that she could have kissed it. Tears ran down Annette's cheeks.

'The shame of it,' she groaned.

'Oh, come now, there's no shame in a bit of Gruyère and a piece of pork.'

Hans sat down and lit a cigarette. Then he passed the packet over to the old man. The farmer hesitated for a moment, but the temptation was too strong for him; he took one and handed back the packet.

'Keep it,' said Hans. 'I can get plenty more.' He inhaled the smoke and blew a cloud of it from his nostrils. 'Why can't we be friends? What's done can't be undone. War is war, and, well, you know what I mean. I know Annette's an educated girl and I want her to think well of me. I expect we shall be in Soissons for quite a while and I can bring you something now and then to help out. You know, we do all we can to make friends with the townspeople, but they won't let us. They won't even look at us when we pass them in the street. After all, it was an accident, what happened that time I came here with Willi. You needn't be afraid of me. I'll respect Annette as if she was my own sister.'

'Why do you want to come here? Why can't you leave us alone?' asked Annette.

He really didn't know. He didn't like to say that he wanted a little human friendship. The silent hostility that surrounded them all at Soissons got on his nerves so that sometimes he wanted to go up to a Frenchman who looked at him as if he wasn't there and knock him down, and sometimes it affected him so that he was almost inclined to cry. It would be nice if he had some place to go where he was welcome. He spoke the truth when he said he had no desire for Annette. She wasn't the sort of woman he fancied. He liked women to be tall and full-breasted, blue-eyed, and fair-haired like himself; he liked them to be strong and hefty and well-covered. That refinement which he couldn't account for, that thin fine nose and those dark eyes, the long pale face – there was something intimidating about the girl, so that if he hadn't been excited by the great victories of the German armies, if he hadn't been so tired and yet so elated, if he hadn't drunk all that wine on an empty stomach, it would never have crossed his mind that he could have anything to do with her.

For a fortnight after that Hans couldn't get away. He'd left the food at the farm and he had no doubt that the old people had wolfed it. He wondered if Annette had eaten it too; he wouldn't have been surprised to discover that the moment his back was turned she had set to with the others. These French people, they couldn't resist getting something for nothing. They were weak and decadent. She hated him, yes, God, how she hated him, but pork was pork, and cheese was cheese. He thought of her quite a lot. It tantalized him that she should have such a loathing for him. He was used to being liked by women. It would be funny if one of these days she fell in love with him. He'd been her first lover and he'd heard the students at Munich over their beer saying that it was her first lover a woman loved, after that it was love. When he'd set his mind on getting a girl he'd never failed yet. Hans laughed to himself and a sly look came into his eyes.

At last he got his chance to go to the farm. He got hold of cheese and butter, sugar, a tin of sausages, and some coffee, and set off on his motor-cycle. But that time he didn't see Annette.

She and her father were at work in the fields. The old woman was in the yard and her face lit up when she saw the parcel he was bringing. She led him into the kitchen. Her hands trembled a little as she untied the string and when she saw what he had brought her eyes filled with tears.

'You're very good,' she said.

'May I sit down?' he asked politely.

'Of course.' She looked out of the window and Hans guessed that she wanted to make sure that Annette was not coming. 'Can I offer you a glass of wine.'

'I'd be glad of it.'

He was sharp enough to see that her greed for food had made her, if not friendly to him, at least willing to come to terms with him. That look out of the window made them almost fellow conspirators.

'Did you like the pork?' he asked.

'It was a treat.'

'I'll try to bring you some more next time I come. Did Annette like it?'

'She wouldn't touch a thing you'd left. She said she'd rather starve.'

'Silly.'

'That's what I said to her. As long as the food is there, I said, there's nothing to be gained by not eating it.'

They chatted quite amicably while Hans sipped his wine. He discovered that she was called Madame Périer. He asked her whether there were any other members of the family. She sighed. No, they'd had a son, but he'd been mobilized at the beginning of the war and he'd died. He hadn't been killed, he'd got pneumonia and died in the hospital at Nancy.

'I'm sorry,' said Hans.

'Perhaps he's better off than if he'd lived. He was like Annette in many ways. He could never have borne the shame of defeat.' She sighed again. 'Oh, my poor friend, we've been betrayed.'

'Why did you want to fight for the Poles? What were they to you?'

'You're right. If we had let your Hitler take Poland he would have left us alone.'

When Hans got up to go he said he would come again soon.

'I shan't forget the pork.'

Then Hans had a lucky break; he was given a job that took him twice a week to a town in the vicinity so that he was able to get to the farm much oftener. He took care never to come without bringing something. But he made no headway with Annette. Seeking to ingratiate himself with her, he used the simple wiles that he had discovered went down with women; but they only excited her derision. Thin-lipped and hard, she looked at him as though he were dirt. On more than one occasion she made him so angry that he would have liked to take her by the shoulders and shake the life out of her. Once he found her alone, and when she got up to go he barred her passage.

'Stop where you are. I want to talk to you.'

'Talk. I am a woman and defenceless.'

'What I want to say is this: for all I know I may be here for a long time. Things aren't going to get easier for you French, they're going to get harder. I can be useful to you. Why don't you be reasonable like your father and mother?'

It was true that old Périer had come round. You couldn't say that he was cordial, he was indeed cold and gruff, but he was civil. He had even asked Hans to bring him some tobacco, and when he wouldn't accept payment for it had thanked him. He was pleased to hear the news of Soissons and grabbed the paper that Hans brought him. Hans, a farmer's son, could talk about the farm as one who knew. It was a good farm, not too big and not too small, well watered, for a sizable brook ran through it, and well wooded, with arable land and pasture. Hans listened with understanding sympathy when the old man bewailed himself because without labour, without fertilizers, his stock taken from him, it was all going to rack and ruin.

'You ask me why I can't be reasonable like my father and mother,' said Annette.

She pulled her dress tight and showed herself to him. He couldn't believe his eyes. What he saw caused such a convulsion in his soul as he had never known. The blood rushed to his cheeks.

'You're pregnant.'

She sank back on her chair and leaning her head on her hands began to weep as though her heart would break.

'The shame of it. The shame.'

He sprang towards her to take her in his arms.

'My sweet,' he cried.

But she sprang to her feet and pushed him away.

'Don't touch me. Go away. Go away. Haven't you done me enough harm already?'

She flung out of the room. He waited by himself for a few minutes. He was bewildered. His thoughts in a whirl, he rode slowly back to Soissons, and when he went to bed he couldn't get to sleep for hours. He could think of nothing but Annette and her swollen body. She had been unbearably pathetic as she sat there at the table crying her eyes out. It was his child she bore in her womb. He began to feel drowsy, and then with a start he was once more wide awake, for suddenly it came to him, it came to him with the shattering suddenness of gun-fire: he was in love with her. It was such a surprise, such a shock that he couldn't cope with it. Of course he'd thought of her a lot, but never in that way, he'd thought it would be a great joke if he made her fall in love with him, it would be a triumph if the time came when she offered what he had taken by force; but not for a moment had it occurred to him that she was anything to him but a woman like another. She wasn't his type. She wasn't very pretty. There was nothing to her. Why should he have all of a sudden this funny feeling for her? It wasn't a pleasant feeling either, it was a pain. But he knew what it was all right; it was love, and it made him feel happier than he had ever felt in his life. He wanted to take her in his arms, he wanted to pet her, he wanted to kiss those tear-stained eyes of hers. He didn't desire her, he thought, as a man desires a woman, he wanted to comfort her, he wanted her to smile at him – strange, he had never seen her smile, he wanted to see her eyes – fine eyes they were, beautiful eyes – soft with tenderness.

For three days he could not leave Soissons and for three days, three days and three nights, he thought of Annette and the child she would bear. Then he was able to go to the farm. He wanted to see Madame Périer by herself, and luck was with him, for he met her on the road some way from the house. She had been gathering sticks in the wood and was going home with a great bundle on her back. He stopped his motor-cycle. He knew that the friendliness she showed him was due only to the provisions he brought with him, but he didn't care; it was enough that she was mannerly, and that she was prepared to be so as long as she could get something out of him. He told her he wanted to talk to her and asked her to put her bundle down. She did as he bade. It was a grey, cloudy day, but not cold.

'I know about Annette,' he said.

She started.

'How did you find out? She was set on your not knowing.'

'She told me.'

'That was a pretty job of work you did that evening.'

'I didn't know. Why didn't you tell me sooner?'

She began to talk, not bitterly, not blaming him even, but as though it were a misfortune of nature, like a cow dying in giving birth to a calf or a sharp spring frost nipping the fruit trees and ruining the crop, a misfortune that human kind must accept with resignation and humility. After that dreadful night Annette had been in bed for days with a high fever. They thought she was going out of her mind. She would scream for hours on end. There were no doctors to be got. The village doctor had been called to the colours. Even in Soissons there were only two doctors left, old men both of them, and how could they get to the farm even if it had been possible to send for them? They weren't allowed to leave the town. Even when the fever went down Annette was too ill to leave her bed, and when she got up she was so weak, so pale, it was pitiful. The shock had been terrible, and when a month went by, and another month, without her being unwell she paid no attention. She had always been irregular. It was Madame Périer who first suspected that something was wrong. She questioned Annette. They were terrified, both of them, but they weren't certain and they said nothing to Périer. When the third month came it was impossible to doubt any longer. Annette was pregnant.

They had an old Citroën in which before the war Madame Périer had taken the farm produce into the market at Soissons two mornings a week, but since the German occupation they had had nothing to sell that made the journey worth while. Petrol was almost unobtainable. But now they got it out and drove into town. The only cars to be seen were the military cars of the Germans. German soldiers lounged about. There were German signs in the streets, and on public buildings proclamations in French signed by the Officer Commanding. Many shops were closed. They went to the old doctor they knew, and he confirmed their suspicions. But he was a devout Catholic and would not help them. When they wept he shrugged his shoulders.

'You're not the only one,' he said. '*Il faut souffrir.*'

They knew about the other doctor too and went to see him. They rang the bell and for a long time no one answered. At last the door was opened by a sad-faced woman in black, but when they asked to see the doctor she began to cry. He had been arrested by the Germans because he was a freemason, and was held as a hostage. A bomb had exploded in a café frequented by German officers and two had been killed and several wounded. If the guilty were not handed over before a certain date he was to be shot. The woman seemed kindly and Madame Périer told her of their trouble.

'The brutes,' she said. She looked at Annette with compassion. 'My poor child.'

She gave them the address of a midwife in the town and told them to say that they had come from her. The midwife gave them some medicine. It made Annette so ill that she thought she was going to die, but it had no further effect. Annette was still pregnant.

That was the story that Madame Périer told Hans. For a while he was silent.

'It's Sunday tomorrow,' he said then. 'I shall have nothing to do. I'll come and we'll talk. I'll bring something nice.'

'We have no needles. Can you bring some?'

'I'll try.'

She hoisted the bundle of sticks on her back and trudged down the road. Hans went back to Soissons. He dared not use his motor-cycle, so next day he hired a push-bike. He tied his parcel of food on the carrier. It was a larger parcel than usual because he had put a bottle of champagne into it. He got to the farm when the gathering darkness made it certain that they would all be home from work. It was warm and cosy in the kitchen when he walked in. Madame Périer was cooking and her husband was reading a *Paris-Soir*. Annette was darning stockings.

'Look, I've brought you some needles,' he said, as he undid his parcel. 'And here's some material for you, Annette.'

'I don't want it.'

'Don't you?' he grinned. 'You'll have to begin making things for the baby.'

'That's true, Annette,' said her mother, 'and we have nothing.' Annette did not look up from her sewing. Madame Périer's greedy eyes ran over the contents of the parcel. 'A bottle of champagne.'

Hans chuckled.

'I'll tell you what that's for presently. I've had an idea.' He hesitated for a moment, then drew up a chair and sat down facing Annette. 'I don't know quite how to begin. I'm sorry for what I did that night, Annette. It wasn't my fault, it was the circumstances. Can't you forgive me?'

She threw him a look of hatred.

'Never. Why don't you leave me alone? Isn't it enough that you've ruined my life?'

'Well, that's just it. Perhaps I haven't. When I knew you were going to have a baby it had a funny effect on me. It's all different now. It's made me so proud.'

'Proud?' she flung at him viciously.

'I want you to have the baby, Annette. I'm glad you couldn't get rid of it.'

'How dare you say that?'

'But listen to me. I've been thinking of nothing else since I knew. The war will be over in six months. We shall bring the English to their knees in the spring. They haven't got a chance. And then I shall be demobilized and I'll marry you.'

'You? Why?'

He blushed under his tan. He could not bring himself to say it in French, so he said it in German. He knew she understood it.

'*Ich liebe dich.*'

'What does he say?' asked Madame Périer.

'He says he loves me.'

Annette threw back her head and broke into a peal of harsh laughter. She laughed louder and louder and she couldn't stop and tears streamed from her eyes. Madame Périer slapped her sharply on both cheeks.

'Don't pay any attention,' she said to Hans. 'It's hysteria. Her condition, you know.'

Annette gasped. She gained control over herself.

'I brought the bottle of champagne to celebrate our engagement,' said Hans.

'That's the bitterest thing of all,' said Annette, 'that we were beaten by fools, by such fools.'

Hans went on speaking in German.

'I didn't know I loved you till that day when I found out that you were going to have a baby. It came like a clap of thunder, but I think I've loved you all the time.'

'What does he say?' asked Madame Périer.

'Nothing of importance.'

He fell back into French. He wanted Annette's parents to hear what he had to say.

'I'd marry you now, only they wouldn't let me. And don't think I'm nothing at all. My father's well-to-do and we're well thought of in our commune. I'm the eldest son and you'd want for nothing.'

'Are you a Catholic?' asked Madame Périer.

'Yes, I'm a Catholic.'

'That's something.'

'It's pretty, the country where we live and the soil's good. There's not better farming land between Munich and Innsbruck, and it's our own. My grandfather bought it after the war of '70.

And we've got a car and a radio, and we're on the telephone.'

Annette turned to her father.

'He has all the tact in the world, this gentleman,' she cried ironically. She eyed Hans. 'It would be a nice position for me, the foreigner from the conquered country with a child born out of wedlock. It offers me a chance of happiness, doesn't it? A fine chance.'

Périer, a man of few words, spoke for the first time.

'No. I don't deny that it's a fine gesture you're making. I went through the last war and we all did things we wouldn't have done in peace time. Human nature is human nature. But now that our son is dead, Annette is all we have. We can't let her go.'

'I thought you might feel that way,' said Hans, 'and I've got my answer to that. I'll stay here.'

Annette gave him a quick look.

'What do you mean?' asked Madame Périer.

'I've got another brother. He can stay and help my father. I like this country. With energy and initiative a man could make a good thing of your farm. When the war's over a lot of Germans will be settling here. It's well known that you haven't got enough men in France to work the land you've got. A fellow gave us a lecture the other day at Soissons. He said that a third of the farms were left uncultivated because there aren't the men to work them.'

Périer and his wife exchanged glances and Annette saw that they were wavering. That was what they'd wanted since their son had died, a son-in-law who was strong and hefty and could take over when they grew too old to do more than potter about.

'That changes the case,' said Madame Périer. 'It's a proposition to consider.'

'Hold your tongue,' cried Annette roughly. She leant forward and fixed her burning eyes on the German. 'I'm engaged to a teacher who worked in the boys' school in the town where I taught, we were to be married after the war. He's not strong and big like you, or handsome; he's small and frail. His only beauty is the intelligence that shines in his face, his only strength is the greatness of his soul. He's not a barbarian, he's civilized; he has a thousand years of civilization behind him. I love him. I love him with all my heart and soul.'

Hans's face grew sullen. It had never occurred to him that Annette might care for anyone else.

'Where is he now?'

'Where do you suppose he is? In Germany. A prisoner and

starving. While you eat the fat of our land. How many times have I got to tell you that I hate you? You ask me to forgive you. Never. You want to make reparation. You fool.' She threw her head back and there was a look of intolerable anguish on her face. 'Ruined. Oh, he'll forgive me. He's tender. But I'm tortured by the thought that one day the suspicion may come to him that perhaps I hadn't been forced – that perhaps I'd given myself to you for butter and cheese and silk stockings. I shouldn't be the only one. And what would our life be with that child between us, your child, a German child? Big like you, and blond like you, and blue-eyed like you. Oh, my God, why do I have to suffer this?'

She got up and went swiftly out of the kitchen. For a minute the three were left in silence. Hans looked ruefully at his bottle of champagne. He sighed and rose to his feet. When he went out Madame Périer accompanied him.

'Did you mean it when you said you would marry her?' she asked him, speaking in a low voice.

'Yes. Every word. I love her.'

'And you wouldn't take her away? You'd stay here and work on the farm?'

'I promise you.'

'Evidently my old man can't last for ever. At home you'd have to share with your brother. Here you'd share with nobody.'

'There's that too.'

'We never were in favour of Annette marrying that teacher, but our son was alive then and he said, if she wants to marry him, why shouldn't she? Annette was crazy about him. But now that our son's dead, poor boy, it's different. Even if she wanted to, how could she work the farm alone?'

'It would be a shame if it was sold. I know how one feels about one's own land.'

They had reached the road. She took his hand and gave it a little squeeze.

'Come again soon.'

Hans knew that she was on his side. It was a comfort to him to think that as he rode back to Soissons. It was a bother that Annette was in love with somebody else. Fortunately he was a prisoner; long before he was likely to be released the baby would be born. That might change her: you could never tell with a woman. Why, in his village there'd been a woman who was so much in love with her husband that it had been a joke, and then she had a baby and after that she couldn't bear the sight of him.

Well, why shouldn't the contrary happen too? And now that he'd offered to marry her she must see that he was a decent sort of fellow. God, how pathetic she'd looked with her head flung back, and how well she'd spoken! What language! An actress on the stage couldn't have expressed herself better, and yet it had all sounded so natural. You had to admit that, these French people knew how to talk. Oh, she was clever. Even when she lashed him with that bitter tongue it was a joy to listen to her. He hadn't had a bad education himself, but he couldn't hold a candle to her. Culture, that's what she had.

'I'm a donkey,' he said out loud as he rode along. She'd said he was big and strong and handsome. Would she have said that if it hadn't meant something to her? And she'd talked of the baby having fair hair and blue eyes like his own. If that didn't mean that his colouring had made an impression on her he was a Dutchman. He chuckled. 'Give me time. Patience, and let nature go to work.'

The weeks went by. The C.O. at Soissons was an elderly, easy-going fellow and in view of what the spring had in store for them he was content not to drive his men too hard. The German papers told them that England was being wrecked by the Luftwaffe and the people were in a panic. Submarines were sinking British ships by the score and the country was starving. Revolution was imminent. Before summer it would be all over and the Germans would be masters of the world. Hans wrote home and told his parents that he was going to marry a French girl and with her a fine farm. He proposed that his brother should borrow money to buy him out of his share of the family property so that he could increase the size of his own holding while land, owing to the war and the exchange, could still be bought for a song. He went over the farm with Périer. The old man listened quietly when Hans told him his ideas: the farm would have to be re-stocked and as a German he would have a pull; the motor tractor was old, he would get a fine new one from Germany, and a motor plough. To make a farm pay you had to take advantage of modern inventions. Madame Périer told him afterwards that her husband had said he wasn't a bad lad and seemed to know a lot. She was very friendly with him now and insisted that he should share their midday meal with them on Sundays. She translated his name into French and called him Jean. He was always ready to give a hand, and as time went on and Annette could do less and less it was useful to have a man about who didn't mind doing a job of work.

Annette remained fiercely hostile. She never spoke to him except to answer his direct questions and as soon as it was possible went to her own room. When it was so cold that she couldn't stay there she sat by the side of the kitchen stove, sewing or reading, and took no more notice of him than if he hadn't been there. She was in radiant health. There was colour in her cheeks and in Hans's eyes she was beautiful. Her approaching maternity had given her a strange dignity and he was filled with exultation when he gazed upon her. Then one day when he was on his way to the farm he saw Madame Périer in the road waving to him to stop. He put his brakes on hard.

'I've been waiting for an hour. I thought you'd never come. You must go back. Pierre is dead.'

'Who's Pierre?'

'Pierre Gavin. The teacher Annette was going to marry.'

Hans's heart leapt. What luck! Now he'd have his chance.

'Is she upset?'

'She's not crying. When I tried to say something she bit my head off. If she saw you today she's capable of sticking a knife into you.'

'It's not my fault if he died. How did you hear?'

'A prisoner, a friend of his, escaped through Switzerland and he wrote to Annette. We got the letter this morning. There was a mutiny in the camp because they weren't given enough to eat, and the ringleaders were shot. Pierre was one of them.'

Hans was silent. He could only think it served the man right. What did they think that a prison camp was – the Ritz?

'Give her time to get over the shock,' said Madame Périer. 'When she's calmer I'll talk to her. I'll write you a letter when you can come again.'

'All right. You will help me, won't you?'

'You can be sure of that. My husband and I, we're agreed. We talked it over and we came to the conclusion that the only thing to do was to accept the situation. He's no fool, my husband, and he says the best chance for France now is to collaborate. And take it all in all I don't dislike you. I shouldn't wonder if you didn't make Annette a better husband than that teacher. And with the baby coming and all.'

'I want it to be a boy,' said Hans.

'It's going to be a boy. I know for certain. I've seen it in the coffee grounds and I've put out the cards. The answer is a boy every time.'

301

'I almost forgot, here are some papers for you,' said Hans, as he turned his cycle and prepared to mount.

He handed her three numbers of *Paris-Soir*. Old Périer read every evening. He read that the French must be realistic and accept the new order that Hitler was going to create in Europe. He read that the German submarines were sweeping the sea. He read that the General Staff had organized to the last detail the campaign that would bring England to her knees and that the Americans were too unprepared, too soft and too divided to come to her help. He read that France must take the heaven-sent opportunity and by loyal collaboration with the Reich regain her honoured position in the new Europe. And it wasn't Germans who wrote it all; it was Frenchmen. He nodded his head with approval when he read that the plutocrats and the Jews would be destroyed and the poor man in France would at last come into his own. They were quite right, the clever fellows who said that France was essentially an agricultural country and its backbone was its industrious farmers. Good sense, that was.

One evening, when they were finishing their supper, ten days after the news had come of Pierre Gavin's death, Madame Périer by arrangement with her husband, said to Annette:

'I wrote a letter to Hans a few days ago telling him to come here tomorrow.'

'Thank you for the warning. I shall stay in my room.'

'Oh, come, daughter, the time has passed for foolishness. You must be realistic. Pierre is dead. Hans loves you and wants to marry you. He's a fine-looking fellow. Any girl would be proud of him as a husband. How can we restock the farm without his help? He's going to buy a tractor and a plough with his own money. You must let bygones be bygones.'

'You're wasting your breath, Mother. I earned my living before, I can earn my living again. I hate him. I hate his vanity and his arrogance. I could kill him: his death wouldn't satisfy me. I should like to torture him as he's tortured me. I think I should die happy if I could find a way to wound him as he's wounded me.'

'You're being very silly, my poor child.'

'Your mother's right, my girl,' said Périer. 'We've been defeated and we must accept the consequences. We've got to make the best arrangement we can with the conquerors. We're cleverer than they are and if we play our cards well we shall come out on top. France was rotten. It's the Jews and the plutocrats who ruined the country. Read the papers and you'll see for yourself!'

'Do you think I believe a word in that paper? Why do you think he brings it to you except that it's sold to the Germans? The men who write in it – traitors, traitors. Oh God, may I live to see them torn to pieces by the mob. Bought, bought every one of them – bought with German money. The swine.'

Madame Périer was getting exasperated.

'What have you got against the boy? He took you by force – yes, he was drunk at the time. It's not the first time that's happened to a woman and it won't be the last time. He hit your father and he bled like a pig, but does your father bear him malice?'

'It was an unpleasant incident, but I've forgotten it,' said Périer.

Annette burst into harsh laughter.

'You should have been a priest. You forgive injuries with a spirit truly Christian.'

'And what is there wrong about that?' asked Madame Périer angrily. 'Hasn't he done everything he could to make amends? Where would your father have got his tobacco all these months if it hadn't been for him? If we haven't gone hungry it's owing to him.'

'If you'd had any pride, if you'd had any sense of decency, you'd have thrown his presents in his face.'

'You've profited by them, haven't you?'

'Never. Never.'

'It's a lie and you know it. You've refused to eat the cheese he brought and the butter and the sardines. But the soup you've eaten, you know I put the meat in it that he brought; and the salad you ate tonight, if you didn't have to eat it dry, it's because he brought me oil.'

Annette sighed deeply. She passed her hand over her eyes.

'I know. I tried not to, I couldn't help myself, I was so hungry. Yes, I knew his meat went into the soup and I ate it. I knew the salad was made with his oil. I wanted to refuse it; I had such a longing for it, it wasn't I that ate it, it was a ravenous beast within me.'

'That's neither here nor there. You ate it.'

'With shame. With despair. They broke our strength first with their tanks and their planes, and now when we're defenceless they're breaking our spirit by starving us.'

'You get nowhere by being theatrical, my girl. For an educated woman you have really no sense. Forget the past and give a father to your child, to say nothing of a good workman for the farm who'll be worth two hired men. That is sense.'

Annette shrugged her shoulders wearily and they lapsed into silence. Next day Hans came. Annette gave him a sullen look, but neither spoke nor moved. Hans smiled.

'Thank you for not running away,' he said.

'My parents asked you to come and they've gone down to the village. It suits me because I want to have a definite talk with you. Sit down.'

He took off his coat and his helmet and drew a chair to the table.

'My parents want me to marry you. You've been clever; with your presents, with your promises, you've got round them. They believe all they read in the papers you bring them. I want to tell you that I will never marry you. I wouldn't have thought it possible that I could hate a human being as I hate you.'

'Let me speak in German. You understand enough to know what I'm saying.'

'I ought to. I taught it. For two years I was governess to two little girls in Stuttgart.'

He broke into German, but she went on speaking French.

'It's not only that I love you, I admire you. I admire your distinction and your grace. There's something about you I don't understand. I respect you. Oh, I can see that you don't want to marry me now even if it were possible. But Pierre is dead.'

'Don't speak of him,' she cried violently. 'That would be the last straw.'

'I only want to tell you that for your sake I'm sorry he died.'

'Shot in cold blood by his German jailers.'

'Perhaps in time you'll grieve for him less. You know, when someone you love dies, you think you'll never get over it, but you do. Won't it be better then to have a father for your child?'

'Even if there were nothing else do you think I could ever forget that you are a German and I'm a Frenchwoman? If you weren't as stupid as only a German can be you'd see that that child must be a reproach to me as long as I live. Do you think I have no friends? How could I ever look them in the face with the child I had with a German soldier? There's only one thing I ask you; leave me alone with my disgrace. Go, go – for God's sake go and never come again.'

'But he's my child too. I want him.'

'You?' she cried in astonishment. 'What can a by-blow that

304

you got in a moment of savage drunkenness mean to you?'

'You don't understand. I'm so proud and so happy. It was when I knew you were going to have a baby that I knew I loved you. At first I couldn't believe it; it was such a surprise to me. Don't you see what I mean? That child that's going to be born means everything in the world to me. Oh, I don't know how to put it; it's put feelings in my heart that I don't understand myself.'

She looked at him intently and there was a strange gleam in her eyes. You would have said it was a look of triumph. She gave a short laugh.

'I don't know whether I more loathe the brutality of you Germans or despise your sentimentality.'

He seemed not to have heard what she said.

'I think of him all the time.'

'You've made up your mind it'll be a boy?'

'I know it'll be a boy. I want to hold him in my arms and I want to teach him to walk. And then when he grows older I'll teach him all I know. I'll teach him to ride and I'll teach him to shoot. Are there fish in your brook? I'll teach him to fish. I'm going to be the proudest father in the world.'

She stared at him with hard, hard eyes. Her face was set and stern. An idea, a terrible idea was forming itself in her mind. He gave her a disarming smile.

'Perhaps when you see how much I love our boy, you'll come to love me too. I'll make you a good husband, my pretty.'

She said nothing. She merely kept on gazing at him sullenly.

'Haven't you one kind word for me?' he said.

She flushed. She clasped her hands tightly together.

'Others may despise me. I will never do anything that can make me despise myself. You are my enemy and you will always be my enemy. I only live to see the deliverance of France. It'll come, perhaps not next year or the year after, perhaps not for thirty years, but it'll come. The rest of them can do what they like, I will never come to terms with the invaders of my country. I hate you and I hate this child that you've given me. Yes, we've been defeated. Before the end comes you'll see that we haven't been conquered. Now go. My mind's made up and nothing on God's earth can change it.'

He was silent for a minute or two.

'Have you made arrangements for a doctor? I'll pay all the expenses.'

'Do you suppose we want to spread our shame through the

whole countryside? My mother will do all that's necessary.'

'But supposing there's an accident?'

'And supposing you mind your own business!'

He sighed and rose to his feet. When he closed the door behind him she watched him walk down the pathway that led to the road. She realized with rage that some of the things he said had aroused in her heart a feeling that she had never felt for him before.

'O God, give me strength,' she cried.

Then, as he walked along, the dog, an old dog they'd had for years, ran up to him barking angrily. He had tried for months to make friends with the dog, but it had never responded to his advances; when he tried to pat it, it backed away growling and showing its teeth. And now as the dog ran towards him, irritably giving way to his feeling of frustration, Hans gave it a savage brutal kick and the dog was flung into the bushes and limped yelping away.

'The beast,' she cried. 'Lies, lies, lies. And I was weak enough to be almost sorry for him.'

There was a looking-glass hanging by the side of the door and she looked at herself in it. She drew herself up and smiled at her reflection. But rather than a smile it was a finished grimace.

It was now March. There was a bustle of activity in the garrison at Soissons. There were inspections and there was intensive training. Rumour was rife. There was no doubt they were going somewhere, but the rank and file could only guess where. Some thought they were being got ready at last for the invasion of England, others were of opinion that they would be sent to the Balkans, and others again talked of the Ukraine. Hans was kept busy. It was not till the second Sunday afternoon that he was able to get out to the farm. It was a cold grey day, with sleet that looked as though it might turn to snow falling in sudden windy flurries. The country was grim and cheerless.

'You!' cried Madame Périer when he went in. 'We thought you were dead.'

'I couldn't come before. We're off any day now. We don't know when.'

'The baby was born this morning. It's a boy.'

Hans's heart gave a great leap in his breast. He hung his arms round the old woman and kissed her on both cheeks.

'A Sunday child, he ought to be lucky. Let's open the bottle of champagne. How's Annette?'

'She's as well as can be expected. She had a very easy time.

She began to have pains last night and by five o'clock this morning it was all over.'

Old Périer was smoking his pipe sitting as near the stove as he could get. He smiled quietly at the boy's enthusiasm.

'One's first child, it has an effect on one,' he said.

'He has quite a lot of hair and it's as fair as yours; and blue eyes just like you said he'd have,' said Madame Périer. 'I've never seen a lovelier baby. He'll be just like his papa.'

'Oh, my God, I'm so happy,' cried Hans. 'How beautiful the world is! I want to see Annette.'

'I don't know if she'll see you. I don't want to upset her on account of the milk.'

'No, no, don't upset her on my account. If she doesn't want to see me it doesn't matter. But let me see the baby just for a minute.'

'I'll see what I can do. I'll try to bring it down.'

Madame Périer went out and they heard her heavy tread clumping up the stairs. But in a moment they heard her clattering down again. She burst into the kitchen.

'They're not there. She isn't in her room. The baby's gone.'

Périer and Hans cried out and without thinking what they were doing all three of them scampered upstairs. The harsh light of the winter afternoon cast over the shabby furniture, the iron bed, the cheap wardrobe, the chest of drawers, a dismal squalor. There was no one in the room.

'Where is she?' screamed Madame Périer. She ran into the narrow passage, opening doors, and called the girl's name. 'Annette, Annette. Oh, what madness!'

'Perhaps in the sitting-room.'

They ran downstairs to the unused parlour. An icy air met them as they opened the door. They opened the door of a store-room.

'She's gone out. Something awful has happened.'

'How could she have got out?' asked Hans sick with anxiety.

'Through the front door, you fool.'

Périer went up to it and looked.

'That's right. The bolt's drawn back.'

'Oh, my God, my God, what madness,' cried Madame Périer. 'It'll kill her.'

'We must look for her,' said Hans. Instinctively, because that was the way he always went in and out, he ran back into the kitchen and the others followed him. 'Which way?'

'The brook,' the old woman gasped.

He stopped as though turned to stone with horror. He stared at the old woman aghast.

'I'm frightened,' she cried. 'I'm frightened.'

Hans flung open the door, and as he did so Annette walked in. She had nothing on but her nightdress and a flimsy rayon dressing-gown. It was pink, with pale blue flowers. She was soaked, and her hair, dishevelled, clung damply to her head and hung down her shoulders in bedraggled wisps. She was deathly white. Madame Périer sprang towards her and took her in her arms.

'Where have you been? Oh, my poor child, you're wet through. What madness!'

But Annette pushed her away. She looked at Hans.

'You've come at the right moment, you.'

'Where's the baby?' cried Madame Périer.

'I had to do it at once. I was afraid if I waited I shouldn't have the courage.'

'Annette, what have you done?'

'I've done what I had to do. I took it down to the brook and held it under water till it was dead.'

Hans gave a great cry, the cry of an animal wounded to death; he covered his face with his hands, and staggering like a drunken man flung out of the door. Annette sank into a chair, and leaning her forehead on her two fists burst into passionate weeping.

THE ESCAPE

I HAVE always been convinced that if a woman once made up her mind to marry a man nothing but instant flight could save him. Not always that; for once a friend of mine, seeing the inevitable loom menacingly before him, took ship from a certain port (with a tooth-brush for all his luggage, so conscious was he of his danger and the necessity for immediate action) and spent a year travelling round the world; but when, thinking himself safe (women are fickle, he said, and in twelve months she will have forgotten all about me), he landed at the selfsame port the first person he saw gaily waving to him from the quay was the little lady from whom he had fled. I have only once known a man who in such circumstances managed to extricate himself. His name was Roger Charing. He was no longer young when he fell in love with Ruth Barlow and he had had sufficient experience to make him careful; but Ruth Barlow had a gift (or should I call it a quality?) that renders most men defenceless, and it was this that dispossessed Roger of his commonsense, his prudence, and his worldly wisdom. He went down like a row of ninepins. This was the gift of pathos. Mrs Barlow, for she was twice a widow, had splendid dark eyes and they were the most moving I ever saw; they seemed to be ever on the point of filling with tears; they suggested that the world was too much for her, and you felt that, poor dear, her sufferings had been more than anyone should be asked to bear. If, like Roger Charing, you were a strong, hefty fellow with plenty of money, it was almost inevitable that you should say to yourself: I must stand between the hazards of life and this helpless little thing, oh, how wonderful it would be to take the sadness out of those big and lovely eyes! I gathered from Roger that everyone had treated Mrs Barlow very badly. She was apparently one of those unfortunate persons with whom nothing by any chance goes right. If she married a husband he beat her; if she employed a broker he cheated her; if she engaged a cook she drank. She never had a little lamb but it was sure to die.

When Roger told me that he had at last persuaded her to marry him, I wished him joy.

'I hope you'll be good friends,' he said. 'She's a little afraid of you, you know; she thinks you're callous.'

'Upon my word I don't know why she should think that.'

'You do like her, don't you?'

'Very much.'

'She's had a rotten time, poor dear. I feel so dreadfully sorry for her.'

'Yes,' I said.

I couldn't say less. I knew she was stupid and I thought she was scheming. My own belief was that she was as hard as nails.

The first time I met her we had played bridge together and when she was my partner she twice trumped my best card. I behaved like an angel, but I confess that I thought if the tears were going to well up into anybody's eyes they should have been mine rather than hers. And when, having by the end of the evening lost a good deal of money to me, she said she would send me a cheque and never did, I could not but think that I and not she should have worn a pathetic expression when next we met.

Roger introduced her to his friends. He gave her lovely jewels. He took her here, there, and everywhere. Their marriage was announced for the immediate future. Roger was very happy. He was committing a good action and at the same time doing something he had very much a mind to. It is an uncommon situation and it is not surprising if he was a trifle more pleased with himself than was altogether becoming.

Then, on a sudden, he fell out of love. I do not know why. It could hardly have been that he grew tired of her conversation, for she had never had any conversation. Perhaps it was merely that this pathetic look of hers ceased to wring his heart-strings. His eyes were opened and he was once more the shrewd man of the world he had been. He became acutely conscious that Ruth Barlow had made up her mind to marry him and he swore a solemn oath that nothing would induce him to marry Ruth Barlow. But he was in a quandary. Now that he was in possession of his senses he saw with clearness the sort of woman he had to deal with and he was aware that, if he asked her to release him, she would (in her appealing way) assess her wounded feelings at an immoderately high figure. Besides, it is always awkward for a man to jilt a woman. People are apt to think he has behaved badly.

Roger kept his own counsel. He gave neither by word nor gesture an indication that his feelings towards Ruth Barlow had changed. He remained attentive to all her wishes; he took her to dine at restaurants, they went to the play together, he sent her flowers; he was sympathetic and charming. They had made up their minds that they would be married as soon as they found a house that suited them, for he lived in chambers and she in furnished rooms; and they set about looking at desirable residences. The agents sent Roger orders to view and he took Ruth to see a number of houses. It was very hard to find anything that was quite satisfactory. Roger applied to more agents. They visited house after house. They went over them thoroughly, examining them from the cellars in the basement to the attics under the roof. Sometimes they were too large and sometimes they were too small; sometimes they were too far from the centre of things and sometimes they were too close; sometimes they were too expensive and sometimes they wanted too many repairs; sometimes they were too stuffy and sometimes they were too airy; sometimes they were too dark and sometimes they were too bleak. Roger always found a fault that made the house unsuitable. Of course he was hard to please; he could not bear to ask his dear Ruth to live in any but the perfect house, and the perfect house wanted finding. House-hunting is a tiring and a tiresome business and presently Ruth began to grow peevish. Roger begged her to have patience; somewhere, surely, existed the very house they were looking for, and it only needed a little perseverance and they would find it. They looked at hundreds of houses; they climbed thousands of stairs; they inspected innumerable kitchens. Ruth was exhausted and more than once lost her temper.

'If you don't find a house soon,' she said, 'I shall have to reconsider my position. Why, if you go on like this we shan't be married for years.'

'Don't say that,' he answered, 'I beseech you to have patience. I've just received some entirely new lists from agents I've only just heard of. There must be at least sixty houses on them.'

They set out on the chase again. They looked at more houses and more houses. For two years they looked at houses. Ruth grew silent and scornful: her pathetic, beautiful eyes acquired an expression that was almost sullen. There are limits to human endurance. Mrs Barlow had the patience of an angel, but at last she revolted.

'Do you want to marry me or do you not?' she asked him.

There was an unaccustomed hardness in her voice, but it did not affect the gentleness of his reply.

'Of course I do. We'll be married the very moment we find a house. By the way, I've just heard of something that might suit us.'

'I don't feel well enough to look at any more houses just yet.'

'Poor dear, I was afraid you were looking rather tired.'

Ruth Barlow took to her bed. She would not see Roger and he

had to content himself with calling at her lodgings to inquire and sending her flowers. He was as ever assiduous and gallant. Every day he wrote and told her that he had heard of another house for them to look at. A week passed and then he received the following letter:

Roger –
I do not think you really love me. I have found someone who is anxious to take care of me and I am going to be married to him today.
                                                                                              Ruth

He sent back his reply by special messenger:

Ruth –
Your news shatters me. I shall never get over the blow, but of course your happiness must be my first consideration. I send you herewith seven orders to view; they arrived by this morning's post and I am quite sure you will find among them a house that will exactly suit you.
                                                                                              Roger

THE JUDGEMENT SEAT

THEY awaited their turn patiently, but patience was no new thing to them; they had practised it, all three of them, with grim determination, for thirty years. Their lives had been a long preparation for this moment and they looked forward to the issue now, if not with self-confidence, for that on so awful an occasion would have been misplaced, at all events with hope and courage. They had taken the strait and narrow path when the flowery meads of sin stretched all too invitingly before them; with heads held high, though with breaking hearts, they had resisted temptation; and now, their arduous journey done, they expected their reward. There was no need for them to speak, since each knew the others' thoughts, and they felt that in all three of them the same emotion of relief filled their bodiless souls with thanksgiving. With what anguish now would they have been wrung if they had yielded to the passion which then had seemed so nearly irresistible and what a madness it would have been if for a few short years of bliss they had sacrificed that Life Everlasting which with so bright a light at long last shone before them! They felt like men who with the skin of their teeth have escaped a sudden and violent death and touch their feet and hands and, scarce able to believe that they are still alive, look about them in amazement. They had done nothing with which they could reproach themselves and when presently their angels came and told them that the moment was come, they would advance, as they had passed through the world that was now so far behind, happily conscious that they had done their duty. They stood a little on one side, for the press was great. A terrible war was in progress and for years the soldiers of all nations, men in the full flush of their gallant youth, had marched in an interminable procession to the Judgement Seat; women and children too, their lives brought to a wretched end by violence or, more unhappily, by grief, disease, and starvation; and there was in the courts of heaven not a little confusion.

It was on account of this war, too, that these three wan, shivering ghosts stood in expectation of their doom. For John and Mary had been passengers on a ship which was sunk by the torpedo of a submarine; and Ruth, broken in health by the arduous work to which she had so nobly devoted herself, hearing of the death of the man whom she had loved with all her heart, sank beneath the blow and died. John, indeed, might have saved himself if he had not tried to save his wife; he hated her; he had hated her to the depths of his soul for thirty years; but he had always done his duty by her and now, in the moment of dreadful peril, it never occurred to him that he could do otherwise.

At last their angels took them by the hand and led them to the Presence. For a little while the Eternal took not the slightest notice of them. If the truth must be told he was in a bad humour. A moment before there had come up for judgement a philosopher, deceased full of years and honours, who had told the Eternal to his face that he did not believe in him. It was not this that would have disturbed the serenity of the Kings of Kings, this could only have made him smile; but the philosopher, taking perhaps an unfair advantage of the regrettable happenings just then upon Earth, had asked him how, considering them dispassionately, it was possible to reconcile his All-Power with his All-Goodness.

'No one can deny the fact of Evil,' said the philosopher, sententiously. 'Now, if God cannot prevent Evil he is not all-powerful, and if he can prevent it and will not, he is not all-good.'

This argument was of course not new to the Omniscient, but he had always refused to consider the matter; for the fact is, though he knew everything, he did not know the answer to this. Even God cannot make two and two five. But the philosopher, pressing his advantage, and, as philosophers often will, drawing from a reasonable premise an unjustifiable inference – the philosopher had finished with a statement that in the circumstances was surely preposterous.

'I will not believe,' he said, 'in a God who is not All-Powerful and All-Good.'

It was not then perhaps without relief that the Eternal turned his attention to the three shades who stood humbly and yet hopefully before him. The quick, with so short a time to live, when they talk of themselves, talk too much; but the dead, with eternity before them, are so verbose that only angels could listen to them with civility. But this in brief is the story that these three recounted. John and Mary had been happily married for five years and till John met Ruth they loved each other, as married couples for the most part do, with sincere affection and mutual respect. Ruth was eighteen, ten years younger than he was, a charming, graceful animal, with a sudden and all-conquering loveliness; she was as healthy in mind as she was in body, and, eager for the natural happiness of life, was capable of achieving that greatness which is beauty of soul. John fell in love with her and she with him. But it was no ordinary passion that seized them; it was something so overwhelming that they felt as if the whole long history of the world signified only because it had led to the time and place that had brought them together. They loved as Daphnis and Chloe or as Paolo and Francesca. But after that first moment of ecstasy when each discovered the other's love they were seized with dismay. They were decent people and they respected themselves, the beliefs in which they had been bred, and the society in which they lived. How could he betray an innocent girl, and what had she to do with a married man? Then they grew conscious that Mary was aware of their love. The confident affection with which she had regarded her husband was shaken; and there arose in her feelings of which she would never have thought herself capable, jealousy and the fear that he would desert her, anger because her possession of his heart was threatened, and a strange hunger of the soul which was more painful than love. She felt that she would die if he left her; and yet she knew that if he loved it was because love had come to him, not because he had sought it. She did not blame him. She prayed for strength; she wept silent, bitter tears. John and Ruth saw her pine away before their eyes. The struggle was long and bitter. Sometimes their hearts failed them and they felt that they could not resist the passion that burned the marrow of their bones. They resisted. They wrestled with evil as Jacob wrestled with the angel of God and at last they conquered. With breaking hearts, but proud in their innocence, they parted. They offered up to God, as it were a sacrifice, their hopes of happiness, the joy of life, and the beauty of the world.

Ruth had loved too passionately ever to love again, and with a stony heart she turned to God and to good works. She was indefatigable. She tended the sick and assisted the poor. She founded orphanages and managed charitable institutions. And little by little her beauty which she cared for no longer left her and her face grew as hard as her heart. Her religion was fierce and narrow; her very kindness was cruel because it was founded not on love but on reason; she became domineering, intolerant, and vindictive. And John, resigned, but sullen and angry, dragged himself along the weary years waiting for the release of death. Life lost its meaning to him; he had made his effort and in conquering was conquered; the only emotion that remained with him was the unceasing, secret hatred with which he looked upon his wife. He used her with kindness and consideration; he did everything that could be expected of a man who was a Christian and a gentleman. He did his duty. Mary, a good, faithful and (it must be confessed) exceptional wife, never thought to reproach her husband for the madness that had seized him; but all the same she could not forgive him for the sacrifice he had made for her sake. She grew acid and querulous. Though she hated herself for it, she could not refrain from saying the things that she knew would wound him. She would willingly have sacrificed her life for him, but she could not bear that he should enjoy a moment's happiness when she was so wretched that a hundred times she had wished she was dead. Well, now she was and so were they; grey and drab had life been, but that was passed; they had not sinned and now their reward was at hand.

They finished and there was silence. There was silence in all the courts of heaven. Go to hell were the words that came to the Eternal's lips, but he did not utter them, for they had a colloquial association that he rightly thought unfitting to the solemnity of the occasion. Nor indeed would such a decree have met the merits of the case. But his brows darkened. He asked himself if it was for this that he had made the rising sun shine on the boundless sea and the snow glitter on the mountain tops; was it for this that the brooks sang blithely as they hastened down the hillsides and the golden corn waved in the evening breeze?

'I sometimes think,' said the Eternal, 'that the stars never shine more brightly than when reflected in the muddy waters of a wayside ditch.'

But the three shades stood before him and now that they had unfolded their unhappy story they could not but feel a certain satisfaction. It had been a bitter struggle, but they had done their duty. The Eternal blew lightly, he blew as a man might blow out a lighted match, and, behold! where the three poor souls had stood – was nothing. The Eternal annihilated them.

'I have often wondered why men think I attach so much importance to sexual irregularity,' he said. 'If they read my works more attentively they would see that I have always been sympathetic to that particular form of human frailty.'

Then he turned to the philosopher, who was still waiting for a reply to his remarks.

'You cannot but allow,' said the Eternal, 'that on this occasion I have very happily combined my All-Power with my All-Goodness.'

MR KNOW-ALL

I WAS prepared to dislike Max Kelada even before I knew him. The war had just finished and the passenger traffic in the ocean-going liners was heavy. Accommodation was very hard to get and you had to put up with whatever the agents chose to offer you. You could not hope for a cabin to yourself and I was thankful to be given one in which there were only two berths. But when I was told the name of my companion my heart sank. It suggested closed port-holes and the night air rigidly excluded. It was bad enough to share a cabin for fourteen days with anyone (I was going from San Francisco to Yokohama), but I should have looked upon it with less dismay if my fellow-passenger's name had been Smith or Brown.

When I went on board I found Mr Kelada's luggage already below. I did not like the look of it; there were too many labels on the suitcases, and the wardrobe trunk was too big. He had un-packed his toilet things, and I observed that he was a patron of the excellent Monsieur Coty; for I saw on the washing-stand his scent, his hair-wash, and his brilliantine. Mr Kelada's brushes, ebony with his monogram in gold, would have been all the better for a scrub. I did not at all like Mr Kelada. I made my way into the smoking-room. I called for a pack of cards and began to play patience. I had scarcely started before a man came up to me and asked me if he was right in thinking my name was so-and-so.

'I am Mr Kelada,' he added, with a smile that showed a row of flashing teeth, and sat down.

'Oh, yes, we're sharing a cabin, I think.'

'Bit of luck, I call it. You never know who you're going to be put in with. I was jolly glad when I heard you were English. I'm all for us English sticking together when we're abroad, if you understand what I mean.'

I blinked.

'Are you English?' I asked, perhaps tactlessly.

'Rather. You don't think I look an American, do you? British to the backbone, that's what I am.'

To prove it, Mr Kelada took out of his pocket a passport and airily waved it under my nose.

King George has many strange subjects. Mr Kelada was short and of a sturdy build, clean-shaven and dark-skinned, with a fleshy, hooked nose and very large, lustrous and liquid eyes. His long black hair was sleek and curly. He spoke with a fluency in which there was nothing English and his gestures were exuberant. I felt pretty sure that a closer inspection of that British passport would have betrayed the fact that Mr Kelada was born under a bluer sky than is generally seen in England.

'What will you have?' he asked me.

I looked at him doubtfully. Prohibition was in force and to all appearances the ship was bone-dry. When I am not thirsty I do not know which I dislike more, ginger-ale or lemon-squash. But Mr Kelada flashed an oriental smile at me.

'Whisky and soda or a dry Martini, you have only to say the word.'

From each of his hip-pockets he fished a flask and laid them on the table before me. I chose the Martini, and calling the steward he ordered a tumbler of ice and a couple of glasses.

'A very good cocktail,' I said.

'Well, there are plenty more where that came from, and if you've got any friends on board, you tell them you've got a pal who's got all the liquor in the world.'

Mr Kelada was chatty. He talked of New York and of San Francisco. He discussed plays, pictures, and politics. He was patriotic. The Union Jack is an impressive piece of drapery, but when it is flourished by a gentleman from Alexandria or Beirut, I cannot but feel that it loses somewhat in dignity. Mr Kelada was familiar. I do not wish to put on airs, but I cannot help feeling that it is seemly in a total stranger to put mister before my name when he addresses me. Mr Kelada, doubtless to set me at my ease, used no such formality. I did not like Mr Kelada. I had put aside the cards when he sat down, but now, thinking that for this first occasion our conversation had lasted long enough, I went on with my game.

'The three on the four,' said Mr Kelada.

There is nothing more exasperating when you are playing patience than to be told where to put the card you have turned up before you have had a chance to look for yourself.

'It's coming out, it's coming out,' he cried. 'The ten on the knave.'

With rage and hatred in my heart I finished. Then he seized the pack.

'Do you like card tricks?'

'No, I hate card tricks,' I answered.

'Well, I'll just show you this one.'

He showed me three. Then I said I would go down to the dining-room and get my seat at table.

'Oh, that's all right,' he said. 'I've already taken a seat for you. I thought that as we were in the same state-room we might just as well sit at the same table.'

I did not like Mr Kelada.

I not only shared a cabin with him and ate three meals a day at the same table, but I could not walk round the deck without his joining me. It was impossible to snub him. It never occurred to him that he was not wanted. He was certain that you were as glad to see him as he was to see you. In your own house you might have kicked him downstairs and slammed the door in his face without the suspicion dawning on him that he was not a welcome visitor. He was a good mixer, and in three days knew everyone on board. He ran everything. He managed the sweeps, conducted the auctions, collected money for prizes at the sports, got up quoit and golf matches, organized the concert, and arranged the fancy-dress ball. He was everywhere and always. He was certainly the best-hated man in the ship. We called him Mr Know-All, even to his face. He took it as a compliment. But it was at meal times that he was most intolerable. For the better part of an hour then he had us at his mercy. He was hearty, jovial, loquacious and argumentative. He knew everything better than anybody else, and it was an affront to his overweening vanity that you should disagree with him. He would not drop a subject, however unimportant, till he had brought you round to his way of thinking. The possibility that he could be mistaken never occurred to him. He was the chap who knew. We sat at the doctor's table. Mr Kelada would certainly have had it all his own way, for the doctor was lazy and I was frigidly indifferent, except for a man called Ramsay who sat there also. He was as dogmatic as Mr Kelada and resented bitterly the Levantine's cocksureness. The discussions they had were acrimonious and interminable.

Ramsay was in the American Consular Service, and was stationed at Kobe. He was a great heavy fellow from the Middle West, with loose fat under a tight skin, and he bulged out of his ready-made clothes. He was on his way back to resume his post, having been on a flying visit to New York to fetch his wife, who had been spending a year at home. Mrs Ramsay was a very pretty little thing, with pleasant manners and a sense of humour. The Consular Service is ill paid, and she was dressed always very simply; but she knew how to wear her clothes. She achieved an effect of quiet distinction. I should not have paid any particular attention to her but that she possessed a quality that may be common enough in women, but nowadays is not obvious in their demeanour. You could not look at her without being struck by her modesty. It shone in her like a flower on a coat.

One evening at dinner the conversation by chance drifted to the subject of pearls. There had been in the papers a good deal of talk about the culture pearls which the cunning Japanese were making, and the doctor remarked that they must inevitably diminish the value of real ones. They were very good already; they would soon be perfect. Mr Kelada, as was his habit, rushed the new topic. He told us all that was to be known about pearls. I do not believe Ramsay knew anything about them at all, but he could not resist the opportunity to have a fling at the Levantine, and in five minutes we were in the middle of a heated argument. I had seen Mr Kelada vehement and voluble before, but never so voluble and vehement as now. At last something that Ramsay said stung him, for he thumped the table and shouted:

'Well, I ought to know what I am talking about. I'm going to Japan just to look into this Japanese pearl business. I'm in the trade and there's not a man in it who won't tell you that what I say about pearls goes. I know all the best pearls in the world, and what I don't know about pearls isn't worth knowing.'

Here was news for us, for Mr Kelada, with all his loquacity, had never told anyone what his business was. We only knew vaguely that he was going to Japan on some commercial errand. He looked round the table triumphantly.

'They'll never be able to get a culture pearl that an expert like me can't tell with half an eye.' He pointed to a chain that Mrs Ramsay wore. 'You take my word for it, Mrs Ramsay, that chain you're wearing will never be worth a cent less than it is now.'

Mrs Ramsay in her modest way flushed a little and slipped the chain inside her dress. Ramsay leaned forward. He gave us all a look and a smile flickered in his eyes.

'That's a pretty chain of Mrs Ramsay's, isn't it?'

'I noticed it at once,' answered Mr Kelada. 'Gee, I said to myself, those are pearls all right.'

'I didn't buy it myself, of course. I'd be interested to know how much you think it cost.'

'Oh, in the trade somewhere round fifteen thousand dollars. But if it was bought on Fifth Avenue I shouldn't be surprised to hear that anything up to thirty thousand was paid for it.'

Ramsay smiled grimly.

'You'll be surprised to hear that Mrs Ramsay bought that string at a department store the day before we left New York, for eighteen dollars.'

Mr Kelada flushed.

'Rot. It's not only real, but it's as fine a string for its size as I've ever seen.'

'Will you bet on it? I'll bet you a hundred dollars it's imitation.'

'Done.'

'Oh, Elmer, you can't bet on a certainty,' said Mrs Ramsay. She had a little smile on her lips and her tone was gently deprecating.

'Can't I? If I get a chance of easy money like that I should be all sorts of a fool not to take it.'

'But how can it be proved?' she continued. 'It's only my word against Mr Kelada's.'

'Let me look at the chain, and if it's imitation I'll tell you quickly enough. I can afford to lose a hundred dollars,' said Mr Kelada.

'Take it off, dear. Let the gentleman look at it as much as he wants.'

Mrs Ramsay hesitated a moment. She put her hands to the clasp.

'I can't undo it,' she said. 'Mr Kelada will just have to take my word for it.'

I had a sudden suspicion that something unfortunate was about to occur, but I could think of nothing to say.

Ramsay jumped up.

'I'll undo it.'

He handed the chain to Mr Kelada. The Levantine took a magnifying glass from his pocket and closely examined it. A smile of triumph spread over his smooth and swarthy face. He handed back the chain. He was about to speak. Suddenly he caught sight of Mrs Ramsay's face. It was so white that she looked as though she were about to faint. She was staring at him with wide and terrified eyes. They held a desperate appeal; it was so clear that I wondered why her husband did not see it.

Mr Kelada stopped with his mouth open. He flushed deeply. You could almost *see* the effort he was making over himself.

'I was mistaken,' he said. 'It's a very good imitation, but of course as soon as I looked through my glass I saw that it wasn't real. I think eighteen dollars is just about as much as the damned thing's worth.'

321

He took out his pocket-book and from it a hundred-dollar note. He handed it to Ramsay without a word.

'Perhaps that'll teach you not to be so cocksure another time, my young friend,' said Ramsay as he took the note.

I noticed that Mr Kelada's hands were trembling.

The story spread over the ship as stories do, and he had to put up with a good deal of chaff that evening. It was a fine joke that Mr Know-All had been caught out. But Mrs Ramsay retired to her state-room with a headache.

Next morning I got up and began to shave. Mr Kelada lay on his bed smoking a cigarette. Suddenly there was a small scraping sound and I saw a letter pushed under the door. I opened the door and looked out. There was nobody there. I picked up the letter and saw that it was addressed to Max Kelada. The name was written in block letters. I handed it to him.

'Who's this from?' He opened it. 'Oh!'

He took out of the envelope, not a letter, but a hundred-dollar note. He looked at me and again he reddened. He tore the envelope into little bits and gave them to me.

'Do you mind just throwing them out of the port-hole?'

I did as he asked, and then I looked at him with a smile.

'No one likes being made to look a perfect damned fool,' he said.

'Were the pearls real?'

'If I had a pretty little wife I shouldn't let her spend a year in New York while I stayed at Kobe,' said he.

At that moment I did not entirely dislike Mr Kelada. He reached out for his pocket-book and carefully put in it the hundred-dollar note.

THE HAPPY MAN

IT is a dangerous thing to order the lives of others and I have often wondered at the self-confidence of politicians, reformers and suchlike who are prepared to force upon their fellows measures that must alter their manners, habits, and points of view. I have always hesitated to give advice, for how can one advise another how to act unless one knows that other as well as one knows oneself? Heaven knows, I know little enough of myself: I know nothing of others. We can only guess at the thoughts and emotions of our neighbours. Each one of us is a prisoner in a solitary tower and he communicates with the other prisoners, who form mankind, by conventional signs that have not quite the same meaning for them as for himself. And life, unfortunately, is something that you can lead but once; mistakes are often irreparable, and who am I that I should tell this one and that how he should lead it? Life is a difficult business and I have found it hard enough to make my own a complete and rounded thing; I have not been tempted to teach my neighbour what he should do with his. But there are men who flounder at the journey's start, the way before them is confused and hazardous, and on occasion, however unwillingly, I have been forced to point the finger of fate. Sometimes men have said to me, what shall I do with my life? and I have seen myself for a moment wrapped in the dark cloak of Destiny.

Once I know that I advised well.

I was a young man and I lived in a modest apartment in London near Victoria Station. Late one afternoon, when I was beginning to think that I had worked enough for that day, I heard a ring at the bell. I opened the door to a total stranger. He asked me my name; I told him. He asked if he might come in.

'Certainly.'

I led him into my sitting-room and begged him to sit down. He seemed a trifle embarrassed. I offered him a cigarette and he had some difficulty in lighting it without letting go of his hat. When he had satisfactorily achieved this feat I asked him if I should not put it on a chair for him. He quickly did this and while doing it dropped his umbrella.

'I hope you don't mind my coming to see you like this,' he said. 'My name is Stephens and I am a doctor. You're in the medical, I believe?'

323

'Yes, but I don't practise.'

'No, I know. I've just read a book of yours about Spain and I wanted to ask you about it.'

'It's not a very good book, I'm afraid.'

'The fact remains that you know something about Spain and there's no one else I know who does. And I thought perhaps you wouldn't mind giving me some information.'

'I shall be very glad.'

He was silent for a moment. He reached out for his hat and holding it in one hand absent-mindedly stroked it with the other. I surmised that it gave him confidence.

'I hope you won't think it very odd for a perfect stranger to talk to you like this.' He gave an apologetic laugh. 'I'm not going to tell you the story of my life.'

When people say this to me I always know that it is precisely what they are going to do. I do not mind. In fact I rather like it.

'I was brought up by two old aunts. I've never been anywhere. I've never done anything. I've been married for six years. I have no children. I'm a medical officer at the Camberwell Infirmary. I can't stick it any more.'

There was something very striking in the short, sharp sentences he used. They had a forcible ring. I had not given him more than a cursory glance, but now I looked at him with curiosity. He was a little man, thick-set and stout, of thirty perhaps, with a round red face from which shone small, dark and very bright eyes. His black hair was cropped close to a bullet-shaped head. He was dressed in a blue suit a good deal the worse for wear. It was baggy at the knees and the pockets bulged untidily.

'You know what the duties are of a medical officer in an infirmary. One day is pretty much like another. And that's all I've got to look forward to for the rest of my life. Do you think it's worth it?'

'It's a means of livelihood,' I answered.

'Yes, I know. The money's pretty good.'

'I don't exactly know why you've come to me.'

'Well, I wanted to know whether you thought there would be any chance for an English doctor in Spain?'

'Why Spain?'

'I don't know, I just have a fancy for it.'

'It's not like *Carmen*, you know.'

'But there's sunshine there, and there's good wine, and there's colour, and there's air you can breathe. Let me say what I have to say straight out. I heard by accident that there was no English doctor in Seville. Do you think I could earn a living there? Is it madness to give up a good safe job for an uncertainty?'

'What does your wife think about it?'

'She's willing.'

'It's a great risk.'

'I know. But if you say take it, I will: if you say stay where you are, I'll stay.'

He was looking at me intently with those bright dark eyes of his and I knew that he meant what he said. I reflected for a moment.

'Your whole future is concerned: you must decide for yourself. But this I can tell you: if you don't want money but are content to earn just enough to keep body and soul together, then go. For you will lead a wonderful life.'

He left me, I thought about him for a day or two, and then forgot. The episode passed completely from my memory.

Many years later, fifteen at least, I happened to be in Seville and having some trifling indisposition asked the hotel porter whether there was an English doctor in the town. He said there was and gave me the address. I took a cab and as I drove up to the house a little fat man came out of it. He hesitated when he caught sight of me.

'Have you come to see me?' he said. 'I'm the English doctor.'

I explained my errand and he asked me to come in. He lived in an ordinary Spanish house, with a patio, and his consulting room which led out of it was littered with papers, books, medical appliances, and lumber. The sight of it would have startled a squeamish patient. We did our business and then I asked the doctor what his fee was. He shook his head and smiled.

'There's no fee.'

'Why on earth not?'

'Don't you remember me? Why, I'm here because of something you said to me. You changed my whole life for me. I'm Stephens.'

I had not the least notion what he was talking about. He reminded me of our interview, he repeated to me what we had said, and gradually, out of the night, a dim recollection of the incident came back to me.

'I was wondering if I'd ever see you again,' he said, 'I was wondering if ever I'd have a chance of thanking you for all you've done for me.'

'It's been a success then?'

I looked at him. He was very fat now and bald, but his eyes

twinkled gaily and his fleshy, red face bore an expression of perfect good-humour. The clothes he wore, terribly shabby they were, had been made obviously by a Spanish tailor and his hat was the wide-brimmed sombrero of the Spaniard. He looked to me as though he knew a good bottle of wine when he saw it. He had a dissipated, though entirely sympathetic, appearance. You might have hesitated to let him remove your appendix, but you could not have imagined a more delightful creature to drink a glass of wine with.

'Surely you were married?' I said.

'Yes. My wife didn't like Spain, she went back to Camberwell, she was more at home there.'

'Oh, I'm sorry for that.'

His black eyes flashed a bacchanalian smile. He really had somewhat the look of a young Silenus.

'Life is full of compensations,' he murmured.

The words were hardly out of his mouth when a Spanish woman, no longer in her first youth, but still boldly and voluptuously beautiful, appeared at the door. She spoke to him in Spanish, and I could not fail to perceive that she was the mistress of the house.

As he stood at the door to let me out he said to me:

'You told me when last I saw you that if I came here I should earn just enough money to keep body and soul together, but that I should lead a wonderful life. Well, I want to tell you that you were right. Poor I have been and poor I shall always be, but by heaven I've enjoyed myself. I wouldn't exchange the life I've had with that of any king in the world.'

THE ROMANTIC YOUNG LADY

ONE of the many inconveniences of real life is that it seldom gives you a complete story. Some incident has excited your interest, the people who are concerned in it are in the devil's own muddle, and you wonder what on earth will happen next. Well, generally nothing happens. The inevitable catastrophe you foresaw wasn't inevitable after all, and high tragedy, without any regard to artistic decency, dwindles into drawing-room comedy. Now, growing old has many disadvantages, but it has this compensation (among, let us admit, not a few others), that sometimes it gives you the opportunity of seeing what was the outcome of certain events you had witnessed long ago. You had given up the hope of ever knowing what was the end of the story, and then, when you least expected it, it is handed to you on a platter.

These reflections occurred to me when, having escorted the Marquesa de San Esteban to her car, I went back into the hotel and sat down again in the lounge. I ordered a cocktail, lit a cigarette, and composed myself to order my recollections. The hotel was new and splendid, it was like every other first-class hotel in Europe, and I had been regretting that for the sake of its modern plumbing I had deserted the old-fashioned, picturesque Hotel de Madrid to which I generally went when I stayed in Seville. It was true that from my hotel I had a view of the noble river, the Guadalquivir, but that did not make up for the *thés dansants* that filled the bar-lounge two or three days a week with a fashionable crowd whose exuberant conversation almost drowned the strident din of a jazz orchestra.

I had been out all the afternoon, and coming in found myself in the midst of a seething mob. I went to the desk and asked for my key so that I might go straight up to my room. But the porter, handing it to me, said that a lady had been asking for me.

'For me?'

'She wants to see you very much. It's the Marquesa de San Esteban.'

I knew no one of that name.

'It must be some mistake.'

As I said the words, looking rather vaguely around, a lady came up to me with outstretched hands and a bright smile on her lips. To the best of my knowledge I had never seen her before in my life. She seized my hands, both of them, and shook them warmly. She spoke in fluent French.

'How very nice to see you again after all these years. I saw by the paper that you were staying here and I said to myself: I must look him up. How many years is it since we danced together? I daren't think. Do you still dance? I do. And I'm a grandmother. I'm fat of course, I don't care, and it keeps me from getting fatter.'

She talked with such a rush that it took my breath away to listen to her. She was a stout, more than middle-aged woman, very much made up, with dark red hair, obviously dyed, cut short; and she was dressed in the height of Parisian fashion, which never suits Spanish women very well. But she had a gay, fruity laugh that made you feel you wanted to laugh too. It was quite obvious that she thoroughly enjoyed life. She was a fine figure of a woman and I could well believe that in youth she had been beautiful. But I could not place her.

'Come and drink a glass of champagne with me and we will talk of old times. Or will you have a cocktail? Our dear old Seville has changed, you see. *Thés dansants* and cocktails. It's just like Paris and London now. We've caught up. We're a civilized people.'

She led me to a table near the space where they were dancing and we sat down. I could not go on pretending I was at ease; I thought I should only get into a fearful mess.

'It's terribly stupid of me, I'm afraid,' I said, 'but I don't seem able to remember ever having known anyone of your name in the old days in Seville.'

'San Esteban?' she interrupted before I could go on. 'Naturally. My husband came from Salamanca. He was in the diplomatic service. I'm a widow. You knew me as Pilar Carreon. Of course having my hair red changes me a little, but otherwise I don't think I've altered much.'

'Not at all,' I said quickly. 'It was only the name that bothered me.'

Of course now I remembered her, but I was concerned at the moment only with the effort to conceal from her the mingled consternation and amusement that filled me as I realized that the Pilar Carreon I had danced with at the Countess de Marbella's parties and at the Fair had turned into this stout, flaunting dowager. I could not get over it. But I had to watch my step. I wondered if she knew how well I recollected the story that had shaken Seville to its foundations, and I was glad when after she had finally bidden me an effusive farewell I was able to recall it at ease.

In those days, forty years ago, Seville had not become a prosperous commercial city. It had quiet, white streets, paved with cobbles, with a multitude of churches on the belfries of which storks built their nests. Bull-fighters, students, and loungers sauntered in the Sierpes all day long. Life was easy. This of course, was before the time of motor-cars, and the Sevillan would live in penury, practising every possible economy, in order to have a carriage. For this luxury he was willing to sacrifice the necessities of life. Everyone who had any claim to gentility drove up and down the Delicias, the park-like gardens by the Guadalquivir, every blessed afternoon from five till seven. You saw carriages of all sorts, from fashionable London victorias to old broken-down shays that seemed as though they would fall to pieces, magnificent horses and wretched hacks whose tragic end in the bull-ring was near at hand. But there was one equipage that could not fail to attract the stranger's attention. It was a victoria, very smart and new, drawn by two beautiful mules; and the coachman and the footman wore the national costume of Andalusia in pale grey. It was the most splendid turn-out Seville had ever known, and it belonged to the Countess de Marbella. She was a Frenchwoman married to a Spaniard, who had enthusiastically adopted the manners and customs of her husband's country, but with a Parisian elegance that gave them a peculiar distinction. The rest of the carriages went at a snail's pace so that their occupants could see and be seen, but the countess, behind her mules, dashed up between the two crawling lines at a fast trot, went to the end of the Delicias and back twice and then drove away. The proceeding savoured somewhat of royalty. When you looked at her gracefully seated in that swift victoria, her head handsomely poised, her hair of too brilliant a gold to be natural, you did not wonder that her French vivacity and determination had given her the position she held. She made the fashion. Her decrees were law. But the countess had too many adorers not to have as many enemies, and the most determined of these was the widowed Duchess de Dos Palos, whose birth and social consequence made her claim as a right the first place in Society which the Frenchwoman had won by grace, wit and character.

Now the duchess had an only daughter. This was Doña Pilar. She was twenty when I first knew her and she was very beautiful. She had magnificent eyes and a skin that, however hard you tried to find a less hackneyed way to describe it, you could only call peach-like. She was very slim, rather tall for a Spanish girl, with a red mouth and dazzlingly white teeth. She wore her abundant, shining black hair dressed very elaborately in the Spanish style of the period. She was infinitely alluring. The fire in her black eyes, the warmth of her smile, the seductiveness of her movements suggested so much passion that it really wasn't quite fair. She belonged to the generation which was straining to break the old conventions that had kept the Spanish girl of good family hidden away till it was time for her to be married. I often played tennis with her and I used to dance with her at the Countess de Marbella's parties. The duchess considered the Frenchwoman's parties, with champagne and a sit-down supper, ostentatious, and when she opened her own great house to Society, which was only twice a year, it was to give them lemonade and biscuits. But she bred fighting-bulls, as her husband had done, and on the occasions when the young bulls were tried out, she gave picnic luncheons to which her friends were asked, very gay and informal, but with a sort of feudal state which fascinated my romantic imagination. Once, when the duchess's bulls were to fight at a *corrida* in Seville, I rode in with them at night as one of the men escorting Doña Pilar, dressed in a costume that reminded one of a picture by Goya, who headed the cavalcade. It was a charming experience to ride through the night, on those prancing Andalusian horses, with the six bulls, surrounded by oxen, thundering along behind.

A good many men, rich or noble and sometimes both, had asked Doña Pilar's hand in marriage, but, notwithstanding her mother's remonstrances, she had refused them. The duchess had been married at fifteen and it seemed to her really indecent that her daughter at twenty should be still single. The duchess asked her what she was waiting for; it was absurd to be too difficult. It was her duty to marry. But Pilar was stubborn. She found reasons to reject every one of her suitors.

Then the truth came out.

During the daily drives in the Delicias which the duchess, accompanied by her daughter, took in a great old-fashioned landau, they passed the countess as she was twice swiftly driven up and down the promenade. The ladies were on such bad terms that they pretended not to see one another, but Pilar could not keep her eyes off that smart carriage and the two beautiful grey mules and, not wishing to catch the countess's somewhat ironic glance, her own fell on the coachman who drove her. He was the handsomest man in Seville and in his beautiful uniform he was a sight to see. Of course no one knew exactly what happened, but apparently the more Pilar looked at the coachman the more she liked the look of him, and somehow or other, for all this part of the story remained a mystery, the pair met. In Spain the classes are strangely mingled and the butler may have in his veins much nobler blood than the master. Pilar learnt, not I think without satisfaction, that the coachman belonged to the ancient family of León, than which there is none in Andalusia more distinguished; and really so far as birth went there was little to choose between them. Only her life had been passed in a ducal mansion, while fate had forced him to earn his living on the box of a victoria. Neither could regret this, since only in that exalted place could he have attracted the attention of the most difficult young woman in Seville. They fell madly in love with one another. It so happened that just then a young man called the Marqués de San Esteban, whom they had met at San Sebastian the summer before, wrote to the duchess and asked for Pilar's hand in marriage. He was extremely eligible and the two families had formed alliances from time to time ever since the reign of Philip II. The duchess was determined not to stand any more nonsense, and when she told Pilar of the proposal added that she had shilly-shallied long enough. She must either marry him or she should go into a convent.

'I'm not going to either the one or the other,' said Pilar.

'What are you going to do then? I have given you a home long enough.'

'I'm going to marry José León.'

'Who is he?'

Pilar hesitated for a moment and it may be, it is indeed to be hoped, that she blushed a little.

'He's the countess's coachman.'

'What countess?'

'The Countess de Marbella.'

I remembered the duchess well and I am sure that when roused she stuck at little. She raged, she implored, she cried, she argued. There was a terrific scene. People said that she slapped her daughter and pulled her hair, but I have an impression that Pilar in such a pass was capable of hitting back. She repeated that she loved José León and he loved her. She was determined to marry him. The duchess called a family council. The matter was put before them and it was decided that to save them all from disgrace Pilar should be taken away to the country and kept there till she had recovered from her infatuation. Pilar got wind of the scheme and put a stop to it by slipping out of the window of her room one night when everyone was asleep and going to live with her lover's parents. They were respectable persons who inhabited a small apartment on the unfashionable side of the Guadalquivir, in the quarter called Triana.

After that no concealment was possible. The fat was in the fire and the clubs along the Sierpes buzzed with the scandal. Waiters were kept busy bringing trays of little glasses of Manzanilla to the members from the neighbouring wine-shops. They gossiped and laughed over the scandal, and Pilar's rejected suitors were the recipients of many congratulations. What an escape! The duchess was in despair. She could think of nothing better to do than go to the Archbishop, her trusted friend and former confessor, and beg him himself to reason with the infatuated girl. Pilar was summoned to the episcopal palace, and the good old man, used to intervening in family quarrels, did his utmost to show her the folly of her course. But she would not be persuaded. Nothing that anyone could say would induce her to forsake the man she loved. The duchess, waiting in an adjoining room, was sent for and made a final appeal to her daughter. In vain. Pilar returned to her humble lodging and the duchess in tears was left alone with the Archbishop. The Archbishop was no less astute than he was pious, and when he saw that the distracted woman was in a fit state to listen to him, advised her as a last resource to go to the Countess de Marbella. She was the cleverest woman in Seville and it might be that she could do something.

At first the duchess indignantly refused. She would never suffer the humiliation of appealing to her greatest enemy. Sooner might the ancient house of Dos Palos fall in ruin. The Archbishop was accustomed to dealing with tiresome women. He set himself with gentle cunning to induce her to change her mind and presently she consented to throw herself on the Frenchwoman's mercy. With rage in her heart she sent a message asking if she might see her, and that afternoon was ushered into her drawing-room. The countess of course had been one of the first to hear the story, but she listened to the unhappy mother as though she had not known a thing about it. She relished the situation enormously. It was the crowning triumph to have the vindictive duchess on her knees before her. But she was at heart a good-natured woman and she had a sense of humour.

'It's a most unfortunate situation,' she said. 'And I'm sorry that one of my servants should be the occasion of it. But I don't exactly see what I can do.'

The duchess would have liked to slap her painted face and her voice trembled a little with the effort she made to control her anger.

'It is not for my own sake I'm asking you to help. It's for Pilar's. I know, we all know, that you are the cleverest woman in the city. It seemed to me, it seemed to the Archbishop, that if there was a way out, your quick wit would find it.'

The countess knew she was being grossly flattered. She did not mind. She liked it.

'You must let me think.'

'Of course, if he'd been a gentleman I could have sent for my son and he would have killed him, but the Duke of Dos Palos cannot fight a duel with the Countess de Marbella's coachman.'

'Perhaps not.'

'In the old days it would have been so simple. I should merely have hired a couple of ruffians and had the brute's throat cut one night in the street. But with all these laws they have nowadays decent people have no way of protecting themselves from insult.'

'I should deplore any method of settling the difficulty that deprived me of the services of an excellent coachman,' murmured the countess.

'But if he married my daughter he cannot continue to be your coachman,' cried the duchess indignantly.

'Are you going to give Pilar an income for them to live on?'

'Me? Not a peseta. I told Pilar at once that she should get nothing from me. They can starve for all I care.'

'Well, I should think rather than do that he will prefer to stay on as my coachman. There are very nice rooms over my stables.'

The duchess went pale. The duchess went red.

'Forget all that has passed between us. Let us be friends. You can't expose me to such a humiliation. If I've ever done things to affront you I ask you on my knees to forgive me.'

The duchess cried.

'Dry your eyes, Duchess,' the Frenchwoman said at last. 'I will do what I can.'

'Is there anything you can do?'

'Perhaps. Is it true that Pilar has and will have no money of her own?'

'Not a penny if she marries without my consent.'

The countess gave her one of her brightest smiles.

'There is a common impression that southern people are romantic and northern people matter-of-fact. The reverse is true. It is the northerners who are incurably romantic. I have lived long enough among you Spaniards to know that you are nothing if not practical.'

The duchess was too broken to resent openly these unpleasant remarks, but, oh, how she hated the woman! The Countess de Marbella rose to her feet.

'You shall hear from me in the course of the day.'

She firmly dismissed her visitor.

The carriage was ordered for five o'clock and at ten minutes to, the countess, dressed for her drive, sent for José. When he came into the drawing-room, wearing his pale grey livery with such an air, she could not deny that he was very good to look upon. If he had not been her own coachman – well, it was not the moment for ideas of that sort. He stood before her, holding himself easily, but with a gallant swagger. There was nothing servile in his bearing.

'A Greek god,' the countess murmured to herself. 'It is only Andalusia that can produce such types.' And then aloud: 'I hear that you are going to marry the daughter of the Duchess of Dos Palos.'

'If the countess does not object.'

She shrugged her shoulders.

'Whoever you marry is a matter of complete indifference to me. You know of course that Doña Pilar will have no fortune.'

'Yes, madam. I have a good place and I can keep my wife. I love her.'

'I can't blame you for that. She is a beautiful girl. But I think it only right to tell you that I have a rooted objection to married coachmen. On your wedding-day you leave my service. That is all I had to say to you. You can go.'

She began to look at the daily paper that had just arrived from Paris, but José, as she expected, did not stir. He stared down at the floor. Presently the countess looked up.

'What are you waiting for?'

'I never knew madam would send me away,' he answered in a troubled tone.

'I have no doubt you'll find another place.'

'Yes, but . . .'

'Well, what is it?' she asked sharply.

He sighed miserably.

'There's not a pair of mules in the whole of Spain to come up to ours. They're almost human beings. They understand every word I say to them.'

The countess gave him a smile that would have turned the head of anyone who was not madly in love already.

'I'm afraid you must choose between me and your betrothed.'

He shifted from one foot to the other. He put his hand to his pocket to get himself a cigarette, but then, remembering where he was, restrained the gesture. He glanced at the countess and that peculiar shrewd smile came over his face which those who have lived in Andalusia know so well.

'In that case, I can't hesitate. Pilar must see that this alters my position entirely. One can get a wife any day of the week, but a place like this is found only once in a lifetime. I should be a fool to throw it up for a woman.'

That was the end of the adventure. José León continued to drive the Countess de Marbella, but she noticed when they sped up and down the Delicias that henceforward as many eyes were turned on her handsome coachman as on her latest hat: and a year later Pilar married the Marqués de San Esteban.

THE POINT OF HONOUR

SOME years ago, being engaged on writing a book about Spain in the Golden Age, I had occasion to read again the plays of Calderón. Among others I read one called *El Médico de su Honra*, which means the Physician of his Honour. It is a cruel play and you can hardly read it without a shudder. But re-reading it, I was reminded of an encounter I had had many years before which has always remained in my memory as one of the strangest I have ever known. I was quite young then and I had gone to Seville on a short visit to see the celebration of the Feast of Corpus Christi. It was the height of summer and the heat was terrific. Great sail-cloths were drawn across the narrow streets, giving a grateful shade, but in the squares the sun beat down mercilessly. In the morning I watched the procession. It was splendid and impressive. The crowd knelt down as the Host was solemnly carried past, and the Civil Guards in full uniform stood at salute to do homage to the heavenly King. And in the afternoon I joined the dense throng which was making its way to the bull-ring. The cigarette girls and the sewing girls wore carnations in their dark hair and their young men were dressed in all their best. It was just after the Spanish-American war, and the short, embroidered jacket, the skin-tight trousers, and the broad-brimmed, low-crowned hat were still worn. Sometimes the crowd was scattered by a picador on the wretched hack that would never survive the afternoon, and the rider, with conscious pride in his picturesque costume, exchanged pleasantries with the facetious. A long line of carriages, dilapidated and shabby, overfilled with *aficionados*, drove noisily along.

I went early, for it amused me to see the people gradually filling the vast arena. The cheaper seats in the sun were already packed, and it was a curious effect that the countless fans made, like the fluttering of a host of butterflies, as men and women restlessly fanned themselves. In the shade, where I was sitting, the places were taken more slowly, but even there, an hour before the fight began, one had to look rather carefully for a seat. Presently a man stopped in front of me and with a pleasant smile asked if I could make room for him. When he had settled down, I took a sidelong glance at him and noticed that he was well-dressed, in English clothes, and looked like a gentleman. He had beautiful hands, small but resolute, with thin, long fingers.

336

Wanting a cigarette, I took out my case and thought it would be polite to offer him one. He accepted. He had evidently seen that I was a foreigner, for he thanked me in French.

'You are English?' he went on.

'Yes.'

'How is it you haven't run away from the heat?'

I explained that I had come on purpose to see the Feast of Corpus Christi.

'After all, it's something you must come to Seville for.'

Then I made some casual remark about the vast concourse of people.

'No one would imagine that Spain was bleeding from the loss of all that remained of her Empire and that her ancient glory is now nothing but a name.'

'There's a great deal left.'

'The sunshine, the blue sky, and the future.'

He spoke dispassionately, as though the misfortunes of his fallen country were no concern of his. Not knowing what to reply, I remained silent. We waited. The boxes began to fill up. Ladies in their mantillas of black or white lace entered them and spread their Manila shawls over the balustrade so as to form a gay and many-coloured drapery. Now and then, when one of them was of particular beauty, a round of applause would greet her appearance and she would smile and bow without embarrassment. At last the president of the bull-fight made his entry, the band struck up, and the fighters, all glittering in their satin and gold and silver, marched swaggering across the ring. A minute later a great black bull charged in. Carried away by the horrible excitement of the contest, I noticed, notwithstanding, that my neighbour remained cool. When a man fell and only escaped by a miracle the horns of the furious beast, and with a gasp thousands sprang to their feet, he remained motionless. The bull was killed and the mules dragged out the huge carcass. I sank back exhausted.

'Do you like bull-fighting?' he asked me. 'Most English do, though I have noticed that in their own country they say hard enough things about it.'

'Can one like something that fills one with horror and loathing? Each time I come to a fight I swear I will never go to another. And yet I do.'

'It's a curious passion that leads us to delight in the peril of others. Perhaps it's natural to the human race. The Romans had their gladiators and the moderns have their melodramas. It may be that it is an instinct in man to find pleasure in bloodshed and torture.'

I did not answer directly.

'Don't you think that the bull-fight is the reason why human life is of so little account in Spain?'

'And do you think human life is of any great account?' he asked.

I gave him a quick look, for there was an ironical tone in his voice that no one could have missed, and I saw that his eyes were full of mockery. I flushed a little, for he made me on a sudden feel very young. I was surprised at the change of his expression. He had seemed rather an amiable man, with his large soft friendly eyes, but now his face bore a look of sardonic hauteur which was a trifle disquieting. I shrank back into my shell. We said little to one another during the rest of the afternoon, but when the last bull was killed and we all rose to our feet he shook hands with me and expressed the hope that we might meet again. It was a mere politeness and neither of us, I imagine, thought that there was even a remote possibility of it.

But quite by chance, two or three days later, we did. I was in a quarter of Seville that I did not know very well. I had been that afternoon to the palace of the Duke of Alba, which I knew had a fine garden and in one of the rooms a magnificent ceiling reputed to have been made by Moorish captives before the fall of Granada. It was not easy to gain admittance, but I wanted very much to see it and thought that now, in the height of summer when there were no tourists, with two or three pesetas I might be allowed in. I was disappointed. The man in charge told me that the house was under repair and no stranger could visit it without a written permission from the Duke's agent. So, having nothing else to do, I went to the royal garden of the Alcázar, the old palace of Don Pedro the Cruel, whose memory lives still among the people of Seville. It was very pleasant among the orange trees and cypresses. I had a book with me, a volume of Calderón, and I sat there for a while and read. Then I went for a stroll. In the older parts of Seville the streets are narrow and tortuous. It is delicious to wander along them under the awnings that stretch above, but not easy to find one's way. I lost mine. When I had just made up my mind that I had no notion in which direction to turn I saw a man walking towards me and recognized my acquaintance of the bull-ring. I stopped him and asked whether he could direct me. He remembered me.

'You'll never find your way,' he smiled, turning round. 'I'll walk a little with you until you can't mistake it.'

I protested, but he would not listen. He assured me it was no trouble.

'You haven't gone away then?' he said.

'I'm leaving tomorrow. I've just been to the Duke of Alba's house. I wanted to see that Moorish ceiling of his, but they wouldn't let me in.'

'Are you interested in Arabic art?'

'Well, yes. I've heard that that ceiling is one of the finest things in Seville.'

'I think I could show you one as good.'

'Where?'

He looked at me for a moment reflectively as though wondering what sort of a person I was. If he was, he evidently came to a satisfactory decision.

'If you have ten minutes to spare I will take you to it.'

I thanked him warmly and we turned back and retraced our steps. We chatted of indifferent things till we came to a large house, washed in pale green, with the Arabic look of a prison, the windows on the street heavily barred, which so many houses in Seville have. My guide clapped his hands at the gateway and a servant looked out from a window into the patio, and pulled a cord.

'Whose house is this?'

'Mine.'

I was surprised, for I knew how jealously Spaniards guarded their privacy and how little inclined they were to admit strangers into their houses. The heavy iron gate swung open and we walked into the courtyard; we crossed it and went through a narrow passage. Then I found myself suddenly in an enchanted garden. It was walled on three sides, with walls as high as houses; and their old red brick, softened by time, was covered with roses. They clad every inch in wanton, scented luxuriance. In the garden, growing wildly, as if the gardeners had striven in vain to curb the exuberance of nature, were palm-trees rising high into the air in their passionate desire for the sun, dark orange-trees and trees in flower whose names I did not know, and among them roses and more roses. The fourth wall was a Moorish loggia, with horseshoe arches heavily decorated with tracery, and when we entered this I saw the magnificent ceiling. It was like a little bit of the Alcázar, but it had not suffered the restorations that have taken all the charm from that palace, and the colours were exquisitely tender. It was a gem.

'Believe me, you need not regret that you have not been able to see the duke's house. Further, you can say that you have seen something that no other foreigner has seen within living memory.'

'It's very kind of you to have shown it to me. I'm infinitely grateful.'

He looked about him with a pride with which I could sympathize.

'It was built by one of my own ancestors in the time of Don Pedro the Cruel. It is very likely that the King himself more than once caroused under this ceiling with my ancestor.'

I held out the book I was carrying.

'I've just been reading a play in which Don Pedro is one of the important characters.'

'What is the book?'

I handed it to him and he glanced at the title. I looked about me.

'Of course, what adds to the beauty is that wonderful garden,' I said. 'The whole impression is awfully romantic.'

The Spaniard was evidently pleased with my enthusiasm. He smiled. I had already noticed how grave his smile was. It hardly dispelled the habitual melancholy of his expression.

'Would you like to sit down for a few minutes and smoke a cigarette?'

'I should love to.'

We walked out into the garden and came upon a lady sitting on a bench of Moorish tiles like those in the gardens of the Alcázar. She was working at some embroidery. She looked up quickly, evidently taken aback to see a stranger, and gave my companion an inquiring stare.

'Allow me to present you to my wife,' he said.

The lady gravely bowed. She was very beautiful, with magnificent eyes, a straight nose with delicate nostrils, and a pale smooth skin. In her black hair, abundant as with most Spanish women, there was a broad white streak. Her face was quite unlined and she could not have been more than thirty.

'You have a very lovely garden, Señora,' I said because I had to say something.

She gave it an indifferent glance.

'Yes, it is pretty.'

I felt suddenly embarrassed. I did not expect her to show me any cordiality, and I could not blame her if she thought my intrusion merely a nuisance. There was something about her that I could not quite make out. It was not an active hostility. Absurd as it seemed, since she was a young woman and beautiful, I felt that there was something dead in her.

'Are you going to sit here?' she asked her husband.

'With your permission. Only for a few minutes.'

'I won't disturb you.'

She gathered her silks and the canvas on which she had been working and rose to her feet. When she stood up I saw that she was taller than Spanish women generally are. She gave me an unsmiling bow. She carried herself with a sort of royal composure and her gait was stately. I was flippant in those days, and I remember saying to myself that she was not the sort of girl you could very well think of being silly with. We sat down on the multi-coloured bench and I gave my host a cigarette. I held a match to it. He still had my volume of Calderón in his hands, and now he idly turned the pages.

'Which of the plays have you been reading?'

'*El Médico de su Honra.*'

He gave me a look, and I thought I discerned in his large eyes a sardonic glint.

'And what do you think of it?'

'I think it's revolting. The fact is, of course, that the idea is so foreign to our modern notions.'

'What idea?'

'The point of honour and all that sort of thing.'

I should explain that the point of honour is the mainspring of much of the Spanish drama. It is the nobleman's code that impels a man to kill his wife, in cold blood, not only if she has been unfaithful to him, but even if, however little she was to blame, her conduct has given rise to scandal. In this particular play there is an example of this more deliberate than any I have ever read: the physician of his honour takes vengeance on his wife, though aware that she is innocent, simply as a matter of decorum.

'It's in the Spanish blood,' said my friend. 'The foreigner must just take it or leave it.'

'Oh, come, a lot of water has flowed down the Guadalquivir since Calderón's day. You're not going to pretend that any man would behave like that now.'

'On the contrary I pretend that even now a husband who finds himself in such a humiliating and ridiculous position can only regain his self-respect by the offender's death.'

I did not answer. It seemed to me that he was pulling a romantic gesture, and within me I murmured, Bosh. He gave me an ironic smile.

'Have you ever heard of Don Pedro Aguria?'

'Never.'

'The name is not unknown in Spanish history. An ancestor was Admiral of Spain under Philip II and another was bosom friend to Philip IV. By royal command he sat for his portrait to Velasquez.'

My host hesitated a moment. He gave me a long, reflective stare before he went on.

'Under the Philips the Agurias were rich, but by the time my friend Don Pedro succeeded his father their circumstances were much reduced. But still he was not poor, he had estates between Cordova and Aguilar, and in Seville his house retained at least traces of its ancient splendour. The little world of Seville was astonished when he announced his engagement to Soledad, the daughter of the ruined Count of Acaba, for though her family was distinguished her father was an old scamp. He was crippled with debts, and the shifts he resorted to in order to keep his head above water were none too nice. But Soledad was beautiful and Don Pedro in love with her. They were married. He adored her with the vehement passion of which perhaps only a Spaniard is capable. But he discovered to his dismay that she did not love him. She was kind and gentle. She was a good wife and a good housekeeper. She was grateful to him. But that was all. He thought that when she had a child she would change, but the child came, and it made no difference. The barrier between them that he had felt from the beginning was still there. He suffered. At last he told himself that she had a character too noble, a spirit too delicate, to descend to earthly passion, and he resigned himself. She was too high above him for mortal love.'

I moved a little uneasily in my seat. I thought the Spaniard was unduly rhetorical. He went on.

'You know that here in Seville the Opera House is open only for the six weeks after Easter, and since the Sevillans don't care very much for European music we go more to meet our friends than to listen to the singers. The Agurias had a box, like everybody else, and they went on the opening night of the season. *Tannhäuser* was being given. Don Pedro and his wife, like typical Spaniards, with nothing to do all day but always late, did not arrive till nearly the end of the first act. In the interval the Count of Acaba, Soledad's father, came into the box accompanied by a young officer of artillery whom Don Pedro had never seen before. But Soledad seemed to know him well.

'"Here is Pepe Alvarez," said the Count. "He's just come back from Cuba and I insisted on bringing him to see you."

'Soledad smiled and held out her hand, then introduced the newcomer to her husband.

'"Pepe is the son of the attorney at Carmona. We used to play together when we were children."

'Carmona is a small town near Seville, and it was here that the Count had retired when his creditors in the city grew too troublesome. The house he owned there was almost all that was left him of the fortune he had squandered. He lived in Seville now through Don Pedro's generosity. But Don Pedro did not like him and he bowed stiffly to the young officer. He guessed that his father the attorney and the count had been concerned together in transactions that were none too reputable. In a minute he left the box to talk with his cousin, the Duchess of Santaguador, whose box was opposite his own. A few days later he met Pepe Alvarez at his club in the Sierpes and had a chat with him. To his surprise he found him a very pleasant young fellow. He was full of his exploits in Cuba and he related them with humour.

'The six weeks about Easter and the great Fair are the gayest in Seville, and the world meets to exchange gossip and laughter, at one festivity after another. Pepe Alvarez with his good nature and high spirits was in great request and the Agurias met him constantly. Don Pedro saw that he amused Soledad. She was more vivacious when he was there, and her laughter, which he had so seldom heard, was a delight to him. Like other members of the aristocracy he took a booth for the Fair, where they danced, supped, and drank champagne till dawn. Pepe Alvarez was always the life and soul of the parties.

'One night Don Pedro was dancing with the Duchess of Santaguador and they passed Soledad with Pepe Alvarez.

'"Soledad is looking very beautiful this evening," she remarked.

'"And happy," he replied.

'"Is it true that once she was engaged to be married to Pepe Alvarez?"

'"Of course not."

'But the question startled him. He had known that Soledad and Pepe had known one another when they were children, but it had never crossed his mind that there could have been anything between them. The Count of Acaba, though a rogue, was a gentleman by birth, and it was inconceivable that he could have thought of marrying his daughter to the son of a provincial attorney. When they got home Don Pedro told his wife what the duchess had said and what he had replied.

'"But I was engaged to Pepe," she said.

'"Why did you never tell me?"

'"It was finished and done with. He was in Cuba. I never expected to see him again."

'"There must be people who know you were engaged to him."

'"I daresay. Does it matter?"

'"Very much. You shouldn't have renewed your acquaintance with him when he returned."

'"Does that mean that you have no confidence in me?"

'"Of course not. I have every confidence in you. All the same I wish you to discontinue it now."

'"And if I refuse?"

'"I shall kill him."

'They looked long into one another's eyes. Then she gave him a little bow and went to her room. Don Pedro sighed. He wondered whether she still loved Pepe Alvarez and whether it was on account of this that she had never loved him. But he would not allow himself to give way to the unworthy emotion of jealousy. He looked into his heart and was sure that it harboured no feeling of hatred for the young artilleryman. On the contrary, he liked him. This was not an affair of love or hate, but of honour. On a sudden he remembered that a few days before when he went to his club he noticed that the conversation suddenly failed, and, looking back, he seemed to remember that several of the group who were sitting there and chatting eyed him curiously. Was it possible that he had been the subject of their conversation? He shivered a little at the thought.

'The Fair was drawing to its end, and when it was over the Agurias had arranged to go to Cordova, where Don Pedro had an estate which it was necessary for him to visit from time to time. He looked forward to the peace of a country life after the turmoil of Seville. The day after this conversation Soledad, saying she was not well, stayed in the house, and she did the same the day following. Don Pedro visited her in her room morning and evening and they talked of indifferent things. But on the third day his cousin Conchita de Santaguador was giving a ball. It was the last of the season and everyone in her exclusive set would be there. Soledad, saying she was still indisposed, announced that she would stay at home.

'"Are you refusing to go because of our conversation of the other night?" Don Pedro asked.

'"I have been thinking over what you said. I think your demand unreasonable, but I shall accede to it. The only way I can cease my friendship with Pepe is by not going to places where I am likely to meet him." A tremor of pain passed over her lovely face. "Perhaps it is best."

'"Do you love him still?"

'"Yes."

'Don Pedro felt himself go cold with anguish.

'"Then why did you marry me?"

'"Pepe was away, in Cuba, no one knew when he would come back. Perhaps never. My father said that I must marry you."

'"To save him from ruin?"

'"From worse than ruin."

'"I am very sorry for you."

'"You have been kind to me. I have done everything in my power to prove to you that I am grateful."

'"And does Pepe love you?"

'She shook her head and smiled sadly.

'"Men are different. He's young. He's too gay to love anyone very long. No, to him I'm just the friend whom he used to play with when he was a child and flirt with when he was a boy. He can make jokes about the love he once had for me."

'He took her hand and pressed it, then kissed it and left her. He went to the ball by himself. His friends were sorry to hear of Soledad's indisposition, but after expressing a proper sympathy devoted themselves to the evening's amusement. Don Pedro drifted into the card-room. There was room at a table, and he sat down to play *chemin de fer*. He played with extraordinary luck and made a good deal of money. One of the players laughingly asked where Soledad was that evening. Don Pedro saw another give him a startled glance, but he laughed and answered that she was safely in bed and asleep. Then an unlucky incident occurred. Some young man came into the room, and addressing an artillery officer who was playing asked where Pepe Alvarez was.

'"Isn't he here?" said the officer.

'"No."

'An odd silence fell upon the party. Don Pedro exercised all his self-control to prevent his face from showing what he suddenly felt. The thought flashed through his mind that those men at the table suspected that Pepe was with Soledad, his wife. Oh, the shame! The indignity! He forced himself to go on playing for another hour and still he won. He could not go wrong. The game broke up and he returned to the ballroom. He went up to his cousin.

'"I've hardly had a word with you," he said. "Come into another room and let us sit down for a little."

'"If you like."

'The room, Conchita's boudoir, was empty.

'"Where is Pepe Alvarez tonight?" he asked casually.

'"I can't think."

'"You were expecting him?"

'"Of course."

'She was smiling as he was, but he noticed that she looked at him sharply. He dropped his mask of casualness and, though they were alone, lowered his voice.

'"Conchita, I beseech you to tell me the truth. Are they saying that he is Soledad's lover?"

'"Pedrito, what a monstrous question to put to me!"

'But he had seen the terror in her eyes and the sudden instinctive movement of her hand to her face.

'"You've answered it."

'He got up and left her. He went home and looking up from the patio saw a light in his wife's room. He went upstairs and knocked at the door. There was no answer, but he went in. To his surprise, for it was late, she was sitting up working at the embroidery upon which much of her time was spent.

'"Why are you working at this hour?"

'"I couldn't sleep, I couldn't read. I thought it would distract my mind if I worked."

'He did not sit down.

'"Soledad, I have something to tell you that must cause you pain. I must ask you to be brave. Pepe Alvarez was not at Conchita's tonight."

'"What is that to me?"

'"It is unfortunate that you were not there either. Everyone at the ball thought that you were together."

'"That's preposterous."

'"I know, but that doesn't help matters. You could have opened the gate for him yourself and let him out, or you could have slipped out yourself without anyone seeing you go or come."

'"But do you believe it?"

'"No. I agreed with you that the thing was preposterous. Where was Pepe Alvarez?"

'"How do I know? How should I know?"

'"It is very strange that he should not have come to the most brilliant party, the last party, of the season."

'She was silent for a minute.

'"The night after you spoke to me about him I wrote and told him that in view of the circumstances I thought it would be better if in future we saw no more of one another than could be helped. It may be that he did not go to the ball for the same reason that I did not."

'They were silent for a while. He looked down at the ground, but he felt that her eyes were fixed on him. I should have told you before that Don Pedro possessed one accomplishment which raised him above his fellows, but at the same time was a drawback. He was the best shot in Andalusia. Everyone knew this and it would have been a brave man who ventured to offend him. A few days earlier there had been pigeon-shooting at Tablada, the wide common outside Seville along the Guadalquivir, and Don Pedro had carried all before him. Pepe Alvarez on the other hand had shown himself so indifferent a marksman that everyone had laughed at him. The young artilleryman had borne the chaff with good-humour. Cannon were his weapon, he said.

'"What are you going to do?" Soledad asked.

'"You know that there is only one thing I can do."

'She understood. But she tried to treat what he said as a pleasantry.

'"You're childish. We're not living any more in the sixteenth century."

'"I know. That is why I am talking to you now. If I have to challenge Pepe I shall kill him. I don't want to do that. If he will resign his commission and leave Spain I will do nothing."

'"How can he? Where is he to go?"

'"He can go to South America. He may make his fortune."

'"Do you expect me to tell him that?"

'"If you love him."

'"I love him too much to ask him to run away like a coward. How could he face life without honour?"

'Don Pedro laughed.

'"What has Pepe Alvarez, the son of the attorney at Carmona, to do with honour?"

'She did not answer, but in her eyes he saw the fierce hatred she bore him. That look stabbed his heart, for he loved her, he loved her as passionately as ever.

'Next day he went to his club and joined a group who were sitting at the window looking out at the crowd passing up and down the Sierpes. Pepe Alvarez was in it. They were talking of last night's party.

'"Where were you, Pepe?" someone asked.

'"My mother was ill. I had to go to Carmona," he answered. "I was dreadfully disappointed, but perhaps it was all for the best." He turned laughingly to Don Pedro. "I hear you were in luck and won everybody's money."

'"When are you going to give us our revenge, Pedrito?" asked another.

'"I'm afraid you'll have to wait for that," he answered. "I have to go to Cordova. I find that my attorney has been robbing me. I know that all attorneys are thieves, but I stupidly thought this one was honest."

'He seemed to speak quite lightly, and it was as lightly that Pepe Alvarez put in his word.

'"I think you exaggerate, Pedrito. Don't forget that my father is an attorney and he at least is honest."

'"I don't believe it for a minute," laughed Don Pedro. "I have no doubt that your father is as big a thief as any."

'The insult was so unexpected and so unprovoked that for a moment Pepe Alvarez was staggered. The others were startled into sudden seriousness.

'"What do you mean, Pedrito?"

'"Exactly what I say."

'"It's a lie and you know it's a lie. You must withdraw that at once."

'Don Pedro laughed.

'"Of course I shall not withdraw. Your father is a thief and a rascal."

'Pepe did the only thing he could do. He sprang from his chair and with his open hand hit Don Pedro in the face. The outcome was inevitable. Next day the two men met on the frontier of Portugal. Pepe Alvarez, the attorney's son, died like a gentleman with a bullet in his heart.'

The Spaniard ended his story on such a casual note that for the first moment I hardly took it in. But when I did I was profoundly shocked.

'Barbarous,' I said. 'It was just cold-blooded murder.'

My host got up.

'You're talking nonsense, my young friend. Don Pedro did the only thing he could do in the circumstances.'

I left Seville next day, and from then till now have never been able to discover the name of the man who told me this strange story. I have often wondered whether the lady I saw, the lady with the pale face and the lock of white hair, was the unhappy Soledad.

THE POET

I AM not much interested in the celebrated and I have never had
patience with the passion that afflicts so many to shake hands
with the great ones of the earth. When it is proposed to me to
meet some person distinguished above his fellows by his rank or
his attainments, I seek for a civil excuse that may enable me to
avoid the honour; and when my friend Diego Torre suggested
giving me an introduction to Santa Aña I declined. But for once
the excuse I made was sincere; Santa Aña was not only a great
poet but also a romantic figure and it would have amused me to
see in his decrepitude a man whose adventures (in Spain at least)
were legendary; but I knew that he was old and ill and I could
not believe that it would be anything but a nuisance to him to
meet a stranger and a foreigner. Calisto de Santa Aña was the
last descendant of the Grand School; in a world unsympathetic
to Byronism he had led a Byronic existence and he had narrated
his hazardous life in a series of poems that had brought him a
fame unknown to his contemporaries. I am no judge of their
value, for I read them first when I was three-and-twenty and
then was enraptured by them; they had a passion, a heroic
arrogance and a multi-coloured vitality that swept me off my
feet, and to this day, so intermingled are those ringing lines and
haunting cadences with the charming memories of my youth, I
cannot read them without a beating heart. I am inclined to think
that Calisto de Santa Aña deserves the reputation he enjoys
among the Spanish-speaking peoples. In those days his verses
were on the lips of all young men and my friends would talk to
me endlessly of his wild ways, his vehement speeches (for he was
a politician as well as a poet), his incisive wit, and his amours.
He was a rebel and sometimes an outlaw, daring and adven-
turous; but above all he was a lover. We knew all about his
passion for this great actress or that divine singer – had we not
read till we knew them by heart the burning sonnets in which he
described his love, his anguish, and his wrath? – and we were
aware that an infanta of Spain, the proudest descendant of the
Bourbons, having yielded to his entreaties, had taken the veil
when he ceased to love her. When the Philips, her royal ancestors,
tired of a mistress she entered a convent, for it was unfitting that
one whom the King had loved should be loved by another, and
was not Calisto de Santa Aña greater than any earthly king? We

350

applauded the lady's romantic gesture; it was creditable to her and flattering to our poet.

But all this took place many years ago and for a quarter of a century Don Calisto, disdainfully withdrawing from a world that had nothing more to offer, had lived in seclusion in his native town of Ecija. It was when I announced my intention of going there (I had been spending a week or two in Seville) not because of him, but because it is a charming little Andalusian town with associations that endear it to me, that Diego Torre offered me this introduction. It appeared that Don Calisto allowed the younger men of letters occasionally to visit him and now and then would talk to them with the fire that had electrified his hearers in the great days of his prime.

'What does he look like now?' I asked.

'Magnificent.'

'Have you a photograph of him?'

'I wish I had. He has refused to face the camera since he was thirty-five. He says he does not wish posterity to know him other than young.'

I confess that I found this suggestion of vanity not a little touching. I knew that in early manhood he was of extraordinary beauty, and that moving sonnet of his written when he grew conscious that youth had for ever left him shows with what a bitter and sardonic pang he must have watched the passing of those looks that had been so fantastically admired.

But I refused my friend's offer; I was quite satisfied to read once more the poems I had known so well and for the rest I preferred to wander about the silent and sunswept streets of Ecija in freedom. It was with some consternation therefore that on the evening of my arrival I received a note from the great man himself. Diego Torre had written to him of my visit, he said, and it would give him great pleasure if I would call on him at eleven next morning. In the circumstances there was nothing for me to do but to present myself at his house at the appointed hour.

My hotel was in the Plaza and on that spring morning it was animated, but as soon as I left it I might have walked in a deserted city. The streets, the tortuous white streets, were empty but for a woman in black now and then who returned with measured steps from her devotions. Ecija is a town of churches and you can seldom go far without seeing a crumbling façade or a tower in which storks have built their nests. Once I paused to watch a string of little donkeys pass by. Their red caparisons were faded and they carried I know not what in their panniers. But Ecija has been a place of consequence in its day and many of these white houses have gateways of stone surmounted by imposing coats of arms, for to this remote spot flowed the riches of the New World and adventurers who had gathered wealth in the Americas spent here their declining years. It was in one of these houses that Don Calisto lived and as I stood at the *reja* after pulling the bell, I was pleased to think that he lived in such a fitting style. There was a dilapidated grandeur about the massive gateway that suited my impression of the flamboyant poet. Though I heard the bell peal through the house no one answered it and I rang a second and then a third time: at last an old woman with a heavy moustache came to the gate.

'What do you want?' she said.

She had fine black eyes, but a sullen look, and I supposed that it was she who took care of the old man. I gave her my card.

'I have an appointment with your master.'

She opened the iron gateway and bade me enter. Asking me to wait she left me and went upstairs. The patio was pleasantly cool after the street. Its proportions were noble and you surmised that it had been built by some follower of the *conquistadores*; but the paint was tarnished, the tiles on the floor broken, and here and there great flakes of plaster had fallen away. There was about everything an air of poverty but not of squalor. I knew that Don Calisto was poor. Money had come to him easily at times but he had never attached any importance to it and had spent it profusely. It was plain that he lived now in a penury that he disdained to notice. In the middle of the patio was a table with a rocking-chair on each side of it, and on the table newspapers a fortnight old. I wondered what dreams occupied his fancy as he sat there on the warm summer nights, smoking cigarettes. On the walls under the colonnade were Spanish pictures, dark and bad, and here and there stood an ancient dusty *bargueño* and on it a mended lustre plate. By the side of a door hung a pair of old pistols, and I had a pleasant fancy that they were the weapons he had used when in the most celebrated of his many duels, for the sake of Pepa Montañez the dancer (now, I suppose, a toothless and raddled hag), he had killed the Duke of Dos Hermanos.

The scene, with its associations which I vaguely divined, so aptly fitted the romantic poet that I was overcome by the spirit of the place. Its noble indigence surrounded him with a glory as great as the magnificence of his youth; in him too there was the spirit of the old *conquistadores*, and it was becoming that he should finish his famous life in that ruined and magnificent house. Thus surely should a poet live and die. I had arrived cool enough and even somewhat bored at the prospect of my meeting, but now I began to grow a trifle nervous. I lit a cigarette. I had come at the time appointed and wondered what detained the old man The silence was strangely disturbing. Ghosts of the past thronged the silent patio and an age dead and gone gained a sort of shadowy life for me. The men of that day had a passion and a wildness of spirit that are gone out of the world for ever. We are no longer capable of their reckless deeds or their theatrical heroics.

I heard a sound and my heart beat quickly. I was excited now and when at last I saw him coming slowly down the stairs I caught my breath. He held my card in his hand. He was a tall old man and exceedingly thin, with a skin the colour of old ivory; his hair was abundant and white, but his bushy eyebrows were dark still; they made his great eyes flash with a more sombre fire. It was wonderful that at his age those black eyes should still preserve their brilliance. His nose was aquiline, his mouth close-set. His unsmiling eyes rested on me as he approached and there was in them a look of cool appraisal. He was dressed in black and in one hand held a broad-brimmed hat. There was in his bearing assurance and dignity. He was as I should have wished him to be and as I watched him I understood how he had swayed men's minds and touched their hearts. He was every inch a poet.

He had reached the patio and came slowly towards me. He had really the eyes of an eagle. It seemed to me a tremendous moment, for there he stood, the heir of the great old Spanish poets, the magnificent Herrera, the nostalgic and moving Fray Luis, Juan de la Cruz, the mystic, and the crabbed and obscure Góngora. He was the last of that long line and he trod in their steps not unworthily. Strangely in my heart sang the lovely and tender song which is the most famous of Don Calisto's lyrics.

I was abashed. It was fortunate for me that I had prepared beforehand the phrase with which I meant to greet him.

'It is a wonderful honour, Maestro, for a foreigner such as I to make the acquaintance of so great a poet.'

A flicker of amusement passed through those piercing eyes and a smile for an instant curved the lines of that stern mouth.

'I am not a poet, Señor, but a bristle merchant. You have made a mistake, Don Calisto lives next door.'

I had come to the wrong house.

THE MOTHER

Two or three people, hearing sounds of a quarrel in the patio, came out of their rooms and listened.

'It's the new lodger,' said a woman. 'She's having a row with the porter who brought her things.'

It was a tenement house of two storeys, built round a patio, in a back street of La Macarena, which is the roughest quarter in Seville. The rooms were let to working men and the small functionaries with whom Spain is overrun, postmen, policemen, or tram-conductors, and the place swarmed with children. There were twenty families there. They squabbled and made it up; they chattered their heads off; they helped one another when help was needed; for the Andalusians are good-natured people, and on the whole they got on well enough together. One room had been for some time unlet. A woman had taken it that morning, and an hour later had brought her bits and pieces, carrying as much as she could herself, a *gallego* – the Galicians are the general porters of Spain – laden with the rest.

But the quarrel was growing more violent, and the two women above, on the first floor, anxious not to miss a word, leant over the balcony.

They heard the newcomer's shrill voice raised in a torrent of abuse and the man's sullen interjections. The two women nudged one another.

'I shan't go till you pay me,' he kept on saying.

'But I've paid you already. You said you'd do it for three *reales*.'

'Never! You promised me four.'

They were haggling over rather less than twopence halfpenny.

'Four *reales* for moving those few things? You're crazy.'

She tried to push him away.

'I shan't go till you pay me,' he repeated.

'I'll give you a penny more.'

'I won't take it.'

The dispute grew more and more noisy. The woman screamed at the porter and cursed him. She shook her fist in his face. At last he lost patience.

'Oh, all right, give me the penny and I'll go. I'm not going to waste time on a slut like you.'

She paid him, and the man, throwing down her mattress, left

her. She flung a filthy word at him as he went. She came out of the room to drag the things in, and the two women in the balcony saw her face.

'*Carai*, what an evil face! She looks like a murderess.'

A girl came up the stairs at that moment, and her mother called out: 'Did you see her, Rosalia?'

'I asked the *gallego* where she came from, he says he brought the things from Triana. She promised him four *reales* and then wouldn't pay.'

'Did he tell you her name?'

'He didn't know. But in Triana they called her La Cachirra.'

The vixen appeared again to fetch a bundle she had forgotten. She glanced at the women in the balcony watching her unconcernedly, but said nothing. Rosalia shuddered.

'She frightens me.'

La Cachirra was forty, haggard and very thin, with bony hands and fingers like a vulture's claws. Her cheeks were sunken and her skin wrinkled and yellow. When she opened her mouth, with its pale, heavy lips, she showed teeth that were pointed like those of a beast of prey. Her hair was black and coarse; she wore it in a clumsy knot, which seemed on the point of falling over her shoulders, and in front of each ear fell a straight wisp. Her eyes, deep-set in their sockets, large and black, shone fiercely. Her face bore an expression of such ferocity that no one dared come near to speak with her. She kept entirely to herself. The curiosity of the neighbours was aroused. They knew she was very poor, for her clothes were wretched. She went out every morning at six and did not return till night; but they could not even find out how she earned her living. They urged a policeman who lived in the house to make inquiries.

'As long as she doesn't break the peace, I have nothing to do with her,' said he.

But in Seville scandal travels quickly and in a few days a mason who lived in an upper room brought the news that a friend in Triana knew her story. La Cachirra had only come out of prison one month before, and she had spent seven years there – for murder. She had lodged in a house in Triana, but the children, finding out what had happened, threw stones at her and called her names; and she, turning upon them with foul words and with blows, had filled the whole place with such tumult that the landlord gave her notice. Cursing him and all who had turned her out, La Cachirra one morning suddenly disappeared.

'And whom did she murder?' asked Rosalia.

'They say it was her lover,' replied the mason.

'She can never have had one,' said Rosalia, with a laugh of scorn.

'*Santa María!*' cried Pilar, her mother, 'I hope she won't kill any of us. I said she looked like a murderess!'

Rosalia, shivering, crossed herself. At that moment La Cachirra came in from her day's work and a sudden oppression fell upon the talkers. They made a movement as if to huddle together and looked nervously at the wild-eyed woman. She seemed to see something ominous in their silence and gave them a rapid, suspicious glance. The policeman, to make conversation, bade her good evening.

'*Buena sera*,' she replied, with a scowl, and, passing quickly into her room, slammed the door.

They heard her lock it. The evil, sullen eyes had cast a gloom over them and they talked in whispers as if under a mischievous spell.

'She has the devil in her,' said Rosalia.

'I'm glad you're here to protect us, Manuel,' added her mother to the policeman.

But La Cachirra seemed indisposed to give trouble. She went her way, unbending, never addressing so much as a word to anyone, and brusquely cut short every attempt at friendliness. She felt that the neighbours had discovered her secret, the homicide and the long years of imprisonment; and the lines in her face grew sterner, the expression of her deep-set eyes more inhuman. But gradually the anxiety she had caused was dispelled. Even the garrulous Pilar ceased to pay attention to the silent gaunt figure who occasionally passed through the group sitting in the patio.

'I dare say the prison has sent her mad, they say it often does.'

But one day an event occurred to revive the gossip. A youth came to the *reja* – the wrought-iron gate that serves as front door to the Sevillan house – and asked for Antonia Sánchez. Pilar, who was mending a skirt in the patio, looked up at her daughter and shrugged her shoulders.

'No one of that name lives here,' she said.

'Yes, she does,' the young man answered; then, after a pause: 'They call her La Cachirra.'

'Ah!' Rosalia opened the gate and pointed to the door. 'She's in there.'

'Thank you.'

The youth gave her a smile. She was a pretty girl, with a high colour and fine bold eyes. A red carnation threw up the glossy blackness of her hair. Her breasts were full and the nipples were prominent under her blouse.

'Blessed be the mother that bore you,' he said, using a hackneyed phrase.

'*Vaya Usted con Dios*, go you with God,' answered Pilar.

He passed on and knocked at the door. The two women looked after him curiously.

'Who can he be?' asked Pilar. 'La Cachirra's never had a visitor before.'

There was no reply to his knocking, and he knocked again. They heard La Cachirra's rasping voice ask who was there.

'*Madre*!' he cried. 'Mother.'

There was a shriek. The door was burst open.

'Currito!'

The woman threw her arms round his neck and kissed him passionately. She fondled him and with a loving gesture stroked his face with both her hands. The girl and her mother who watched would never have thought her capable of such tenderness. At last, with little sobs of joy, she dragged him into her room.

'He's her son,' said Rosalia, with surprise. 'Who'd have thought it! And a fine fellow like that.'

Currito had a lean face and white, even teeth; his hair was cut very close, shaved on the temples, and set on the scalp with a truly Andalusian perfection. The shadow of his precocious beard showed blue beneath his brown skin. And of course he was a dandy. He had the national love of fine clothes, and his trousers were skin-tight; his short jacket and his frilled shirt were as new as new could be. He wore a broad-brimmed hat.

At last the door of La Cachirra's room was opened and she appeared, hanging on her son's arm.

'You'll come again next Sunday?' she asked.

'If nothing stops me.'

He glanced at Rosalia and, having bidden his mother good night, nodded to her also.

'*Vaya Usted con Dios!*' said she.

She gave him a smile and a flash of her dark eyes. La Cachirra intercepted the look; and the sullenness which her intense joy had driven away suddenly darkened her face like a thunder-cloud. She scowled fiercely at the handsome girl.

'Is that your son?' asked Pilar, when the youth was gone.

357

'Yes, he's my son,' answered La Cachirra gruffly, going back to her room.

Nothing could soften her, and even when her heart was brimming over with happiness she repelled the overtures of friendship.

'He's a good-looking fellow,' said Rosalia; and she thought of him more than once during the next few days.

It was a terrible love that La Cachirra had for her son. He was all she had in the world and she adored him with a fiery, jealous passion that demanded in return impossible devotion. She wished to be all in all to him. On account of his work they could not live together and it tortured her to imagine what he did when he was away from her. She could not bear him to look at a woman and she writhed at the bare idea that he might pay court to some girl. No amusement is more common in Seville than the long flirtation in which the maid sits at her window half the night long, guarded by iron bars, or stands at the gate, while her lover in the street pours his rapture into her willing ear. La Cachirra asked the boy if he had a *novia*, a sweetheart, aware that so attractive a youth must enjoy the smiles of women, and she knew he lied when he swore he spent his evenings at work. But his denials gave her a fierce delight.

When she saw Rosalia's provoking glance and Currito's answering smile, rage leapt to her throat. She had hated her neighbours before, because they were happy and she was wretched, because they knew her terrible secret; but now she hated them more, already fancying, half crazily, that they were conspiring to rob her of her son. On the following Sunday, in the afternoon, La Cachirra came out of her room, crossed the patio and stood at the gate. This was a proceeding so unusual that the neighbours commented upon it.

'Don't you know why she's there?' said Rosalia, with a stifled laugh. 'Her precious son is coming, and she doesn't want us to see him.'

'Does she think we'll eat him?'

Currito arrived and his mother took him quickly to her room.

'She's as jealous of him as if he was her lover,' said Pilar.

Rosalia looked at the closed door, laughing again, and her shining eyes were filled with mischief. It occurred to her that it would be very amusing to have a word with Currito. Rosalia's white teeth gleamed at the thought of La Cachirra's anger. She stationed herself at the gate, so that the pair, when they came out, could not help crossing her; but La Cachirra, seeing the girl, moved to the other side of her son so that not even a glance should pass between them. Rosalia shrugged her shoulders.

'You won't beat me so easily as that,' she thought.

The Sunday after, when La Cachirra took up her place at the gate, Rosalia went out into the street and strolled along in the direction from which she guessed he would come. In a minute she saw Currito, and walked on, elaborately ignoring him.

'*Hola!*' said he, stopping.

'Is it you? I thought you were afraid to speak to me.'

'I'm afraid of nothing,' he answered boastingly.

'Except mamma!'

She walked on, as if she wanted him to leave her; but she knew very well he would do no such thing.

'Where are you going?' he asked.

'What has that to do with you, Currito? Go to your mother, my son, or she'll beat you. You're afraid to look at me when she's with you.'

'What nonsense.'

'Well, *vaya Usted con Dios!* I have commissions.'

He went off rather sheepishly, and Rosalia laughed to herself. She was in the courtyard once more when he passed through with La Cachirra on his way out; and this time, shamed into courage, he stopped and said good night. La Cachirra turned red with anger.

'Come, Currito,' she cried, with a rasping voice, 'what are you waiting for?'

He went away, and the woman stopped a moment in front of Rosalia as if she were going to speak, but, with a visible effort, she restrained herself, and went back to her dark, silent room.

A few days later was the feast of San Isidoro, the patron saint of Seville, and to celebrate the holiday the mason and one or two others had put a string of Chinese lanterns in the patio. They glowed warmly in the clear summer night. The sky was soft against the shining stars. The people of the house were gathered in the middle of the patio, sitting on chairs; and the women, some with babies at their breasts, fanned themselves with little paper fans, interrupting their ceaseless chattering to fling a word of abuse at some older child who was making a nuisance of himself. The cool air was very pleasant after the day's breathless heat. Those who had been to the bull-fight were telling the less fortunate all about it. They described with precise detail a wonderful feat that Belmonte, the famous matador, had performed. With their vivid imaginations, the particulars gained every minute in variety and colour, so that it appeared that never in the history of Seville had there been a more excellent *corrida*. Everyone was present but La Cachirra, and in her room they saw the light of a solitary candle.

'And her son?'

'He's in there,' answered Pilar. 'I saw him pass an hour ago.'

'He must be amusing himself,' said Rosalia, with a laugh.

'Oh, don't bother about La Cachirra,' said another. 'Give us a dance, Rosalia.'

'Yes, yes,' they cried. 'Go on, my girl. You dance.'

In Spain they love dancing and they love to look at dancing. Years and years ago it was said that there was never a Spanish woman that was not born to dance.

The chairs were quickly set in a ring. The mason and the tram conductor fetched their guitars. Rosalia got her castanets, and stepping forward with another girl, began.

Currito, in the poky room, pricked up his ears when he heard the music.

'They're dancing,' he said, and an itching shot down his limbs.

He looked through the curtain and saw the group in the mellow light of the Chinese lanterns. He saw the two girls dancing. Rosalia wore her Sunday clothes, and, as is customary, she was heavily powdered. A splendid carnation gleamed in her hair. Currito's heart beat quickly. Love in Spain grows fast, and he had thought often of the handsome girl since that day on which he first spoke to her. He moved towards the door.

'What are you doing?' asked La Cachirra.

'I'm going to look at them dance. You never wish me to amuse myself.'

'It's Rosalia you want to see.'

He pushed her away as she tried to stop him, and joined the group that watched the dancers. La Cachirra followed a step or two, and then stood, half hidden by the gloom, with fury gnawing at her heart. Rosalia saw him.

'Aren't you frightened to look at me?' she whispered, as she passed him.

The dancing had made her light-headed and she felt no fear of La Cachirra. When the measure ended and her partner sank into a chair, Rosalia marched up to Currito and stood in front of him, upright, with her head thrown back and her breast heaving with the rapid motion.

'Of course, you don't know how to dance,' she said.

'Yes, I do.'

'Well, come then.'

She smiled provokingly, but he hesitated. He looked over his shoulder at his mother, whom he divined, rather than saw, in the darkness. Rosalia caught the glance and its meaning.

'Are you afraid?'

'What should I be afraid of?' he asked with a shrug of the shoulders.

He stepped into the ring. The guitarists strummed away and the onlookers rhythmically clapped their hands, punctuating the time with an occasional cry of *Olé*. A girl gave Currito a pair of castanets and the pair began to dance. They heard a little hiss, as of a serpent in the darkness, and Rosalia, quite reckless now, looked with a laugh at the face, ghastly white, that gleamed from the shadows. La Cachirra did not move. She watched the movements of the dance, the swaying of the bodies, the intricate steps; she saw Rosalia lean back with a graceful gesture and smile in Currito's face as he wound about her, clapping his castanets. Her eyes glowed like coals of fire and she felt them burning in the sockets; but no one noticed her, and she gave a groan of rage. The dance came to an end, and Rosalia, smiling with pleasure at the applause, told Currito she did not know he could dance so well.

La Cachirra flung herself into her room and bolted the door. She gave no answer when Currito came and bade her open.

'Well, I shall go home,' he said.

Her heart bled with pain, but she would not speak. He was all she had, all she loved in the world; and yet she hated him. She could not sleep that night, but lay thinking, half-madly, that they were robbing her of her son. In the morning she did not go to work, but lay in wait for Rosalia. The girl came out at last, rather bedraggled after the night's festivities, and she started when La Cachirra suddenly faced her.

'What do you want with my son?'

'What do you mean?' replied Rosalia, assuming an expression of surprise.

La Cachirra quivered with passion and she bit her hand to keep herself quiet.

'Oh, you know what I mean. You're stealing him from me.'

'Do you think I want your son? Keep him away from me. I can't help it if he runs after me wherever I go.'

'That's a lie!'

'Ask him!' And now Rosalia's voice was so scornful that La

Cachirra could hardly contain herself. 'He waits an hour in the street to see me. Why don't you keep him to yourself?'

'You lie, you lie! You throw yourself in his way.'

'If I wanted lovers I could get them without asking. I don't want the son of a murderess.'

Then everything grew confused to La Cachirra; the blood leaped to her head and choked her eyes. She sprang at Rosalia and tore her hair. The girl gave a shrill cry and sought to defend herself, but immediately a passer-by wrenched them apart.

'If you don't leave Currito alone, I'll kill you!' cried La Cachirra.

'Do you think I'm frightened? Keep him from me if you can. You fool, don't you see that he loves me better than his eyes?'

'Now then, go away,' said the man. 'Don't answer her, Rosalia.'

La Cachirra gave a little roar of passion, like a wild beast baulked of its prey, and pushed past into the street.

But the dance had left Currito madly in love with Rosalia, and all next day he thought of her red lips; the light of her eyes shone in his heart and filled him with enchantment. He passionately desired her. At nightfall he wandered towards the Macarena and presently found himself at her house. He waited in the darkness of the porch till he saw her in the patio. At the other end burned his mother's lonely light.

'Rosalia,' he called in a low voice.

She turned, stifling a cry of surprise.

'Why are you here today,' she whispered, going towards him.

'I couldn't keep away from you.'

'Why?' she smiled.

'Because I love you.'

'Do you know your mother nearly killed me this morning?'

And with the embellishments necessary to the Andalusian temperament, she related the occurrence, omitting, however, the final taunt which had enraged La Cachirra beyond endurance.

'She's got the temper of the devil,' said Currito; and then, with bravado: 'I shall tell her that you're my sweetheart.'

'She will be pleased,' said Rosalia ironically.

'Will you come to the *reja* tomorrow?'

'Perhaps,' she answered.

He gave a little chuckle, for he knew by her tone that she would. He swaggered even more than usual when he walked through the Sierpes on his way home. She was waiting for him when he came next day and, as is the way with lovers in Seville,

362

they talked for hours under their breath, with the iron gate between them, and it never even occurred to Currito that it was a needless impediment. When he asked Rosalia if she loved him she answered with a little amorous sigh. They tried to see the passion that burnt hotly in one another's eyes. Then he went every night.

But fearing that his mother knew of his visits, Currito did not go to see her on the following Sunday. The wretched woman waited for him with an aching heart. She was ready to fall on her knees and beg him to forgive her, but then, when he did not come, she hated him; she would have liked to see him dead at her feet. Her heart sank when she thought that another week must pass before she could even hope to see him.

The week passed and still he did not come. She could not bear it. Anguish, anguish! She loved him as no sweetheart could ever love him. She told herself that this was Rosalia's doing and when she thought of her, rage filled her heart. At last Currito plucked up his courage and went to see his mother; but she had waited too long. It seemed as though her love was dead. She pushed him away when he wanted to kiss her.

'Why haven't you come before?'

'You locked the door on me. I thought you didn't want me!'

'Was it only that? Had you no other reason?'

'I've been busy,' he said, shrugging his shoulders.

'Busy? An idle loafer like you. What have you been doing? You wouldn't have been too busy to come and see Rosalia.'

'Why did you hit her?'

'How do you know I hit her? Have you seen her?' La Cachirra strode up to her son; her eyes flashed. 'She called me a murderess.'

'Well, what of it?'

'What of it?' she screamed, so that they heard her in the patio. 'And if I am a murderess – it was for you. Yes, I killed Pepe Santi; but it was because he was beating you. It was for your sake that I lay in prison for seven years – for seven years. Oh, you fool, you think she cares for you, and every night she spends hours at the gate.'

'I know,' Currito answered with a grin.

La Cachirra started violently. She shot a puzzled look at him and then she understood. She gasped with pain and wrath; she clutched at her heart as though the agony were too intense to bear.

'You've been coming every night to the *reja* and you never

came near me? Oh, how cruel! I've done everything in the world for you. Do you think I loved Pepe Santi? I endured his blows so that I could give you bread; and I killed him when he beat you. Oh, God, I only lived for you. But for the thought of you I would have died rather than suffer those years of prison.'

'Come, woman, be reasonable. I'm twenty. What d'you expect? If it wasn't Rosalia it would be another.'

'You beast. I hate you. Get out.'

She pushed him violently to the door. Currito shrugged his shoulders.

'You needn't think I want to stay.'

He walked jauntily through the patio and slammed the iron gate behind him. La Cachirra stalked to and fro in her tiny room. The hours passed slowly. For a long while she remained at the window, watching with the horrible steadfastness of a savage beast ready to spring. She stood motionless, repressing the convulsive restlessness that tore at her heart-strings. There was a clapping of hands at the *reja* as a signal that someone was without, and she peered forward with panting mouth, her fiery eyes almost starting from her head. But it was only the mason. She waited longer, and Pilar, Rosalia's mother, came in and walked slowly up the stairs to her room. La Cachirra clutched at her throat to relieve the intolerable oppression of her breath. Still she waited. Now and then an extraordinary quiver travelled through all her limbs.

At last! There was a clap of light hands at the gate, and a voice above called out: 'Who is it?'

'Peace!'

La Cachirra recognized Rosalia's voice. She gave a gasp of triumph. The door was opened from above, and Rosalia, entering, crossed the courtyard with a buoyant and easy step. The joy of life was in her every motion. She was about to put her foot on the stair when La Cachirra sprang forward and stopped her. She caught hold of her arm and the girl could not shake herself free.

'What do you want?' said Rosalia. 'Let me pass.'

'What have you been doing with my son?'

'Let me pass, or I shall call out.'

'Is it true that you meet at the *reja* every night?'

'Mother, help! Antonio!' Rosalia cried out shrilly.

'Answer me.'

'Well, if you want the truth, you can have it. He's going to marry me. He loves me, and I – I love him with all my heart.'

She turned on La Cachirra, trying to free herself from the vicious grip. 'D'you think you can prevent us? D'you think he's frightened of you? He hates you, he told me so. He wishes you'd never come out of prison.'

'He told you that?'

La Cachirra shrank back. Rosalia pursued the advantage.

'Yes, he told me that; and he told me much more. He told me that you murdered Pepe Santi; and that you were in prison for seven years; and he wished you were dead.'

Rosalia hissed the words venomously, laughing with a shrill voice when she saw the wretched woman shrink as though struck by palpable blows.

'And you ought to be proud that I don't refuse to marry the son of a murderess.'

Then, giving La Cachirra a push, she leapt to the stairs; but the movement revived the woman, stunned by the horrible taunts, and with a cry of brutal rage she sprang upon Rosalia and caught her by the shoulders and dragged her down. Rosalia turned and hit her in the face. La Cachirra drew a knife from her bosom, and with an oath buried it in the girl's neck. Rosalia shrieked.

'Mother, she's killed me.'

She fell to the bottom of the stairs and lay huddled up on the stones. Blood made a little pool on the ground.

Half a dozen doors were flung open at the despairing cry, and people rushed to seize La Cachirra; but she backed against the wall and faced them, with an expression of such ferocity on her face that no one dared approach her. The hesitation was momentary, but Pilar ran from the balcony shrieking, and the common attention for an instant was distracted. La Cachirra saw the opportunity and ran forward. She reached her room and locked and bolted the door behind her.

Suddenly the court was filled with people. Pilar with loud dreadful cries flung herself down on her daughter and would not let herself be dragged away. Someone rushed for a doctor and someone else went for the police. The crowd surged in from the street and collected round the door. The doctor hurried in with a black bag in his hand. When the police came a dozen people at once excitedly explained what had happened. They pointed to the door of La Cachirra's room, and the police broke in. There was a scuffle and they came out with La Cachirra handcuffed. The mob rushed forward, but the police surrounded her and with their scabbards beat the people off; but they shook their fists and hurled curses at her. She looked at them scornfully. She deigned to make no answer. Her eyes shone with triumph. The policemen led her through the patio and they passed by the body of Rosalia.

'Is she dead?' asked La Cachirra.

'Yes,' the doctor answered gravely.

'Thanks be to God!' she said.

A MAN FROM GLASGOW

IT is not often that anyone entering a great city for the first time has the luck to witness such an incident as engaged Shelley's attention when he drove into Naples. A youth ran out of a shop pursued by a man armed with a knife. The man overtook him and with one blow in the neck laid him dead on the road. Shelley had a tender heart. He didn't look upon it as a bit of local colour; he was seized with horror and indignation. But when he expressed his emotions to a Calabrian priest who was travelling with him, a fellow of gigantic strength and stature, the priest laughed heartily and attempted to quiz him. Shelley says he never felt such an inclination to beat anyone.

I have never seen anything so exciting as that, but the first time I went to Algeciras I had an experience that seemed to me far from ordinary. Algeciras was then an untidy, neglected town. I arrived somewhat late at night and went to an inn on the quay. It was rather shabby, but it had a fine view of Gibraltar, solid and matter-of-fact, across the bay. The moon was full. The office was on the first floor, and a slatternly maid, when I asked for a room, took me upstairs. The landlord was playing cards. He seemed little pleased to see me. He looked me up and down, curtly gave me a number, and then, taking no further notice of me, went on with his game.

When the maid had shown me to my room I asked her what I could have to eat.

'What you like,' she answered.

I knew well enough the unreality of the seeming profusion.

'What have you got in the house?'

'You can have eggs and ham.'

The look of the hotel had led me to guess that I should get little else. The maid led me to a narrow room with white-washed walls and a low ceiling in which was a long table laid already for the next day's luncheon. With his back to the door sat a tall man, huddled over a *brasero*, the round brass dish of hot ashes which is erroneously supposed to give sufficient warmth for the temperate winter of Andalusia. I sat down at table and waited for my scanty meal. I gave the stranger an idle glance. He was looking at me, but meeting my eyes he quickly turned away. I waited for my eggs. When at last the maid brought them he looked up again.

'I want you to wake me in time for the first boat,' he said.

'*Si, señor.*'

His accent told me that English was his native tongue, and the breadth of his build, his strongly marked features, led me to suppose him a northerner. The hardy Scot is far more often found in Spain than the Englishman. Whether you go to the rich mines of Rio Tinto, or to the *bodegas* of Jerez, to Seville or to Cadiz, it is the leisurely speech of beyond the Tweed that you hear. You will meet Scotsmen in the olive groves of Carmona, on the railway between Algeciras and Bobadilla, and even in the remote cork woods of Merida.

I finished eating and went over to the dish of burning ashes. It was midwinter and the windy passage across the bay had chilled my blood. The man pushed his chair away as I drew mine forwards.

'Don't move,' I said. 'There's heaps of room for two.'

I lit a cigar and offered one to him. In Spain the Havana from Gib is never unwelcome.

'I don't mind if I do,' he said, stretching out his hand.

I recognized the singing speech of Glasgow. But the stranger was not talkative, and my efforts at conversation broke down before his monosyllables. We smoked in silence. He was even bigger than I had thought, with great broad shoulders and ungainly limbs; his face was sunburned, his hair short and grizzled. His features were hard; mouth, ears and nose were large and heavy and his skin much wrinkled. His blue eyes were pale. He was constantly pulling his ragged, grey moustache. It was a nervous gesture that I found faintly irritating. Presently I felt that he was looking at me, and the intensity of his stare grew so irksome that I glanced up expecting him, as before, to drop his eyes. He did, indeed, for a moment, but then raised them again. He inspected me from under his long, bushy eyebrows.

'Just come from Gib?' he asked suddenly.

'Yes.'

'I'm going tomorrow – on my way home. Thank God.'

He said the last two words so fiercely that I smiled.

'Don't you like Spain?'

'Oh, Spain's all right.'

'Have you been here long?'

'Too long. Too long.'

He spoke with a kind of gasp. I was surprised at the emotion my casual inquiry seemed to excite in him. He sprang to his feet and walked backwards and forwards. He stamped to and fro like a caged beast pushing aside a chair that stood in his way, and now and again repeated the words in a groan. 'Too long. Too long.' I sat still. I was embarrassed. To give myself countenance I stirred the *brasero* to bring the hotter ashes to the top, and he stood suddenly still, towering over me, as though my movement had brought back my existence to his notice. Then he sat down heavily in his chair.

'D'you think I'm queer?' he asked.

'Not more than most people,' I smiled.

'You don't see anything strange in me?'

He leant forward as he spoke so that I might see him well.

'No.'

'You'd say so if you did, wouldn't you?'

'I would.'

I couldn't quite understand what all this meant. I wondered if he was drunk. For two or three minutes he didn't say anything and I had no wish to interrupt the silence.

'What's your name?' he asked suddenly. I told him.

'Mine's Robert Morrison.'

'Scotch?'

'Glasgow. I've been in this blasted country for years. Got any baccy?'

I gave him my pouch and he filled his pipe. He lit it from a piece of burning charcoal.

'I can't stay any longer. I've stayed too long. Too long.'

He had an impulse to jump up again and walk up and down, but he resisted it, clinging to his chair. I saw on his face the effort he was making. I judged that his restlessness was due to chronic alcoholism. I find drunks very boring, and I made up my mind to take an early opportunity of slipping off to bed.

'I've been managing some olive groves,' he went on. 'I'm here working for the Glasgow and South of Spain Olive Oil Company Limited.'

'Oh, yes.'

'We've got a new process for refining oil, you know. Properly treated, Spanish oil is every bit as good as Lucca. And we can sell it cheaper.'

He spoke in a dry, matter-of-fact, business-like way. He chose his words with Scotch precision. He seemed perfectly sober.

'You know, Ecija is more or less the centre of the olive trade, and we had a Spaniard there to look after the business. But I found he was robbing us right and left, so I had to turn him out. I used to live in Seville; it was more convenient for shipping the

oil. However, I found I couldn't get a trustworthy man to be at
Ecija, so last year I went there myself. D'you know it?'

'No.'

'The firm has got a big estate two miles from the town, just
outside the village of San Lorenzo, and it's got a fine house on
it. It's on the crest of a hill, rather pretty to look at, all white,
you know, and straggling, with a couple of storks perched on the
roof. No one lived there, and I thought it would save the rent of
a place in town if I did.'

'It must have been a bit lonely,' I remarked.

'It was.'

Robert Morrison smoked on for a minute or two in silence.
I wondered whether there was any point in what he was telling
me.

I looked at my watch.

'In a hurry?' he asked sharply.

'Not particularly. It's getting late.'

'Well, what of it?'

'I suppose you didn't see many people?' I said, going back.

'Not many. I lived there with an old man and his wife who
looked after me, and sometimes I used to go down to the village
and play *tresillo* with Fernández, the chemist, and one or two
men who met at his shop. I used to shoot a bit and ride.'

'It doesn't sound such a bad life to me.'

'I'd been there two years last spring. By God, I've never known
such heat as we had in May. No one could do a thing. The
labourers just lay about in the shade and slept. Sheep died and
some of the animals went mad. Even the oxen couldn't work.
They stood around with their backs all humped up and gasped
for breath. That blasted sun beat down and the glare was so
awful, you felt your eyes would shoot out of your head. The
earth cracked and crumbled, and the crops frizzled. The olives
went to rack and ruin. It was simply hell. One couldn't get a
wink of sleep. I went from room to room, trying to get a breath
of air. Of course I kept the windows shut and had the floors
watered, but that didn't do any good. The nights were just as
hot as the days. It was like living in an oven.

'At last I thought I'd have a bed made up for me downstairs
on the north side of the house in a room that was never used
because in ordinary weather it was damp. I had an idea that I
might get a few hours' sleep there at all events. Anyhow it was
worth trying. But it was no damned good; it was a washout. I
turned and tossed and my bed was so hot that I couldn't stand

it. I got up and opened the doors that led to the veranda and walked out. It was a glorious night. The moon was so bright that I swear you could read a book by it. Did I tell you the house was on the crest of a hill? I leant against the parapet and looked at the olive-trees. It was like the sea. I suppose that's what made me think of home. I thought of the cool breeze in the fir-trees and the racket of the streets in Glasgow. Believe it or not, I could smell them, and I could smell the sea. By God, I'd have given every bob I had in the world for an hour of that air. They say it's a foul climate in Glasgow. Don't you believe it. I like the rain and the grey sky and that yellow sea and the waves. I forgot that I was in Spain, in the middle of the olive country, and I opened my mouth and took a long breath as though I were breathing in the sea-fog.

'And then all of a sudden I heard a sound. It was a man's voice. Not loud, you know, low. It seemed to creep through the silence like – well, I don't know what it was like. It surprised me. I couldn't think who could be down there in the olives at that hour. It was past midnight. It was a chap laughing. A funny sort of laugh. I suppose you'd call it a chuckle. It seemed to crawl up the hill – disjointedly.'

Morrison looked at me to see how I took the odd word he used to express a sensation that he didn't know how to describe.

'I mean, it seemed to shoot up in little jerks, something like shooting stones out of a pail. I leant forward and stared. With the full moon it was almost as light as day, but I'm dashed if I could see a thing. The sound stopped, but I kept on looking at where it had come from in case somebody moved. And in a minute it started off again, but louder. You couldn't have called it a chuckle any more, it was a real belly laugh. It just rang through the night. I wondered it didn't wake my servants. It sounded like someone who was roaring drunk.

'"Who's there?" I shouted.

'The only answer I got was a roar of laughter. I don't mind telling you I was getting a bit annoyed. I had half a mind to go down and see what it was all about. I wasn't going to let some drunken swine kick up a row like that on my place in the middle of the night. And then suddenly there was a yell. By God, I was startled. Then cries. The man had laughed with a deep bass voice, but his cries were – shrill, like a pig having his throat cut.

'"My God," I cried.

'I jumped over the parapet and ran down towards the sound.

I thought somebody was being killed. There was silence and then one piercing shriek. After that sobbing and moaning. I'll tell you what it sounded like, it sounded like someone at the point of death. There was a long groan and then nothing. Silence. I ran from place to place. I couldn't find anyone. At last I climbed the hill again and went back to my room.

'You can imagine how much sleep I got that night. As soon as it was light, I looked out of the window in the direction from which the row had come and I was surprised to see a little white house in a sort of dale among the olives. The ground on that side didn't belong to us and I'd never been through it. I hardly ever went to that part of the house and so I'd never seen the house before. I asked José who lived there. He told me that a madman had inhabited it, with his brother and a servant.'

'Oh, was that the explanation?' I said. 'Not a very nice neighbour.'

The Scot bent over quickly and seized my wrist. He thrust his face into mine and his eyes were starting out of his head with terror.

'The madman had been dead for twenty years,' he whispered.

He let go my wrist and leant back in his chair panting.

'I went down to the house and walked all round it. The windows were barred and shuttered and the door was locked. I knocked. I shook the handle and rang the bell. I heard it tinkle, but no one came. It was a two-storey house and I looked up. The shutters were tight closed, and there wasn't a sign of life anywhere.'

'Well, what sort of condition was the house in?' I asked.

'Oh, rotten. The whitewash had worn off the walls and there was practically no paint left on the door or the shutters. Some of the tiles off the roof were lying on the ground. They looked as though they'd been blown away in a gale.'

'Queer,' I said.

'I went to my friend Fernàndez, the chemist, and he told me the same story as José. I asked about the madman and Fernàndez said that no one ever saw him. He was more or less comatose ordinarily, but now and then he had an attack of acute mania and then he could be heard from ever so far laughing his head off and then crying. It used to scare people. He died in one of his attacks and his keepers cleared out at once. No one had ever dared to live in the house since.

'I didn't tell Fernàndez what I'd heard. I thought he'd only laugh at me. I stayed up that night and kept watch. But nothing happened. There wasn't a sound. I waited about till dawn and then I went to bed.'

'And you never heard anything more?'

'Not for a month. The drought continued and I went on sleeping in the lumber-room at the back. One night I was fast asleep, when something seemed to happen to me; I don't exactly know how to describe it, it was a funny feeling as though some-one had given me a little nudge, to warn me, and suddenly I was wide awake. I lay there in my bed and then in the same way as before I heard a long, low gurgle, like a man enjoying an old joke. It came from away down in the valley and it got louder. It was a great bellow of laughter. I jumped out of bed and went to the window. My legs began to tremble. It was horrible to stand there and listen to the shouts of laughter that rang through the night. Then there was the pause, and after that a shriek of pain and that ghastly sobbing. It didn't sound human. I mean, you might have thought it was an animal being tortured. I don't mind telling you I was scared stiff. I couldn't have moved if I'd wanted to. After a time the sounds stopped, not suddenly, but dying away little by little. I strained my ears, but I couldn't hear a thing. I crept back to bed and hid my face.

'I remembered then that Fernàndez had told me that the mad-man's attacks only came at intervals. The rest of the time he was quite quiet. Apathetic, Fernàndez said. I wondered if the fits of mania came regularly. I reckoned out how long it had been between the two attacks I'd heard. Twenty-eight days. It didn't take me long to put two and two together; it was quite obvious that it was the full moon that set him off. I'm not a nervous man really and I made up my mind to get to the bottom of it, so I looked out in the calendar which day the moon would be full next and that night I didn't go to bed. I cleaned my revolver and loaded it. I prepared a lantern and sat down on the parapet of my house to wait. I felt perfectly cool. To tell you the truth, I was rather pleased with myself because I didn't feel scared. There was a bit of a wind, and it whistled about the roof. It rustled over the leaves of the olive trees like waves swishing on the pebbles of the beach. The moon shone on the white walls of the house in the hollow. I felt particularly cheery.

'At last I heard a little sound, the sound I knew, and I almost laughed. I was right; it was the full moon and the attacks came as regular as clockwork. That was all to the good. I threw myself over the wall into the olive grove and ran straight to the house. The chuckling grew louder as I came near. I got to the house and looked up. There was no light anywhere. I put my ears to the door and listened. I heard the madman simply laughing his bloody head off. I beat on the door with my fist and I pulled the bell. The sound of it seemed to amuse him. He roared with laughter. I knocked again, louder and louder, and the more I knocked the more he laughed. Then I shouted at the top of my voice.

'"Open the blasted door, or I'll break it down."'

'I stepped back and kicked the latch with all my might. I flung myself at the door with the whole weight of my body. It cracked. Then I put all my strength into it and the damned thing smashed open.

'I took the revolver out of my pocket and held my lantern in the other hand. The laughter sounded louder now that the door was opened. I stepped in. The stink nearly knocked me down. I mean, just think, the windows hadn't been opened for twenty years. The row was enough to raise the dead, but for a moment I didn't know where it was coming from. The walls seemed to throw the sound backwards and forwards. I pushed open a door by my side and went into a room. It was bare and white and there wasn't a stick of furniture in it. The sound was louder and I followed it. I went into another room, but there was nothing there. I opened a door and found myself at the foot of a staircase. The madman was laughing just over my head. I walked up, cautiously, you know, I wasn't taking any risks, and at the top of the stairs there was a passage. I walked along it, throwing my light ahead of me, and I came to a room at the end. I stopped. He was in there. I was only separated from the sound by a thin door.

'It was awful to hear it. A shiver passed through me and I cursed myself because I began to tremble. It wasn't like a human being at all. By Jove, I very nearly took to my heels and ran. I had to clench my teeth to force myself to stay. But I simply couldn't bring myself to turn the handle. And then the laughter was cut, cut with a knife you'd have said, and I heard a hiss of pain. I hadn't heard that before, it was too low to carry to my place, and then a gasp.

'"Ay!" I heard the man speak in Spanish. "You're killing me. Take it away. O God, help me!"

'He screamed. The brutes were torturing him. I flung open the door and burst in. The draught blew a shutter back and the moon streamed in so bright that it dimmed my lantern. In my ears, as clearly as I hear you speak and as close, I heard the wretched chap's groans. It was awful, moaning and sobbing, and frightful gasps. No one could survive that. He was at the point of death. I tell you I heard his broken, choking cries right in my ears. And the room was empty.'

Robert Morrison sank back in his chair. That huge solid man had strangely the look of a lay figure in a studio. You felt that if you pushed him he would fall over in a heap on to the floor.

'And then?' I asked.

He took a rather dirty handkerchief out of his pocket and wiped his forehead.

'I felt I didn't much want to sleep in that room on the north side, so, heat or no heat, I moved back to my own quarters. Well, exactly four weeks later, about two in the morning, I was waked up by the madman's chuckle. It was almost at my elbow. I don't mind telling you that my nerve was a bit shaken by then, so next time the blighter was due to have an attack, next time the moon was full, I mean, I got Fernàndez to come and spend the night with me. I didn't tell him anything. I kept him up playing cards till two in the morning, and then I heard it again. I asked him if he heard anything. "Nothing," he said. "There's somebody laughing," I said. "You're drunk, man," he said, and he began laughing too. That was too much. "Shut up, you fool," I said. The laughter grew louder and louder. I cried out. I tried to shut it out by putting my hands to my ears, but it wasn't a damned bit of good. I heard it and I heard the scream of pain. Fernàndez thought I was mad. He didn't dare say so, because he knew I'd have killed him. He said he'd go to bed, and in the morning I found he'd slunk away. His bed hadn't been slept in. He'd taken himself off when he left me.

'After that I couldn't stop in Ecija. I put a factor there and went back to Seville. I felt myself pretty safe there, but as the time came near I began to get scared. Of course I told myself not to be a damned fool, but, you know, I damned well couldn't help myself. The fact is, I was afraid the sounds had followed me, and I knew if I heard them in Seville I'd go on hearing them all my life. I've got as much courage as any man, but damn it all, there are limits to everything. Flesh and blood couldn't stand it. I knew I'd go stark staring mad. I got in such a state that I began drinking, the suspense was so awful, and I used to lie awake counting the days. And at last I knew it'd come. And it came. I heard those sounds in Seville – sixty miles away from Ecija.'

I didn't know what to say. I was silent for a while.

'When did you hear the sounds last?' I asked.

'Four weeks ago.'

I looked up quickly. I was startled.

'What d'you mean by that? It's not full moon tonight?'

He gave me a dark, angry look. He opened his mouth to speak and then stopped as though he couldn't. You would have said his vocal cords were paralysed, and it was with a strange croak that at last he answered.

'Yes, it is.'

He stared at me and his pale blue eyes seemed to shine red. I have never seen in a man's face a look of such terror. He got up quickly and stalked out of the room, slamming the door behind him.

I must admit that I didn't sleep any too well that night myself.

BEFORE THE PARTY

MRS SKINNER liked to be in good time. She was already dressed, in black silk as befitted her age and the mourning she wore for her son-in-law, and now she put on her toque. She was a little uncertain about it, since the egrets' feathers which adorned it might very well arouse in some of the friends she would certainly meet at the party acid expostulations; and of course it was shocking to kill those beautiful white birds, in the mating season too, for the sake of their feathers; but there they were, so pretty and stylish, and it would have been silly to refuse them, and it would have hurt her son-in-law's feelings. He had brought them all the way from Borneo and he expected her to be so pleased with them. Kathleen had made herself rather unpleasant about them, she must wish she hadn't now, after what had happened, but Kathleen had never really liked Harold. Mrs Skinner, standing at her dressing-table, placed the toque on her head, it was after all the only nice hat she had, and put in a pin with a large jet knob. If anybody spoke to her about the ospreys she had her answer.

'I know it's dreadful,' she would say, 'and I wouldn't dream of buying them, but my poor son-in-law brought them back the last time he was home on leave.'

That would explain her possession of them and excuse their use. Everyone had been very kind. Mrs Skinner took a clean handkerchief from a drawer and sprinkled a little eau de Cologne on it. She never used scent, and she had always thought it rather fast, but eau de Cologne was so refreshing. She was very nearly ready now, and her eyes wandered out of the window behind her looking-glass. Canon Heywood had a beautiful day for his garden-party. It was warm and the sky was blue; the trees had not yet lost the fresh green of the spring. She smiled as she saw her little granddaughter in the strip of garden behind the house busily raking her very own flower-bed. Mrs Skinner wished Joan were not quite so pale, it was a mistake to have kept her so long in the tropics; and she was so grave for her age, you never saw her run about; she played quiet games of her own invention and watered her garden. Mrs Skinner gave the front of her dress a little pat, took up her gloves, and went downstairs.

Kathleen was at the writing-table in the window busy with lists she was making, for she was honorary secretary of the Ladies'

Golf Club, and when there were competitions had a good deal to do. But she too was ready for the party.

'I see you've put on your jumper after all,' said Mrs Skinner.

They had discussed at luncheon whether Kathleen should wear her jumper or her black chiffon. The jumper was black and white, and Kathleen thought it rather smart, but it was hardly mourning. Millicent, however, was in favour of it.

'There's no reason why we should all look as if we'd just come from a funeral,' she said. 'Harold's been dead eight months.'

To Mrs Skinner it seemed rather unfeeling to talk like that. Millicent was strange since her return from Borneo.

'You're not going to leave off your weeds yet, darling?' she asked.

Millicent did not give a direct answer.

'People don't wear mourning in the way they used,' she said. She paused a little and when she went on there was a tone in her voice which Mrs Skinner thought quite peculiar. It was plain that Kathleen noticed it too, for she gave her sister a curious look. 'I'm sure Harold wouldn't wish me to wear mourning for him indefinitely.'

'I dressed early because I wanted to say something to Millicent,' said Kathleen in reply to her mother's observation.

'Oh?'

Kathleen did not explain. But she put her lists aside and with knitted brows read for the second time a letter from a lady who complained that the committee had most unfairly marked down her handicap from twenty-four to eighteen. It requires a good deal of tact to be honorary secretary to a ladies' golf club. Mrs Skinner began to put on her new gloves. The sun-blinds kept the room cool and dark. She looked at the great wooden hornbill, gaily painted, which Harold had left in her safekeeping; and it seemed a little odd and barbaric to her, but he had set much store on it. It had some religious significance and Canon Heywood had been greatly struck by it. On the wall, over the sofa, were Malay weapons, she forgot what they were called, and here and there on occasional tables pieces of silver and brass which Harold at various times had sent to them. She had liked Harold and involuntarily her eyes sought his photograph which stood on the piano with photographs of her two daughters, her grandchild, her sister, and her sister's son.

'Why, Kathleen, where's Harold's photograph?' she asked.

Kathleen looked round. It no longer stood in its place.

'Someone's taken it away,' said Kathleen.

Surprised and puzzled, she got up and went over to the piano. The photographs had been rearranged so that no gap should show.

'Perhaps Millicent wanted to have it in her bedroom,' said Mrs Skinner.

'I should have noticed it. Besides, Millicent has several photographs of Harold. She keeps them locked up.'

Mrs Skinner had thought it very peculiar that her daughter should have no photographs of Harold in her room. Indeed she had spoken of it once, but Millicent had made no reply. Millicent had been strangely silent since she came back from Borneo, and had not encouraged the sympathy Mrs Skinner would have been so willing to show her. She seemed unwilling to speak of her great loss. Sorrow took people in different ways. Her husband had said the best thing was to leave her alone. The thought of him turned her ideas to the party they were going to.

'Father asked if I thought he ought to wear a top-hat,' she said. 'I said I thought it was just as well to be on the safe side.'

It was going to be quite a grand affair. They were having ices, strawberry and vanilla, from Boddy, the confectioner, but the Heywoods were making the iced coffee at home. Everyone would be there. They had been asked to meet the Bishop of Hong Kong, who was staying with the Canon, an old college friend of his, and he was going to speak on the Chinese missions. Mrs Skinner, whose daughter had lived in the East for eight years and whose son-in-law had been Resident of a district in Borneo, was in a flutter of interest. Naturally it meant more to her than to people who had never had anything to do with the Colonies and that sort of thing.

'What can they know of England who only England know?' as Mr Skinner said.

He came into the room at that moment. He was a lawyer, as his father had been before him, and he had offices in Lincoln's Inn Fields. He went up to London every morning and came down every evening. He was only able to accompany his wife and daughters to the Canon's garden-party because the Canon had very wisely chosen a Saturday to have it on. Mr Skinner looked very well in his tail-coat and pepper-and-salt trousers. He was not exactly dressy, but he was neat. He looked like a respectable family solicitor, which indeed he was; his firm never touched work that was not perfectly above board, and if a client went to him with some trouble that was not quite nice, Mr Skinner would look grave.

'I don't think this is the sort of case that we very much care to undertake,' he said. 'I think you'd do better to go elsewhere.'

He drew towards him his writing-block and scribbled a name and address on it. He tore off a sheet of paper and handed it to his client.

'If I were you I think I would go and see these people. If you mention my name I believe they'll do anything they can for you.'

Mr Skinner was clean-shaven and very bald. His pale lips were tight and thin, but his blue eyes were shy. He had no colour in his cheeks and his face was much lined.

'I see you've put on your new trousers,' said Mrs Skinner.

'I thought it would be a good opportunity,' he answered. 'I was wondering if I should wear a buttonhole.'

'I wouldn't, father,' said Kathleen. 'I don't think it's awfully good form.'

'A lot of people will be wearing them,' said Mrs Skinner.

'Only clerks and people like that,' said Kathleen. 'The Heywoods have had to ask everybody, you know. And besides, we are in mourning.'

'I wonder if there'll be a collection after the Bishop's address,' said Mr Skinner.

'I should hardly think so,' said Mrs Skinner.

'I think it would be rather bad form,' agreed Kathleen.

'It's as well to be on the safe side,' said Mr Skinner. 'I'll give for all of us. I was wondering if ten shillings would be enough or if I must give a pound.'

'If you give anything I think you ought to give a pound, father,' said Kathleen.

'I'll see when the time comes. I don't want to give less than anyone else, but on the other hand I see no reason to give more than I need.'

Kathleen put away her papers in the drawer of the writing-table and stood up. She looked at her wrist-watch.

'Is Millicent ready?' asked Mrs Skinner.

'There's plenty of time. We're only asked at four, and I don't think we ought to arrive much before half past. I told Davis to bring the car round at four-fifteen.'

Generally Kathleen drove the car, but on grand occasions like this Davis, who was the gardener, put on his uniform and acted as chauffeur. It looked better when you drove up, and naturally Kathleen didn't much want to drive herself when she was wearing her new jumper. The sight of her mother forcing her fingers one by one into her new gloves reminded her that she must put on her own. She smelt them to see if any odour of the cleaning still clung to them. It was very slight. She didn't believe anyone would notice.

At last the door opened and Millicent came in. She wore her widow's weeds. Mrs Skinner never could get used to them, but of course she knew that Millicent must wear them for a year. It was a pity they didn't suit her; they suited some people. She had tried on Millicent's bonnet once, with its white band and long veil, and thought she looked very well in it. Of course she hoped dear Alfred would survive her, but if he didn't she would never go out of weeds. Queen Victoria never had. It was different for Millicent; Millicent was a much younger woman; she was only thirty-six: it was very sad to be a widow at thirty-six. And there wasn't much chance of her marrying again. Kathleen wasn't very likely to marry now, she was thirty-five; last time Millicent and Harold had come home she had suggested that they should have Kathleen to stay with them; Harold had seemed willing enough, but Millicent said it wouldn't do. Mrs Skinner didn't know why not. It would give her a chance. Of course they didn't want to get rid of her, but a girl ought to marry, and somehow all the men they knew at home were married already. Millicent said the climate was trying. It was true she was a bad colour. No one would think now that Millicent had been the prettier of the two. Kathleen had fined down as she grew older, of course some people said she was too thin, but now that she had cut her hair, with her cheeks red from playing golf in all weathers, Mrs Skinner thought her quite pretty. No one could say that of poor Millicent; she had lost her figure completely; she had never been tall, and now that she had filled out she looked stocky. She was a good deal too fat; Mrs Skinner supposed it was due to the tropical heat that prevented her from taking exercise. Her skin was sallow and muddy; and her blue eyes, which had been her best feature, had gone quite pale.

'She ought to do something about her neck,' Mrs Skinner reflected. 'She's becoming dreadfully jowly.'

She had spoken of it once or twice to her husband. He remarked that Millicent wasn't as young as she was; that might be, but she needn't let herself go altogether. Mrs Skinner made up her mind to talk to her daughter seriously, but of course she must respect her grief, and she would wait till the year was up. She was just as glad to have this reason to put off a conversation the thought of which made her slightly nervous. For Millicent was certainly changed. There was something sullen in her face which made her mother not quite at home with her. Mrs Skinner liked to say aloud all the thoughts that passed through her head, but Millicent when you made a remark (just to say something, you know) had an awkward habit of not answering, so that you wondered whether she had heard. Sometimes Mrs Skinner found it so irritating, that not to be quite sharp with Millicent she had to remind herself that poor Harold had only been dead eight months.

The light from the window fell on the widow's heavy face as she advanced silently, but Kathleen stood with her back to it. She watched her sister for a moment.

'Millicent, there's something I want to say to you,' she said. 'I was playing golf with Gladys Heywood this morning.'

'Did you beat her?' asked Millicent.

Gladys Heywood was the Canon's only unmarried daughter.

'She told me something about you which I think you ought to know.'

Millicent's eyes passed beyond her sister to the little girl watering flowers in the garden.

'Have you told Annie to give Joan her tea in the kitchen, mother?' she said.

'Yes, she'll have it when the servants have theirs.'

Kathleen looked at her sister coolly.

'The Bishop spent two or three days at Singapore on his way home,' she went on. 'He's very fond of travelling. He's been to Borneo, and he knows a good many of the people that you know.'

'He'll be interested to see you, dear,' said Mrs Skinner. 'Did he know poor Harold?'

'Yes, he met him at Kuala Solor. He remembers him very well. He says he was shocked to hear of his death.'

Millicent sat down and began to put on her black gloves. It seemed strange to Mrs Skinner that she received these remarks with complete silence.

'Oh, Millicent,' she said, 'Harold's photo has disappeared. Have you taken it?'

'Yes, I put it away.'

'I should have thought you'd like to have it out.'

Once more Millicent said nothing. It really was an exasperating habit.

Kathleen turned slightly in order to face her sister.

'Millicent, why did you tell us that Harold died of fever?'

The widow made no gesture, she looked at Kathleen with

steady eyes, but her sallow skin darkened with a flush. She did not reply.

'What *do* you mean, Kathleen?' asked Mr Skinner, with surprise.

'The Bishop says that Harold committed suicide.'

Mrs Skinner gave a startled cry, but her husband put out a deprecating hand.

'Is it true, Millicent?'

'It is.'

'But why didn't you tell us?'

Millicent paused for an instant. She fingered idly a piece of Brunei brass which stood on the table by her side. That too had been a present from Harold.

'I thought it better for Joan that her father should be thought to have died of fever. I didn't want her to know anything about it.'

'You've put us in an awfully awkward position,' said Kathleen, frowning a little. 'Gladys Heywood said she thought it rather nasty of me not to have told her the truth. I had the greatest difficulty in getting her to believe that I knew absolutely nothing about it. She said her father was rather put out. He says, after all the years we've known one another, and considering that he married you, and the terms we've been on, and all that, he does think we might have had confidence in him. And at all events, if we didn't want to tell him the truth we needn't have told him a lie.'

'I must say I sympathize with him there,' said Mr Skinner, acidly.

'Of course I told Gladys that we weren't to blame. We only told them what you told us.'

'I hope it didn't put you off your game,' said Millicent.

'Really, my dear, I think that is a most improper observation,' exclaimed her father.

He rose from his chair, walked over to the empty fireplace, and from force of habit stood in front of it with parted coat-tails.

'It was my business,' said Millicent, 'and if I chose to keep it to myself I didn't see why I shouldn't.'

'It doesn't look as if you had any affection for your mother if you didn't even tell her,' said Mrs Skinner.

Millicent shrugged her shoulders.

'You might have known it was bound to come out,' said Kathleen.

'Why? I didn't expect that two gossiping old parsons would have nothing else to talk about than me.'

'When the Bishop said he'd been to Borneo it's only natural that the Heywoods should ask him if he knew you and Harold.'

'All that's neither here nor there,' said Mr Skinner. 'I think you should certainly have told us the truth, and we could have decided what was the best thing to do. As a solicitor I can tell you that in the long run it only makes things worse if you attempt to hide them.'

'Poor Harold,' said Mrs Skinner, and the tears began to trickle down her raddled cheeks. 'It seems dreadful. He was always a good son-in-law to me. Whatever induced him to do such a dreadful thing?'

'The climate.'

'I think you'd better give us all the facts, Millicent,' said her father.

'Kathleen will tell you.'

Kathleen hesitated. What she had to say really was rather dreadful. It seemed terrible that such things should happen to a family like theirs.

'The Bishop says he cut his throat.'

Mrs Skinner gasped and she went impulsively up to her bereaved daughter. She wanted to fold her in her arms.

'My poor child,' she sobbed.

But Millicent withdrew herself.

'Please don't fuss me, mother. I really can't stand being mauled about.'

'Really, Millicent,' said Mr Skinner, with a frown.

He did not think she was behaving very nicely.

Mrs Skinner dabbed her eyes carefully with her handkerchief and with a sigh and a little shake of the head returned to her chair. Kathleen fidgeted with the long chain she wore round her neck.

'It does seem rather absurd that I should have to be told the details of my brother-in-law's death by a friend. It makes us all look such fools. The Bishop wants very much to see you, Millicent; he wants to tell you how much he feels for you.' She paused, but Millicent did not speak. 'He says that Millicent had been away with Joan and when she came back she found poor Harold lying dead on his bed.'

'It must have been a great shock,' said Mr Skinner.

Mrs Skinner began to cry again, but Kathleen put her hand gently on her shoulder.

'Don't cry, mother,' she said. 'It'll make your eyes red and people will think it so funny.'

They were all silent while Mrs Skinner, drying her eyes, made a successful effort to control herself. It seemed very strange to her that at this very moment she should be wearing in her toque the ospreys that poor Harold had given her.

'There's something else I ought to tell you,' said Kathleen.

Millicent looked at her sister again, without haste, and her eyes were steady, but watchful. She had the look of a person who is waiting for a sound which he is afraid of missing.

'I don't want to say anything to wound you, dear,' Kathleen went on, 'but there's something else and I think you ought to know it. The Bishop says that Harold drank.'

'Oh, my dear, how dreadful!' cried Mrs Skinner. 'What a shocking thing to say. Did Gladys Heywood tell you? What did you say?'

'I said it was entirely untrue.'

'This is what comes of making secrets of things,' said Mr Skinner, irritably. 'It's always the same. If you try and hush a thing up all sorts of rumours get about which are ten times worse than the truth.'

'They told the Bishop in Singapore that Harold had killed himself while he was suffering from delirium tremens. I think for all our sakes you ought to deny that, Millicent.'

'It's such a dreadful thing to have said about anyone who's dead,' said Mrs Skinner. 'And it'll be so bad for Joan when she grows up.'

'But what is the foundation of this story, Millicent?' asked her father. 'Harold was always very abstemious.'

'Here,' said the widow.

'Did he drink?'

'Like a fish.'

The answer was so unexpected, and the tone so sardonic, that all three of them were startled.

'Millicent, how can you talk like that of your husband when he's dead?' cried her mother, clasping her neatly gloved hands. 'I can't understand you. You've been so strange since you came back. I could never have believed that a girl of mine could take her husband's death like that.'

'Never mind about that, mother,' said Mr Skinner. 'We can go into all that later.'

He walked to the window and looked out at the sunny little garden, and then walked back into the room. He took his pince-nez out of his pocket and, though he had no intention of putting them on, wiped them with his handkerchief. Millicent looked at him and in her eyes, unmistakably, was a look of irony which was quite cynical. Mr Skinner was vexed. He had finished his week's work and he was a free man till Monday morning. Though he had told his wife that this garden-party was a great nuisance and he would much sooner have tea quietly in his own garden, he had been looking forward to it. He did not care very much about Chinese missions, but it would be interesting to meet the Bishop. And now this! It was not the kind of thing he cared to be mixed up in; it was most unpleasant to be told on a sudden that his son-in-law was a drunkard and a suicide. Millicent was thoughtfully smoothing her white cuffs. Her coolness irritated him; but instead of addressing her he spoke to his younger daughter.

'Why don't you sit down, Kathleen? Surely there are plenty of chairs in the room.'

Kathleen drew forward a chair and without a word seated herself. Mr Skinner stopped in front of Millicent and faced her.

'Of course I see why you told us Harold had died of fever. I think it was a mistake, because that sort of thing is bound to come out sooner or later. I don't know how far what the Bishop has told the Heywoods coincides with the facts, but if you will take my advice you will tell us everything as circumstantially as you can, then we can see. We can't hope that it will go no further now that Canon Heywood and Gladys know. In a place like this people are bound to talk. It will make it easier for all of us if we at all events know the exact truth.'

Mrs Skinner and Kathleen thought he put the matter very well. They waited for Millicent's reply. She had listened with an impassive face; that sudden flush had disappeared and it was once more, as usual, pasty and sallow.

'I don't think you'll much like the truth if I tell it you,' she said.

'You must know that you can count on our sympathy and understanding,' said Kathleen gravely.

Millicent gave her a glance and the shadow of a smile flickered across her set mouth. She looked slowly at the three of them. Mrs Skinner had an uneasy impression that she looked at them as though they were mannequins at a dressmaker's. She seemed to live in a different world from theirs and to have no connexion with them.

'You know, I wasn't in love with Harold when I married him,' she said reflectively.

Mrs Skinner was on the point of making an exclamation when a rapid gesture of her husband, barely indicated, but after so many years of married life perfectly significant, stopped her.

Millicent went on. She spoke with a level voice, slowly, and there was little change of expression in her tone.

'I was twenty-seven, and no one else seemed to want to marry me. It's true he was forty-four, and it seemed rather old, but he had a very good position, hadn't he? I wasn't likely to get a better chance.'

Mrs Skinner felt inclined to cry again, but she remembered the party.

'Of course I see now why you took his photograph away,' she said dolefully.

'Don't, mother,' exclaimed Kathleen.

It had been taken when he was engaged to Millicent and was a very good photograph of Harold. Mrs Skinner had always thought him quite a fine man. He was heavily built, tall and perhaps a little too fat, but he held himself well, and his presence was imposing. He was inclined to be bald, even then, but men did go bald very early nowadays, and he said that topees, sun-helmets, you know, were very bad for the hair. He had a small dark moustache, and his face was deeply burned by the sun. Of course his best feature was his eyes; they were brown and large, like Joan's. His conversation was interesting. Kathleen said he was pompous, but Mrs Skinner didn't think him so, she didn't mind it if a man laid down the law; and when she saw, as she very soon did, that he was attracted by Millicent she began to like him very much. He was always very attentive to Mrs Skinner, and she listened as though she were really interested when he spoke of his district, and told her of the big game he had killed. Kathleen said he had a pretty good opinion of himself, but Mrs Skinner came of a generation which accepted without question the good opinion that men had of themselves. Millicent saw very soon which way the wind blew, and though she said nothing to her mother, her mother knew that if Harold asked her she was going to accept him.

Harold was staying with some people who had been thirty years in Borneo and they spoke well of the country. There was no reason why a woman shouldn't live there comfortably; of course the children had to come home when they were seven; but Mrs Skinner thought it unnecessary to trouble about that yet. She asked Harold to dine, and she told him they were always in to tea. He seemed to be at a loose end, and when his visit to his old friends was drawing to a close, she told him they would be very much pleased if he would come and spend a fortnight with them. It was towards the end of this that Harold and Millicent became engaged. They had a very pretty wedding, they went to Venice for their honeymoon, and then they started for the East. Millicent wrote from various ports at which the ship touched. She seemed happy.

'People were very nice to me at Kuala Solor,' she said. Kuala Solor was the chief town of the state of Sembulu. 'We stayed with the Resident and everyone asked us to dinner. Once or twice I heard men ask Harold to have a drink, but he refused; he said he had turned over a new leaf now he was a married man. I didn't know why they laughed. Mrs Gray, the Resident's wife, told me they were all so glad Harold was married. She said it was dreadfully lonely for a bachelor on one of the outstations. When we left Kuala Solor Mrs Gray said good-bye to me so funnily that I was quite surprised. It was as if she was solemnly putting Harold in my charge.'

They listened to her in silence. Kathleen never took her eyes off her sister's impassive face; but Mr Skinner stared straight in front of him at the Malay arms, krises and parangs, which hung on the wall above the sofa on which his wife sat.

'It wasn't till I went back to Kuala Solor a year and a half later, that I found out why their manner had seemed so odd.' Millicent gave a queer little sound like the echo of a scornful laugh. 'I knew then a good deal that I hadn't known before. Harold came to England that time in order to marry. He didn't much mind who it was. Do you remember how we spread ourselves out to catch him, mother? We needn't have taken so much trouble.'

'I don't know what you mean, Millicent,' said Mrs Skinner, not without acerbity, for the insinuation of scheming did not please her. 'I saw he was attracted by you.'

Millicent shrugged her heavy shoulders.

'He was a confirmed drunkard. He used to go to bed every night with a bottle of whisky and empty it before morning. The Chief Secretary told him he'd have to resign unless he stopped drinking. He said he'd give him one more chance. He could take his leave then and go to England. He advised him to marry so that when he got back he'd have someone to look after him. Harold married me because he wanted a keeper. They took bets in Kuala Solor on how long I'd make him stay sober.'

'But he was in love with you,' Mrs Skinner interrupted. 'You don't know how he used to speak to me about you, and at that time you're speaking of, when you went to Kuala Solor to have Joan, he wrote me such a charming letter about you.'

388

Millicent looked at her mother again and a deep colour dyed her sallow skin. Her hands, lying on her lap, began to tremble a little. She thought of those first months of her married life. The government launch took them to the mouth of the river, and they spent the night at the bungalow which Harold said jokingly was their seaside residence. Next day they went up-stream in a prahu. From the novels she had read she expected the rivers of Borneo to be dark and strangely sinister, but the sky was blue, dappled with little white clouds, and the green of the mangroves and the nipahs, washed by the flowing water, glistened in the sun. On each side stretched the pathless jungle, and in the distance, silhouetted against the sky, was the rugged outline of a mountain. The air in the early morning was fresh and buoyant. She seemed to enter upon a friendly, fertile land, and she had a sense of spacious freedom. They watched the banks for monkeys sitting on the branches of the tangled trees, and once Harold pointed out something that looked like a log and said it was a crocodile. The Assistant Resident, in ducks and a topee, was at the landing-stage to meet them, and a dozen trim little soldiers were lined up to do them honour. The Assistant Resident was introduced to her. His name was Simpson.

'By Jove, sir,' he said to Harold. 'I'm glad to see you back. It's been deuced lonely without you.'

The Resident's bungalow, surrounded by a garden in which grew wildly all manner of gay flowers, stood on the top of a low hill. It was a trifle shabby and the furniture was sparse, but the rooms were cool and of generous size.

'The kampong is down there,' said Harold, pointing.

Her eyes followed his gesture, and from among the coconut trees rose the beating of a gong. It gave her a queer little sensation in the heart.

Though she had nothing much to do the days passed easily enough. At dawn a boy brought them their tea and they lounged about the veranda, enjoying the fragrance of the morning (Harold in a singlet and a sarong, she in a dressing-gown) till it was time to dress for breakfast. Then Harold went to his office and she spent an hour or two learning Malay. After tiffin he went back to his office while she slept. A cup of tea revived them both, and they went for a walk or played golf on the nine-hole links which Harold had made on a level piece of cleared jungle below the bungalow. Night fell at six and Mr Simpson came along to have a drink. They chatted till their late dinner hour, and sometimes Harold and Mr Simpson played chess. The balmy evenings were enchanting. The fireflies turned the bushes just below the veranda into coldly-sparkling, tremulous beacons, and flowering trees scented the air with sweet odours. After dinner they read the papers which had left London six weeks before and presently went to bed. Millicent enjoyed being a married woman, with a house of her own, and she was pleased with the native servants, in their gay sarongs, who went about the bungalow, with bare feet, silent but friendly. It gave her a pleasant sense of importance to be the wife of the Resident. Harold impressed her by the fluency with which he spoke the language, by his air of command, and by his dignity. She went into the court-house now and then to hear him try cases. The multifariousness of his duties and the competent way in which he performed them aroused her respect. Mr Simpson told her that Harold understood the natives as well as any man in the country. He had the combination of firmness, tact, and good-humour which was essential in dealing with that timid, revengeful, and suspicious race. Millicent began to feel a certain admiration for her husband.

They had been married nearly a year when two English naturalists came to stay with them for a few days on their way to the interior. They brought a pressing recommendation from the governor, and Harold said he wanted to do them proud. Their arrival was an agreeable change. Millicent asked Mr Simpson to dinner (he lived at the Fort and only dined with them on Sunday nights) and after dinner the men sat down to play bridge. Millicent left them presently and went to bed, but they were so noisy that for some time she could not get to sleep. She did not know at what hour she was awakened by Harold staggering into the room. She kept silent. He made up his mind to have a bath before getting into bed; the bath-house was just below their room, and he went down the steps that led to it. Apparently he slipped, for there was a great clatter, and he began to swear. Then he was violently sick. She heard him sluice the buckets of water over himself and in a little while, walking very cautiously this time, he crawled up the stairs and slipped into bed. Millicent pretended to be asleep. She was disgusted. Harold was drunk. She made up her mind to speak about it in the morning. What would the naturalists think of him? But in the morning Harold was so dignified that she hadn't quite the determination to refer to the matter. At eight Harold and she, with their two guests, sat down to breakfast. Harold looked round the table.

'Porridge,' he said. 'Millicent, your guests might manage a little Worcester Sauce for breakfast, but I don't think they'll much fancy anything else. Personally I shall content myself with a whisky and soda.'

The naturalists laughed, but shamefacedly.

'Your husband's a terror,' said one of them.

'I should not think I had properly performed the duties of hospitality if I sent you sober to bed on the first night of your visit,' said Harold, with his round, stately way of putting things.

Millicent, smiling acidly, was relieved to think that her guests had been as drunk as her husband. The next evening she sat up with them and the party broke up at a reasonable hour. But she was glad when the strangers went on with their journey. Their life resumed its placid course. Some months later Harold went on a tour of inspection of his district and came back with a bad attack of malaria. This was the first time she had seen the disease of which she had heard so much, and when he recovered it did not seem strange to her that Harold was very shaky. She found his manner peculiar. He would come back from the office and stare at her with glazed eyes; he would stand on the veranda, swaying slightly, but still dignified, and make long harangues about the political situation in England; losing the thread of his discourse, he would look at her with an archness which his natural stateliness made somewhat disconcerting and say:

'Pulls you down dreadfully, this confounded malaria. Ah, little woman, you little know the strain it puts upon a man to be an empire builder.'

She thought that Mr Simpson began to look worried, and once or twice, when they were alone, he seemed on the point of saying something to her which his shyness at the last moment prevented. The feeling grew so strong that it made her nervous, and one evening when Harold, she knew not why, had remained later than usual at the office she tackled him.

'What have you got to say to me, Mr Simpson?' she broke out suddenly.

He blushed and hesitated.

'Nothing. What makes you think I have anything in particular to say to you?'

Mr Simpson was a thin, weedy youth of four and twenty, with a fine head of waving hair which he took great pains to plaster down very flat. His wrists were swollen and scarred with mosquito bites. Millicent looked at him steadily.

'If it's something to do with Harold don't you think it would be kinder to tell me frankly?'

He grew scarlet now. He shuffled uneasily on his rattan chair. She insisted.

'I'm afraid you'll think it awful cheek,' he said at last. 'It's rotten of me to say anything about my chief behind his back. Malaria's a rotten thing, and after one's had a bout of it one feels awfully down and out.'

He hesitated again. The corners of his mouth sagged as if he were going to cry. To Millicent he seemed like a little boy.

'I'll be as silent as the grave,' she said with a smile, trying to conceal her apprehension. 'Do tell me.'

'I think it's a pity your husband keeps a bottle of whisky at the office. He's apt to take a nip more often than he otherwise would.'

Mr Simpson's voice was hoarse with agitation. Millicent felt a sudden coldness shiver through her. She controlled herself, for she knew that she must not frighten the boy if she were to get out of him all there was to tell. He was unwilling to speak. She pressed him, wheedling, appealing to his sense of duty, and at last she began to cry. Then he told her that Harold had been drunk more or less for the last fortnight, the natives were talking about it, and they said that soon he would be as bad as he had been before his marriage. He had been in the habit of drinking a good deal too much then, but details of that time, notwithstanding all her attempts, Mr Simpson resolutely declined to give her.

'Do you think he's drinking now?' she asked.

'I don't know.'

Millicent felt herself on a sudden hot with shame and anger. The Fort, as it was called because the rifles and the ammunition were kept there, was also the court-house. It stood opposite the Resident's bungalow in a garden of its own. The sun was just about to set and she did not need a hat. She got up and walked across. She found Harold sitting in the office behind the large hall in which he administered justice. There was a bottle of whisky in front of him. He was smoking cigarettes and talking to three or four Malays who stood in front of him listening with obsequious and at the same time scornful smiles. His face was red.

The natives vanished.

'I came to see what you were doing,' she said.

He rose, for he always treated her with elaborate politeness, and lurched. Feeling himself unsteady he assumed an elaborate stateliness of demeanour.

'Take a seat, my dear, take a seat. I was detained by press of work.'

She looked at him with angry eyes.

'You're drunk,' she said.

He stared at her, his eyes bulging a little, and a haughty look gradually traversed his large and fleshy face.

'I haven't the remotest idea what you mean,' he said.

She had been ready with a flow of wrathful expostulation, but suddenly she burst into tears. She sank into a chair and hid her face. Harold looked at her for an instant, then the tears began to trickle down his own cheeks; he came towards her with outstretched arms and fell heavily on his knees. Sobbing, he clasped her to him.

'Forgive me, forgive me,' he said. 'I promise you it shall not happen again. It was that damned malaria.'

'It's so humiliating,' she moaned.

He wept like a child. There was something very touching in the self-abasement of that big dignified man. Presently Millicent looked up. His eyes, appealing and contrite, sought hers.

'Will you give me your word of honour that you'll never touch liquor again?'

'Yes, yes. I hate it.'

It was then she told him that she was with child. He was overjoyed.

'That is the one thing I wanted. That'll keep me straight.'

They went back to the bungalow. Harold bathed himself and had a nap. After dinner they talked long and quietly. He admitted that before he married her he had occasionally drunk more than was good for him; in outstations it was easy to fall into bad habits. He agreed to everything that Millicent asked. And during the months before it was necessary for her to go to Kuala Solor for her confinement, Harold was an excellent husband, tender, thoughtful, proud, and affectionate; he was irreproachable. A launch came to fetch her, she was to leave him for six weeks, and he promised faithfully to drink nothing during her absence. He put his hands on her shoulders.

'I never break a promise,' he said in his dignified way. 'But even without it, can you imagine that while you are going through so much, I should do anything to increase your troubles?'

Joan was born. Millicent stayed at the Resident's, and Mrs Gray, his wife, a kindly creature of middle age, was very good to her. The two women had little to do during the long hours they were alone but to talk, and in course of time Millicent learnt everything there was to know of her husband's alcoholic past. The fact which she found most difficult to reconcile herself to was that Harold had been told that the only condition upon which he would be allowed to keep his post was that he should bring back a wife. It caused in her a dull feeling of resentment. And when she discovered what a persistent drunkard he had been, she felt vaguely uneasy. She had a horrid fear that during her absence he would not have been able to resist the craving. She went home with her baby and a nurse. She spent a night at the mouth of the river and sent a messenger in a canoe to announce her arrival. She scanned the landing-stage anxiously as the launch approached it. Harold and Mr Simpson were standing there. The trim little soldiers were lined up. Her heart sank, for Harold was swaying slightly, like a man who seeks to keep his balance on a rolling ship, and she knew he was drunk.

It wasn't a very pleasant home-coming. She had almost forgotten her mother and father and her sister who sat there silently listening to her. Now she roused herself and became once more aware of their presence. All that she spoke of seemed very far away.

'I knew that I hated him then,' she said. 'I could have killed him.'

'Oh, Millicent, don't say that,' cried her mother. 'Don't forget that he's dead, poor man.'

Millicent looked at her mother, and for a moment a scowl darkened her impassive face. Mr Skinner moved uneasily.

'Go on,' said Kathleen.

'When he found out that I knew all about him he didn't bother very much more. In three months he had another attack of D.T.s.'

'Why didn't you leave him?' said Kathleen.

'What would have been the good of that? He would have been dismissed from the service in a fortnight. Who was to keep me and Joan? I had to stay. And when he was sober I had nothing to complain of. He wasn't in the least in love with me, but he was fond of me; I hadn't married him because I was in love with him, but because I wanted to be married. I did everything I could to keep liquor from him; I managed to get Mr Gray to prevent whisky being sent from Kuala Solor, but he got it from the Chinese. I watched him as a cat watches a mouse. He was too cunning for me. In a little while he had another outbreak. He neglected his duties. I was afraid complaints would be made. We were two days from Kuala Solor and that was our safeguard, but I suppose something was said, for Mr Gray wrote a private letter of warning to me. I showed it to Harold. He stormed and blustered, but I saw he was frightened, and for two or three months he was quite sober. Then he began again. And so it went on till our leave became due.

'Before we came to stay here I begged and prayed him to be careful. I didn't want any of you to know what sort of a man I had married. All the time he was in England he was all right and before we sailed I warned him. He'd grown to be very fond of Joan, and very proud of her, and she was devoted to him. She always liked him better than she liked me. I asked him if he wanted to have his child grow up, knowing that he was a drunkard, and I found out that at last I'd got a hold on him. The thought terrified him. I told him that *I* wouldn't allow it, and if he ever let Joan see him drunk I'd take her away from him at once. Do you know, he grew quite pale when I said it. I fell on my knees that night and thanked God, because I'd found a way of saving my husband.

'He told me that if I would stand by him he would have another try. We made up our minds to fight the thing together. And he tried so hard. When he felt as though he *must* drink he came to me. You know he was inclined to be rather pompous; with me he was so humble, he was like a child; he depended on me. Perhaps he didn't love me when he married me, but he loved me then, me and Joan. I'd hated him, because of the humiliation, because when he was drunk and tried to be dignified and impressive he was loathsome; but now I got a strange feeling in my heart. It wasn't love, but it was a queer, shy tenderness. He was something more than my husband, he was like a child that I'd carried under my heart for long and weary months. He was so proud of me and, you know, I was proud too. His long speeches didn't irritate me any more, and I only thought his stately ways rather funny and charming. At last we won. For two years he never touched a drop. He lost his craving entirely. He was even able to joke about it.

'Mr Simpson had left us then and we had another young man called Francis.

'"I'm a reformed drunkard, you know, Francis," Harold said to him once. "If it hadn't been for my wife I'd have been sacked long ago. I've got the best wife in the world, Francis."

'You don't know what it meant to me to hear him say that. I felt that all I'd gone through was worth while. I was so happy.'

She was silent. She thought of the broad, yellow and turbid river on whose banks she had lived so long. The egrets, white and gleaming in the tremulous sunset, flew down the stream in a flock, flew low and swift, and scattered. They were like a ripple of snowy notes, sweet and pure and spring-like, which an unseen hand drew forth, a divine arpeggio, from an unseen harp. They fluttered along between the green banks, wrapped in the shadows of evening, like the happy thoughts of a contented mind.

'Then Joan fell ill. For three weeks we were very anxious. There was no doctor nearer than Kuala Solor and we had to put up with the treatment of a native dispenser. When she grew well again I took her down to the mouth of the river in order to give her a breath of sea air. We stayed there a week. It was the first time I had been separated from Harold since I went away to have Joan. There was a fishing village, on piles, not far from us, but really we were quite alone. I thought a great deal about Harold, so tenderly, and all at once I knew that I loved him. I was so glad when the prahu came to fetch us back, because I wanted to tell him. I thought it would mean a good deal to him. I can't tell you how happy I was. As we rowed up-stream the headman told me that Mr Francis had had to go up-country to arrest a woman who had murdered her husband. He had been gone a couple of days.

'I was surprised that Harold was not on the landing-stage to meet me; he was always very punctilious about that sort of thing; he used to say that husband and wife should treat one another as politely as they treated acquaintances; and I could not imagine what business had prevented him. I walked up the little hill on which the bungalow stood. The ayah brought Joan behind me. The bungalow was strangely silent. There seemed to be no servants about, and I could not make it out; I wondered if Harold hadn't expected me so soon and was out. I went up the steps. Joan was thirsty and the ayah took her to the servants' quarters to give her something to drink. Harold was not in the sitting-room. I called him, but there was no answer. I was disappointed because I should have liked him to be there. I went into our bedroom. Harold wasn't out after all; he was lying on the bed asleep. I was really very much amused, because he always pretended he never slept in the afternoon. He said it was an unnecessary habit that we white people got into. I went up to the bed softly. I thought I would have a joke with him. I opened the mosquito curtains. He was lying on his back, with nothing on but a sarong, and there was an empty whisky bottle by his side. He was drunk.

'It had begun again. All my struggles for so many years were wasted. My dream was shattered. It was all hopeless. I was seized with rage.'

Millicent's face grew once again darkly red and she clenched the arms of the chair she sat in.

'I took him by the shoulders and shook him with all my might. "You beast," I cried, "you beast." I was so angry I don't know what I did, I don't know what I said. I kept on shaking him. You don't know how loathsome he looked, that large fat man, half naked; he hadn't shaved for days, and his face was bloated and purple. He was breathing heavily. I shouted at him, but he took no notice. I tried to drag him out of bed, but he was too heavy. He lay there like a log. "Open your eyes," I screamed. I shook him again. I hated him. I hated him all the more because for a week I'd loved him with all my heart. He'd let me down. He'd let me down. I wanted to tell him what a filthy beast he was. I could make no impression on him. "You shall open your eyes," I cried. I was determined to make him look at me.'

The widow licked her dry lips. Her breath seemed hurried. She was silent.

'If he was in that state I should have thought it best to have let him go on sleeping,' said Kathleen.

'There was a parang on the wall by the side of the bed. You know how fond Harold was of curios.'

'What's a parang?' said Mrs Skinner.

'Don't be silly, mother,' her husband replied irritably. 'There's one on the wall immediately behind you.'

He pointed to the Malay sword on which for some reason his eyes had been unconsciously resting. Mrs Skinner drew quickly into the corner of the sofa, with a little frightened gesture, as though she had been told that a snake lay curled up beside her.

'Suddenly the blood spurted out from Harold's throat. There was a great red gash right across it.'

'Millicent,' cried Kathleen, springing up and almost leaping towards her, 'what in God's name do you mean?'

Mrs Skinner stood staring at her with wide startled eyes, her mouth open.

'The parang wasn't on the wall any more. It was on the bed. Then Harold opened his eyes. They were just like Joan's.'

'I don't understand,' said Mr Skinner. 'How could he have committed suicide if he was in the state you describe?'

Kathleen took her sister's arm and shook her angrily.

'Millicent, for God's sake explain.'

Millicent released herself.

'The parang was on the wall, I told you. I don't know what happened. There was all the blood, and Harold opened his eyes.

He died almost at once. He never spoke, but he gave a sort of gasp.'

At last Mr Skinner found his voice.

'But, you wretched woman, it was murder.'

Millicent, her face mottled with red, gave him such a look of scornful hatred that he shrank back. Mrs Skinner cried out.

'Millicent, you didn't do it, did you?'

Then Millicent did something that made them all feel as though their blood were turned to ice in their veins. She chuckled.

'I don't know who else did,' she said.

'My God,' muttered Mr Skinner.

Kathleen had been standing bolt upright with her hands to her heart, as though its beating were intolerable.

'And what happened then?' she said.

'I screamed. I went to the window and flung it open. I called for the ayah. She came across the compound with Joan. "Not Joan," I cried. "Don't let her come." She called the cook and told him to take the child. I cried to her to hurry. And when she came I showed her Harold. "The Tuan's killed himself!" I cried. She gave a scream and ran out of the house.

'No one would come near. They were all frightened out of their wits. I wrote a letter to Mr Francis, telling him what had happened and asking him to come at once.'

'How do you mean you told him what had happened?'

'I said, on my return from the mouth of the river, I'd found Harold with his throat cut. You know, in the tropics you have to bury people quickly. I got a Chinese coffin, and the soldiers dug a grave behind the Fort. When Mr Francis came, Harold had been buried for nearly two days. He was only a boy. I could do anything I wanted with him. I told him I'd found the parang in Harold's hand and there was no doubt he'd killed himself in an attack of delirium tremens. I showed him the empty bottle. The servants said he'd been drinking hard ever since I left to go to the sea. I told the same story at Kuala Solor. Everyone was very kind to me, and the government granted me a pension.'

For a little while nobody spoke. At last Mr Skinner gathered himself together.

'I am a member of the legal profession. I'm a solicitor. I have certain duties. We've always had a most respectable practice. You've put me in a monstrous position.'

He fumbled, searching for the phrases that played at hide and seek in his scattered wits. Millicent looked at him with scorn.

'What are you going to do about it?'

'It was murder, that's what it was; do you think I can possibly connive at it?'

'Don't talk nonsense, father,' said Kathleen sharply. 'You can't give up your own daughter.'

'You've put me in a monstrous position,' he repeated.

Millicent shrugged her shoulders again.

'You made me tell you. And I've borne it long enough by myself. It was time that all of you bore it too.'

At that moment the door was opened by the maid.

'Davis has brought the car round, sir,' she said.

Kathleen had the presence of mind to say something, and the maid withdrew.

'We'd better be starting,' said Millicent.

'I can't go to the party now,' cried Mrs Skinner, with horror. 'I'm far too upset. How can we face the Heywoods? And the Bishop will want to be introduced to you.'

Millicent made a gesture of indifference. Her eyes held their ironical expression.

'We must go, mother,' said Kathleen. 'It would look so funny if we stayed away.' She turned on Millicent furiously. 'Oh, I think the whole thing is such frightfully bad form.'

Mrs Skinner looked helplessly at her husband. He went to her and gave her his hand to help her up from the sofa.

'I'm afraid we must go, mother,' he said.

'And me with the ospreys in my toque that Harold gave me with his own hands,' she moaned.

He led her out of the room, Kathleen followed close on their heels, and a step or two behind came Millicent.

'You'll get used to it, you know,' she said quietly. 'At first I thought of it all the time, but now I forget it for two or three days together. It's not as if there was any danger.'

They did not answer. They walked through the hall and out of the front door. The three ladies got into the back of the car and Mr Skinner seated himself beside the driver. They had no self-starter; it was an old car, and Davis went to the bonnet to crank it up. Mr Skinner turned round and looked petulantly at Millicent.

'I ought never to have been told,' he said. 'I think it was most selfish of you.'

Davis took his seat and they drove off to the Canon's garden-party.

LOUISE

I COULD never understand why Louise bothered with me. She disliked me and I knew that behind my back, in that gentle way of hers, she seldom lost the opportunity of saying a disagreeable thing about me. She had too much delicacy ever to make a direct statement, but with a hint and a sigh and a little flutter of her beautiful hands she was able to make her meaning plain. She was a mistress of cold praise. It was true that we had known one another almost intimately, for five-and-twenty years, but it was impossible for me to believe that she could be affected by the claims of old association. She thought me a coarse, brutal, cynical, and vulgar fellow. I was puzzled at her not taking the obvious course and dropping me. She did nothing of the kind; indeed, she would not leave me alone; she was constantly asking me to lunch and dine with her and once or twice a year invited me to spend a week-end at her house in the country. At last I thought that I had discovered her motive. She had an uneasy suspicion that I did not believe in her; and if that was why she did not like me, it was also why she sought my acquaintance: it galled her that I alone should look upon her as a comic figure and she could not rest till I acknowledged myself mistaken and defeated. Perhaps she had an inkling that I saw the face behind the mask and because I alone held out was determined that sooner or later I too should take the mask for the face. I was never quite certain that she was a complete humbug. I wondered whether she fooled herself as thoroughly as she fooled the world or whether there was some spark of humour at the bottom of her heart. If there was it might be that she was attracted to me, as a pair of crooks might be attracted to one another, by the knowledge that we shared a secret that was hidden from everybody else.

I knew Louise before she married. She was then a frail, delicate girl with large and melancholy eyes. Her father and mother worshipped her with an anxious adoration, for some illness, scarlet fever I think, had left her with a weak heart and she had to take the greatest care of herself. When Tom Maitland proposed to her they were dismayed, for they were convinced that she was much too delicate for the strenuous state of marriage. But they were not too well off and Tom Maitland was rich. He promised to do everything in the world for Louise and finally they entrusted her to him as a sacred charge. Tom Maitland was a big, husky fellow, very good-looking and a fine athlete. He doted on Louise. With her weak heart he could not hope to keep her with him long and he made up his mind to do everything he could to make her few years on earth happy. He gave up the games he excelled in, not because she wished him to, she was glad that he should play golf and hunt, but because by a coincidence she had a heart attack whenever he proposed to leave her for a day. If they had a difference of opinion she gave in to him at once, for she was the most submissive wife a man could have, but her heart failed her and she would be laid up, sweet and uncomplaining, for a week. He could not be such a brute as to cross her. Then they would have quite a little tussle about which should yield and it was only with difficulty that at last he persuaded her to have her own way. On one occasion seeing her walk eight miles on an expedition that she particularly wanted to make, I suggested to Tom Maitland that she was stronger than one would have thought. He shook his head and sighed.

'No, no, she's dreadfully delicate. She's been to all the best heart specialists in the world and they all say that her life hangs on a thread. But she has an unconquerable spirit.'

He told her that I had remarked on her endurance.

'I shall pay for it tomorrow,' she said to me in her plaintive way. 'I shall be at death's door.'

'I sometimes think that you're quite strong enough to do the things you want to,' I murmured.

I had noticed that if a party was amusing she could dance till five in the morning, but if it was dull she felt very poorly and Tom had to take her home early. I am afraid she did not like my reply, for though she gave me a pathetic little smile I saw no amusement in her large blue eyes.

'You can't very well expect me to fall down dead just to please you,' she answered.

Louise outlived her husband. He caught his death of cold one day when they were sailing and Louise needed all the rugs there were to keep her warm. He left her a comfortable fortune and a daughter. Louise was inconsolable. It was wonderful that she managed to survive the shock. Her friends expected her speedily to follow poor Tom Maitland to the grave. Indeed they already felt dreadfully sorry for Iris, her daughter, who would be left an orphan. They redoubled their attentions towards Louise. They would not let her stir a finger; they insisted on doing everything in the world to save her trouble. They had to, because if she was called upon to do anything tiresome or inconvenient her heart went back on her and there she was at death's door. She was entirely lost without a man to take care of her, she said, and she did not know how, with her delicate health, she was going to bring up her dear Iris. Her friends asked why she did not marry again. Oh, with her heart it was out of the question, though of course she knew that dear Tom would have wished her to, and perhaps it would be the best thing for Iris if she did; but who would want to be bothered with a wretched invalid like herself? Oddly enough more than one young man showed himself quite ready to undertake the charge and a year after Tom's death she allowed George Hobhouse to lead her to the altar. He was a fine, upstanding fellow and he was not at all badly off. I never saw anyone so grateful as he for the privilege of being allowed to take care of this frail little thing.

'I shan't live to trouble you long,' she said.

He was a soldier and an ambitious one, but he resigned his commission. Louise's health forced her to spend the winter at Monte Carlo and the summer at Deauville. He hesitated a little at throwing up his career, and Louise at first would not hear of it; but at last she yielded as she always yielded, and he prepared to make his wife's last few years as happy as might be.

'It can't be very long now,' she said. 'I'll try not to be trouble-some.'

For the next two or three years Louise managed, notwith-standing her weak heart, to go beautifully dressed to all the most lively parties, to gamble very heavily, to dance and even to flirt with tall slim young men. But George Hobhouse had not the stamina of Louise's first husband and he had to brace himself now and then with a stiff drink for his day's work as Louise's second husband. It is possible that the habit would have grown on him, which Louise would not have liked at all, but very fortunately (for her) the war broke out. He rejoined his regiment and three months later was killed. It was a great shock to Louise. She felt, however, that in such a crisis she must not give way to a private grief; and if she had a heart attack nobody heard of it. In order to distract her mind she turned her villa at Monte Carlo into a hospital for convalescent officers. Her friends told her that she would never survive the strain.

'Of course it will kill me,' she said, 'I know that. But what does it matter? I must do my bit.'

It didn't kill her. She had the time of her life. There was no convalescent home in France that was more popular. I met her by chance in Paris. She was lunching at the Ritz with a tall and very handsome young Frenchman. She explained that she was there on business connected with the hospital. She told me that the officers were too charming to her. They knew how delicate she was and they wouldn't let her do a single thing. They took care of her, well – as though they were all her husbands. She sighed.

'Poor George, who would ever have thought that I with my heart should survive him?'

'And poor Tom!' I said.

I don't know why she didn't like my saying that. She gave me her plaintive smile and her beautiful eyes filled with tears.

'You always speak as though you grudged me the few years that I can expect to live.'

'By the way, your heart's much better, isn't it?'

'It'll never be better. I saw a specialist this morning and he said I must be prepared for the worst.'

'Oh, well, you've been prepared for that for nearly twenty years now, haven't you?'

When the war came to an end Louise settled in London. She was now a woman of over forty, thin and frail still, with large eyes and pale cheeks, but she did not look a day more than twenty-five. Iris, who had been at school and was now grown up, came to live with her.

'She'll take care of me,' said Louise. 'Of course, it'll be hard on her to live with such a great invalid as I am, but it can only be for such a little while, I'm sure she won't mind.'

Iris was a nice girl. She had been brought up with the knowledge that her mother's health was precarious. As a child she had never been allowed to make a noise. She had always realized that her mother must on no account be upset. And though Louise told her now that she would not hear of her sacrificing herself for a tiresome old woman the girl simply would not listen. It wasn't a question of sacrificing herself, it was a happiness to do what she could for her poor dear mother. With a sigh her mother let her do a great deal.

'It pleases the child to think she's making herself useful,' she said.

'Don't you think she ought to go out and about more?' I asked.

'That's what I'm always telling her. I can't get her to enjoy herself. Heaven knows, I never want anyone to put themselves out on my account.'

And Iris, when I remonstrated with her, said: 'Poor dear mother, she wants me to go and stay with friends and go to parties, but the moment I start off anywhere she has one of her heart attacks, so I much prefer to stay at home.'

But presently she fell in love. A young friend of mine, a very good lad, asked her to marry him and she consented. I liked the child and was glad that she was to be given at last the chance to lead a life of her own. She had never seemed to suspect that such a thing was possible. But one day the young man came to me in great distress and told me that his marriage was indefinitely postponed. Iris felt that she could not desert her mother. Of course it was really no business of mine, but I made the opportunity to go and see Louise. She was always glad to receive her friends at tea-time and now that she was older she cultivated the society of painters and writers.

'Well, I hear that Iris isn't going to be married,' I said after a little.

'I don't know about that. She's not going to be married quite as soon as I could have wished. I've begged her on my bended knees not to consider me, but she absolutely refuses to leave me.'

'Don't you think it's rather hard on her?'

'Dreadfully. Of course it can only be for a few months, but I hate the thought of anyone sacrificing themselves for me.'

'My dear Louise, you've buried two husbands, I can't see the least reason why you shouldn't bury at least two more.'

'Do you think that's funny?' she asked me in a tone that she made as offensive as she could.

'I suppose it's never struck you as strange that you're always strong enough to do anything you want to and that your weak heart only prevents you from doing things that bore you?'

'Oh, I know, I know what you've always thought of me. You've never believed that I had anything the matter with me, have you?'

I looked at her full and square.

'Never. I think you've carried out for twenty-five years a stupendous bluff. I think you're the most selfish and monstrous woman I have ever known. You ruined the lives of those two wretched men you married and now you're going to ruin the life of your daughter.'

I should not have been surprised if Louise had had a heart attack then. I fully expected her to fly into a passion. She merely gave me a gentle smile.

'My poor friend, one of these days you'll be so dreadfully sorry you said this to me.'

'Have you quite determined that Iris shall not marry this boy?'

'I've begged her to marry him. I know it'll kill me, but I don't mind. Nobody cares for me. I'm just a burden to everybody.'

'Did you tell her it would kill you?'

'She made me.'

'As if anyone ever made you do anything that you were not yourself quite determined to do.'

'She can marry her young man tomorrow if she likes. If it kills me, it kills me.'

'Well, let's risk it, shall we?'

'Haven't you got any compassion for me?'

'One can't pity anyone who amuses one as much as you amuse me,' I answered.

A faint spot of colour appeared on Louise's pale cheeks and though she smiled still her eyes were hard and angry.

'Iris shall marry in a month's time,' she said, 'and if anything happens to me I hope you and she will be able to forgive yourselves.'

Louise was as good as her word. A date was fixed, a trousseau of great magnificence was ordered, and invitations were issued. Iris and the very good lad were radiant. On the wedding-day, at ten o'clock in the morning, Louise, that devilish woman, had one of her heart attacks – and died. She died gently forgiving Iris for having killed her.

THE PROMISE

My wife is a very unpunctual woman, so when, having arranged to lunch with her at Claridge's, I arrived there ten minutes late and did not find her I was not surprised. I ordered a cocktail. It was the height of the season and there were but two or three vacant tables in the lounge. Some of the people after an early meal were drinking their coffee, others like myself were toying with a dry Martini; the women in their summer frocks looked gay and charming and the men debonair; but I could see no one whose appearance sufficiently interested me to occupy the quarter of an hour I was expecting to wait. They were slim and pleasant to look upon, well dressed and carelessly at ease, but they were for the most part of a pattern and I observed them with tolerance rather than with curiosity. But it was two o'clock and I felt hungry. My wife tells me that she can wear neither a turquoise nor a watch, for the turquoise turns green and the watch stops; and this she attributes to the malignity of fate. I have nothing to say about the turquoise, but I sometimes think the watch might go if she wound it. I was engaged with these reflections when an attendant came up and with that hushed significance that hotel attendants affect (as though their message held a more sinister meaning than their words suggested) told me that a lady had just telephoned to say that she had been detained and could not lunch with me.

I hesitated. It is not very amusing to eat in a crowded restaurant by oneself, but it was late to go to a club and I decided that I had better stay where I was. I strolled into the dining-room. It has never given me any particular satisfaction (as it appears to do to so many elegant persons) to be known by name to the head waiters of fashionable restaurants, but on this occasion I should certainly have been glad to be greeted by less stony an eye. The *maître d'hôtel* with a set and hostile face told me that every table was occupied. I looked helplessly round the large and stately room and on a sudden to my pleasure caught sight of someone I knew. Lady Elizabeth Vermont was an old friend. She smiled and noticing that she was alone I went up to her.

'Will you take pity on a hungry man and let me sit with you?' I asked.

'Oh, do. But I've nearly finished.'

She was at a little table by the side of a massive column and when I took my place I found that notwithstanding the crowd we sat almost in privacy.

'This is a bit of luck for me,' I said. 'I was on the point of fainting from hunger.'

She had a very agreeable smile; it did not light up her face suddenly, but seemed rather to suffuse it by degrees with charm. It hesitated for a moment about her lips and then slowly travelled to those great shining eyes of hers and there softly lingered. No one surely could say that Elizabeth Vermont was cast in the common mould. I never knew her when she was a girl, but many have told me that then she was so lovely, it brought the tears to one's eyes, and I could well believe it; for now, though fifty, she was still incomparable. Her ravaged beauty made the fresh and blooming comeliness of youth a trifle insipid. I do not like these painted faces that look all alike; and I think women are foolish to dull their expression and obscure their personality with powder, rouge, and lipstick. But Elizabeth Vermont painted not to imitate nature, but to improve it; you did not question the means but applauded the result. The flaunting boldness with which she used cosmetics increased rather than diminished the character of that perfect face. I suppose her hair was dyed; it was black and sleek and shining. She held herself upright as though she had never learned to loll and she was very slim. She wore a dress of black satin, the lines and simplicity of which were admirable, and about her neck was a long rope of pearls. Her only other jewel was an enormous emerald which guarded her wedding-ring, and its sombre fire emphasized the whiteness of her hand. But it was in her hands with their reddened nails that she most clearly betrayed her age; they had none of a girl's soft and dimpled roundness; and you could not but look at them with a certain dismay. Before very long they would look like the talons of a bird of prey.

Elizabeth Vermont was a remarkable woman. Of great birth, for she was the daughter of the seventh Duke of St Erth, she married at the age of eighteen a very rich man and started at once upon a career of astounding extravagance, lewdness, and dissipation. She was too proud to be cautious, too reckless to think of consequences, and within two years her husband in circumstances of appalling scandal divorced her. She married then one of the three co-respondents named in the case and eighteen months later ran away from him. Then followed a succession of lovers. She became notorious for her profligacy. Her startling beauty and her scandalous conduct held her in the public eye and it was never very long but that she gave the gossips something to talk about. Her name stank in the nostrils of decent people. She was a gambler, a spendthrift, and a wanton. But though unfaithful to her lovers she was constant to her friends and there always remained a few who would never allow, whatever she did, that she was anything but a very nice woman. She had candour, high spirits, and courage. She was never a hypocrite. She was generous and sincere. It was at this period of her life that I came to know her; for great ladies, now that religion is out of fashion, when they are very much blown upon take a flattering interest in the arts. When they receive the cold shoulder from members of their own class they condescend sometimes to the society of writers, painters, and musicians. I found her an agreeable companion. She was one of those blessed persons who say quite fearlessly what they think (thus saving much useful time), and she had a ready wit. She was always willing to talk (with a diverting humour) of her lurid past. Her conversation, though uninstructed, was good, because, notwithstanding everything, she was an honest woman.

Then she did a very surprising thing. At the age of forty, she married a boy of twenty-one. Her friends said it was the maddest act of all her life, and some who had stuck to her through thick and thin, now for the boy's sake, because he was nice and it seemed shameful thus to take advantage of his inexperience, refused to have anything more to do with her. It really was the limit. They prophesied disaster, for Elizabeth Vermont was incapable of sticking to any man for more than six months, nay, they hoped for it, since it seemed the only chance for the wretched youth that his wife should behave so scandalously that he must leave her. They were all wrong. I do not know whether time was responsible for a change of heart in her, or whether Peter Vermont's innocence and simple love touched her, but the fact remains that she made him an admirable wife. They were poor, and she was extravagant, but she became a thrifty housewife; she grew on a sudden so careful of her reputation that the tongue of scandal was silenced. His happiness seemed her only concern. No one could doubt that she loved him devotedly. After being the subject of so much conversation for so long Elizabeth Vermont ceased to be talked about. It looked as though her story were told. She was a changed woman, and I amused myself with the notion that when she was a very old lady, with many years of perfect respectability behind her, the past, the lurid past, would seem to belong not to her but to someone long since dead whom once she had vaguely known. For women have an enviable faculty of forgetting.

But who can tell what the fates have in store? In the twinkling of an eye all was changed. Peter Vermont, after ten years of an ideal marriage, fell madly in love with a girl called Barbara Canton. She was a nice girl, the youngest daughter of Lord Robert Canton who was at one time Under-Secretary for Foreign Affairs, and she was pretty in a fair and fluffy way. Of course she was not for a moment to be compared with Lady Elizabeth. Many people knew what had happened, but no one could tell whether Elizabeth Vermont had any inkling of it, and they wondered how she would meet a situation that was so foreign to her experience. It was always she who had discarded her lovers; none had deserted her. For my part I thought she would make short work of little Miss Canton; I knew her courage and her adroitness. All this was in my mind now while we chatted over our luncheon. There was nothing in her demeanour, as gay, charming, and frank as usual, to suggest that anything troubled her. She talked as she always talked, lightly but with good sense and a lively perception of the ridiculous, of the various topics which the course of conversation brought forward. I enjoyed myself. I came to the conclusion that by some miracle she had no notion of Peter's changed feelings, and I explained this to myself by the supposition that her love for him was so great, she could not conceive that his for her might be less.

We drank our coffee and smoked a couple of cigarettes, and she asked me the time.

'A quarter to three.'

'I must ask for my bill.'

'Won't you let me stand you lunch?'

'Of course,' she smiled.

'Are you in a hurry?'

'I'm meeting Peter at three.'

'Oh, how is he?'

'He's very well.'

She gave a little smile, that tardy and delightful smile of hers, but I seemed to discern in it a certain mockery. For an instant she hesitated and she looked at me with deliberation.

'You like curious situations, don't you?' she said. 'You'd never guess the errand I'm bound on. I rang up Peter this morning and asked him to meet me at three. I'm going to ask him to divorce me.'

'You're not,' did I cried. I felt myself flush and not know what to say. 'I thought you got on so well together.'

'Do you think it's likely that I shouldn't know what all the world knows? I'm really not such a fool as all that.'

She was not a woman to whom it was possible to say what one did not believe and I could not pretend that I did not know what she meant. I remained silent for a second or two.

'Why should you allow yourself to be divorced?'

'Robert Canton is a stuffy old thing. I very much doubt if he'd let Barbara marry Peter if I divorced him. And for me, you know, it isn't of the smallest consequence: one divorce more or less . . .'

She shrugged her pretty shoulders.

'How do you know he wants to marry her?'

'He's head over ears in love with her.'

'Has he told you so?'

'No. He doesn't even know that I know. He's been so wretched, poor darling. He's been trying so hard not to hurt my feelings.'

'Perhaps it's only a momentary infatuation,' I hazarded. 'It may pass.'

'Why should it? Barbara's young and pretty. She's quite nice. They're very well suited to one another. And besides, what good would it do if it did pass? They love each other now and the present in love is all that matters. I'm nineteen years older than Peter. If a man stops loving a woman old enough to be his mother do you think he'll ever come to love her again? You're a novelist, you must know more about human nature than that.'

'Why should you make this sacrifice?'

'When he asked me to marry him ten years ago I promised him that when he wanted his release he should have it. You see there was so great a disproportion between our ages I thought that was only fair.'

'And are you going to keep a promise that he hasn't asked you to keep?'

She gave a little flutter of those long thin hands of hers and now I felt that there was something ominous in the dark glitter of that emerald.

'Oh, I must, you know. One must behave like a gentleman. To tell you the truth, that's why I'm lunching here today. It was at this table that he proposed to me; we were dining together, you know, and I was sitting just where I am now. The nuisance is that I'm just as much in love with him now as I was then.'

She paused for a minute and I could see that she clenched her teeth. 'Well, I suppose I ought to go. Peter hates one to keep him waiting.'

She gave me a sort of little helpless look and it struck me that she simply could not bring herself to rise from her chair. But she smiled and with an abrupt gesture sprang to her feet.

'Would you like me to come with you?'

'As far as the hotel door,' she smiled.

We walked through the restaurant and the lounge and when we came to the entrance a porter swung round the revolving doors. I asked if she would like a taxi.

'No, I'd sooner walk, it's such a lovely day.' She gave me her hand. 'It's been so nice to see you. I shall go abroad tomorrow, but I expect to be in London all the autumn. Do ring me up.'

She smiled and nodded and turned away. I watched her walk up Davies Street. The air was still bland and springlike, and above the roofs little white clouds were sailing leisurely in a blue sky. She held herself very erect and the poise of her head was gallant. She was a slim and lovely figure so that people looked at her as they passed. I saw her bow graciously to some acquaintance who raised his hat, and I thought that never in a thousand years would it occur to him that she had a breaking heart. I repeat, she was a very honest woman.

'WHAT a bit of luck that I'm placed next to you,' said Laura, as we sat down to dinner.

'For me,' I replied politely.

'That remains to be seen. I particularly wanted to have the chance of talking to you. I've got a story to tell you.'

At this my heart sank a little.

'I'd sooner you talked about yourself,' I answered. 'Or even about me.'

'Oh, but I must tell you the story. I think you'll be able to use it.'

'If you must, you must. But let's look at the menu first.'

'Don't you want me to?' she said, somewhat aggrieved. 'I thought you'd be pleased.'

'I am. You might have written a play and wanted to read me that.'

'It happened to some friends of mine. It's perfectly true.'

'That's no recommendation. A true story is never quite so true as an invented one.'

'What does that mean?'

'Nothing very much,' I admitted. 'But I thought it sounded well.'

'I wish you'd let me get on with it.'

'I'm all attention. I'm not going to eat the soup. It's fattening.'

She gave me a pinched look and then glanced at the menu. She uttered a little sigh.

'Oh, well, if you're going to deny yourself I suppose I must too. Heaven knows, I can't afford to take liberties with my figure.'

'And yet is there any soup more heavenly than the sort of soup in which you put a great dollop of cream?'

'Bortsch,' she sighed. 'It's the only soup I really like.'

'Never mind. Tell me your story and we'll forget about food till the fish comes.'

'Well, I was actually there when it happened. I was dining with the Livingstones. Do you know the Livingstones?'

'No, I don't think I do.'

'Well, you can ask them and they'll confirm every word I say. They'd asked their governess to come in to dinner because some woman had thrown them over at the last moment – you know how inconsiderate people are – and they would have been thirteen at table. Their governess was a Miss Robinson, quite a nice girl, young, you know, twenty or twenty-one, and rather pretty. Personally I would never engage a governess who was young and pretty. One never knows.'

'But one hopes for the best.'

Laura paid no attention to my remark.

'The chances are that she'll be thinking of young men instead of attending to her duties and then, just when she's got used to your ways, she'll want to go and get married. But Miss Robinson had excellent references, and I must allow that she was a very nice, respectable person. I believe in point of fact she was a clergyman's daughter.

'There was a man at dinner whom I don't suppose you've ever heard of, but who's quite a celebrity in his way. He's a Count Borselli and he knows more about precious stones than anyone in the world. He was sitting next to Mary Lyngate, who rather fancies herself on her pearls, and in the course of conversation she asked him what he thought of the string she was wearing. He said it was very pretty. She was rather piqued at this and told him it was valued at eight thousand pounds.

'"Yes, it's worth that," he said.

'Miss Robinson was sitting opposite to him. She was looking rather nice that evening. Of course I recognized her dress, it was one of Sophie's old ones; but if you hadn't known Miss Robinson was the governess you would never have suspected it.

'"That's a very beautiful necklace that young lady has on," said Borselli.

'"Oh, but that's Mrs Livingstone's governess," said Mary Lyngate.

'"I can't help that," he said. "She's wearing one of the finest strings of pearls for its size that I've ever seen in my life. It must be worth fifty thousand pounds."

'"Nonsense."

'"I give you my word it is."

'Mary Lyngate leant over. She has rather a shrill voice.

'"Miss Robinson, do you know what Count Borselli says?" she exclaimed. "He says that string of pearls you're wearing is worth fifty thousand pounds."

'Just at that moment there was a sort of pause in the conversation so that everybody heard. We all turned and looked at Miss Robinson. She flushed a little and laughed.

'"Well, I made a very good bargain," she said, "because I paid fifteen shillings for it."

'"You certainly did."

'We all laughed. It was of course absurd. We've all heard of wives palming off on their husbands as false a string of pearls that was real and expensive. That story is as old as the hills.'

'Thank you,' I said, thinking of a little narrative of my own.

'But it was too ridiculous to suppose that a governess would remain a governess if she owned a string of pearls worth fifty thousand pounds. It was obvious that the Count had made a bloomer. Then an extraordinary thing happened. The long arm of coincidence came in.'

'It shouldn't,' I retorted. 'It's had too much exercise. Haven't you seen that charming book called *A Dictionary of English Usage*?'

'I wish you wouldn't interrupt just when I'm really getting to the exciting point.'

But I had to do so again, for just then a young grilled salmon was insinuated round my left elbow.

'Mrs Livingstone is giving us a heavenly dinner,' I said.

'Is salmon fattening?' asked Laura.

'Very,' I answered as I took a large helping.

'Bunk,' she said.

'Go on,' I begged her. 'The long arm of coincidence was about to make a gesture.'

'Well, at that very moment the butler bent over Miss Robinson and whispered something in her ear. I thought she turned a trifle pale. It's such a mistake not to wear rouge; you never know what tricks nature will play on you. She certainly looked startled. She leant forwards.

'"Mrs Livingstone, Dawson says there are two men in the hall who want to speak to me at once."

'"Well, you'd better go," said Sophie Livingstone.

'Miss Robinson got up and left the room. Of course the same thought flashed through all our minds, but I said it first.

'"I hope they haven't come to arrest her," I said to Sophie. "It would be too dreadful for you, my dear."

'"Are you sure it was a real necklace, Borselli?" she asked.

'"Oh, quite."

'"She could hardly have had the nerve to wear it tonight if it were stolen," I said.

'Sophie Livingstone turned as pale as death under her make-up, and I saw she was wondering if everything was all right in her jewel case. I only had on a little chain of diamonds, but instinctively I put my hand up to my neck to feel if it was still there.

'"Don't talk nonsense," said Mr Livingstone. "How on earth would Miss Robinson have had the chance of sneaking a valuable string of pearls?"

'"She may be a receiver," I said.

'"Oh, but she had such wonderful references," said Sophie.

'"They always do," I said.'

I was positively forced to interrupt Laura once more.

'You don't seem to have been determined to take a very bright view of the case,' I remarked.

'Of course I knew nothing against Miss Robinson, and I had every reason to think her a very nice girl, but it would have been rather thrilling to find out that she was a notorious thief and a well-known member of a gang of international crooks.'

'Just like a film. I'm dreadfully afraid that it's only in films that exciting things like that happen.'

'Well, we waited in breathless suspense. There was not a sound. I expected to hear a scuffle in the hall or at least a smothered shriek. I thought the silence very ominous. Then the door opened and Miss Robinson walked in. I noticed at once that the necklace was gone. I could see that she was pale and excited. She came back to the table, sat down and with a smile threw on it . . .'

'On what?'

'On the table, you fool. A string of pearls.'

'"There's my necklace," she said.

'Count Borselli leant forwards.

'"Oh, but those are false," he said.

'"I told you they were," she laughed.

'"That's not the same string that you had on a few moments ago," he said.

'She shook her head and smiled mysteriously. We were all intrigued. I don't know that Sophie Livingstone was so very much pleased at her governess making herself the centre of interest like that and I thought there was a suspicion of tartness in her manner when she suggested that Miss Robinson had better explain. Well, Miss Robinson said that when she went into the hall she found two men who said they'd come from Jarrot's Stores. She'd bought her string there, as she said, for fifteen shillings, and she'd taken it back because the clasp was loose and had only fetched it that afternoon. The men said they had given her the wrong string. Someone had left a string of real pearls to be re-strung and the assistant had made a mistake. Of course I can't understand how anyone could be so stupid as to take a really valuable string to Jarrot's, they aren't used to dealing with that sort of thing, and they wouldn't know real pearls from false; but you know what fools some women are. Anyhow, it was the string Miss Robinson was wearing, and it was valued at fifty thousand pounds. She naturally gave it back to them – she couldn't do anything else, I suppose, though it must have been a wrench – and they returned her own string to her; then they said that although of course they were under no obligation – you know the silly, pompous way men talk when they're trying to be businesslike – they were instructed, as a solatium or whatever you call it, to offer her a cheque for three hundred pounds. Miss Robinson actually showed it to us. She was as pleased as Punch.'

-'Well, it was a piece of luck, wasn't it?'

'You'd have thought so. As it turned out it was the ruin of her.'

'Oh, how was that?'

'Well, when the time came for her to go on her holiday she told Sophie Livingstone that she'd made up her mind to go to Deauville for a month and blue the whole three hundred pounds. Of course Sophie tried to dissuade her, and begged her to put the money in the savings bank, but she wouldn't hear of it. She said she'd never had such a chance before and would never have it again and she meant for at least four weeks to live like a duchess. Sophie couldn't really do anything and so she gave way. She sold Miss Robinson a lot of clothes that she didn't want; she'd been wearing them all through the season and was sick to death of them; she says she gave them to her, but I don't suppose she quite did that – I dare say she sold them very cheap – and Miss Robinson started off, entirely alone, for Deauville. What do you think happened then?'

'I haven't a notion,' I replied. 'I hope she had the time of her life.'

'Well, a week before she was due to come back she wrote to Sophie and said that she'd changed her plans and had entered another profession, and hoped that Mrs Livingstone would forgive her if she didn't return. Of course poor Sophie was furious. What had actually happened was that Miss Robinson had picked up a rich Argentine in Deauville and had gone off to Paris with him. She's been in Paris ever since. I've seen her myself at Florence's, with bracelets right up to her elbow and ropes of pearls round her neck. Of course I cut her dead. They say she has a house in the Bois de Boulogne and I know she has a Rolls. She threw over the Argentine in a few months and then got hold of a Greek; I don't know who she's with now, but the long and short of it is that she's far and away the smartest cocotte in Paris.'

'When you say she was ruined you use the word in a purely technical sense, I conclude,' said I.

'I don't know what you mean by that,' said Laura. 'But don't you think you could make a story out of it?'

'Unfortunately I've already written a story about a pearl necklace. One can't go on writing stories about pearl necklaces.'

'I've got half a mind to write it myself. Only, of course, I should change the end.'

'Oh, how would you end it?'

'Well, I should have had her engaged to a bank clerk who had been badly knocked about in the war, with only one leg, say, or half his face shot away; and they'd be dreadfully poor and there would be no prospect of their marriage for years, and he would be putting all his savings into buying a little house in the suburbs, and they'd have arranged to marry when he had saved the last instalment. And then she takes him the three hundred pounds and they can hardly believe it, they're so happy, and he cries on her shoulder. He just cries like a child. And they get the little house in the suburbs and they marry, and they have his old mother to live with them, and he goes to the bank every day, and if she's careful not to have babies she can still go out as a daily governess, and he's often ill – with his wound, you know – and she nurses him, and it's all very pathetic and sweet and lovely.'

'It sounds rather dull to me,' I ventured.

'Yes, but moral,' said Laura.

THE YELLOW STREAK

THE two prahus were dropping easily down-stream, one a few yards ahead of the other, and in the first sat the two white men. After seven weeks on the rivers they were glad to know that they would lodge that night in a civilized house. To Izzart, who had been in Borneo since the war, the Dyak houses and their feasts were of course an old story; but Campion, though new to the country and at first amused by the strangeness, hankered too now for chairs to sit on and a bed to sleep in. The Dyaks were hospitable, but no one could say that there was much comfort to be found in their houses, and there was a monotony in the entertainment they offered a guest which presently grew somewhat wearisome. Every evening, as the travellers reached the landing-place, the headman, bearing a flag, and the more important members of the household came down to the river to fetch them. They were led up to the long-house – a village really under one roof, built on piles, to which access was obtained by climbing up the trunk of a tree rudely notched into steps – and to the beating of drums and gongs walked up and down the whole length of it in long procession. On both sides serried throngs of brown people sat on their haunches and stared silently as the white men passed. Clean mats were unrolled and the guests seated themselves. The headman brought a live chicken, and, holding it by the legs, waved it three times over their heads, called the spirits loudly to witness and uttered an invocation. Then various persons brought eggs. Arak was drunk. A girl, a very small shy thing with the grace of a flower but with something hieratic in her immobile face, held a cup to the white man's lips till it was empty and then a great shout arose. The men began to dance, one after the other, each treading his little measure, with his shield and his parang, to the accompaniment of drum and gong. After this had gone on for some time the visitors were taken into one of the rooms that led off the long platform on which was led the common life of the household and found their supper prepared for them. The girls fed them with Chinese spoons. Then everyone grew a little drunk and they all talked till the early hours of the morning.

But now their journey was done and they were on their way to the coast. They had started at dawn. The river then was very shallow and ran clear and bright over a shingly bottom; the trees leaned over it so that above there was only a strip of blue sky;

but now it had broadened out, and the men were poling no longer but paddling. The trees, bamboos, wild sago like huge bunches of ostrich feathers, trees with enormous leaves and trees with feathery foliage like the acacia, coconut trees and areca palms, with their long straight white stems, the trees on the banks were immensely and violently luxuriant. Here and there, gaunt and naked, was the bare skeleton of a tree struck by lightning or dead of old age, and its whiteness against all that green was vivid. Here and there, rival kings of the forest, tall trees soared above the common level of the jungle. Then there were the parasites; in the fork of two branches great tufts of lush green leaves, or flowering creepers that covered the spreading foliage like a bride's veil; sometimes they wound round a tall trunk, a sheath of splendour, and threw long flowering arms from branch to branch. There was something thrilling in the passionate wildness of that eager growth; it had the daring abandon of the nomad rioting in the train of the god.

The day wore on, and now the heat was no longer so oppressive. Campion looked at the shabby silver watch on his wrist. It could not be long now before they reached their destination.

'What sort of a chap is Hutchinson?' he asked.

'I don't know him. I believe he's a very good sort.'

Hutchinson was the Resident in whose house they were to spend the night, and they had sent on a Dyak in a canoe to announce their arrival.

'Well, I hope he's got some whisky. I've drunk enough arak to last me a lifetime.'

Campion was a mining engineer whom the Sultan on his way to England had met at Singapore, and finding him at a loose end had commissioned to go to Sembulu and see whether he could discover any mineral which might be profitably worked. He sent Willis, the Resident at Kuala Solor, instructions to afford him every facility, and Willis had put him in the care of Izzart because Izzart spoke both Malay and Dyak like a native. This was the third trip they had made into the interior, and now Campion was to go home with his reports. They were to catch the *Sultan Ahmed*, which was due to pass the mouth of the river at dawn on the next day but one, and with any luck they should reach Kuala Solor on the same afternoon. They were both glad to get back to it. There was tennis and golf there, and the club with its billiard tables, food which was relatively good, and the comforts of civilization. Izzart was glad, too, that he would have other society than Campion's. He gave him a sidelong glance. He was a little man with a big, bald head, and though certainly fifty, strong and wiry; he had quick, shining blue eyes and a stubbly, grey moustache. He was seldom without an old briar pipe between his broken and discoloured teeth. He was neither clean nor neat, his khaki shorts were ragged and his singlet torn; he was wearing now a battered topee. He had knocked about the world since he was eighteen and had been in South Africa, in China and in Mexico. He was good company; he could tell a story well, and he was prepared to drink and drink again with anyone he met. They had got on very well together, but Izzart had never felt quite at home with him. Though they joked and laughed together, got drunk together, Izzart felt that there was no intimacy between them: for all the cordiality of their relations they remained nothing but acquaintances. He was very sensitive to the impression he made on others, and behind Campion's joviality he had felt a certain coolness; those shining blue eyes had summed him up; and it vaguely irritated Izzart that Campion had formed an opinion of him, and he did not quite know what it was. He was exasperated by the possibility that this common little man did not think entirely well of him. He desired to be liked and admired. He wanted to be popular. He wished the people he met to take an inordinate fancy to him, so that he could either reject them or a trifle condescendingly bestow his friendship on them. His inclination was to be familiar with all and sundry, but he was held back by the fear of a rebuff; sometimes he had been uneasily conscious that his effusiveness surprised the persons he lavished it on.

By some chance he had never met Hutchinson, though of course he knew all about him just as Hutchinson knew all about *him*, and they would have many common friends to talk of. Hutchinson had been at Winchester, and Izzart was glad that he could tell him that he had been at Harrow. . . .

The prahu rounded a bend in the river and suddenly, standing on a slight eminence, they saw the bungalow. In a few minutes they caught sight of the landing-stage and on it, among a little group of natives, a figure in white waving to them.

Hutchinson was a tall, stout man with a red face. His appearance led you to expect that he was breezy and self-confident, so that it was not a little surprising to discover quickly that he was diffident and even a trifle shy. When he shook hands with his guests – Izzart introduced himself and then Campion – and led them up the pathway to the bungalow, though he was plainly anxious to be civil it was not hard to see that he found it difficult to make conversation. He took them out on to the veranda and here they found on the table glasses and whisky and soda. They made themselves comfortable on long chairs. Izzart, conscious of Hutchinson's slight embarrassment with strangers, expanded; he was very hearty and voluble. He began to speak of their common acquaintances at Kuala Solor, and he managed very soon to slip in casually the information that he had been at Harrow.

'You were at Winchester, weren't you?' he asked.

'Yes.'

'I wonder if you knew George Parker. He was in my regiment. He was at Winchester. I daresay he was younger than you.'

Izzart felt that it was a bond between them that they had been at these particular schools, and it excluded Campion, who obviously had enjoyed no such advantage. They drank two or three whiskies. Izzart in half an hour began to call his host Hutchie. He talked a good deal about 'my regiment' in which he had got his company during the war, and what good fellows his brother officers were. He mentioned two or three names which could hardly be unknown to Hutchinson. They were not the sort of people that Campion was likely to have come across, and he was not sorry to administer to him a neat snub when he claimed acquaintance with someone he spoke of.

'Billie Meadows? I knew a fellow called Billie Meadows in Sinaloa many years ago,' said Campion.

'Oh, I shouldn't think it could be the same,' said Izzart, with a smile. 'Billie's by way of being a peer of the realm. He's the Lord Meadows who races. Don't you remember, he owned Spring Carrots?'

Dinner time was approaching, and after a wash and brush-up they drank a couple of gin pahits. They sat down. Hutchinson had not been to Kuala Solor for the best part of a year, and had not seen another white man for three months. He was anxious to make the most of his visitors. He could give them no wine, but there was plenty of whisky and after dinner he brought out a precious bottle of Benedictine. They were very gay. They laughed and talked a great deal. Izzart was getting on famously. He thought he had never liked a fellow more than Hutchinson, and he pressed him to come down to Kuala Solor as soon as he could. They would have a wonderful beano. Campion was left out of the conversation by Izzart with the faintly malicious intention of putting him in his place, and by Hutchinson through shyness; and presently, after yawning a good deal, he said he would go to bed. Hutchinson showed him to his room, and when he returned Izzart said to him:

'You don't want to turn in yet, do you?'

'Not on your life. Let's have another drink.'

They sat and talked. They both grew a little drunk. Presently Hutchinson told Izzart that he lived with a Malay girl, and had a couple of children by her. He had told them to keep out of sight while Campion was there.

'I expect she's asleep now,' said Hutchinson, with a glance at the door which Izzart knew led into his room, 'but I'd like you to see the kiddies in the morning.'

Just then a faint wail was heard and Hutchinson with a 'Hullo, the little devil's awake', went to the door and opened it. In a moment or two he came out of the room with a child in his arms. A woman followed him.

'He's cutting his teeth,' said Hutchinson. 'It makes him restless.'

The woman wore a sarong and a thin white jacket and she was barefoot. She was young, with fine dark eyes, and she gave Izzart when he spoke to her a bright and pleasant smile. She sat down and lit a cigarette. She answered the civil questions Izzart put to her without embarrassment, but also without effusion. Hutchinson asked her if she would have a whisky and soda, but she refused. When the two men began to talk again in English she sat on quite quietly, faintly rocking herself in her chair, and occupied with none could tell what calm thoughts.

'She's a very good girl,' said Hutchinson. 'She looks after the house and she's no trouble. Of course it's the only thing to do in a place like this.'

'I shall never do it myself,' said Izzart. 'After all, one may want to get married and then it means all sorts of botherations.'

'But who wants to get married? What a life for a white woman. I wouldn't ask a white woman to live here for anything in the world.'

'Of course it's a matter of taste. If I have any kiddies I'm going to see that they have a white mother.'

Hutchinson looked down at the little dark-skinned child he held in his arms. He gave a faint smile.

'It's funny how you get to like them,' he said. 'When they're your own it doesn't seem to matter that they've got a touch of the tar-brush.'

The woman gave the child a look, and getting up said she would take it back to bed.

'I should think we'd better all turn in,' said Hutchinson. 'God knows what the time is.'

Izzart went to his room and threw open the shutters which his boy Hassan, whom he was travelling with, had closed. Blowing out the candle so that it should not attract the mosquitoes, he sat down at the window and looked at the soft night. The whisky he had drunk made him feel very wide awake, and he was not inclined to go to bed. He took off his ducks, put on a sarong and lit a cheroot. His good-humour was gone. It was the sight of Hutchinson looking fondly at the half-caste child which had upset him.

'They've got no right to have them,' he said to himself. 'They've got no chance in the world. Ever.'

He passed his hands reflectively along his bare and hairy legs. He shuddered a little. Though he had done everything he could to develop the calves, his legs were like broomsticks. He hated them. He was uneasily conscious of them all the time. They were like a native's. Of course they were the very legs for a top-boot. In his uniform he had looked very well. He was a tall, powerful man, over six feet high, and he had a neat black moustache and neat black hair. His dark eyes were fine and mobile. He was a good-looking fellow and he knew it, and he dressed well, shabbily when shabbiness was good form, and smartly when the occasion demanded. He had loved the army, and it was a bitter blow to him when, at the end of the war, he could not remain in it. His ambitions were simple. He wanted to have two thousand a year, give smart little dinners, go to parties, and wear a uniform. He hankered after London.

Of course his mother lived there, and his mother cramped his style. He wondered how on earth he could produce her if ever he got engaged to the girl of good family (with a little money) whom he was looking for to make his wife. Because his father had been dead so long and during the later part of his career was stationed in the most remote of the Malay States, Izzart felt fairly sure that no one in Sembulu knew anything about her, but he lived in terror lest someone, running across her in London, should write over to tell people that she was a half-caste. She had been a beautiful creature when Izzart's father, an engineer in the government service, had married her; but now she was a fat old woman with grey hair who sat about all day smoking cigarettes. Izzart was twelve years old when his father died and then he could speak Malay much more fluently than English. An aunt offered to pay for his education and Mrs Izzart accompanied her son to

England. She lived habitually in furnished apartments, and her rooms with their Oriental draperies and Malay silver were over-heated and stuffy. She was for ever in trouble with her landladies because she would leave cigarette-ends about. Izzart hated the way she made friends with them: she would be shockingly familiar with them for a time, then there would be a falling-out, and after a violent scene she would flounce out of the house. Her only amusement was the pictures, and to these she went every day in the week. At home she wore an old and tawdry dressing-gown, but when she went out she dressed herself – but, oh, how untidily – in extravagant colours, so that it was a mortification to her dapper son. He quarrelled with her frequently, she made him impatient and he was ashamed of her; and yet he felt for her a deep tenderness; it was almost a physical bond between them, something stronger than the ordinary feeling of mother and son, so that notwithstanding the failings that exasperated him she was the only person in the world with whom he felt entirely at home.

It was owing to his father's position and his own knowledge of Malay, for his mother always spoke it to him, that after the war, finding himself with nothing to do, he had managed to enter the service of the Sultan of Sembulu. He had been a success. He played games well, he was strong and a good athlete; in the rest-house at Kuala Solor were the cups which he had won at Harrow for running and jumping, and to these he had added since others for golf and tennis. With his abundant fund of small-talk he was an asset at parties and his cheeriness made things go. He ought to have been happy and he was wretched. He wanted so much to be popular, and he had an impression, stronger than ever at this moment, that popularity escaped him. He wondered whether by any chance the men at Kuala Solor with whom he was so hail-fellow-well-met suspected that he had native blood in him. He knew very well what to expect if they ever found out. They wouldn't say he was gay and friendly then, they would say he was damned familiar; and they would say he was inefficient and care-less, as the half-castes were, and when he talked of marrying a white woman they would snigger. Oh, it was so unfair! What difference could it make, that drop of native blood in his veins, and yet because of it they would always be on the watch for the expected failure at the critical moment. Everyone knew that you couldn't rely on Eurasians, sooner or later they would let you down; he knew it too, but now he asked himself whether they didn't fail because failure was expected of them. They were never given a chance, poor devils.

But a cock crew loudly. It must be very late and he was beginning to feel chilly. He got into bed. When Hassan brought him his tea next morning he had a racking headache, and when he went into breakfast he could not look at the porridge and the bacon and eggs which were set before him. Hutchinson too was feeling none too well.

'I fancy we made rather a night of it,' said his host, with a smile to conceal his faint embarrassment.

'I feel like hell,' said Izzart.

'I'm going to breakfast off a whisky and soda myself,' added Hutchinson.

Izzart asked for nothing better, and it was with distaste that they watched Campion eat with healthy appetite a substantial meal. Campion chaffed them.

'By God, Izzart, you're looking green about the gills,' he said. 'I never saw such a filthy colour.'

Izzart flushed. His swarthiness was always a sensitive point with him. But he forced himself to give a cheery laugh.

'You see, I had a Spanish grandmother,' he answered, 'and when I'm under the weather it always comes out. I remember at Harrow I fought a boy and licked him, because he called me a damned half-caste.'

'You are dark,' said Hutchinson. 'Do Malays ever ask you if you have any native blood in you?'

'Yes, damn their impudence.'

A boat with their kit had started early in the morning in order to get to the mouth of the river before them, and tell the skipper of the *Sultan Ahmed*, if by chance he arrived before he was due, that they were on their way. Campion and Izzart were to set out immediately after tiffin in order to arrive at the place where they were to spend the night before the Bore passed. A Bore is a tidal wave that, by reason of a peculiarity in the lie of the land, surges up certain rivers, and there happened to be one on the river on which they were travelling. Hutchinson had talked to them of it the night before and Campion, who had never seen such a thing, was much interested.

'This is one of the best in Borneo. It's worth looking at,' said Hutchinson.

He told them how the natives, waiting the moment, rode it and were borne up the river on its crest at a breathless and terrifying speed. He had done it once himself.

'Never no more for me,' he said. 'I was scared out of my wits.'

'I should like to try it once,' said Izzart.

'It's exciting enough, but my word, when you're in a flimsy dug-out and you know that if the native doesn't get the right moment you'll be flung in that seething torrent and you won't have a chance in a million . . . no, it's not my idea of sport.'

'I've shot a good many rapids in my day,' said Campion.

'Rapids be damned. You wait till you see the Bore. It's one of the most terrifying things I know. D'you know that at least a dozen natives are drowned in it in this river alone every year?'

They lounged about on the veranda most of the morning and Hutchinson showed them the court-house. Then gin pahits were served. They drank two or three. Izzart began to feel himself, and when at length tiffin was ready he found that he had an excellent appetite. Hutchinson had boasted of his Malay curry and when the steaming, succulent dishes were placed before them they all set to ravenously. Hutchinson pressed them to drink.

'You've got nothing to do but sleep. Why shouldn't you get drunk?'

He could not bear to let them go so soon, it was good after so long to have white men to talk to, and he lingered over the meal. He urged them to eat. They would have a filthy meal that night at the long-house and nothing to drink but arak. They had better make hay while the sun shone. Campion suggested once or twice that they should start, but Hutchinson, and Izzart too, for now he was feeling very happy and comfortable, assured him there was plenty of time. Hutchinson sent for his precious bottle of Benedictine. They had made a hole in it last night; they might as well finish it before they went.

When at last he walked down with them to the river they were all very merry and none of them was quite steady on his legs. Over the middle of the boat was an attap awning, and under this Hutchinson had had a mattress laid. The crew were prisoners who had been marched down from the jail to row the white men, and they wore dingy sarongs with the prison mark. They waited at their oars. Izzart and Campion shook hands with Hutchinson and threw themselves down on the mattress. The boat pushed off. The turbid river, wide and placid, glistened in the heat of that brilliant afternoon like polished brass. In the distance ahead of them they could see the bank with its tangle of green trees. They felt drowsy, but Izzart at least found a curious enjoyment in resisting for a little while the heaviness that was creeping over him, and he made up his mind that he would not let himself fall asleep till he had finished his cheroot. At last the stub began to burn his fingers and he flung it into the river.

'I'm going to have a wonderful snooze,' he said.

'What about the Bore?' asked Campion.

'Oh, that's all right. We needn't worry about that.'

He gave a long and noisy yawn. His limbs felt like lead. He had one moment in which he was conscious of his delicious drowsiness and then he knew nothing more. Suddenly he was awakened by Campion shaking him.

.'I say, what's that?'

'What's what?'

He spoke irritably, for sleep was still heavy upon him, but with his eyes he followed Campion's gesture. He could hear nothing, but a good way off he saw two or three white-crested waves following one another. They did not look very alarming.

'Oh, I suppose that's the Bore.'

'What are we going to do about it?' cried Campion.

Izzart was scarcely yet quite awake. He smiled at the concern in Campion's voice.

'Don't worry. These fellows know all about it. They know exactly what to do. We may get a bit splashed.'

But while they were saying these few words the Bore came nearer, very quickly, with a roar like the roar of an angry sea, and Izzart saw that the waves were much higher than he had thought. He did not like the look of them and he tightened his belt so that his shorts should not slip down if the boat were upset. In a moment the waves were upon them. It was a great wall of water that seemed to tower over them, and it might have been ten or twelve feet high, but you could measure it only with your horror. It was quite plain that no boat could weather it. The first wave dashed over them, drenching them all, half filling the boat with water, and then immediately another wave struck them. The boatmen began to shout. They pulled madly at their oars and the steersman yelled an order. But in that surging torrent they were helpless, and it was frightening to see how soon they lost all control of the boat. The force of the water turned it broadside on and it was carried along, helter skelter, upon the crest of the Bore. Another great wave dashed over them and the boat began to sink. Izzart and Campion scrambled out of the covered place in which they had been lying and suddenly the boat gave way under their feet and they found themselves struggling in the water. It surged and stormed around them. Izzart's first impulse was to swim for the shore, but his boy, Hassan, shouted to him to cling to the boat. For a minute or two they all did this.

'Are you all right?' Campion shouted to him.

'Yes, enjoying the bath,' said Izzart.

He imagined that the waves would pass by as the Bore ascended the river, and in a few minutes at the outside they would find themselves in calm water once more. He forgot that they were being carried along on its crest. The waves dashed over them. They clung to the gunwale and the base of the structure which supported the attap awning. Then a larger wave caught the boat as it turned over, falling upon them so that they lost their hold; there seemed nothing but a slippery bottom to cling to and Izzart's hands slithered helplessly on the greasy surface. But the boat continued to turn and he made a desperate grab at the gunwale, only to feel it slip out of his hands as the turn went on, then he caught the framework of the awning, and still it turned, turned slowly right round and once more he sought for a hand-hold on the bottom. The boat went round and round with a horrible regularity. He thought this must be because everyone was clinging to one side of it, and he tried to make the crew go round to the other. He could not make them understand. Everyone was shouting and the waves beat against them with a dull and angry roar. Each time the boat rolled over on them Izzart was pushed under water, only to come up again as the gunwale and the framework of the awning gave him something to cling to. The struggle was awful. Presently he began to get terribly out of breath, and he felt his strength leaving him. He knew that he could not hold on much longer, but he did not feel frightened, for his fatigue by now was so great that he did not very much care what happened. Hassan was by his side and he told him he was growing very tired. He thought the best thing was to make a dash for the shore, it did not look more than sixty yards away, but Hassan begged him not to. Still they were being carried along amid those seething, pounding waves. The boat went round and round and they scrambled over it like squirrels in a cage. Izzart swallowed a lot of water. He felt he was very nearly done. Hassan could not help him, but it was a comfort that he was there, for Izzart knew that his boy, used to the water all his life, was a powerful swimmer. Then, Izzart did not know why, for a minute or two the boat held bottom downwards, so that he was able to hold on to the gunwale. It was a precious thing to be able to get his breath. At that moment two dug-outs, with Malays in them riding the Bore, passed swiftly by them. They shouted for help, but the Malays averted their faces and went on. They saw the white men, and did not want to be concerned in any trouble that might befall them. It was agonizing to see them go past, callous and indifferent in their safety. But on a sudden the boat rolled round again, round and round, slowly, and the miserable, exhausting scramble repeated itself. It took the heart out of you. But the short respite had helped Izzart, and he was able to struggle a little longer. Then once more he found himself so terribly out of breath that he thought his chest would burst. His strength was all gone, and he did not know now whether he had enough to try to swim for the shore. Suddenly he heard a cry.

'Izzart, Izzart. Help. Help.'

It was Campion's voice. It was a scream of agony. It sent a shock all through Izzart's nerves. Campion, Campion, what did he care for Campion? Fear seized him, a blind animal fear, and it gave him a new strength. He did not answer.

'Help me, quick, quick,' he said to Hassan.

Hassan understood him at once. By a miracle one of the oars was floating quite close to them and he pushed it into Izzart's reach. He placed a hand under Izzart's arm and they struck away from the boat. Izzart's heart was pounding and his breath came with difficulty. He felt horribly weak. The waves beat in his face. The bank looked dreadfully far away. He did not think he could ever reach it. Suddenly the boy cried that he could touch bottom and Izzart put down his legs; but he could feel nothing; he swam a few more exhausted strokes, his eyes fixed on the bank, and then, trying again, felt his feet sink into thick mud. He was thankful. He floundered on and there was the bank within reach of his hands, black mud in which he sank to his knees: he scrambled up, desperate to get out of the cruel water, and when he came to the top he found a little flat with tall rank grass all about it. He and Hassan sank down on it and lay for a while stretched out like dead men. They were so tired that they could not move. They were covered with black mud from head to foot.

But presently Izzart's mind began to work, and a pang of anguish on a sudden shook him. Campion was drowned. It was awful. He did not know how he was going to explain the disaster when he got back to Kuala Solor. They would blame him for it; he ought to have remembered the Bore and told the steersman to make for the bank and tie up the boat when he saw it coming. It wasn't his fault, it was the steersman's, he knew the river; why in God's name hadn't he had the sense to get into safety? How could he have expected that it was possible to ride that horrible torrent? Izzart's limbs shook as he remembered the wall of seething water that rushed down upon them. He must get the body and take it back to Kuala Solor. He wondered whether any of the crew were drowned too. He felt too weak to move, but Hassan now rose and wrung the water out of his sarong; he looked over the river and quickly turned to Izzart.

'Tuan, a boat is coming.'

The lalang grass prevented Izzart from seeing anything.

'Shout to them,' he said.

Hassan slipped out of view and made his way along the branch of a tree that overhung the water; he cried out and waved. Presently Izzart heard voices. There was a rapid conversation between the boy and the occupants of the boat, and then the boy came back.

'They saw us capsize, Tuan,' he said, 'and they came as soon as the Bore passed. There's a long-house on the other side. If you will cross the river they will give us sarongs and food and we can sleep there.'

Izzart for a moment felt that he could not again trust himself on the face of the treacherous water.

'What about the other tuan?' he asked.

'They do not know.'

'If he's drowned they must find the body.'

'Another boat has gone up-stream.'

Izzart did not know what to do. He was numb. Hassan put his arm round his shoulder and raised him to his feet. He made his way through the thick grass to the edge of the water, and there he saw a dug-out with two Dyaks in it. The river now once more was calm and sluggish; the great wave had passed on and no one would have dreamed that so short a while before the placid surface was like a stormy sea. The Dyaks repeated to him what they had already told the boy. Izzart could not bring himself to speak. He felt that if he said a word he would burst out crying. Hassan helped him to get in, and the Dyaks began to pull across. He fearfully wanted something to smoke, but his cigarettes and his matches, both in a hip-pocket, were soaking. The passage of the river seemed endless. The night fell and when they reached the bank the first stars were shining. He stepped ashore and one of the Dyaks took him up to the long-house. But Hassan seized the paddle he had dropped and with the other pushed out into the stream. Two or three men and some children came down to meet Izzart and he climbed to the house amid a babel of conversation. He went up the ladder and was led with greetings and excited comment to the space where the young men slept. Rattan mats were hurriedly laid to make him a couch and he sank down on them. Someone brought him a jar of arak and he took a long drink; it was rough and fiery, burning his throat, but it warmed his heart. He slipped off his shirt and trousers and put on a dry sarong which someone lent him. By chance he caught sight of the yellow new moon lying on her back, and it gave him a keen, almost a sensual, pleasure. He could not help thinking that he might at that moment be a corpse floating up the river with the tide. The moon had never looked to him more lovely. He began to feel hungry and he asked for rice. One of the women went into a room to prepare it. He was more himself now, and he began to think again of the explanations he would make at Kuala Solor. No one could really blame him because he had gone to sleep; he certainly wasn't drunk, Hutchinson would bear him out there, and how was he to suspect that the steersman would be such a damned fool? It was just rotten luck. But he couldn't think of Campion without a shudder. At last a platter of rice was brought him, and he was just about to start eating when a man ran hurriedly along and came up to him.

'The tuan's come,' he cried.

'What tuan?'

He jumped up. There was a commotion about the doorway and he stepped forward. Hassan was coming quickly towards him out of the darkness, and then he heard a voice.

'Izzart. Are you there?'

Campion advanced towards him.

'Well, here we are again. By God, that was a pretty near thing, wasn't it? You seem to have made yourself nice and comfortable. My heavens, I could do with a drink.'

His dank clothes clung round him, and he was muddy and dishevelled. But he was in excellent spirits.

'I didn't know where the hell they were bringing me. I'd made up my mind that I should have to spend the night on the bank. I thought you were drowned.'

'Here's some arak,' said Izzart.

Campion put his mouth to the jar and drank and spluttered and drank again.

'Muck, but by God it's strong.' He looked at Izzart with a grin of his broken and discoloured teeth. 'I say, old man, you look as though you'd be all the better for a wash.'

'I'll wash later.'

'All right, so will I. Tell them to get me a sarong. How did you get out?' He did not wait for an answer. 'I thought I was done for. I owe my life to these two sportsmen here.' He indicated with a cheery nod two of the Dyak prisoners whom Izzart vaguely recognized as having been part of their crew. 'They were hanging on to that blasted boat on each side of me and somehow they cottoned on to it that I was down and out. I couldn't have lasted another minute. They made signs to me that we could risk having a shot at getting to the bank, but I didn't think I had the strength. By George, I've never been so blown in all my life. I don't know how they managed it, but somehow they got hold of the mattress we'd been lying on, and they made it into a roll. They're sportsmen they are. I don't know why they didn't just save themselves without bothering about me. They gave it me. I thought it a damned poor lifebelt, but I saw the force of the proverb about a drowning man clutching at a straw. I caught hold of the damned thing and between them somehow or other they dragged me ashore.'

The danger from which he had escaped made Campion excited and voluble; but Izzart hardly listened to what he said. He heard once more, as distinctly as though the words rang now through the air, Campion's agonized cry for help, and he felt sick with terror. The blind panic raced down his nerves. Campion was talking still, but was he talking to conceal his thoughts? Izzart looked into those bright blue eyes and sought to read the sense behind the flow of words. Was there a hard glint in them or something of cynical mockery? Did he know that Izzart, leaving him to his fate, had cut and run? He flushed deeply. After all, what was there that he could have done? At such a moment it was each for himself and the devil take the hindmost. But what would they say in Kuala Solor if Campion told them that Izzart had deserted him? He ought to have stayed, he wished now with all his heart that he had, but then, then it was stronger than himself, he couldn't. Could anyone blame him? No one who had seen that fierce and seething torrent. Oh, the water and the exhaustion, so that he could have cried!

'If you're as hungry as I am you'd better have a tuck in at this rice,' he said.

Campion ate voraciously, but when Izzart had taken a mouthful or two he found that he had no appetite. Campion talked and talked. Izzart listened suspiciously. He felt that he must be alert and he drank more arak. He began to feel a little drunk.

'I shall get into the devil of a row at K. S.' he said tentatively.

'I don't know why.'

'I was told off to look after you. They won't think it was very clever of me to let you get nearly drowned.'

'It wasn't your fault. It was the fault of the damned fool of a steersman. After all, the important thing is that we're saved. By George, I thought I was finished once. I shouted out to you. I don't know if you heard me.'

'No, I didn't hear anything. There was such a devil of a row, wasn't there?'

'Perhaps you'd got away before. I don't know exactly when you did get away.'

Izzart looked at him sharply. Was it his fancy that there was an odd look in Campion's eyes?

'There was such an awful confusion,' he said. 'I was just about down and out. My boy threw me over an oar. He gave me to understand you were all right. He told me you'd got ashore.'

The oar! He ought to have given Campion the oar and told Hassan, the strong swimmer, to give *him* his help. Was it his fancy again that Campion gave him a quick and searching glance?

'I wish I could have been of more use to you,' said Izzart.

'Oh, I'm sure you had enough to do to look after yourself,' answered Campion.

The headman brought them cups of arak, and they both drank a great deal. Izzart's head began to spin and he suggested that they should turn in. Beds had been prepared for them and mosquito nets fixed. They were to set out at dawn on the rest of their journey down the river. Campion's bed was next to his, and in a few minutes he heard him snoring. He had fallen asleep the moment he lay down. The young men of the long-house and the prisoners of the boat's crew went on talking late into the night. Izzart's head now was aching horribly and he could not think. When Hassan roused him as day broke it seemed to him that he had not slept at all. Their clothes had been washed and dried, but they were bedraggled objects as they walked along the narrow pathway to the river where the prahu was waiting for them. They rowed leisurely. The morning was lovely and the great stretch of placid water gleamed in the early light.

'By George, it's fine to be alive,' said Campion.

He was grubby and unshaved. He took long breaths, and his twisted mouth was half open with a grin. You could tell that he found the air singularly good to breathe. He was delighted with the blue sky and the sunshine and the greenness of the trees. Izzart hated him. He was sure that this morning there was a difference in his manner. He did not know what to do. He had a mind to throw himself on his mercy. He had behaved like a cad, but he was sorry, he would give anything to have the chance

433

again, but anyone might have done what he did, and if Campion gave him away he was ruined. He could never stay in Sembulu; his name would be mud in Borneo and the Straits Settlements. If he made his confession to Campion he could surely get Campion to promise to hold his tongue. But would he keep his promise? He looked at him, a shifty little man: how could he be relied on? Izzart thought of what he had said the night before. It wasn't the truth, of course, but who could know that? At all events who could prove that he hadn't honestly thought that Campion was safe? Whatever Campion said, it was only his word against Izzart's; he could laugh and shrug his shoulders and say that Campion had lost his head and didn't know what he was talking about. Besides, it wasn't certain that Campion hadn't accepted his story; in that frightful struggle for life he could be very sure of nothing. He had a temptation to go back to the subject, but he was afraid if he did that he would excite suspicion in Campion's mind. He *must* hold his tongue. That was his only chance of safety. And when they got to K. S. he would get in his story first.

'I should be completely happy now,' said Campion, 'if I only had something to smoke.'

'We shall be able to get some stinkers on board.'

Campion gave a little laugh.

'Human beings are very unreasonable,' he said. 'At the first moment I was so glad to be alive that I thought of nothing else, but now I'm beginning to regret the loss of my notes and my photographs and my shaving tackle.'

Izzart formulated the thought which had lurked at the back of his mind, but which all through the night he had refused to admit into his consciousness.

'I wish to God he'd been drowned. Then I'd have been safe.'

'There she is,' cried Campion suddenly.

Izzart looked round. They were at the mouth of the river and there was the *Sultan Ahmed* waiting for them. Izzart's heart sank: he had forgotten that she had an English skipper and that he would have to be told the story of their adventure. What would Campion say? The skipper was called Bredon, and Izzart had met him often at Kuala Solor. He was a little bluff man, with a black moustache, and a breezy manner.

'Hurry up,' he called out to them, as they rowed up, 'I've been waiting for you since dawn.' But when they climbed on board his face fell. 'Hullo, what's the matter with you?'

'Give us a drink and you shall hear all about it,' said Campion, with his crooked grin.

'Come along.'

They sat down under the awning. On a table were glasses, a bottle of whisky and soda-water. The skipper gave an order and in a few minutes they were noisily under way.

'We were caught in the Bore,' said Izzart.

He felt he must say something. His mouth was horribly dry notwithstanding the drink.

'Were you, by Jove? You're lucky not to have been drowned. What happened?'

He addressed himself to Izzart because he knew him, but it was Campion who answered. He related the whole incident, accurately, and Izzart listened with strained attention. Campion spoke in the plural when he told the early part of the story, and then, as he came to the moment when they were thrown into the water, changed to the singular. At first it was what *they* had done and now it was what happened to *him*. He left Izzart out of it. Izzart did not know whether to be relieved or alarmed. Why did he not mention him? Was it because in that mortal struggle for life he had thought of nothing but himself or – did he *know*?

'And what happened to you?' said Captain Bredon, turning to Izzart.

Izzart was about to answer when Campion spoke.

'Until I got over to the other side of the river I thought he was drowned. I don't know how he got out. I expect he hardly knows himself.'

'It was touch and go,' said Izzart with a laugh.

Why had Campion said that? He caught his eye. He was sure now that there was a gleam of amusement in it. It was awful not to be certain. He was frightened. He was ashamed. He wondered if he could not so guide the conversation, either now or later, as to ask Campion whether that was the story he was going to tell in Kuala Solor. There was nothing in it to excite anyone's suspicions. But if nobody else knew, Campion knew. He could have killed him.

'Well, I think you're both of you damned lucky to be alive,' said the skipper.

It was but a short run to Kuala Solor, and as they steamed up the Sembulu river Izzart moodily watched the banks. On each side were the mangroves and the nipahs washed by the water, and behind, the dense green of the jungle; here and there, among fruit trees, were Malay houses on piles. Night fell as they docked.

Goring, of the police, came on board and shook hands with them. He was living at the rest-house just then, and as he set about his work of seeing the native passengers he told them they would find another man, Porter by name, staying there too. They would all meet at dinner. The boys took charge of their kit, and Campion and Izzart strolled along. They bathed and changed, and at half past eight the four of them assembled in the common-room for gin pahits.

'I say, what's this Bredon tells me about your being nearly drowned?' said Goring as he came in.

Izzart felt himself flush, but before he could answer Campion broke in, and it seemed certain to Izzart that he spoke in order to give the story as he chose. He felt hot with shame. Not a word was spoken in disparagement of him, not a word was said of him at all; he wondered if those two men who listened, Goring and Porter, thought it strange that he should be left out. He looked at Campion intently as he proceeded with his narration; he told it rather humorously; he did not disguise the danger in which they had been, but he made a joke of it, so that the two listeners laughed at the quandary in which they found themselves.

'A thing that's tickled me since,' said Campion, 'is that when I got over to the other bank I was black with mud from head to foot. I felt I really ought to jump in the river and have a wash, but you know I felt I'd been in that damned river as much as ever I wanted, and I said to myself: No, by George, I'll go dirty. And when I got into the long-house and saw Izzart as black as I was, I knew he'd felt just like I did.'

They laughed and Izzart forced himself to laugh too. He noticed that Campion had told the story in precisely the same words as he had used when he told it to the skipper of the *Sultan Ahmed*. There could be only one explanation of that; he knew, he knew everything, and had made up his mind exactly what story to tell. The ingenuity with which Campion gave the facts and yet left out what must be to Izzart's discredit was devilish. But why was he holding his hand? It wasn't in him not to feel contempt and resentment for the man who had callously deserted him in that moment of dreadful peril. Suddenly, in a flash of inspiration Izzart understood: he was keeping the truth to tell to Willis, the Resident. Izzart had gooseflesh as he thought of confronting Willis. He could deny, but would his denials serve him? Willis was no fool, and he would get at Hassan; Hassan could not be trusted to be silent; Hassan would give him away. Then he would be done for. Willis would suggest that he had better go home.

He had a racking headache, and after dinner he went to his room, for he wanted to be alone so that he could devise a plan of action. And then a thought came to him which made him go hot and cold: he knew that the secret which he had guarded so long was a secret to nobody. He was on a sudden certain of it. Why should he have those bright eyes and that swarthy skin? Why should he speak Malay with such ease and have learned Dyak so quickly? Of course they knew. What a fool he was ever to think that they believed that story of his, about the Spanish grandmother! They must have laughed up their sleeves when he told it, and behind his back they had called him a damned nigger. And now another thought came to him, torturing, and he asked himself whether it was on account of that wretched drop of native blood in him that when he heard Campion cry out his nerve failed him. After all, anyone might at that moment have been seized with panic; and why in God's name should he sacrifice his life to save a man's whom he cared nothing for? It was insane. But of course in K. S. they would say it was only what they expected; they would make no allowances.

At last he went to bed, but when, after tossing about recklessly for God knows how long, he fell asleep, he was awakened by a fearful dream; he seemed to be once more in that raging torrent, with the boat turning, turning; and then there was the desperate clutching at the gunwale, and the agony as it slipped out of his hands, and the water that roared over him. He was wide awake before dawn. His only chance was to see Willis and get his story in first; and he thought over carefully what he was going to say, and chose the very words he meant to use.

He got up early, and in order not to see Campion went out without breakfast. He walked along the high road till such time as he knew the Resident would be in his office, and then walked back again. He sent in his name and was ushered into Willis's room. He was a little elderly man with thin grey hair and a long yellow face.

'I'm glad to see you back safe and sound,' he said, shaking hands with Izzart. 'What's this I hear about your being nearly drowned?'

Izzart, in clean ducks, his topee spotless, was a fine figure of a man. His black hair was neatly brushed, and his moustache was trimmed. He had an upright and soldierly bearing.

'I thought I'd better come and tell you at once, sir, as you told me to look after Campion.'

'Fire away.'

437

Izzart told his story. He made light of the danger. He gave Willis to understand that it had not been very great. They would never have been upset if they had not started so late.

'I tried to get Campion away earlier, but he'd had two or three drinks and the fact is, he didn't want to move.'

'Was he tight?'

'I don't know about that,' smiled Izzart good-humouredly. 'I shouldn't say he was cold sober.'

He went on with his story. He managed to insinuate that Campion had lost his head a little. Of course it was a very frightening business to a man who wasn't a decent swimmer: he, Izzart, had been more concerned for Campion than for himself; he knew the only chance was to keep cool, and the moment they were upset he saw that Campion had got the wind up.

'You can't blame him for that,' said the Resident.

'Of course I did everything I possibly could for him, sir, but the fact is, there wasn't anything much I could do.'

'Well, the great thing is that you both escaped. It would have been very awkward for all of us if he'd been drowned.'

'I thought I'd better come and tell you the facts before you saw Campion, sir. I fancy he's inclined to talk rather wildly about it. There's no use exaggerating.'

'On the whole your stories agree pretty well,' said Willis, with a little smile.

Izzart looked at him blankly.

'Haven't you seen Campion this morning? I heard from Goring that there'd been some trouble, and I looked in last night on my way home from the Fort after dinner. You'd already gone to bed.'

Izzart felt himself trembling, and he made a great effort to preserve his composure.

'By the way, you got away first, didn't you?'

'I don't really know, sir. You see, there was a lot of confusion.'

'You must have if you got over to the other side before he did.'

'I suppose I did then.'

'Well, thanks for coming to tell me,' said Willis, rising from his chair.

As he did so he knocked some books on the floor. They fell with a sudden thud. The unexpected sound made Izzart start violently, and he gave a gasp. The Resident looked at him quickly.

'I say, your nerves are in a pretty state.'

Izzart could not control his trembling.

'I'm very sorry, sir,' he murmured.

'I expect it's been a shock. You'd better take it easy for a few days. Why don't you get the doctor to give you something?'

'I didn't sleep very well last night.'

The Resident nodded as though he understood. Izzart left the room, and as he passed out some man he knew stopped and congratulated him on his escape. They all knew of it. He walked back to the rest-house. And as he walked, he repeated to himself the story he had told the Resident. Was it really the same story that Campion had told? He had never suspected that the Resident had already heard it from Campion. What a fool he had been to go to bed! He should never have let Campion out of his sight. Why had the Resident listened without telling him that he already knew? Now Izzart cursed himself for having suggested that Campion was drunk and had lost his head. He had said this in order to discredit him, but he knew now that it was a stupid thing to do. And why had Willis said that about his having got away first? Perhaps he was holding his hand too; perhaps he was going to make inquiries; Willis was very shrewd. But what exactly had Campion said? He must know that; at whatever cost he must know. Izzart's mind was seething, so that he felt he could hardly keep a hold on his thoughts, but he must keep calm. He felt like a hunted animal. He did not believe that Willis liked him; once or twice in the office he had blamed him because he was careless; perhaps he was just waiting till he got all the facts. Izzart was almost hysterical.

He entered the rest-house and there, sitting on a long chair, with his legs stretched out, was Campion. He was reading the papers which had arrived during their absence in the jungle. Izzart felt a blind rush of hatred well up in him as he looked at the little, shabby man who held him in the hollow of his hand.

'Hullo,' said Campion, looking up. 'Where have you been?'

To Izzart it seemed that there was in his eyes a mocking irony. He clenched his hands, and his breath came fast.

'What have you been saying to Willis about me?' he asked abruptly.

The tone in which he put the unexpected question was so harsh that Campion gave him a glance of faint surprise.

'I don't think I've been saying anything very much about you. Why?'

'He came here last night.'

Izzart looked at him intently. His brows were drawn together in an angry frown as he tried to read Campion's thoughts.

'I told him you'd gone to bed with a headache. He wanted to know about our mishap.'

'I've just seen him.'

Izzart walked up and down the large and shaded room; now, though it was still early, the sun was hot and dazzling. He felt himself in a net. He was blind with rage; he could have seized Campion by the throat and strangled him, and yet, because he did not know what he had to fight against, he felt himself powerless. He was tired and ill, and his nerves were shaken. On a sudden the anger which had given him a sort of strength left him, and he was filled with despondency. It was as though water and not blood ran through his veins; his heart sank and his knees seemed to give way. He felt that if he did not take care, he would begin to cry. He was dreadfully sorry for himself.

'Damn you, I wish to God I'd never set eyes on you,' he cried pitifully.

'What on earth's the matter?' asked Campion, with astonishment.

'Oh, don't pretend. We've been pretending for two days, and I'm fed up with it.' His voice rose shrilly, it sounded odd in that robust and powerful man. 'I'm fed up with it. I cut and run. I left you to drown. I know I behaved like a skunk. I couldn't help it.'

Campion rose slowly from his chair.

'What *are* you talking about?'

His tone was so genuinely surprised that it gave Izzart a start. A cold shiver ran down his spine.

'When you called for help I was panic-stricken. I just caught hold of an oar and got Hassan to help me get away.'

'That was the most sensible thing you could do.'

'I couldn't help you. There wasn't a thing I could do.'

'Of course not. It was damned silly of me to shout. It was waste of breath, and breath was the very thing I wanted.'

'Do you mean to say you didn't know?'

'When those fellows got me the mattress, I thought you were still clinging to the boat. I had an idea that I got away before you did.'

Izzart put both his hands to his head, and gave a hoarse cry of despair.

'My God, what a fool I've been.'

The two men stood for a while staring at one another. The silence seemed endless.

'What are you going to do now?' asked Izzart at last.

'Oh, my dear fellow, don't worry. I've been frightened too often myself to blame anyone who shows the white feather. I'm not going to tell a soul.'

'Yes, but you *know*.'

'I promise you, you can trust me. Besides, my job's done here and I'm going home. I want to catch the next boat to Singapore.' There was a pause, and Campion looked for a while reflectively at Izzart. 'There's only one thing I'd like to ask you: I've made a good many friends here, and there are one or two things I'm a little sensitive about; when you tell the story of our upset, I should be grateful if you wouldn't make out that I had behaved badly. I wouldn't like the fellows here to think that I'd lost my nerve.'

Izzart flushed darkly. He remembered what he had said to the Resident. It almost looked as though Campion had been listening over his shoulder. He cleared his throat.

'I don't know why you think I should do that.'

Campion chuckled good-naturedly, and his blue eyes were gay with amusement.

'The yellow streak,' he replied, and then, with a grin that showed his broken and discoloured teeth: 'Have a cheroot, dear boy.'

MORE ABOUT PENGUINS

If you have enjoyed reading this book you may wish to know that *Penguin Book News* appears every month. It is an attractively illustrated magazine containing a complete list of books published by Penguins and still in print, together with details of the month's new books. A specimen copy will be sent free on request.

Penguin Book News is obtainable from most bookshops; but you may prefer to become a regular subscriber at 3s. for twelve issues. Just write to Dept EP, Penguin Books Ltd, Harmondsworth, Middlesex, enclosing a cheque or postal order, and you will be put on the mailing list.

Some other books published by Penguins are described on the following pages.

Note: *Penguin Book News* is not available in the U.S.A., Canada or Australia

THE SNOWS OF KILIMANJARO

AND OTHER STORIES

Ernest Hemingway

Where Somerset Maugham had been clinical and dispassionate and Katherine Mansfield passive and poetical, Hemingway seized the short story and injected violence, brutality, passion, blood, and death into it. As a journalist he had learned to pare his style down to a verbal photography of action. His threading of strong and simple words on to short, staccato sentences became the envy of a whole school of imitators. But very few managed to suggest the compassion that lies between the lines of clipped action and laconic dialogue in Hemingway's stories.

'The Snows of Kilimanjaro' is probably the best short story he ever wrote. Face to face with death a writer on safari contemplates all the stories there will now be no time to write. The other stories in this volume are all early ones, and those which feature Nick Adams are at least in part autobiographical.

'They are stamped with the urgency of Mr Hemingway's style. That style, at its best, is a superb vehicle for revealing tenderness beneath descriptions of brutality' – Ivor Brown in the *Guardian*

Also available

MEN WITHOUT WOMEN

THE SHORT HAPPY LIFE OF
FRANCIS MACOMBER AND OTHER STORIES

TO HAVE AND HAVE NOT

W. SOMERSET MAUGHAM

'To say that Maugham's work spans three literary generations, and embraces almost every form of the literary craft except poetry, still does not exhaust its versatility. He has the exceedingly rare distinction of commanding the interest of all kinds of readers' – John Brophy.

Eight other works by Maugham were published by Penguins at the same time as this volume, as follows:

The Narrow Corner

A drama of the East Indian Islands which recalls many of his best short stories.

Of Human Bondage

Based in part on the author's youth, this fine novel is likely to survive as his masterpiece.

The Razor's Edge

His last great novel is concerned, on the grand level, with religion and mysticism.

The Summing Up

Maugham's impartial judgement on Maugham, with his considered comment on life and on his own life's work.

Collected Short Stories Volume 2

Twenty-four more stories set in many quarters of the world and including 'The Vessel of Wrath'.

Collected Short Stories Volume 3

Contains the famous Ashenden series of stories of a Secret Service agent of the First World War.

Collected Short Stories Volume 4

Thirty stories set mainly in Malaya and South-East Asia, including such masterpieces as 'The Outstation'.

Selected Plays

This selection contains Sheppey, The Sacred Flame, The Circle, The Constant Wife, and Our Betters.

NOT FOR SALE IN THE U.S.A.

Also by W. Somerset Maugham

Cakes and Ale

Of all Somerset Maugham's novels *Cakes and Ale* is the gayest. The entrancing character of Rosie, a barmaid with a history and a heart of gold, places the book, as creative literature, on a level with *Of Human Bondage*.

Rosie, in less decorous days, had been married to a famous author whose second wife later nursed him into the position of Grand Old Man of English letters. Some have professed to see a likeness to Thomas Hardy in Edward Driffield, and Hugh Walpole in Alroy Kear, the ambitious but untalented biographer. Maugham, however, has denied any such connexion.

The Painted Veil

The Painted Veil is probably the only novel that Somerset Maugham based on a story rather than a character. Nevertheless, on publication in 1925, it was twice threatened with libel actions.

Maugham gives a modern setting to the curious plot which was suggested by a few lines of Dante. Detected in an affair with the Assistant Colonial Secretary of Hong Kong, Kitty Fane is forced by her husband, a bacteriologist, to accompany him to the heart of a cholera epidemic. In the course of this harsh penance she learns the true meaning of love. But her discovery comes too late.

The Moon and Sixpence

The Moon and Sixpence, published in 1919, confirmed Maugham's reputation as a novelist and is probably his best-known book. In the single-minded character of Charles Strickland, the London stockbroker who suddenly abandons family and career to become a painter, he drew a harsh but credible likeness of the mentality of genius. The story, suggested by the life of Paul Gauguin, is mainly set in Paris, but the closing chapters describe the artist's primitive life in Tahiti and his lingering death from leprosy. We are left with the disturbing impression of a man possessed by demonic forces.

BERNARD SHAW

IN THE PENGUIN PLAYS

All the plays are complete with Shaw's original prefaces

Androcles and the Lion
The Apple Cart
Back to Methuselah
The Doctor's Dilemma
Heartbreak House
Major Barbara
Man and Superman
The Millionairess

Plays Pleasant
ARMS AND THE MAN · CANDIDA
THE MAN OF DESTINY · YOU NEVER CAN TELL

Plays Unpleasant
MRS WARREN'S PROFESSION
THE PHILANDERER · WIDOWERS' HOUSES

Pygmalion

Saint Joan

Three Plays for Puritans
THE DEVIL'S DISCIPLE · CAESAR AND CLEOPATRA
CAPTAIN BRASSBOUND'S CONVERSION

Selected One Act Plays Vol. 1
Selected One Act Plays Vol. 2

NOT FOR SALE IN THE U.S.A.